RAVES FOR CHARLIE CARILLO

Raising Jake

The best kind of story because it is a page-turner you don't want to end . . . written in a smart, funny, moving way in the special language of fathers and sons. I want my own three sons to read it, as well.
—Mike Lupica, *New York Times*–bestselling author of *Travel Team* and *Heat*

Charlie Carillo has long been a superb comic novelist but in *Raising Jake* he hits a perfect page-turning stride. It's scathingly hilarious, vengeful, and truthful, and should come with a warning: *Beware: this book is potentially life-altering.*
—Sally Jenkins, *Washington Post* sports columnist and *New York Times*–bestselling author of *It's Not About the Bike: My Journey Back to Life* with Lance Armstrong

In the tradition of Tom Perrotta, Carillo explores the strength of the family bond, the power of forgiveness, and the hope that comes from embracing second chances . . . truthful, and hilarious.
—Alison Grambs, author of *The Smart Girl's Guide to Getting Even*

I don't like funny, touching novels because they make me wish I'd written them myself. I enjoyed Charlie Carillo's book from beginning to end and now I'm miserable.
—Sherwood Kiraly, author of *Diminished Capacity*

Raising Jake is a literary romp through the minefields of a totally normal, and totally abnormal, family. . . . I actually laughed out loud and kept turning the pages to make absolutely sure that all worked out at the end.
—Cathy Lamb, author of *Henry's Sisters*

I read *Raising Jake* with a smile on my face the whole way through. Sometimes I laughed aloud; always I enjoyed the turnabouts and back-to-front quality of the relationships in this story of a father's coming of age with the help of his son. It's never too late to grow up and no one is ever too old to be young.
—Drusilla Campbell, author of *Blood Orange*

Former *New York Post* reporter Carillo (*My Ride with Gus*) nails the language, the bluster, the rhythm, and the pulse of New York and its denizens. Fans of Jonathan Tropper will go for this one in a big way.
—*Library Journal*

In this coming-of-age tale, there's often a question of who is parenting whom. Carillo, a former reporter for the *New York Post,* has an easy way with breezy prose and likable characters.
—*Publishers Weekly*

Raising Jake was funny, poignant and insightful. Carillo's smooth and steady style brought his characters to life, allowing the reader to experience every moment. Sammy's stories were riveting and heartbreaking; at times I felt I should look away to give him some privacy.
—BookFetish.org

You can take the boy out of the city but you can't take the city out of the boy.
—*New York Post*

If you're not too embarrassed to LOL at the beach, read Charlie Carillo's *Raising Jake.*
—*New York Daily News*

My Ride with Gus

What starts out as a wild ride to get rid of a corpse ends up as a touching and believable story of family love and survival, a testament to Carillo's storytelling abilities.
—*Publishers Weekly*

This nightmarish picaresque novel mixes elements of slapstick, the surreal, and the absurd, all delivered in rambunctious, wildly profane Brooklynese . . . Carillo generates more than enough wacky energy.
—*Booklist*

My Ride with Gus makes Charles Carillo a writer to watch.
—*New York Daily News*

Outrageously funny . . . Charles Carillo's writing is light, fast-paced and yet thought-provoking . . . a fulfilling ride.
—*The Post and Courier* (Charleston, South Carolina)

A plot which hinges on the disposal of an inconvenient corpse is not a new idea, but Charles Carillo manages to make it fresh . . . as well as extremely funny . . . Carillo sustains his deliberately improbable narrative with élan, piling up the jokes in the best comic thriller tradition.
—*The Times of London*

If laughter is good medicine, Charles Carillo's novel is a treatment as well as a treat . . . the best part of the story is the witty contrast between Gus the gangster and Jimmy the Citizen . . . Carillo's book is an inspired marriage of the picaresque narrative and the road movie in which Gus, worldly wise and world weary, and Jimmy, his paranoid straight man, move through a series of hilarious near-disasters.
—*Daily Press Inc.* (Newport News, Virginia)

one hit wonder

Also by Charlie Carillo

Raising Jake

Published by Kensington Publishing Corp.

one hit wonder

CHARLIE CARILLO

KENSINGTON BOOKS
www.kensingtonbooks.com

Once again to Kim

Acknowledgments

Every laugh you laugh is an illness you don't get. My special thanks go to these guys, whose humor cheated innumerable doctors out of my money.

Roll Call:

Pat Cook, Dennis O'Brien, Paul Patrick, Bill Hoffmann, Charles Lachman, Bill Barrett, Phil Tangel, Kimmy Gorden, Matt Meagher, Matt DeNinno, Rob Nieto, Chris Dukas, Jimmy Malhame, Mike Pearl, Michael Shain, David Ng, Leo Standora, Arty Pomerantz, Don Halasy, Sean Delonas, Phil Spellane, Gordon Mitchell, Phil Parrish, Brian ("Dog") Kramer, James Bohrsmann, Frank O'Mahony, Kevin O'Mahony, John Chigounis, Anthony Chigounis, Al Canaletich, Bill Kelly, Randy Glick, Gary Goldstein, Malcolm Pink, Simon ("Dr. Fellenstein") Fell, Derek DeBowski and Darren Stewart.

Also: Tony Carillo, my father; Sal Carillo, my uncle; and Rafael Richardson-Carillo, my son. I guess it's in the blood.

And a farewell salute to Brian Walls and Michael Norcia, both gone long before their time, both so damn funny they made me double over with laughter. By the time I straightened up, my troubles didn't seem nearly as bad.

CHAPTER ONE

The woman sitting beside me on the red-eye recognized me. She had the window seat and I was on the aisle, trying to sleep, but I never could sleep on planes, not even in those long-gone days when I flew first class.

She was just the right age for someone that might know who I was, a slightly overweight thirty-something woman with crinkly brown hair and deep dark eyes, obviously a serious professional of some kind. She stared at me half convinced that it was me, and half afraid of making a fool of herself by asking.

This is what being a has-been celebrity is like—you get stared at, wide-eyed and then narrow-eyed. They wonder if you could be who they're thinking you could be. They wonder if you might have died. They look at you as if you're a ghost.

Then they hesitate, debating with themselves over whether it's actually worth the trouble to find out. This woman decided to give it a shot.

"Excuse me. Are you Mickey DeFalco?"

Picture what it must be like to be ashamed to admit who you are, to know that whoever recognizes you is going to want to know about all the wasted years that have passed since you burst onto the scene.

I didn't answer immediately. The woman continued staring at me, willing herself to be right. I sighed, nodded, shrugged.

"Yes, ma'am, that's me."

She covered her mouth with her hands, as if to stifle a scream of excitement. The hands fell away, the mouth was agape. For a few magical moments, she was no longer a serious professional hurtling toward middle age. She was a groupie.

"Oh my God, I can't *believe* I'm meeting you!"

"Nice meeting you, too."

"God, I *loved* 'Sweet Days'!"

"Well, thanks."

"I was sixteen when it came out. I played it so many times that the tape finally broke! That's how long ago it was—the song was on a cassette! Remember cassettes?"

"Yes, I remember cassettes."

"Oh, God, *Mickey DeFalco!!*"

She was getting loud. I was starting to panic. I had to calm her down. The last thing I needed was for everybody on the plane to know who I was.

And when I say "was," I mean *"was."*

"Sweet Days" is the name of the bubblegum love song I wrote and recorded in 1988. You'll remember it if you were anywhere near an A.M. radio that year. For two straight weeks, I was number one on the charts.

However, things have not gone nearly as well for me in the ensuing thousand or so weeks, give or take a few.

At age eighteen I was a hot ticket. Riding on the crest of my hit song, I moved from my parents' home in Little Neck, Queens, to Los Angeles to star in a TV pilot called *Sweet Days*. It was dropped after three episodes.

Which would have been all right, except that my follow-up record, *Sweeter Days,* went right into the toilet.

Even that would have been okay, except I got married at twenty, divorced at twenty and a half, and lost half my assets to my ex, L.A. style.

Then I got talked into investing in a chain of drive-in ice cream parlors called Sweet Days, a venture that lasted six months and took the other half of my assets.

After that, things got a little frantic.

I tried to stick with the music, but with the passing years it was clear that I was the very definition of a one hit wonder. Once in a while I played the piano and sang my song at country fairs, birthday parties, and bar mitzvahs. (I usually announced the winner of the raffle at such events, and sometimes I called the bingo numbers.)

For a while I sold cars, trading on my fading name often enough to make the sale that made my commission.

When the car dealership went belly-up I became a pool maintenance man. (Yes, ladies and gentlemen, step right up and have Mickey DeFalco check your pH levels and skim those dead dragonflies off the surface!)

Hardly anybody knew who I was out there in my white overalls, which means the horny housewives who lured me inside—in three years on the job, maybe half a dozen—were simply lonely, and not starfuckers. (Fuckers of faded stars? Whatever.)

Anyway, that particular gig came to an abrupt halt after I put too much chlorine in a pool that happened to belong to a vice president at Warner Brothers. His much younger wife dove in brunette, climbed out blond, and demanded the head of the idiot responsible for this atrocity.

Would you believe I only took the pool man job because I thought I would have access to show-biz people whose pools needed cleaning?

This is what it had come to. It was my only way in. Nobody in the music world would even take my calls.

Of course I was fired, and that ended the last of my regular-paying jobs in the City of Angels.

After that, I scrounged any kind of work I could find. I had nothing—no woman, no prospects, no hope. My California dream was a total nightmare.

When I boarded the red-eye from Los Angeles to JFK I was thirty-eight years old, and I was moving back home with Mom and Dad. They didn't even know it yet. I hadn't known it myself, until about two hours before takeoff.

You can move pretty fast when you're desperate.

Of course, I told none of this to the woman on the plane. All I said was that I'd been doing a lot of different things, and now I was relocating to the East Coast to be close to my family.

Luckily for me she wanted to talk about herself. She was a corporate lawyer, and she looked as if she should have been sitting up in business class—good shoes, a smart black pantsuit, a brown leather briefcase that probably cost more than my one-way plane ticket.

I wore jeans and a gray T-shirt. Her brow furrowed as she noticed something on my elbow.

"Hey, what's that?"

I looked. It was a splotch of white. My heart jumped.

"It's paint," I said.

"Paint?"

I hesitated. The less I said about it, the better. On the other hand, I didn't want to seem as if I were hiding something.

"I was painting a house earlier today," I finally said.

She couldn't believe it. She didn't want to believe it.

"Mickey DeFalco, a *house painter?*"

"I was doing a favor for a friend."

She was stunned. She began shaking her head, a sad grin on her face.

"Man, if anybody had told me I'd be flying home with Mickey DeFalco, and he turned out to be a housepainter—"

"Hey! I said it was a favor for a friend!"

The woman was stunned by my tone, but I couldn't help it. Pride dies hard. I was tired of strangers being disappointed by my life. Who the fuck were they to feel this way about me?

"Hey, man," she said, "don't get defensive."

"I'm sorry. I'm just tired."

"All right, then."

She called for the flight attendant. I figured she wanted to change her seat, and that would have been fine with me, but what she did instead was to order a bottle of champagne, as if it were the kind of thing she did every time she flew. The flight attendant went to get it and the woman turned to me.

"I'd like to apologize and I hope you'll join me in a toast," she said. "Your song meant a lot to me, back in the day. Will you clink glasses with me?"

I clinked glasses with her. The champagne tasted as good as airline champagne can taste at thirty thousand feet. We polished off the bottle as she talked about her business trip, how well it had gone, how impressed the L.A. office was with her work, how badly they wanted her to relocate to the West Coast. Ah, to be wanted . . .

It was the middle of the night, and we were somewhere over Kansas. Everybody else on the plane seemed to be asleep. She leaned close, not for a kiss but to whisper. Her breath was hot in my ear. It was the perfect time and place for a tightly wound person like her to become somebody else, a person she could forget all about when the plane landed.

"I'll bet," she began, and then she broke down giggling and had to begin again: "I'll bet you're in the Mile-High Club."

Oh boy. This. I could almost see it coming. Once a groupie, always a groupie.

"Yeah, I'm a member." I sighed. "But it's been a long time," I added truthfully. "A very long time."

"Do you remember how it works?"

"There's not much to remember."

She stared at me seriously. "I'm not a member, Mickey, but I'd like to join."

There was a crinkling sound from her hand. She was clutching a condom, a Trojan, the brand I'd always sworn by. Jesus Christ. Did she carry them around all the time, like breath mints?

I shut my eyes, thought about fame. Even faded fame counts for something, I realized. My name hadn't meant a damn thing for twenty years, but here I was, being offered sex in the sky by a not-bad-looking woman who'd treated me to a bottle of champagne.

"Mickey?"

I opened my eyes. She was staring at me all doe-eyed, waiting for my reply. I was either going to make her a member of the Mile-High Club, or I wasn't. She'd done her part, gotten herself drunk to have an excuse for such behavior, and now it was up to me.

I gestured toward the front of the plane. "Go to that bathroom up on the left," I said. "Close the door, but don't lock it. I'll be there in five minutes."

She did as she was told, drunkenly bumping seat backs as she walked. There were a few drops left in the champagne bottle. I brought it to my lips and downed them. Then I got up from my seat to make a thirty-something lawyer's pop-star fantasy come true.

I didn't even know her name. It was the eighties all over again.

The term "Mile-High Club" implies something merry and giddy, but the truth of it is, you've got your bare ass planted atop a chemical toilet with very little straddle room for the woman on your lap, especially if you're flying coach.

She'd taken off her slacks and was reluctant to drop them on the floor, wet with the splashings of those who'd preceded us. I rolled up her slacks protectively inside my jeans and set the bundle down in the tiny bathroom's driest corner. I set our shoes neatly beside the bundle, side by side. It was an oddly sad sight. You should never set your shoes beside those of anybody you don't love.

She climbed aboard and seemed to be enjoying herself. She clung tightly and buried her nose in my neck, rocking to the sound of music only she could hear. She kept repeating my name, which might have been all right, except it was my full name she repeated.

"Mickey DeFalco . . . Mickey DeFalco . . ."

She had to justify this wild, wanton deed by telling herself that at least it was happening with somebody who used to be famous.

Unfortunately I was now old enough to think past the thrill of the hump. I looked into the future, to a girly night at this woman's apartment six months, maybe a year from now. A room full of her female friends, sitting cross-legged and barefoot on her living room floor, getting silly on white wine and chowing down on Cheetos and potato chips, the kind of stuff women like that never eat—and if they do, they double the workout at the gym the next day to sweat out those poisons. . . .

But this isn't the next day. This is tonight, a night for wild truths to be shared, things they've never told each other, and will she ever have a story to tell! Of course she'd let her friends go first—stories about one-night stands behind their boyfriends' backs, the usual tennis pro or ski instructor boinks, and she'd wait until all these tales were told before casually dropping the bomb. . . .

Be quiet, everybody, be quiet and listen to me!! . . . Do you remember Mickey DeFalco, the guy who sang "Sweet Days"?

Yeah, sure, I remember him! He was cute!
Well . . . I did him on a flight from L.A. to New York!
You did not!!!
Bullshit!
I swear to God it happened!
Was he still cute?
Sort of, I guess . . . we were both sooooo drunk. . . .

I could hear the squealing and the laughter . . . and there I'd be, the big punch line on hen night. . . .

I stood up. It's not an easy thing to do in an airplane toilet with a woman wrapped around you, but fury gives you strength you never imagined you could have. She gasped with shocked pleasure, or maybe it was pleasured shock, and then I turned and completed this ridiculous deed up against the bathroom door, bumping her against it with as many thrusts as it took to finish myself off.

By this time she'd stopped saying my name, switching instead to "They'll hear us! They'll hear us!"

I knew it would bother her. That's why I did it. Anything to get her to stop repeating my name.

Her feet found the floor. She pushed herself away from me, shoved her hair back, and began to dress.

"Mickey," she hissed, "why did you *do* that?"

"The angle on the toilet bowl wasn't working for me."

"We were banging against the door!"

"Don't worry about it."

"What if somebody heard us?"

"What could they do? Stop worrying."

She wanted to be mad at me but the whole thing had been her idea, so she probably didn't feel entitled to her anger. Beyond that, I'm sure she felt lonely. I know I did. We were two semi-naked strangers in a chemical toilet high in the sky, and that's as lonely as lonely gets.

I peeled off the condom, knotted it, and dropped it in the receptacle for used paper towels.

"Is that the best thing to do with that?"

She was worried about evidence. Typical lawyer.

"Nobody's going to inspect the garbage," I said. "Look, I'll drop some paper towels over it. See? It's buried."

There were tears in her eyes. I touched her cheek, forced a smile. "Listen. That was nice. . . . You come okay?"

She blinked back the tears, blushed, nodded. "Several times, in fact."

"Good."

"How do we . . . get out of here?"

"What do you mean?"

"Well, who goes first?"

"It really doesn't matter."

"You came in here *after* me. If somebody saw you, it might look funny if I go out first."

"I'll go first, then."

"What if somebody's waiting right outside to use the toilet? I'll be in here when they come in!"

"So I guess we'll just stay here for the rest of the flight, huh?"

I was trying to loosen her up, but it wasn't working. She was worried. The champagne buzz had faded, and the gleeful aspect of the experience had totally evaporated. Now she wanted her respectability back, as badly as she'd thought she wanted sex ten minutes earlier.

"I'll go first," she decided. "I've got the window seat. I'd have to climb over you if you went first."

"That's very logical of you."

She looked at herself in the mirror and took a deep breath before hopping out of the bathroom as if she had a parachute on her back.

I locked the door after her, sat on the toilet seat and buried my face in my hands. I thought about spending the rest of the flight in here, but the chemical stink would have killed me.

How many women had I tasted since "Sweet Days" hit the charts? The answer was a blur, like trying to count snowflakes in a blizzard. Unlike snowflakes, the women were all alike, except for one, the one who'd inspired the song. Sadly, she wasn't the one I'd married.

She was the one who ran away and broke my heart. Things were getting better, though. Twenty years on, I didn't think about her more than once or twice an hour.

A tap on the bathroom door—it was a flight attendant, asking that I please return to my seat and put my seat belt on, as the captain was anticipating turbulence.

I put my jeans on and went back to my seat. When I got there she was fast asleep with her head against the window, the airline blindfold over her eyes, a blanket tucked up under her chin.

Pretty smart. She was going to pretend it had all been a dream. She slept the rest of the way to JFK, greeting me cordially when she awoke.

Fine with me. I wanted to pretend it hadn't happened, too. It would be easier all around.

We got off the plane and walked together down a long ramp toward the luggage carousel. She had baggage to pick up but I had nothing but my carry-on bag, so this was a perfect departure point. We stopped walking and shook hands, as if one of us had just sold life insurance to the other.

"It was really nice meeting you," I said, well aware that the verb in that statement was a lot milder than it could have been.

She seemed to appreciate it, though. She hesitated before handing me a card.

"If you ever want to get together," she said, leaving the sentence incomplete as she turned and headed for the carousel.

I watched her go, then looked at the card. Rosalind Pomer, Attorney at Law. Now I knew her name.

It was well past midnight in New York. I was exhausted in every way a body and soul can be exhausted. I couldn't just show up at my parents' house, unannounced and reeking of a sky hump. I decided to check into one of those cheap airport motels, the ones you drive past and wonder who in their right mind would stay in dumps like those.

It was only forty-eight bucks for the night, tax included. For the first time in ages I was rolling in money, plenty of money, so I paid in cash. They gave me a boxy room near the ice machine in the hallway, and between the clunking of the ice cubes and the roar of planes it wasn't a particularly restful night.

But there was a good strong shower, and I must have stood beneath its hot spray for twenty minutes, scrubbing away paint stains, Rosalind Pomer, and, I hoped, all the sins I'd committed in the City of Angels.

CHAPTER TWO

I slept late, almost late enough to be charged for another day. It was Sunday afternoon, just past two P.M. I got dressed, packed up, and went to the front desk to check out. The pathetic rubble of a complimentary breakfast was available if I wanted it, coffee in Styrofoam cups and one solitary Entenmann's doughnut, alone in a pile of crumbs.

I took a cup of black coffee, got some change from the desk clerk and went to the pay phone. The coffee was like battery acid but it packed the kick I needed. Two swallows and I was wide awake, ready to do what I had to do. The phone number hadn't changed since my childhood.

"Hello?"

"Mom, it's Mickey."

"Oh my God, you sound so *close!*"

I swallowed. "I'm in New York, Mom."

"Oh, my God! My *God!!*"

"Mom—"

"Are you all right? What happened? What's wrong?"

"Why do you ask if something's wrong?"

"You just show up out of the blue, and I'm not supposed to *wonder?*"

"Listen, Mom, I'm coming home for a while, okay? Would that be all right?"

She made a weird sound, the marriage of a cry and a laugh. "You don't need *permission* to come home!"

"Well . . . thanks."

"Where are you?"

"The airport."

"Which one? Want your father to pick you up?"

"I'll take a cab."

"They're so *expensive!*"

"I'm on my way, Mom."

She had more to say but I hung up the phone, half sorry that I'd called. Now there was no turning back. My mother was waiting for me.

I hailed a yellow cab and of course the Muslim driver wasn't delighted to be taking me to an address on the edge of Queens, knowing he probably wouldn't get a return fare. As we got rolling I thought he was muttering about it to himself, but then I saw that he had a small cell phone clamped onto his ear and was chattering away to someone in his native language. I asked him to please hang up until the end of the ride. He nodded and did as he was asked but his eyes flashed with anger. Maybe he was a terrorist, talking about plans for another attack on the city, and I'd interrupted him. Maybe I was a hero.

I tipped him four bucks, and as he roared away I stood in front of my childhood home and stared in wonder at the little green asbestos-shingled house on Glenwood Street.

I had not been home in twenty years.

In the early days of my career I stayed at places like the Plaza Hotel whenever I came to New York (and sometimes wangled a room for my parents).

But I'd avoided the old neighborhood until now, until I had no choice.

The house seemed to have shrunk. Be it ever so humble, it was fully paid for, thanks to me. When the "Sweet Days" money rolled in I paid off the balance on my old man's mortgage, $22,000. That was probably the only smart thing I did with my money.

So I had a right to be here, if only for that. My knees trembled as I approached the front door, climbed the three cement steps to the stoop and froze.

I didn't know whether to walk right in, or knock on the door. How ridiculous was *this?* How many thousands of times had I barged in after school, dropped my books on the kitchen table, and headed straight for the chocolate milk in the refrigerator?

But that was a long, long time ago. Things had changed. Everything had changed.

Like a timid salesman I tapped on the door, almost inaudibly, but my mother heard it, all right. The door swung open and there she was, looking up at me as if I were a star in the night sky she was trying to recognize.

I'd forgotten about how short she was, barely five feet when I was in my teens, maybe four-eleven now with the shrinkage of time. But her wide-set eyes were still as I remembered them, radiant beneath a wide brow. Her short hair had gone salt and peppery but she still combed it straight back, like a duchess of discipline in a British boarding school.

"Michael," she said, and then her arms were around me, briefly but tightly, as if she'd just pulled me in off the ledge of a skyscraper. She's never once called me "Mickey," hating it when the promoters decided my nickname would sell more records than my proper name.

Her hair was rich with the smell of the meat loaf she'd been cooking, and when she let me go she said, "Is that it?"

She was referring to my luggage. I nodded, setting down my green duffel bag.

"Yeah, this is it."

"You're shipping the rest of it?"

"Mom, there *is* no rest of it. This is it."

Her nostrils widened with an insuck of breath, just as they used to when I was a child showing her a math test with a failing grade. After all this time it was nice to know I hadn't lost my gift for disappointing her, and who wouldn't be disappointed by a son who had nothing but socks, skivvies and T-shirts to show for himself after thirty-eight trips around the sun?

"Well," she said, "come in, come in. Dinner is ready."

My mother called the Sunday afternoon meal "dinner," even though she always served it at four in the afternoon.

I realized I was still standing on the stoop. I took a deep breath, picked up my bag and stepped inside the house.

My father was standing by the tiny gas-jet fireplace they never used, hands hovering over the side pockets of his jeans, as if he were ready to reach for a pair of six-shooters.

"Hello, Dad."

"Mick."

We approached each other but stopped a few feet apart. He seemed shorter, too, and beefier, but he still had Popeye forearms. He's an auto mechanic, and he's always had these amazingly powerful forearms. He never missed a day of work, and that's why he was known around Little Neck as Steady Eddie De-Falco.

His hair had gone totally gray but it was all there, and those brown eyes still burned out of his face with a weird kind of sorrow, the sorrow of a disappointed man who can't even remember what it was he wanted and never got.

"I could have picked you up, you know."

"The cab ride was fine."

"Yeah, but they rob you."

"Not so bad."

"How much?"

"Twenty-eight."

"Fucking crooks."

"Eddie!"

He ignored my mother's outcry.

"A twenty-minute ride, a dollar's worth of gas. How do they hit you for twenty-eight bucks?"

"You got me, Dad."

"That include the tip?"

"No."

"Jeez, I hope you didn't tip him more than three."

"Four."

"Big shot, eh?"

"Used to be."

"Hug your son!" my mother commanded. "For heaven's sake!"

An embarrassed grin crossed his face. He came to me as if to embrace me, but instead he grabbed me by the elbows of my dangling arms, squeezing tightly enough to make me tingle. It was a welcome home, a real welcome home.

"All right, come, let's sit," my mother said. "It's on the table. Michael, you might want to wash your hands."

I was home. Good God in heaven, I was home, and it really hit me hardest as I washed my hands in the downstairs bathroom, where a blue-green mineral drip stain on the porcelain sink had grown like an obscene tongue beneath the hot water spout.

I remembered when that sink was as white as snow. That's how long I'd been away.

We ate at the kitchen table, the only place meals were ever eaten in this house. Nothing much had changed. There was a new coat of linoleum on the floor, and my mother had discovered refrigerator magnets, but the refrigerator they clung to was the same one I'd raided after school, and instead of my spelling tests there were coupons up on display. Back then the refrigerator was silent, but now it ran with an ominous hum, as if to warn that it could be just days, hours, minutes before it broke down once and for all. . . .

"How was your flight?"

My mother was trying to jump-start a conversation. The three of us had been sitting there eating meat loaf and mashed potatoes, silent foods, mushy foods that made no noise when you chewed them. The silent food made the other silence all the more excruciating.

I swallowed the meat loaf, tangy with paprika. "It was all right."

"Do you feel jet-lagged?"

"Mom. It's three hours *earlier* in California."

"Well, you know what I mean. Tired. Do you feel tired?"

If they knew I'd checked into a local motel for a night's sleep they both would have had fits. Paying good money just to sleep! The *waste!*

"Nahh, I'm all right."

I watched my father cut his meat loaf and bring his fork to his mouth. He has exquisite table manners, my old man. I never saw him gulp a drink or wolf a meal, and not until he'd chewed and swallowed did he speak.

"The pool thing didn't work out, huh?"

In my sporadic communications with my parents about my working life I'd exaggerated what I'd been doing. I'd told them I'd been running a pool maintenance business that went bust. They had no idea I was just a hired bug-skimmer.

I shrugged. "I got run out of business by a big outfit. They undercut everybody's prices."

"Bastards!"

"Eddie!"

"Well, it's rotten, that's all. What's the point? Why kill the little man?"

"It's business, Eddie."

"That's not business, Donna. That's *murder,* when you take away a man's living."

"Business is business."

My old man let it go at that. He always let her get the last word, as long as his own words had been read into the record. I always admired him for that, even though I could never work that trick myself. I like getting the last word. I like getting the first word, too, and all the words in the middle. I'm like my mother that way.

She turned to me. "You want coffee, Michael?"

"No thanks, Mom."

"It's made."

(Translation: I made it, don't waste it, there are under-caffeinated children yawning away in Africa.)

"All right, I'll have a cup."

She cleared the plates away and set mugs of coffee, milked and sugared, in front of me and my father. That's the way she did things. You got what you wanted all ready to eat or drink. Nobody ever asked anybody to pass the string beans or the mashed potatoes, because my mother loaded up the plates at the stove and carried them over.

It was like a diner. When I was sixteen I once left her a tip under my plate, and she didn't think it was one bit funny.

While she did the dishes I sat back with the man who'd sired me and sipped coffee, coffee with absolutely no punch.

"Is this decaf, Mom?"

"Do you want regular? We don't drink regular."

"No, no, this is fine."

"There's a Starbucks now on Northern Boulevard," my father said. "They line up for it. *Latte.* They need latte, these kids. Three bucks."

My mother's eyebrows rose. "How do you know how much it is?"

"I checked it out. Three bucks. More than that, if you want a *grande*."

"You had a latte?"

"No, I didn't have a *latte*. Calm down. I said I checked it out, that's all."

"A whole can of Maxwell House is two eighty-nine," my mother said from the sink, where she had begun to wash the dishes.

My father nodded, turned to me. "Hear that?"

"I sure did."

"A can costs less than a cup. Crazy."

Having exhausted the coffee topic, we sat and looked at each other. Something was different about my father, really different, and at last it hit me. This was the longest I'd ever seen him without a cigarette in his mouth.

"You quit smoking, Dad?"

He laughed out loud, not in a happy way. Then he lifted a pack of Camels from his shirt pocket, just long enough for me to get a peek at it before shoving it back.

"I quit smoking *indoors*. Your mother doesn't allow it in the house anymore."

"Why should *I* breathe *your* smoke?"

"No reason I can think of."

She turned to me. "It's good for him. He smokes a lot less this way."

"Yeah. Nineteen a day instead of twenty. That oughta keep the tumors away."

He stood, shook a butt into his mouth, and turned to go outside.

"Welcome home, Mick," he said before leaving.

Home. It's supposed to be a comforting word, isn't it? Everybody wants to go home. Home is where they can't get you. Home is safety.

So why did the very sound of the word make me knock over my coffee?

In a flash my mother was there, mopping up the mess as if she'd expected it to happen. She was so quick on the scene that not a drop of coffee made it off the table to the floor.

"I'm sorry, Mom."

"It's all right, you're jet-lagged."

"I'm *not* jet-lagged."

She tossed the wad of paper towels into the trash and reached for my empty mug. "I'll give you a refill."

"No, no. I think I'll just take my stuff upstairs."

"Your room's made up!" my mother called after me as I climbed the stairs.

The air in my room was tart with the smell of Lemon Pledge. My mother had obviously run up here and given it the once-over right after I called from the airport.

Here was my bed, narrow as a monk's, with the same pebbly-patterned red bedspread that left an imprint on your cheek if you fell asleep with your face against it. My Hardy Boys books were still lined up in a row on the windowsill, and beyond them was the little desk where I'd done my homework by the light of a black twist-neck lamp . . . still there, of course. There were clean towels at the foot of my bed, hotel-ready for my needs.

I closed the door to my room and wished it had a lock. Then I made sure they were both downstairs before opening my duffel bag.

Nestled among my clothes was an old coffee can with a taped-on lid. I peeled off the tape and dumped the contents of the can on my bedspread.

It was piles and piles of cash, neatly rolled up and rubber-banded, an absolutely obscene sight. I didn't even know how much it was.

Hoping and praying that my parents would stay downstairs, I

took off the rubber bands and counted the money. The grand total came to $5,740.

This was funny money. I hadn't exactly stolen it, but at the same time, it wasn't exactly mine. I was going to have to think long and hard before I decided what to do with it.

I realized how stupid I was. My duffel bag had gone through the X-ray machine at LAX. What if the security guards had been alarmed by the bomb-like outline of the can? I was lucky I'd gotten through. I was also lucky that nobody had robbed me at that shitty airport hotel where I'd spent the night.

But then, people have always said I was a lucky guy.

Now I faced the biggest hurdle of all—figuring out a place to stash the cash.

I didn't know what my mother's housecleaning habits were like these days but she used to fine-tooth the place once or twice a week, and how was I going to explain a coffee-can fortune? She'd think her only begotten son had become a drug dealer, and who could blame her, the way I'd landed on them out of the blue in need of a roof, a shave, and a soul, not necessarily in that order?

And then I remembered something, and I knew what I had to do.

I stuffed the cash back into the coffee can, taped the lid in place, and dragged the desk chair to my closet.

Way up inside the closet, higher than its highest shelf, was a kind of a hole in the wall, a deep gap in the bricks where I used to hide *Playboy* magazines. I had to climb up on a chair and stand on tiptoe to reach it, which meant it was completely out of my mother's radar range.

I got up on tiptoe, set the can into the hole, and told myself she'd never find it. Then I unpacked my duffel bag, putting my clothes neatly in the bureau drawers.

And then a funny thing happened. I was suddenly completely exhausted, as if I hadn't slept in weeks.

It was a warm night. I opened the window, stripped down to my skivvies and got into bed. Then I noticed something I hadn't noticed earlier, hanging on the wall over the foot of my bed.

It was the jacket from my one and only hit record, hung in a gold frame, as if it were some kind of religious icon. My hair had been barbered into a sort of punkish buzz cut, with slanted sideburns and a glaze of gel. My head seemed almost to be ablaze, as the photo was taken with the sun setting behind me. I stood on a beach with my arms folded across my chest, the top two buttons of a snug black silk shirt undone ("Let the chest hair peek out!" the photographer had shouted).

I stared at myself on that wall, twenty years younger and twenty pounds lighter. Young Me stared back just as hard, grinning as if God had just whispered in his ear that the rest of his life was going to be a toboggan ride down Whipped Cream Mountain.

"The fuck you lookin' at?" I asked the record jacket, but I got no answer.

I was just about asleep when a coughing sound jolted me. I got up, went to the window and looked out at the backyard, where my father was lighting up a fresh cigarette. He shifted his weight from foot to foot, like a man waiting for a bus that was never coming.

I got back in bed and shut my eyes. I could smell cigarette smoke and hear the clatter of pots being scrubbed by my mother down in the kitchen.

Smoke and clatter. I was home, all right.

CHAPTER THREE

I guess we never know how or when the key moments of our lives are happening. Musically speaking, my inspirational life had just one big day. More like an hour, really.

I wrote "Sweet Days" one dreamy afternoon in September of 1987 on the inside flap of my American History notebook, right above the printed chart they give you to lay out your class schedule. While Mr. Malecki droned on about the Civil War, I jotted down the first few words of the song that would change my life.

> Sweet days . . .
> Feel like a haze . . .
> A summertime craze . . .
> But it ain't just a phase . . .

That afternoon when I got home I went straight to the piano my mother had insisted we have for the lessons I'd taken with Dot Molloy, a kooky neighborhood character whose pedigree included a claim that she'd once played at Carnegie Hall. Mrs. Molloy was a longtime widow, and a lot of Little Neck mothers made their sons take piano lessons with her because, as my mother used to say, "She's on a fixed income." She was past sixty but she had wild bleached blond hair and wore bright red lipstick that smeared beyond the boundaries of her lips. She may have looked like a clown, but she was dead serious about music.

I had talent but no discipline, according to Mrs. Molloy, who said she could tell I never practiced between piano lessons. As a matter of fact she was right, but on this particular afternoon I did voluntarily put my ass on the piano bench and pick out the tickly tune that was buzzing around in my head.

"What are you doing?"

My mother stood there looking astonished, a dusty rag in one hand, a can of Pledge in the other. By this time my lessons from Mrs. Molloy were long over, and she was the only one in the house who ever played the piano. She'd had classical training when she was a child, and the sounds of Mozart she coaxed from the box weren't half bad, in a stilted sort of way. . . .

"Nothing, Mom."

"What was that song you were playing?"

"It's not a song. I'm just fooling around."

"Well, my *God*. After all these years it's a little bit of a shock to see you playing the piano of your own accord."

"Mrs. Molloy was an influential woman. It just took time for me to become influenced."

"Michael, you never do pass up an opportunity to be sarcastic, do you?"

"It's an Irish thing. The smart-ass gene. I get it from you."

She shook her head. "The way you speak to me."

"Did you want to play the piano, Mom? Am I in your way?"

To which she leaned over the side of the piano, spritzed the keys with Pledge and gave them a musical wipe before turning on her heel and striding off to the dining room, where I heard the fizz of the Pledge and the snap of the rag.

Over the next hour I fooled around with the melody, singing softly under my breath. It wasn't even as if I'd written it. It was more as if I'd stumbled upon it, an achy, melancholic sound of something precious lost forever.

That night, after we ate and my mother went off to help run a bingo game for the elderly at St. Anastasia's Church, I played and sang the first stanza for my old man, who listened as he gripped a can of Budweiser. It was like he was waiting for some awful lyric accusing him of something horrible he'd done to me, and when I finished playing he was more relieved than impressed.

"You wrote that, huh?"

"Yeah."

"Get out of here!"

"I swear to God."

"It's very . . . uh . . ." He sipped his beer, swallowed, nodded. "Professional," he finally decided.

"It's just the first stanza."

"It's almost like . . . I don't know . . . you're *mourning* something, ain't it?"

"How do you mean?"

He reddened, sipped more beer. "I don't know. This sweet days stuff . . . it's happy and sad at the same time. The words are about happy times, but the music sounds like they're already gone. That make any sense to you?"

My skin tingled. Just like that I was filled with the terror that comes when a teenage boy feels he's really connecting with his father, far from the comfort of the distant camps they usually inhabit under the same roof.

"Yeah, it makes sense," I all but whispered.

He was scared, too—the fear was right there in his dark eyes, as if he were afraid of his own extraordinary perception. To break the mood he drained his beer, crushed the can in one powerful squeeze of his hand. "Anyway, the Yanks are at Cleveland."

"Yeah?"

"Come watch with me when you're through foolin' around there, Mozart," he said over his shoulder.

The next day at school I played the entire song on the warped, weather-beaten old piano they kept for no good reason outside the cafeteria at Holy Cross High School.

The guys didn't believe I'd written it. A big mouth-breathing German kid named Hans Merkle insisted he'd heard Herman's Hermits perform the very same song on *American Bandstand* years earlier. I swore up and down it was mine, until nobody was standing there but a toady student named Ronald Robinski, staring hard at me through the thickest eyeglasses in the entire junior class.

"Is that really your song, DeFalco?"

I shrugged. "What's the difference whose it is?"

"It's not bad."

Robinski was a goofy, squeaky-voiced eccentric, the target of endless pranks played for the sheer thrill of hearing his terrified shriek echo off the walls. It wasn't a good idea to get chummy with the guy. On the other hand, he was the only one being decent about the song.

"Well," I finally said, "what would *you* know about it, Ronald?"

"Play it again."

"I don't do requests."

"Come on. We only have a few minutes 'til the bell. They're all gone."

It was true. It was just the two of us, so I once again played and sang "Sweet Days," a little slower this time, with more feeling.

Robinski was serious until I finished, and then a smile tickled his lips. "That's it. It'll be a hit."

I laughed out loud. "You kill me, Ronald. What're you talking about?"

He took off his glasses and wiped them with a snow-white handkerchief. "Boy oh boy," he said, regarding me through sparkling-clean lenses, "you don't even know who my father is, do you?"

Ronald Robinski's father, it turned out, was Richard Robinski, a record company executive with an ear for the novelty song, the bubblegum pop tune, the kind of music that makes the hip cringe and the un-hip empty their pockets.

The next afternoon Ronald made me come home with him to play the song for his father, and I was astonished to learn that they lived in Manhattan. Nobody else at Holy Cross lived in the big town. Ronald rode the bus and subway back and forth from Central Park West and Seventy-second Street every day.

He actually lived at the Dakota, where John Lennon had been shot dead seven years earlier! As we approached the giant wrought-iron gates I began to feel a new respect for Ronald. The security guard gave him a friendly nod, and then I was tingling all over as we walked over the cobblestones where Lennon fell. We rode the elevator to the sixth floor and walked down a long, gloomy hall.

"Man," I said, "this is too cool for words."

Ronald shrugged, pushing his key into the door. "It's all I've ever known. Hey, Pop! *Pop!*"

His shouting jolted me. We were in a home with a knock-you-on-your-ass view of Central Park, and for the first time in my seventeen years I felt my nose bump up against the barrier that separates the rich from the poor.

I understood that as much as anything else it was about light and air. The long, wide windows of the Robinski living room looked straight out onto the seemingly endless park.

"Mickey, this is my father."

I was shocked to discover that my feet had taken me to the window—my breath was practically fogging the glass. I turned to see Ronald towering over a short, blunt man with a fringe of snow-white hair around a gleaming pink skull. He was coming toward me, hand extended, a diamond pinkie ring glittering.

We shook, and the power of his grip was almost enough to bruise my knuckles.

"You da boy wit' da song."

A rat-a-tat-tat statement, words like bullets. The man was a proud immigrant, doing nothing to hide his Polish roots.

I nodded. "I wrote a song, yeah."

"So let's hear it already," he said, as if I'd kept him waiting for hours.

He gestured toward an enormous Steinway piano I somehow hadn't noticed before. I slid onto the bench and flexed my fingers.

"Dis song you're gonna play, it's a rock song?"

"More like a love song, Pop," Ronald answered for me. "Go ahead, Mick."

The tone of that piano was like nothing I'd ever known. I could barely believe the sound coming from it traced to my trembling hands.

I didn't know where to look as I sang, so I shut my eyes most of the way and opened them only after I'd turned my face to the right, toward the park. The setting sun was turning it into a leafy world of golden wonders, and I realized through my terror that I'd never seen anything quite so beautiful. Not until I finished the song did I turn to look at Mr. Robinski, who stood staring at me with his arms folded tightly across his chest.

"Once more, please."

He said it without enthusiasm, but behind him Ronald's eyes opened wide and he made the A-OK sign with his thumb and forefinger. I shut my eyes and played the song again, and when I opened them this time Mr. Robinski was standing at my shoulder, scowling as if I were a suspect in a police lineup.

"Dis song, you wrote it all by yourself?"

"Yes, sir."

"Wasn't nobody else helped you?"

"No, sir."

"All right." He allowed himself a smile. "All right." He patted my shoulder. "I give you a call, okay?"

And before I could answer he walked off without a word of good-bye. Ronald put his bony arm across my shoulders as he walked me to the door.

"Hot stuff, huh? What'd I tell you? Didn't I tell you it was gonna be a hit?"

I arched my back to make his arm fall away. "Your father's kind of weird, Ronald."

"Oh, totally. *Totally*. But he knows what he's doing. So do I, huh? Guess I can pick 'em, too!"

I nodded, not wanting to dash Ronald's dreams of Robinski & Son Music Moguls, and suddenly I was out on West Seventy-second Street with no idea of how to get home. I got on a subway going uptown instead of downtown and didn't catch my mistake until I was past Harlem, and by the time I got back to Little Neck it was eight o'clock, a full two hours past suppertime.

My mother was out of her mind with worry. I hadn't bothered calling because I'd never really thought about it. I never really thought I was going to follow Ronald home that afternoon in the first place, or that he'd live all the way in Manhattan, or that his father would want to hear the song not only once, but twice.

It was all like a dream, is what I'm trying to say, and who phones home from a dream?

"We thought you were dead," my mother said.

My father rolled his eyes. "No, we didn't. Don't tell him that. You want him to be afraid of the world?"

"I want him to have sense."

"If he grows up afraid, he won't have a chance!"

"If he gets killed he won't have a chance!"

"I didn't get killed," I offered, but I don't think either of them heard me. I was off the radar for a few minutes while they went at each other, and even as they fought, my mother guided me by my shoulders to my place at the kitchen table, where a plate of food awaited me. A clear glass lid covering the chicken croquettes and mashed potatoes was beaded with condensation from the steam that had risen off the food, two hours earlier. *See how long you were missing? Long enough for steam to turn into water!*

I dug into the food, hungrier than I'd ever been.

"I can reheat it if it's cold."

"It's fine, Mom."

When I finally looked up from my plate the two of them were seated there, staring at me, waiting to be told.

"I was in Manhattan."

My mother's hand went to her throat. Manhattan to her meant sex, narcotics, minorities, crime, and rudeness. "Why were you there?"

"It's where Ronald Robinski lives. I went to his house to play my song for his father. He's in the music business."

My father's eyes widened as my mother's narrowed.

"That little song you were playing yesterday?"

"Yeah, Mom, that little song."

"What are you saying, here? You auditioned?"

"I don't know what I did, Mom. I played the song on the school piano and Ronald thought it was pretty good, so I went home with him and played it for his father."

"Where do they live?"

"The Dakota."

She turned to my father. "That's where that Beatle got shot."

"I know that, Donna, I read the papers."

"You make fun of me for worrying, and meanwhile he's at the exact spot where bullets were flying!"

"Seven years ago," I said. "They've stopped flying, Mom."

"Hey." My father slapped the back of my head. "Watch how you talk to your mother."

"For Christ's sake, it's safe there now! They've got security guards all over the place!"

My mother covered her face with her hands. "He talks to me

this way all the time," she said through the forest of her fingers. "Constantly. Never misses a chance to be fresh."

"Fresh?"

"You heard me—"

My father's fist came down hard on the table, making my plate jump. It put us into a shocked silence, and then he was almost whispering when he spoke.

"Did he like the song, Mick?"

His face was bright with wonder at the idea of his son coming up with a song that maybe, just maybe, would be made into a record.

I shrugged, still tingling from the impact of his fist on the table. "He said he'd call me."

"That's not a good sign," my mother said.

"No? Jeez, Ronald thought it was."

My mother held strong and smug, with the patient grin of one who's been there before. "I used to audition," she said calmly. "When they want you, they tell you on the spot."

"Donna, why do you have to discourage him?"

"I'm not. I'm just speaking from experience. It's a rough business."

"Every business is a rough business."

"This one's rougher than most." She stroked my hair. "We'll see what happens."

"Yes, we will, Mom."

It was a funny moment. In a way my mother was trying to cushion the blow for the almost certain failure I was facing. But I suspected that in another way, she was hoping I'd fall on my face.

They were staring at me in a new way, as if I were a stranger who'd been dropped into their lives. All these years I'd been an average student and a marginal athlete, a devoted son and garbage-taker-outer, nothing special, nothing terrible, just another tart-tongued teenager growing up on the edge of Queens.

At the same time, I was their only begotten son, their only

child. No siblings to pick up the slack, or distract them from me. Embarrassment or pride: It was all riding on my shoulders, and until now the future had seemed foggy, at best. I'd be lucky to get into a state university where the tuition wasn't ruinous to study to become . . . what?

That was the big question for me and just about every other kid in the neighborhood. A lawyer? Slim chance. A doctor? No chance at all, with my dismal grades in math and science. Some kind of civil service job was looking more and more likely. . . .

Or maybe I could write songs for a living. What would *that* be like? I couldn't help getting giddy about it, giggling like a child. . . .

"What's so funny?"

"Nothing, Mom."

"You must be laughing about *something*."

"I'm just a little excited. I mean, it's only hitting me now, everything that happened."

"Delayed reaction," my father said.

My mother hesitated. "So tell me about their apartment."

She would never admit it, but despite her fears she'd wondered all her life about what it would be like to live in the big town.

"Amazing place," I said. "Huge windows looking out over Central Park."

"Noisy?"

"Seemed pretty quiet to me. You hear the traffic sounds, but they're pretty faint from the sixth floor."

She was fascinated, and at the same time she needed to find a way to be better than the Robinskis. At last it came to her.

"Did you eat anything while you were there?"

"No."

"Drink?"

"Mom, I played my song twice and I left."

A dark gleam came to her eyes. "See that? These Manhattan big shots don't even offer you a glass of water. No class."

She turned to my father in triumph before going upstairs to take a bath. My father lit up a Camel, considerately blowing the smoke toward the ceiling.

"Play me the whole song," he said when I finished eating.

So I did. The song was two days old, but I felt as if I'd been playing "Sweet Days" for years, and when I finished he was smiling.

"Son of a bitch," he said. "It's about Lynn, isn't it?"

I felt myself redden. "Yeah, I guess so. Hadn't really thought about it."

"Not much you didn't."

He knew I was lying, right through the teeth he'd paid so many thousands of dollars to have straightened.

CHAPTER FOUR

Lynn Mahoney. My love. My life. My obsession.

I was fifteen years old and as shy as a boy could be without actually disappearing. I had an after-school job that seemed just right for a kid with my temperament—delivering the *New York Daily News* to families all around Little Neck.

I shouldered a big canvas bag filled with rolled-up papers and went from house to house, leaving the papers in front of doors. I was conscientious about it. I never threw them from the sidewalk, because that could tear the front page. I had more than fifty regulars on my route and every one of them got their newspapers in good condition Monday through Saturday, rain or shine.

I was quick on my feet and it didn't take more than an hour to run the route each afternoon. It would have been the perfect job for me, except for one thing—collecting day.

Every Friday I had to bang on the doors and ask to be paid for the week's papers. Nobody was ever happy to see me.

"Collecting," I'd murmur. That was my whole speech. Bob Piellusch, the kid who'd turned over his newspaper route to me (in January, right after he'd collected Christmas tips from his customers), said it would help to smile when I said it, but it didn't seem to make much difference. Often I'd wake people from naps, or interrupt them while they were preparing dinner. They acted as if I were being rude and unreasonable for expecting to be paid.

I wasn't. This was the deal. I had to lay out my own money each week to buy the newspapers. The profit margin wasn't huge, so I couldn't afford to carry any deadbeats.

And one family on my route had become the worst deadbeats of all.

I was nervous as I walked up the path to the Mahoney house that chilly Friday in April. Funny thing was that for a long time, this had been one of the best stops on my route, because Mrs. Mahoney had always taken good care of me. She answered the door promptly, had the money in hand, tipped me half a buck, and even offered me cookies.

But one Friday, she didn't answer the door. Nobody answered it. I made a red check mark next to the Mahoney name in my record book and moved on.

The next week, no answer again. Another red check mark, to be followed by two more. The Mahoneys were a month behind. You were allowed to phone your customers if they were real deadbeats, but I didn't dare do that. I was actually willing to take the loss, if it came to that.

The following Friday I almost didn't bother knocking on the Mahoney door. The only reason I did was because the newspapers weren't piling up on their porch. Somebody was taking them inside, so somebody had to be home. Maybe my luck would turn this time. . . .

And it did. The Mahoneys had a very creaky door, and it was opened that Friday afternoon by the most terrifying man I'd ever seen. His shoulders seemed as wide as the door and his angry blue eyes stared out of a massive skull with a gaze that seemed determined to melt me into a puddle.

I'd obviously awakened him from a nap. His steel-gray hair was flat on one side, his socks were halfway down his feet, and loose red suspenders dangled from his hips.

"What the hell do you want?" he growled.

I swallowed. "Collecting."

"Collecting for *what*?"

Instead of answering I handed him a folded newspaper. He took it from me and rubbed his face with his other hand.

"Paperboy . . . what do I owe you?"

I steeled myself for the outburst to come. "Fifteen dollars, sir."

"Fifteen bucks! Are you kiddin' me?"

"It's for five weeks, sir."

He cocked his huge head at me, narrowed one eye. "You sure about that?"

"Yes, sir. It's three dollars a week. Nobody was home for the last four weeks. See?"

I showed him my notebook with the red check marks beside his name. That didn't seem to appease him. He clearly didn't trust me.

"Wife's been sick," he murmured.

"Oh. I'm sorry."

"Did you say fifteen?"

"Uh-huh."

He dug into his pocket and pulled out a twenty. "You got change, kid?"

"Yes, sir."

So much for a tip. I took the twenty and handed back a five. He took it and slammed the door without another word.

I got out my blue pen and conscientiously made a line through the red check marks, clearing the Mahoney account. Those few moments I lingered there for that bit of bookkeeping changed my life forever.

Because while I was doing it the door opened again, and there she stood in cut-off blue jeans and a red T-shirt, her hair pulled back in a ponytail, staring out at me with the biggest, greenest eyes I'd ever seen.

Maybe it's not possible to love a stranger at first sight, but it is possible to be hit so hard by a girl's beauty that you feel as if your heart might explode, and that's pretty much what happened to me that day on the Mahoneys' front stoop.

"Hold on," she said, "this is for you."

She held out three dollar bills, but I was so blown away by the second thing, the sound of her voice, that all I could do was stare at her. If a brook could speak, it would sound like that, soothing and cool and tranquil.

The sight and the sound would have been enough, but then I caught a whiff of whatever perfume she was wearing. As it turned out, she wasn't wearing perfume at all. It was the smell of the girl herself, like a summer flower carried on an ocean breeze, sweet and salty at the same time.

Somehow I managed to clear my throat to say, "I already got paid."

"Yeah, but you didn't get a tip." She looked left, looked right, lowered her voice. "My father's too cheap to tip. Come on, take it."

She didn't want her father to catch her giving me more money. She kept peeking over her shoulder as she held out the bills.

"Will you take it, already?"

"What's your name?"

"Huh?"

"I said, what's your name?"

She rolled her eyes. "I'm Lynn."

"I'm Mickey."

"Take this money, Mickey."

"Listen," I said, "you wanna get a slice tonight?"

She cocked her head in puzzlement. "A slice?"

She didn't know what I meant. It might have sounded like a sexual offer to her. I had to clarify myself, and fast.

"A slice of pizza," I explained.

Those impossibly big green eyes widened even more. She shook her head, as if to clear it of confusing thoughts.

"You're asking me out?"

"I . . . yeah. Yeah, that's what I'm doing."

"You don't seem too sure."

"Did I do it wrong? I've never asked a girl out before. I'm not sure how it's done."

She giggled, not at me but at the comedy of the situation. At last she lowered the hand holding those three bucks.

"Sure, why not. When?"

"Eight o'clock?"

She nodded. "Okay. But please, take this tip."

She held out the money again. I shook my head.

"Keep it," I said. "You can buy the sodas."

She smiled, went back inside and shut the door. I was practically flying as I finished the rest of my paper route. Collecting from the rest of my customers was a breeze that day. Everybody paid up, nobody gave me a hard time.

For the first time in my life I felt at ease in the world, like I belonged, like I fit in, but it wasn't just that. It was a lot more than that.

Suddenly I didn't feel so alone anymore.

She was waiting for me in front of her house at eight o'clock. It was a short walk to Ponti's Pizza, an old-time joint that had containers of stale oregano and dusty Parmesan cheese on red Formica tables. We settled down at a booth with slices and sodas, and I was delighted to see that Lynn knew how to fold a slice so it wouldn't flop over when she lifted it for a bite. It was the first time I noticed something that would always impress me—Lynn never, ever did anything awkwardly. I was always tripping over things and knocking over drinks but she glided through life like a swan, a pizza-nibbling swan who seemed to be enjoying our first date.

We'd hit a silent patch. I felt I had to say something, and what I said couldn't have been more stupid, considering where we were.

"Do you like pizza?"

Lynn nodded. "Who doesn't like pizza?"

Panic. "I don't know. Maybe some people are allergic to it."

"Allergic to pizza? Who?"

"I don't know . . . people who are allergic to tomatoes, maybe."

"There are people who are allergic to *tomatoes?*"

"Well, there *must* be. . . ."

My voice trailed off. I was drowning in my own foolish words, and just then in walked three Italian kids with slicked-back hair. Cigarettes dangled from their lips. I knew one of them from grade school, an indifferent student named Enrico Boccabella. Our ways had parted a few years earlier, when his parents chose not to waste money on a Catholic high school education for Rico. He acknowledged me with a solemn, wordless nod.

Rico was the alpha male of the pack, ordering three slices and three Cokes. Jimmy Ponti seemed relieved when Rico paid up front. The other two carried the food to a round table, where the three of them sat and ate with their sleek heads tilted toward the middle of the table. Gold crosses dangled under their chins as they spoke in soft, urgent voices.

There were rumors that Rico was the leader of a burglary ring that hit rich people's houses in Great Neck, the ritzy town right on the Nassau County/Queens border. They might have been planning their next heist. Now and then they stared at Lynn, but she looked back without fear, the way a truly calm person can stare down a menacing dog.

I was impressed, and glad to have something to talk about besides pizza allergies.

"My fellow Italians," I said, almost in apology.

"Oh, I think Italians are wonderful."

"They are? I'm not so sure about that."

As if to reinforce my point, Rico let out a long, resonant belch, to the delight of his companions. Lynn rolled her eyes.

"I don't mean those guys," she continued. "I mean the Italians in Italy. The world would be a lot less beautiful without the Italians."

"It would?"

"Oh, sure! The paintings, the sculptures . . . it's an unbelievably rich history. I can't wait to see it."

"See what?"

"Italy. I'm saving up for my trip."

I was stunned to hear this. She was fifteen years old, and planning a trip to the other side of the world. The farthest I'd ever been on my own was Yankee Stadium, and I got lost on the way home.

"I want to see Florence, Venice, and Milan," Lynn continued, ticking the cities off on her fingers. "And Rome, of course. The Sistine Chapel."

"When are you going?"

"When I have enough money. I work a cash register at Pathmark on the weekends. I've got a pretty good fund going. . . . Don't you want to see Italy?"

I shrugged. "I don't know."

"You don't *know*? Aren't you *curious*? You're Italian, aren't you?"

"Half."

"Well, then, Italy is your heritage! Don't you care about your *heritage*?"

"What are you gettin' so excited about?"

"Ever heard of Venice? It's this city the Italians built on water! People ride in boats called gondolas to get around! Wouldn't you like to do that?"

"I guess."

She giggled. "You *guess?* We're talking about the most unique city in the world, here! Think you're ever going to ride a gondola in Little Neck?"

"Maybe if we had a flood."

She sat back in her booth and stared at me. "You're smart," she said softly, "but you don't have to be a wise guy, Mickey. It doesn't help anything."

I was burning with humiliation. "How come you know so much about Italy?"

"Books."

"But you're not Italian."

"That's right. I'm Irish on both sides."

"Well, don't you want to go to Ireland?"

"No."

"But that's *your* heritage."

Lynn waved me off. "Irish people drink and they sing sad songs. Who wants to go all the way across the ocean for that?"

Our voices had risen to almost argument levels. It was as if we were booking a trip abroad together and couldn't agree on where to go, two fifteen-year-olds on their first date in Ponti's Pizza Parlor.

Lynn was staring at me. "Listen," she said, "are you busy tomorrow? I want to take you somewhere."

"Where?"

"Are you busy, yes or no?"

"I . . . no. No, I'm not busy. Except for my paper route. I can do that pretty early."

"Well then, is it a date?"

The sparkle in her eyes was dazzling, almost dizzying.

"Yeah, okay, it's a date," I said at last. "What should I wear?"

"Wear your clothes." Lynn Mahoney giggled. "Be good if you wore your clothes."

* * *

The next day Lynn took me to Manhattan, via bus and subway, and through tunnels and transfers she still wouldn't tell me where we were going. I just had to stay at her side until at last we stopped walking at Eighty-second Street and Fifth Avenue.

"We're here," Lynn announced, and then we were climbing the steps to the Metropolitan Museum of Art, my first time there.

I was in Lynn's hands, all the way. There was a Renaissance exhibition, with statues and paintings by the ancestors of me and Enrico Boccabella, long-dead Italians with the kind of talents that apparently did not survive the journey to the New World.

Lynn came all alive as she spoke about the artists, as if they were friends she'd grown up with.

"Are you an artist?" I asked.

She laughed. "God, no! My brother Brendan is the artist in the family. Eight years old, and you should see his watercolors! But I love art. I want to major in art history. I'd like to teach it some day."

She cocked her head at me. "What do you want to do?"

"I have no idea."

"Ever painted?"

"Not since finger paints in kindergarten. I was never much good at it."

"Well, you might be a word person."

A word person. What the hell was a word person?

Lynn continued the tour through the museum, with me following like a loyal puppy.

"There are Little Neckers who've never even been here," she marveled. "Fifteen miles from home, and they never make the trip. I think that's so sad."

"Hang on a second, Lynn."

A painting had literally stopped me in my tracks. We were in the American wing, and I was looking at a nineteenth-century work by Winslow Homer. It showed a bunch of barefooted boys in a country field playing a game called Snap the Whip, running and tumbling with joy. A perfect portrait of an idyllic childhood, the kind nobody really has. You looked at it, and you just wanted to be there.

"Incredible," I breathed.

"Yeah," Lynn agreed, "Winslow Homer was a good painter."

"Is," I gently corrected her.

She laughed. "Mickey, look at the brass plate. He's been dead since 1910."

"No, he hasn't. Not really. See, this painting's in our heads, now, so we keep the artist alive, you and me and everybody else who sees it. Know what I mean? So this Winslow Homer guy . . . he'll never really die."

I couldn't believe what I'd just said. It was a wild thought that had become verbal without my consent.

Lynn was quiet for a long moment. Tears shone in her eyes. "I knew you'd get it," she said. "And I think maybe I was right about you being a word person."

We left the museum and walked downtown through Central Park. The backs of our hands bumped and suddenly, we were holding hands, just like that. We were approaching the zoo when suddenly, Lynn came to a stop.

"This would be a good spot," she announced, as if we'd just reached a desirable campsite and were about to start banging tent pegs into the ground.

I was confused. "A good spot for what?"

"Our first kiss."

My blood tingled. I had never kissed a girl before. Lynn pointed straight overhead at the Delacorte clock, with its menagerie of musical animals frozen in place. It was one minute to three o'clock. I stepped closer to Lynn, but she stopped me.

"Hang on, Mickey, not just yet. The clock's about to strike the hour."

And sure enough it did, and as the animals rotated in a circle around the clock and a carnivalesque tune filled the air, Lynn

Mahoney and I shared our first kiss, and nothing would ever be the same.

A current ran through me, a true circuit, from my lips down to my toes and up my back, over the top of my head and back to my lips. My whole being hummed with the sheer joy of it, this thing I was certain nobody else in the history of the world had ever experienced quite the way I was feeling it.

The kiss lasted as long as the music, and upon the sudden silence we at last broke apart and looked at each other, eyes and hearts wide open.

"Wow," I breathed.

"Yeah," she agreed, "I wanted our first kiss to be special, so we'd both remember it. I didn't want it to happen on Northern Boulevard, outside Ponti's Pizza. Aren't you glad we waited?"

I was. I was even gladder that she'd referred to it as our "first" kiss.

We held hands again as we resumed our downtown walk. What Lynn and I ignited under that clock was the real deal, the only thing in the universe without a price tag, a definition, or a substitute. I was afraid to talk about it, so I talked around it.

"I gotta say, Lynn, I'm really glad . . ."

"Glad about what?"

"Glad your father didn't tip me. Because I wouldn't have met you if he had."

A brief shadow crossed her face at the mention of her father. I wondered if maybe I'd imagined it, because it was gone so fast. It would be years before I realized I hadn't imagined anything.

CHAPTER FIVE

Lynn Mahoney went to an all-girl Catholic school not far from the all-boy Catholic school I attended. She lived three blocks from us with her parents and her four brothers. You should have seen the groceries that went into that house. One entire shelf in the refrigerator contained nothing but milk, carton after carton of it. Whole milk, none of that sissy skimmed stuff. They drained it every day.

Lynn's father was a legend in the New York City Fire Department, known far and wide as the Burning Angel. This was because of a famous photograph taken of him as a young firefighter, running from a blazing slum one cold night with a small child in his arms. His shoulders were literally on fire. The flames looked like wings. He set the child down and rolled on the snowy ground to douse the flames, but not before the picture was taken. The photographer won a Pulitzer Prize, and Walter Mahoney's fearlessness was immortalized.

All of his sons were either firemen or on the way to becoming firemen. They were always in training for the grueling physical exam, running miles and lifting weights. Their mother was a pretty woman, nervous as a bird, and it was hard to believe that

all those large boys had actually come out of her. She was constantly going down the cellar steps with baskets of sweat-soaked
laundry and staggering back up with clean clothes. Every time
you went to their house you heard the washing machine thump-
ing away downstairs. The woman never got a break.

Mrs. Mahoney liked me all right, but her husband hated my
guts. I think it started when he asked me if I was going to take
the fire department test, and I told him I didn't want to be a fireman.

"What are you gonna be, then?"

"I'm not sure yet, sir."

"You might like being a fireman."

"I don't even like barbecues, sir."

I was only trying to kid my way out of it, but he thought I was
being a wise guy, and it wasn't smart to piss off the Captain. He
stood about six-five and must have weighed two-fifty, give or take,
and every pound of it as solid as a fire hydrant. He had a pink
complexion that went red like rare roast beef when he got mad,
and when he frowned down at you it really did feel as if you'd in-
curred the wrath of God Almighty himself.

He loved competition, any kind of competition in which he
could pit his sons against each other, the oldest and the youngest
versus the two middle ones in football games, tag-team wrestling. . . .
The grass in that yard never had much of a chance to grow with
them tearing it up all the time.

Then there were boxing matches, with the Captain standing
on the sidelines barking commands or insults as his sons swung
at each other with pillow-sized gloves. The Captain and his three
oldest boys were in the middle of a boxing competition one Saturday afternoon when I came up the path to take Lynn to the
movies.

"Hey, Mick, you box?"

I'd been waiting for something like this. Before I could say a word he tossed a pair of gloves at me. I caught them against my chest. His sons stood staring at me, breathing as hard as horses.

"Put 'em on, " said the Captain, who pulled the gloves off his oldest son's hands and began putting them on his own.

"Actually, I'm taking Lynn to the movies."

"So you'll miss the coming attractions. Let's go."

There was no getting out of it. I pulled on the gloves, which had no laces and went on like big mittens. I actually felt the whole thing was a little silly, until I looked at the Captain's face. He'd been waiting a long time for this, and there was no compassion in his manic grin.

Gloves up, chins back, we squared off against each other, waltzing around in a circle bordered by his sons' widespread legs. He threw a short jab, which I blocked. He chuckled.

"Hey, not bad. Eddie teach you that?"

"No."

"Eddie never taught you to box?"

"No, sir."

"I mighta known. Italians prefer guns, eh?"

"If you say so, sir."

"Also, they believe in surrendering. World War Two. They were great at wavin' that white flag in Dubya-Dubya *Two!*"

On "two" he let it fly, and I never saw it coming. It caught me on the chin and I went straight back, flopping on the grass like a kid making a snow angel on a winter morning. I don't know how long I was out but I heard Lynn scream in the midst of my swoon, and when I opened my eyes she'd already pulled off my gloves and placed one under my head to make a pillow. She knelt beside me, stroking my forehead as the Captain regarded me from a standing position, his nostrils wide from exertion.

"You dropped your left, Mick," he said evenly. "Never, ever drop your left."

"I'll remember that, sir."

Lynn gazed up at her father, her throat choked with words she couldn't quite release. So he helped her.

"Go on, say it," he invited.

She spoke plainly and calmly, like a doctor giving a diagnosis.

"You're a bully, Dad. You hit him on purpose because you're a bully."

The boys stepped back, as if to give their father room for whatever the hell he was going to do, but there was no need. The guy had taken it right in the heart-lung region. After a long moment he shook his head as if to get rid of a dizzy spell, and pointed a still-gloved hand at me.

"I taught him a valuable lesson in self-defense, is what I did."

"No, you didn't, Dad. You're cruel. It's just the way you are. Maybe you were born that way."

This was even worse than what she'd already said. He was not to blame for his dreadful behavior. It was the result of a birth defect. He was a deformed soul.

All he could do was stand there and take it, suddenly looking silly and cartoonish with his heaving chest and those big gloves on his hands.

Lynn turned to me, so she missed the malevolent gleam in her father's eyes as well as her brothers' horrified faces. Had any of them said such a thing, Jesus Christ, they'd have been decapitated. . . .

"You okay, Mickey?"

"I'm fine." I pushed myself up to a sitting position. "Let's go to the movies."

"Are you up for it?"

"Sure."

I got to my feet, dusted myself off. I grabbed the Captain's gloved right hand with both of my bare hands and pumped it in farewell.

"Thanks for the boxing lesson, sir."

"Get the hell out of here."

We got out of there, holding hands all the way to the Little Neck Theater.

"Jesus, Lynn, I can't believe you said that to him."

"It's the truth."

"Still, the fact that you *said* it!"

"He's a cruel man, period. Do you think he really wanted to teach you how to box?"

"I know now never to drop my left."

"Don't stick up for him!"

"I'm not! I just want to believe . . . I don't know . . . he's got to have *some* good qualities."

"Oh, he knows what to do when a building's on fire. That he's good at. But once the fire's out, he's a menace to all living things."

"Jesus Christ."

"He doesn't like me either, which is fine. Most of the time we can stay out of each other's way."

"What about your mother?"

"She's numb to it. The only hope she has is to outlive the bastard. I hope to God she does that. She's entitled to a few peaceful years, my mom."

She shut her eyes, slid an arm around my waist. "Oh, God . . . Will you come with me to Italy?"

"Sure, baby."

"I'm serious. We're both saving money. I want to make this trip before we're ancient."

"We will, we will."

"Promise?"

"I promise. Some day . . ."

It was about to get even worse between the Captain and me. He'd always loved cracking Italian jokes and I'd always let them slide, but no more. By the time we got back from the movies he'd showered and had a few beers, and was all ready to pick up where we'd left off.

"No hard feelings, Mick?"

"No, sir."

"Good, good. Hey, I got a good one for you. Haddaya know when an Italian wedding is over? They flush the punch bowl!"

He roared with laughter, then put a hand over his mouth. "Whoops! Sorry, Mickey. No offense, huh?"

I was ready for it with a knockout punch of my own.

"That's all right, Captain Mahoney," I replied. "Being half-Irish I'm actually too dumb to get the joke, anyway."

His eyes went pig-small in his squinty face, and from that day on I waited out on the sidewalk for Lynn to meet me.

"I don't want that half-breed in my house anymore," he supposedly said to his wife. (That's what it was like out on the edge of Queens. Irish people were white, Italians were black. And if you happened to be both, you were always just a suntan away from trouble.)

But old man Mahoney couldn't stop Lynn from going out with me. We were teenagers in love, looking to laugh any way we could.

"Why don't you become a fireman?" she teased me.

"Why don't *you* become a fireman?" I countered.

She shook her head. "Not enough money."

"You want money?"

"Oh, yeah. Tons of it."

"How're you gonna get it?"

"I plan on marrying it."

"Whoa. Guess I'd better succeed at something, huh?"

"I would if I were you."

"How much money do you want?"

She thought about it. "Enough to fill a wheelbarrow."

"Singles?"

"No. Hundreds, minimum. A wheelbarrow full of hundreds'd do me."

I pulled a five-dollar bill from my pocket. "This is all I've got."

"All right, then." She took my hand, laced fingers and pulled me to her side. "What the hell, it'd be annoying, pushing that wheelbarrow everywhere. Take me to the movies, big shot."

Kissing and groping was as far as it ever went between Michael Anthony DeFalco and Lynn Ann Mahoney. We'd come close once to going all the way, but something happened to interrupt us. . . .

I didn't despair, though. I always felt there was an inevitability to our being together, someday, somehow. It was a rock, this inevitability, a rock that wasn't about to be washed away in a roaring rush of hormones.

We had time for everything, is what I'm trying to say, except that time ran out on us very suddenly one August day at Jones Beach.

I really must have loved her, because to make bucks in the summertime I was pushing a lawn mower all week long in the broiling sun, and the last thing I needed on the weekend was a day at the beach. But Lynn was cooped up all week punching that supermarket cash register, and she was starved for the sun.

So we went. We'd take the bus to the beach and spend the whole day swimming, lying around, and eating hot dogs.

It was always a good time, until the last time we did it. She was edgy and cranky. I wondered if she might be getting her period. I wondered if she might have met another guy. I didn't dare ask about either thing.

"We've got to even out that tan of yours, Mickey!"

"What do you mean?"

"Look at you! Brown from the elbows out, white from the neck down! It's a workingman's tan!"

I shrugged. "I'm a workingman. What am I supposed to do about it?"

"I don't know."

I knew her as well as I knew myself, maybe better. She wasn't upset about my tan. Something else was bothering her.

"Hey, baby, what's wrong?"

She shook her head, poked my upper lip with her finger. It was something she did a lot. I have a chubby upper lip that sticks out, even now. It's strictly a structural thing, but it makes me look as if I'm always walking around with an attitude. Lynn was always trying to push it back, so it would look like a "normal" lip.

"I keep telling you," I said, "I was born with it this way. It won't stay in place."

"I don't want it to stay in place. I just like to watch it spring back."

"Push it all you want, then."

"There's nothing wrong with me, is there, Mickey?"

I didn't see that coming. I was shocked. I'd always thought of Lynn as the most confident, self-assured person I'd ever known, the last person I'd ever expect to ask such a question.

"You're great, Lynn."

She pressed my upper lip again, let it go. "You don't think I'm strange, or peculiar?"

"You're . . . unique. But that's a good thing."

"How am I unique?"

"I don't know. . . . You're the only girl I could ever talk to. You're the only *person* I could ever talk to."

I was learning it as I was saying it. What I said was true. Lynn looked as if she were about to cry, but she managed a strange smile, the smile of a happy person who's just bitten into a lemon.

"Know something, Mick? Your father is a nice man."

This came out of nowhere. Why the hell was she talking about my father?

"Eddie's a nice guy? Eddie's a frustrated, unhappy ballbreaker, Lynn!"

"Yeah, sometimes, but deep down, he's all right."

"Lynn, what is all this? What's the matter?"

She blinked back tears. "I guess I was just wishing I had a father like yours, instead of the one I got."

"Well, if we get married some day, you'll have Steady Eddie for a father-in-law. That'd be good, wouldn't it?"

I was shocked by my own words. I'd never spoken with Lynn about marriage. I couldn't imagine life without her, but I'd never even thought about marrying her. Marriage, as far as I could tell, was a total fucking mess.

She stared at me wide-eyed, picked up a clamshell, threw it into the water.

"Wow. Mickey DeFalco speaks the M-word!"

"I didn't *mean* it, Lynn. What I mean is, I didn't mean to *upset* you with it."

"I'm not upset about that."

"Think you'd want to get married some time?"

"I'd rather go to Italy with you first."

We stood at the water's edge, watching ravenous seagulls tear into whatever left-behind food scraps they could find.

"If only we had a sailboat, and we knew how to sail, we could do it from here," I said.

Lynn was puzzled. "Do what?"

I pointed toward the horizon. "Sail to Italy."

She looked at me, and I thought for a moment she was going to burst into tears. "That's a sweet idea, Mickey."

I let my imagination go, the way you do when you're with someone you trust to the bone.

"It could be done, right? It's a straight shot across the Atlantic. If we had a big enough boat, with lots of supplies, and if we didn't hit any big storms in the middle of the ocean . . ."

I'd run out of "ifs."

"Well, anyway, I don't see why we couldn't make it," I continued. "We'd have to make sure we had enough food, stuff that wouldn't spoil, like canned goods, because it'd probably take a couple of weeks, and we might have to drink rainwater. . . ."

She embraced me, harder and longer than she'd ever held me before. I wasn't through.

"We'd sail to Genoa, or Naples," I continued over her shoulder. "I think those are the main seaports in Italy. They'd have to take us in, even if we didn't have passports. . . . Hey, how do you get a passport, anyway?"

There I was, seventeen years old, not yet able to drive a car, talking about guiding a sailboat across the Atlantic to start a life in Italy with Lynn Mahoney.

The sun was setting. Ever really watched a sunset? It's a sudden thing, not gradual in the least, and on this evening the sun seemed to slip into the waves as if it were drowning, never to rise again. On the other side of the sky the moon grew brighter and larger, as if it were winning a battle against the sinking sun. It was like a sad wedding of fire and water, and at the moment the last bit of orange was swallowed, Lynn stood beside me, arms folded across her narrow chest, her big green eyes solemn as she took it all in.

"It could be nighttime forever," she said, more to herself than to me. It was what I'd been thinking, almost to the syllable. I was gripped by a sudden fear that I was about to lose her.

That couldn't happen. I could not let that happen.

"I'm in love with you," I blurted. "I want to marry you. I mean, not this minute, but eventually. There. I said it! I'm *glad* I said it. If that scares you, I'm sorry, but there it is."

She stared at me, those big eyes glistening with tears.

"I know it sounds crazy. I don't want to scare you."

"I'm not scared."

"You're crying."

"Yeah." She wiped her eyes, shivered. "Yeah, I'm crying."

I moved to hold her but the set of her shoulders told me to stay away, for my own sake. . . .

"Lynn?"

"My parents were in love once, I suppose." This was a strange voice coming from her, both vulnerable and distant. She giggle-sobbed. "Funny, huh? My father, who won't even let you in the house, was supposedly *crazy* about my mother."

"Lynn—"

"And look what happened. They don't even touch each other. They don't even *talk*."

I swallowed, felt the panicked pulse of my heart in my throat. "That wouldn't happen with us, baby. We could be different."

"There's more to it than that."

"Yeah? Like what?"

"Things I can't even talk about."

And then she broke down in sobs. I put my arm across her shoulders and led her on the long walk through the suddenly cold sand to what turned out to be the last bus home that night.

She was silent the whole way, awake but with her eyes closed. On the short walk from the bus stop to her house she stayed a step ahead of me, no matter how hard I tried to keep up. She didn't stop until she reached her gate, and then it was time for what would turn out to be a final good-bye.

"Lynn, listen. I didn't mean I want to marry you *now*. I meant someday. You know. When I can get that wheelbarrow full of dough, you know?"

She managed a smile. "You know I was only kidding about that."

"I know, but still. Maybe I'll get it anyway. We'll go to Italy, change it all into lire and live like kings."

She nodded. "Maybe. But even if we don't, we've had a lot of sweet days, haven't we, Mick? More than most people get, that's for sure."

I hated what she'd said. It sounded like the end of something, an obituary.

"Yeah, we've had sweet days. And we'll have a lot more."

She hesitated, then got up on her toes to kiss my forehead. "I'll see you, Mickey DeFalco."

She turned and hurried into her house, and I knew by the way she'd used my whole name that something beyond terrible was about to happen.

And it did. In the middle of the night Lynn took off, nobody knew where. No note, nothing. The whole neighborhood was shocked. She seemed to be a loving girl with good grades in a good Catholic school. She seemed to have a stable family life and a boyfriend who adored her. And just like that, she took off.

But that wasn't all. In the early morning hours after Lynn had vanished, a drunken Captain Walter Mahoney went into a rage over her disappearance. He tumbled down the rickety wooden set of stairs to his basement, snapped his spine and was paralyzed from the waist down. He would spend the rest of his life in a wheelchair. The New York City Fire Department built a ramp for the Captain on the front stoop of his house, and there was even a ribbon-cutting ceremony for the ramp.

BURNING ANGEL TRADES WINGS FOR WHEELS, said the photo caption in the *New York Post.*

It was the beginning of the end for the entire Mahoney family. A runaway daughter, a paralyzed father . . . and then, ten years later, all four firefighting Mahoney brothers died in a raging warehouse blaze in the Bronx.

Of course by this time I'd been on the West Coast for a long time, and I'll never forget the phone call I got from my mother regarding the quadruple service at Eruzione's Funeral Home. It was attended by nearly everybody in Little Neck, along with TV crews from three news programs. All of the Burning Angel's sons being laid to rest! Who could resist such an event? At least one person.

"Well," my mother informed me, "there was no sign of Lynn."

"Maybe she doesn't know what happened."

"How could she not know? It's on television!"

"Maybe there's no TV where she is."

"There are no excuses for her absence, unless she's dead."

I swallowed. "You think Lynn is dead?"

"I didn't say that. I said that would be her only excuse for not being here."

I hung up on my mother. The concept that Lynn might be dead was unacceptable. I didn't want to believe it. I *couldn't* believe it. I'd been dangling from a thread of hope since she'd run away, and suddenly that thread was as slender as the strand of a spiderweb . . . ahh, but still strong . . . so strong. . . .

My parents had nothing to do with the Mahoney family, but my mother's bulletins about them continued over the years, like dispatches from a war zone.

The death of his sons took it all out of the Captain, she reported. . . . He began to shrivel and shrink, physically and spiritually. . . . Lynn's mother had to push him everywhere until at last he died of heart failure, nine years after he'd lost his sons, nineteen years after he'd fallen down the stairs.

Lynn missed that funeral, too, as my mother eagerly informed me in one of her last phone calls to me in Los Angeles.

And it occurred to me that maybe my mother was right. Maybe Lynn was dead. Maybe it was time for me to stop thinking about her, once and for all.

Maybe.

A few weeks after Lynn disappeared I lost my virginity in the backseat of a rusting Ford Pinto to a girl named Rosie Gambardello, who worked the cash register next to Lynn's and always went out of her way to flirt with me. We'd both gotten drunk on a jug of homemade red wine from her father's cellar, rough stuff that left an acid tang on your tongue, unless that was the taste of Rosie.

It was fast, it was furious, it meant nothing to me. We hadn't even taken our clothes off. Just unzipped and unbuttoned what we needed to get it done, artichoke style. A flick of her hips and I was out of her, rolling over to my side of the car. It was like I'd stopped for gas. She sat up and lit a cigarette.

"Ya still miss her, huh?"

That's how it is in Little Neck, Queens. Everybody knows everything.

"Yeah, I do miss her."

"She put out?"

"Shut up, Rosie."

"I knew it. I *knew* it! I could tell, just lookin' at her. A snob. Too good for it. Too good for the Little Neck boys. That's why she run off."

"Rosie, you don't know what you're talking about."

"Yeah, well, I could tell you had a good time just now." I saw her smile by the glow of her cigarette, a horrifying, gap-toothed grin. "This was maw like it, huh, Mick?"

I tumbled out of her car and went home to puke, all that red wine coming up like an angry tide. I was crying at the same time, the one and only time I ever cried over Lynn.

A few weeks later I wrote "Sweet Days," the lyrics about my last night with Lynn, giving the song its story. . . .

Spoke too soon . . .
Between the sun and the moon . . .
Words you could not stand . . .
While we stood in the sand . . .
Took the last bus home . . .
And I knew . . . I knew . . .
I knew that you were gonna roam . . .

What can I say? I know it's not Shakespeare, but somehow it touched a chord out there. And all it cost me was an irreparably broken heart.

I'd say my success was a combination of things—a catchy tune, luck, heartfelt lyrics, luck, good timing, luck, superb management, luck, crafty marketing, luck, a cute face, luck, luck, and more luck.

And if I had it to do all over again, I'd probably have saved some of that luck for the rest of my life, instead of shooting my entire wad on that one damn song.

CHAPTER SIX

When I woke up I wondered why the room wasn't brighter, then realized that the sapling my father had planted outside my window when I was a kid had grown into a big, droopy-leafed maple tree that blocked the sun.

By the time I got showered and shaved it was almost nine in the morning. My mother was in the kitchen, and at the sight of me she cracked two eggs into a bowl and went at them with a whisk.

"You certainly slept. Conked out without a word to anyone."

"Yeah, sorry about that."

"There's coffee if you want it."

"Thanks, Mom."

"It's real coffee. I got real coffee for you."

I poured myself a cup, astonished at how my hand shook. It had always been a nervous house, the nervousness deeply ingrained everywhere. The arguments, the silences, the pouting . . . it had all soaked into the pores of the walls and floors, like endless coats of wax.

"Dad at work?"

"Where else would he be?"

"Steady Eddie."

"In some ways he is, yes."

She poured the eggs into a skillet as I sipped my coffee.

"He going to retire anytime soon?"

"Retire? What would he do with himself?"

"I don't know. Take it easy."

"Why are you so eager for your father to retire?"

Just like that, it was a situation. I spread my hands. "Mom, I'm not eager for it. I just wondered if he was thinking about it."

She worked the eggs with a spatula. "He's only fifty-nine, Michael. It's not as if he's an old man."

"Mom, if he's happy working, that's great."

"Who said he was happy?"

"He's not happy?"

"Work is work, Michael. It's not supposed to make you happy."

"It's not?"

"Michael. Sit. Eat."

I obeyed, knowing I was the problem here, the intruder. I'd splashed down into this delicate ecosystem my parents had developed over the past twenty years, like some crazy salmon who'd swum upstream to rejoin his exhausted parents. I hugged my elbows to my rib cage as I sat there, as if to make myself smaller. . . .

"I have a job now, too."

She blurted the words, then stared at me as if she expected me to burst out laughing. I didn't. My mouth fell open, and at last I said, "You're kidding."

"Don't be so surprised!"

"What do you do?"

"I'm helping out at Eruzione's a couple of days a week. I'm on my way there now. I stayed to make you breakfast."

She emptied the pan onto a plate and set the fluffy yellow eggs before me. I tried hard to remember the last time I'd eaten eggs—that whole Los Angeles health food horseshit has a way of penetrating, even if you're not a believer—but mostly I was awed by the idea of my mother working at the Eruzione Funeral Home, which had been planting Little Neckers for more than fifty years. I noticed for the first time that she was dressed in black.

"You don't like eggs anymore?"

"I love 'em." I wolfed down a forkful. "I can't believe you're at Eruzione's."

"Why not?"

"Well. Kinda depressing, isn't it? All those dead people?"

"Everyone has to die, Michael."

"I guess that's true."

"You *guess?*"

I took another forkful of eggs. "Go ahead, Mom, go. I'm sorry I made you late for work." The last thing I wanted to do was be responsible for keeping the dead waiting.

She tied a black scarf over her hair. "Do you remember Ralph Mackell?"

"Who?"

"The old man we always used to see waiting for the bus?"

I had no clue.

"The old man who limped? He had that black cane?"

I still had no clue. She was losing patience. "*You* know. The old man who used to come into church late and sit in the front row?"

It finally hit me. "The white-haired guy who couldn't stop coughing?"

"That's him!"

"What about him?"

"He died."

I put my fork down. "That guy just died? He was dying twenty years ago!"

"Lung cancer. Eighty-eight. A smoker, like your father. We're laying him out today. Not expecting many visitors. He didn't have many friends in this world."

In this world? When had my mother adopted funeralspeak?

"I'm off, Michael. Make yourself . . ." She caught herself, reddened. "You know."

"At home."

"Yes, well, of course. This is your home. That reminds me."

She gave me a shiny brass key, attached to an Eruzione's Funeral Parlor key ring. It was a red plastic tag, shaped like a little coffin.

"For the front door."

She leaned over to kiss my forehead and she was out the door, eager to run the show for Ralph Mackell's final farewell.

It was a relief to be alone, a relief not to have been asked what my plans were.

But it was also shockingly, embarrassingly lonely. Maybe it's just me, or maybe it hits all thirty-eight-year-old males who suddenly find themselves unemployed and alone in their mothers' kitchens on a weekday morning.

I scraped the rest of the eggs into the garbage, washed my plate (she'd already scrubbed the skillet, of course) and walked out of the house, my newly minted key snug in the pocket of my jeans.

When you walk the streets of your old neighborhood your eye picks out the way things have changed, things you can't believe you bothered to remember as having been different. The McElhennys had added a new porch to their house. The Spellanes had changed the color of their trim from midnight blue to apple green. And of course the Lomuscios had added another two rooms to their house, one up and one out, eating up the last bit of yard they'd had left.

When I was a kid the Lomuscio house had been one of the smallest on the block, but every time they got a few dollars ahead they expanded, waking the neighborhood at dawn each Saturday with the banging of hammers and the roar of electric saws.

My mother would hold her hands over her ears every time a saw blade shrieked its way through a pine knot.

"If they want a bigger house why don't they just move, once and for all?"

"That's not it," my old man would say. "Some Italian people just can't leave their houses alone. Gotta keep adding on all the time."

"Not you."

"I'm what you'd call the contented type."

"You certainly are."

Ahh, the memories . . . I walked on past P.S. 94, the local public school I had not attended. But the P.S. 94 schoolyard was special because it was where I'd tasted my first beer one Saturday night when I was fifteen, out by the seesaws with Jimmy Nailer and Tommy Gordon, who'd swiped three cans of Rheingold from his father's cellar refrigerator. I drank the beer and walked home dizzy, chewing a triple-wad of Dubble Bubble grape gum to mask my breath. . . .

"My God, Mickey, is that you?"

I turned to see a woman with her hair up in curlers under a kerchief, her wrinkly hand straining to keep a cocker spaniel on a leash from chasing a squirrel. It was Eileen Kavanagh, whose windows I used to wash for walking-around money.

I offered my hand. "Good to see you, Mrs. Kavanagh."

She clasped my hand with her free one, a pink lipstick smile stretched across her hawklike face. Suddenly, the smile collapsed.

"Why are you here?"

"I beg your pardon?"

"Is somebody dead?"

"Oh! No, nobody died. I'm just visiting."

In Little Neck nobody comes home unless it's to bury a loved one. At least that's how Mrs. Kavanagh figured it. She was a real estate agent, and if one of my parents was dead, their house might go on the market, and she'd want to be on top of that.

She jerked on the leash, told the dog to sit still. "Staying long?"

"A while."

"Your mother never mentioned it."

"Well, it was a spur-of-the-moment thing."

"Hmmm."

The wheels were turning. Once she got back to her house she'd start phoning around about her Mickey DeFalco sighting, eager for the real story. I had to distract her, keep her from digging for more. . . .

"How's Mr. Kavanagh?"

Her cheeks went slack, as if she'd just heard a tasteless joke. "He died six months ago."

"Oh, my God, I'm sorry."

"Your mother never told you?"

"You know, I'm sure she did, but . . ." I tapped myself on the forehead, maybe to let her hear how hollow my skull was. "I forgot. I'm so sorry."

"Thank God your mother was there."

"My mother?"

"At Eruzione's. Let me tell you something, Mickey. That mother of yours really knows how to handle people when they've lost a loved one. She knows just what to say. It's a gift, I tell you. A *gift*. Either you can talk to people at a time like that, or you can't. Your mother can."

I knew Mrs. Kavanagh was right. My mother is great in situations involving dead people. It's the living who've always given her trouble.

The dog squatted to pee on the grass. Mrs. Kavanagh gave the leash another yank to get him out on the curb, and I used the moment to escape.

"Nice seeing you, Mrs. Kavanagh."

"Welcome home," she said, and coming from her it sounded almost like a threat.

I had to get out of the damn neighborhood. I quickened my stride along Northern Boulevard, shocked at the way things had changed. The Asians had found their way to Little Neck—nail salons and neck-massage parlors, and even an acupuncturist whose sign promised cures for everything from baldness to bad breath. Ponti's Pizza had become part of the Domino's Pizza chain, and the old Carvel ice cream shop had given way to a tattoo parlor. The movie theater where Lynn and I used to go was now a check-cashing place, with a scowling attendant behind a Plexiglas barrier. Bernstein's soda fountain and candy story was gone, replaced by the dreaded Starbucks my father had been ranting about.

Soon I crossed the border from Queens into Nassau County, the town of Great Neck: bigger houses, bigger lawns, bigger taxes, bigger attitudes. The roar of lawn mowers drew me toward a cul-de-sac I'd never been down before, but I had a feeling, just a feeling. . . .

The sound of the mowers grew louder with every step, and then there it was, the battered red truck with J. P. FLYNN LAND-SCAPING sprayed in white stenciled letters on the rusting driver's door. An equally battered green trailer was hitched to the truck, jammed full of gardening equipment. Two guys I didn't know were pushing lawn mowers across a spacious front yard, while a

gray-haired guy I did know squatted to fill the crankcase of a
hedge clipper with oil. As in the old days, a Marlboro dangled
from the lips of my old boss, John P. Flynn, for whom I'd toiled
for two summers during high school. He didn't hear me approaching.

"Jesus, these are the same mowers I pushed around. Invest in
some new equipment, for God's sake."

He squinted up at me, and then his eyes went wide in recognition. "My God! Look who it is!"

He stood to greet me, wiping his hand on a rag before extending it for a shake. "What the hell are you doin' back here,
superstar?"

"Visiting."

"Yeah? How's life with all the movie stars?"

"Actually, Mr. Flynn, I never really met any."

"Yeah, bullshit!"

A second thrill went through him, like a spasm, and he
reached out to squeeze my shoulder. "Jesus Christ, it's you! My
one and only rock star!"

I nodded, shrugged. "Sweet Days" was hardly a rock song, but
what the hell.

"Mick, you look good. Heavier, but good."

"You look good, too, Mr. Flynn."

That wasn't exactly the truth. His face had grown seamed and
his belly, once a slight bay window, was now more like a tire in-
flated to the bursting point. He knew I was lying and waved me
off.

"Ahh, I'm just glad I'm on the other side of the hill, goin'
down. This is my last summer with the lawns, Mick. Me and
Charlotte are movin' to Florida in November."

"Good for you."

"Carmine Eruzione ain't gettin' any o' my money. No disre-
spect to your mother. I hear she's great over there."

He dropped his Marlboro butt, ground it out on the sidewalk, and gestured at a young Hispanic kid struggling to push his lawn mower through the tall grass. The red bandana on his head was soaked through with sweat and he breathed heavily through his open mouth.

"See this guy? He's out every night 'til all hours. Nice enough kid, but you can't do that and work for me. Hungover. Dehydrated. He's stoppin' to drink from every hose along the way. I feel bad, but I gotta let him go."

"Could I take his place?"

The words were out before I could stop them. Flynn grinned, then his face went slack when he realized I was serious.

"Hey, Mickey. You all right?"

"I'm fine. I'm good. But what I said before about visiting . . . well, it's going to be a long visit. See, I moved out of L.A. It just wasn't working out."

He stared at me as if I'd just been in a car wreck, and in a funny way it was even worse than the looks I'd gotten from my parents. Of all the guys who'd pushed lawn mowers for this man for the past thirty years, I was the one who'd gone out and done something big, and now suddenly I was right back where I'd started.

I was rocking everything he believed in. Flynn was a war veteran who'd been wounded in Korea, and he loved his country with all his heart and soul. I was the one never-fail story he had to tell his laborers during lunch breaks in the shade of oak trees, the kid who wasn't even out of high school when he scored a number one hit single. . . . *Think that could happen in Russia? Huh?*

Yes, I was always the kicker to his story about America being the land of opportunity, and now, suddenly, I was a punch line to a bad, sad joke.

His eyes were actually wet. I'd forgotten how soulful a man he was, front row of the seven o'clock mass every Sunday morning, always holding hands with Charlotte, according to my mother. . . .

"You really want this job?"

"Only if you need me."

He nodded. "Sure thing, Mick. Be at the garage tomorrow at eight."

"Yeah, I remember the drill."

"Got the shoes you need? Can't do this work in those friggin' cross-trainers!"

"My mother never chucks anything out. I'm sure my work-boots are in the attic."

"All right, then. Tomorrow." He extended his hand for an-other shake, but this time there was a clinical aspect to it—he was sizing up the goods. A grin full of mischief crossed his map.

"Wear gloves, Mick. You've gone soft in the hands."

"Don't I know it."

I watched him limp to the truck. He'd been shot in the hip in Korea, an injury that left one leg shorter than the other. He was entitled to a government-financed artificial hip, but he wouldn't get one. He was proud of his limp. He wanted people to see that men like him were still around, men who did what they had to do and didn't whine about the consequences.

I broke the big news about my new job at the dinner table, and let's just say they didn't break into applause.

Steady Eddie stared at me. My mother's mouth literally fell open. She closed it, swallowed, and sighed.

"You came all the way back here to push a lawn mower?"

I slid my plate of macaroni and cheese toward the center of the table. "I wouldn't put it that way."

"How exactly would you put it?"

"I need work. This is work."

"John Flynn is moving to Florida in a few months. Did you know that?"

"Yes, I know that."

"What will you do when he leaves?"

"Get another job, I guess."

"Where?"

"Why are you breaking his balls?"

My father said it to stop my mother in her tracks. Vulgarity was his stun gun. She retreated from her attack long enough for him to make his point.

"It's good he's doing this, Donna. Let him do it."

She rolled her eyes. "Pushing a lawn mower for seven dollars an hour is good?"

"Eight, Mom. More than twice what it paid last time I had the job."

"That's just wonderful."

"What are they paying you at the stiff parlor?"

Her eyes were as big as baseballs. "Michael!"

"When the Flynn job ends, maybe you could pull a few strings. Get me on as a junior undertaker. No complaints from the customers, right?"

She pointed right at my face. "Do not mock the dead!"

"I'm not! I'm mocking the living who make *their* living off the dead!"

"*Enough!*"

My father had risen to his feet, arms spread wide. He glowered first at me and then at her as he settled back in his chair.

"He'll work outdoors. He'll clear his head. Lot of time for a man to think with a job like that, Donna."

"Think about what?"

"Things. Or nothing. Maybe he just wants a job that'll make him tired enough to sleep at night. Been a while since you've slept good, am I right, Mick?"

I was shocked. Steady Eddie had hit the nail on the head. He shook a Camel out of his cigarette pack and tamped it on the table. He did this to pack down the loose tobacco flakes but also to torment my mother with the fear that he'd light up in the house.

"Am I right?" he repeated.

All I could do was nod in agreement.

My mother tore her gaze from the cigarette and turned to me. "Is that really how you feel about it?"

I had to laugh. "I'll tell you how I feel. I feel that the sooner I earn some money, the better off I'll be."

The coffee can money was off-limits. I didn't know what I was going to do with it, but I knew I wasn't going to spend it.

My mother's face softened. She felt bad for me and mad at me. The two emotions warred briefly within her, fought to a draw, and left her face slack with exhaustion.

"Work is work, Mom," I ventured. "It's not supposed to make you happy, right?"

She almost smiled, and then her eyes welled up. "You had that job when you were in high school!"

I nodded. "Yeah, that's right, Mom. Speaking of high school, you probably also remember that I never graduated. That sort of limits my options, you know? So I guess I've come full circle, here."

My father stuck the cigarette in his mouth, reached for her forearm and gave it a squeeze. "Come on, Donna, don't worry. Let the boy heal."

He caught my eye, winked, went to the kitchen door and opened it, lighting up on the door saddle before stepping into the backyard. We got the barest whiff of smoke before the door slammed shut, enough for my mother to notice but not enough to complain about. The man was a maestro.

I got up from the table. "I'm sorry I made fun of the funeral parlor," I mumbled to my mother, then gave her a clumsy kiss on top of her head before going up to my room.

That night she got my old work shoes out of the attic. I set them beside my bed along with a pair of work gloves I'd found in the garage and went to bed before ten o'clock to be fresh and strong for my first day back on the job.

The very job I was doing when I lost Lynn Mahoney.

CHAPTER SEVEN

While I'm obsessing over the girl I lost, I should probably mention my ex-wife.

Her name is Lois Butler and I doubt very much that I could pick her out of a police lineup if I saw her today, given the toll of time and cosmetic surgeries that have certainly happened since we parted.

I met Lois on the set of the doomed-from-the-start TV pilot for *Sweet Days*. The premise of the show was that an aspiring singer-songwriter (guess who) working as a dishwasher falls in love with a waitress (Lois) who dreams of being an actress. Late at night after work they drink coffee in the deserted hash house kitchen, share their dreams, fall in love, reach their goals, get married, have kids, grow old together, and are buried in adjoining plots.

Kidding, kidding! As I said before, three episodes aired and that was the end of *Sweet Days,* the TV show. The critics crucified it, and one guy even went so far as to say I was "unconvincing" as a dishwasher.

He was probably right. My mother never let me anywhere near the kitchen sink for fear that I'd "splash too much" when I did the dishes, and so the first time I ever had my hands in a sink full of suds was the day the director yelled "Action!" on the *Sweet Days* set. Maybe if I'd played a gardener, the show would have worked. . . .

Lois wasn't half bad as a waitress, having actually put in time supporting herself that way. She was a tall, wiry girl with flame-red hair and a big cobblestone of a chin, the kind of chin you'd expect to see in profile on a coin commemorating some great pioneering feminist.

Lois was no feminist, though. We got involved soon after we got working on the pilot (you spend sixteen hours a day together, things are going to happen) and right from the start she made it clear that a boyfriend was supposed to light a girl's cigarettes, open car doors, and "pay for stuff," as she put it in her giggly way.

So I did. Why not? She was willing and wild in bed, the perfect distraction from a broken heart. We were either on our feet shooting scenes the writers couldn't stop rewriting or flat on our backs at my condo, resting up for the early morning call.

Nine days after *Sweet Days* went belly-up Richard Robinski, my trusted agent, died of a massive heart attack. Suddenly I had no job, and no representation. Meanwhile, Lois started having nightmares about returning to her hometown in West Virginia and waiting tables for real again. Her career was in ruins, her confidence was shot, and there was one other thing.

"Mickey, I'm pregnant."

She broke the news while we were cuddling in bed the day after the show got the axe. At this point she was living with me, though I don't exactly remember having invited her to do that. Each time she came to stay over, another item of clothing or furniture came with her, but I guess I didn't take it seriously until the plants started arriving.

Suddenly, it was serious. Grim, to use a more appropriate word.

I remember my lips going dry and my legs tingling. If I'd been standing up, I certainly would have fallen. Lois peered into my eyes all this while, looking for truths I was trying to hide.

"It's definitely mine, right?"

"Oh, Mickey, how could you even *ask* me that?"

I embraced her, merely to protect myself from that gaze, the way a losing boxer hugs his opponent to stop the rain of punches.

"What are we gonna do, Mickey?"

"I don't know."

"Are you happy about this?"

"Jesus, Lois. . . ."

She was wise to my false hug and broke the embrace, shoving me away to get back in my eyes. "This isn't the greatest thing that ever happened to me either, you know. My career is screwed."

"Take it easy, Lois."

"An actress has a baby in this town and that's it. Kiss it all good-bye."

I hesitated. "There's another way, you know."

Funny, how I couldn't even bring myself to use the word "abortion." Instead I called it "another way," which I'm pretty sure was the title of a catechism they made us study back at St. Anastasia's grammar school.

Lois gasped. "I could never do that, Mickey!"

"All right, all right, forget it."

I was dizzy. At this point I was still trying to write songs, convinced I hadn't been a one hit wonder with a follow-up record that tanked. Maybe I'd write a new song that would burn up the charts, and put another fortune in my pocket. How about "You're Havin' My Baby?" Nah, Paul Anka had already beaten me to it. . . .

Her eyes softened. "I want to marry you, Mickey."

"You do?"

"Don't you want to marry me?"

I swallowed. "I never really thought about it, Lois. We're pretty young."

"Well, now we *have* to think about it, don't we?"

"I guess."

"Will you marry me, Mickey?"

I swear to God she asked me just like that, flat on her back, naked in my bed, her hand snug around my suddenly hardening cock.

Why did I go firm in a situation so horrifying? The prospect of a shotgun wedding should have made me shrivel, not swell, so what was the explanation for it?

I don't know. Being twenty was part of it, I guess, twenty and lonely and terrified of the abyss I was facing in the wake of the TV show disaster.

"Yeah, Lois, I'll marry you," I replied, and we went at it like wildcats. That very night we drove to Las Vegas and got married at a chapel by a preacher in a lime-green tuxedo who looked like a faker but turned out to be absolutely legitimate, as I learned six months later when Lois served me with divorce papers.

The marriage was real. The pregnancy was another matter. Lois claimed to have miscarried a few months into it, but I don't remember any change in her figure or morning sickness or any behavior you could call even remotely motherly from this woman who insisted that smoking a little pot every night was good for the fetus because it relaxed the mother.

At that point I was worth about half a million dollars, and when the fairly uncomplicated divorce proceedings were over (no prenup, so the fifty-fifty California law applied) my lawyer took me aside.

"We're off the clock now, kid, so this is free advice you can take or leave." He put a pudgy hand on my shoulder to cushion the blow. "Next time a girl tells you she's pregnant, get her to piss into a cup. And be there when she pisses into the cup."

My parents met Lois exactly once, right after we were married.

I flew them over for a visit and my mother spent a long weekend sniffing the air for marijuana smoke I'd tried my best to Air Wick away. She cringed when Lois called her "Mom," and my father kept asking about the TV show.

I lied to them, told them I had another pilot in the works. I lied to them again when I told them I loved Lois, and I thought I was lying one more time when my mother cornered me to ask point-blank if Lois was pregnant.

"No way, Mom!"

Anyway, I had to sell my condo to share my assets with my ex. That was painful, but not nearly as painful as something Lois said to me when we parted for the last time on the courthouse steps. It was a brilliantly sunny Los Angeles day, the kind of all-penetrating sun you have to squint against even if you're looking at the ground. Lois grabbed my hand and pulled me close, not for affection but for scrutiny. She lowered her sunglasses to peer into my eyes, this woman I'd known for less than a year who'd just cut a deal worth a quarter of a million dollars.

Honest to God, I was expecting her to thank me for my generosity, but instead her eyes narrowed and her lips went rubbery in that pre-crying state I'd come to know.

"You never did love me, did you, Mickey?"

I hesitated, which was in fact almost as much of an answer as Lois would need. She had half my money, and now she was after a whole truth. So I gave it to her, right between the eyes.

I shook my head. "Not the way a man's supposed to love a wife, Lois."

It felt good to say it, but only for as long as it took to say it. Her eyes twitched with the pain of it, but I also knew she was tough. She took a deep breath, a fighter's breath.

"Do you want to know if I loved you?"

"Do you want to tell me?"

"I did. I do."

"You do?"

"Yeah, damn you, I *do*." Her eyes brimmed with real tears, not the kind she had to summon up on camera.

The smoggy heat was getting to me. I giggled with a weird giddiness. "Lois. Let's try to remember what happened here. *You* filed for divorce against *me*."

"Yes, I did. Because I knew you'd never divorce me. You'd already left me emotionally, but you never would have left the house."

"Funny you should mention the house. I have to sell it now, as you probably know."

But Lois didn't hear those words. She jabbed her forefinger at my chest. "Don't you ever do this to another woman."

"Do what? Split my assets?"

"Don't promise her a future when you're stuck in the past."

My heart was hammering. Lois wasn't stupid, but her intelligence was a kind of organic thing, and words weren't always her best friends. This observation was a rare thing, almost a lyric from a country-western song. I wondered if she'd heard it someplace or if she came up with it herself, but before I could wonder too long, Lois asked, almost casually, "What's her name?"

I sighed, felt my shoulders slump. I had to tell her. I owed her that much.

"Lynn."

I trembled at the sound of my own voice. I couldn't remember the last time I'd spoken her name aloud. I felt as if I were violating a gravesite, just speaking her name.

Lois was breathing hard. "Is she prettier than me?"

I sighed with weariness and impatience over her refusal to let me and herself off the fucking hook.

Prettier? Jesus Christ, it wasn't a question of measure. Lynn was all alone in my mind. There was Lynn, and then there was everybody else.

But try and explain that to your brand-new ex-wife.

"No, she was not prettier than you."

"Where is she? Back in New York?"

"I have no idea. She ran away from home when she was a kid."

"How dramatic."

"As a matter of fact, it was pretty damn dramatic."

"You love her."

"I did, yes."

"No, you mean you do. You *still* do."

I rubbed my face, spoke through the forest of my fingers. "We've been divorced for twenty minutes now, Lois. Why are we even talking about this?"

"Because it's all over and I realize I never even *knew* you, Mickey. God! What are you, man? An actor? A singer? A song-writer? Or maybe you're just a lost soul."

"That last one, yeah. That sounds about right."

"Make jokes. But I want you to understand that I am *not* a joke." She was practically bawling, and shoved the sunglasses back over her eyes. "I have to know all this stuff before I can get rid of you, Mickey. I have to know why you couldn't look me in the eye after we made love. So now I know, okay? Thank you. *Thank* you. We're done now, Mickey. I know it wasn't my fault. I was competing with a ghost, and ghosts always win."

She turned and walked off to her car. I sat on the courthouse steps and watched this normally graceful girl staggering with a clumsiness brought on by fury, and when she got in her car she roared off at such high speed I was sure she'd kill herself and maybe a few other people before she could get home to the hotel I'd been ordered to pay for by the City of Angels.

Two months later the sale of my condo went through and I sent Lois a check for two hundred and fifty thousand bucks.

I never resented her for taking me for half. Without that money, Lois wouldn't even have been in the game to get a second husband. A desperate woman never gets anywhere in Los Angeles.

Funny, though, how Lois got the wheelbarrow full of money

that I'd promised Lynn. And now I was back pushing a lawn mower for a living.

Three hundred and twenty bucks a week, before taxes. It would take me a hundred years to fill up a wheelbarrow, even if the bills were all singles, even if I could live that long.

CHAPTER EIGHT

My return to the first job I'd ever had. Oh, baby.

You forget what it's like to be out there under the sun, damn near forty years old, pushing a roaring machine that's belching gasoline fumes right into your face.

Mow the grass, trim the edges, a quick pass of a tilling rake over the flower beds, and boom, load everything back onto the truck (a backbreaking task in itself) and race to the next lawn.

No fancy work from the J. P. Flynn landscaping crew. We were the McDonald's of gardening, knocking off the lawns like so many Happy Meals.

By ten in the morning there was a delicious ache in my knees and a weariness I hadn't known since I'd last done this job. At the sound of Flynn's shrill fingers-in-the-mouth whistle I all but wept with joy, and my mouth actually watered. How Pavlovian of me to remember this was the way he made himself heard above the roar of the mowers to call the crew in for a coffee break.

At this point in the morning we were cutting the grass at a big Great Neck estate, a long, sloping front lawn divided exactly in half by a slate path. I had less than half of my side cut, while the other guy on the crew had three-quarters of his side done.

He was a big, square, earnest ox of an eighteen-year-old named Patrick Wagner, and I knew I'd be dead before the end of the day if I tried to keep up with him. We joined Flynn under the shade of an oak tree, where he handed me a Styrofoam cup of coffee.

"Light with two sugars, right?"

"I can't believe you remembered."

"Hey, Mickey." He winked. "I'm not just a pretty face." He passed a bottle of bright red fluid to Patrick.

"Gatorade for Patrick."

"Thank you, Mr. Flynn."

"Can't let the star athlete get dehydrated, huh?" Flynn laughed at the sight of Patrick blushing. "Patrick here is gonna play football for Purdue this fall. Tell him, Patrick."

"You already did, Mr. Flynn," Patrick replied softly.

"No kiddin', Mick, he's on a full scholarship."

I hoisted my coffee cup to this kid who had to have been the most famous Little Necker since . . . well, since me. "Congratulations, Patrick."

"Forty grand a year he's savin' his old man. Great country, ain't it, Patrick?"

Patrick shrugged, clearly embarrassed by Flynn's buildup. Now it all made sense—the bulging biceps, the tree-trunk thighs, even the blond crew-cut that made his protuberant ears seem to stick out even more. I was trying to keep up with Captain Marvel.

"Yeah, he's workin' for me this summer to keep in shape for football. Doesn't even want to get paid."

"That's not quite true, Mr. Flynn."

Flynn spread his arms, a look of mock shock on his face. "Whaddya need money for? You got a free ride comin' to ya!"

Patrick swallowed. "Well, not completely." He began ticking things off on his blunt fingers. "I have to pay for my books, plus plane tickets whenever I want to come home from Indiana—"

Flynn howled with laughter, reaching over to slap my knee. "You believe this kid, Mick? He actually takes me seriously! A month workin' for me now, and he *still* takes me seriously. Patrick, Patrick, you gotta wise up, or this world'll swallow you right up."

Flynn stretched, yawned, and stood up. Now as before, it was the signal for his men to return to work. Patrick and I rose to our feet like a pair of altar boys at the sound of the bells.

"All right, Patrick, get back behind that mower!" Flynn barked. "Pretend it's a tackling sled."

On the walk to the mowers I felt I had to speak up.

"I'm sorry I'm a little slow here, Patrick. You have to give me a few days to get used to this work again."

"Mr. Flynn said you were the best man he ever had."

I was both startled and touched to hear it. It had been a long time since anyone had said I was the best at anything.

"He really said that?"

"Yes."

"Well, maybe I was until you got here, Patrick."

At the lunch break I went into a sandwich shop on Northern Boulevard to pick up three meatball heroes. It was a narrow little place, basically a tunnel with a window. A chubby smiling Italian guy in a soiled apron took my order, his few remaining hairs slicked straight back.

"Ayyyy, Mickey, is thatchoo?"

I looked long and hard before I recognized Enrico Boccabella, the onetime leader of the pack at Ponti's Pizza.

"What do you say, Rico?"

"Not much." He jerked his chin toward Flynn's double-parked truck. "You back with Flynn?"

"For a while."

"Wow. Bad luck?"

"Some."

"Well, you got your health, that's the main thing, thank God."

What the hell would *he* know about my health? He slapped meatballs onto Italian bread. "Hey. Look at my Wall O' Fame."

I looked. Framed photos of Italian stars such as Frank Sinatra, Robert De Niro, and Al Pacino adorned the wall, along with one of me.

"How 'bout that, huh? Hey, do me a favor, Mick, take it down and sign it."

There's nothing worse than signing an autograph twenty years after you last did anything autograph-worthy, so I tried to get out of it.

"Jeez, Rico, you got it all framed up and everything."

"Ayyy, just sign the glass. I got a Magic Marker."

He gave it to me. I took my photo down and wiped off the grit and grease with a paper napkin before writing "To Rico, Best Wishes, Mickey DeFalco."

I hung it back on the wall.

"That oughta bring the customers in, huh?" Rico chuckled. He finished wrapping the heroes, took the money and shook my hand. "Hey, God bless you, Mickey, good to have you back."

Back in the truck Flynn filled me in.

"Rico did five years for breakin' and enterin'. Came out all holy, like one of those born-again Christians. Makes a good sandwich, though."

From that day on, I brought my lunch from home.

The workday at last came to an end. Despite the gloves I'd worn, I had bleeding blisters on both hands. The back of my neck burned from the sun and there was a weird clicking sound in my left knee as I walked home, as if a bit of cartilage was loose in there. Patrick walked with me part of the way, and suddenly remembered something.

"Hey, Mr. Flynn said you wrote a really great song."

"Ah, it was a long time ago."

"Mr. Flynn said it was a hit."

"Like I said, a long time ago. Before you were born."

"That is so cool! Could I hear it some time?"

"I doubt it's in the stores anymore."

"But you must have a copy!"

"Actually, Patrick, I don't."

"Can I get it on YouTube?"

"What's that?"

"The Internet."

"I'm an old-timer, kid. I don't know shit about computers."

When we got to the street where Patrick turned to go home, he shook my hand and said it was a pleasure to be working with me.

"See you tomorrow, Patrick. Get some rest."

"Actually, I'm going for a three-mile jog now. Have to keep my legs limber for football."

If I'd had any strength left I might have taken a swing at him.

Dinner was served at six-thirty in the DeFalco house. My mother liked to watch the six o'clock news before we sat to eat. The mayhem and lunacy of the world gave her an appetite, and she gave a running commentary on whatever was being reported.

"God help him," she'd say if the story was about somebody who needed a kidney transplant.

"God bless him," she'd say about the sibling who was donating a kidney.

"God forgive him," she'd say at the sight of a murder suspect being led away in handcuffs.

Each plea to God earned an eye-roll from my old man.

"Can we sit and eat before God gets annoyed with all your coaching?" he'd ask.

On that night, we were watching the news when a story came on about the sinking of a cruise ship off the California coast. There was footage of people in lifeboats rowing toward a Coast

Guard cutter. Then there was stock footage of the cruise ship itself, a sleek vessel with the words *Barca D'Amore* in swirly script
along its side.

The words meant "Love Boat." I guess it sounded a lot less
corny in Italian.

I sat up straight. The anchorman went on about how four passengers were still missing in the wake of the mysterious sinking,
which had apparently been caused by an engine explosion.

My mother was staring at me. "You're smiling," she said in
wonder. "What in the world are you smiling about?"

"I'm *not* smiling!"

"I'm looking at you, and you are smiling at a story about four
dead people!"

"Missing," my father corrected. "They're missing, they're not
dead."

"They're *probably* dead, and our son seems to think that's
funny!"

"I don't think it's funny, Mom."

"Maybe he's smiling about something else," my father suggested.

It was time to put an end to it.

"I worked on that cruise ship once," I blurted.

They both stared at me. My mother went pale.

"Oh my God," she said, crossing herself, "you could have been
killed!"

"Mom. This was more than a year ago."

"Oh my God, my *God!*"

"Donna," my father said, "he's sitting here in the living room,
alive and well and dry. Calm the hell down."

My mother got up and hugged me. "Thank God you weren't
on that ship!" she cried, refusing to let go.

My father didn't consider my survival of the *Barca D'Amore*
sinking nearly as miraculous.

"What the hell were you doin' on that ship, Mick?"

"Playing the piano," I said. "Matter of fact, it was my last professional gig."

"No kiddin'? How's the pay for somethin' like that?"

"So-so."

We watched the rest of the news, which ended with a bulletin saying the four missing passengers from the *Barca D'Amore* had been safely rescued.

"Thank God!" my mother said.

It was time for dinner. My mother was so relieved that I hadn't died on the *Barca D'Amore* that she forgot all about the way I'd been smiling over that news report.

I was smiling over the memory of a passenger named Sharon Sherman.

CHAPTER NINE

The offer had come up suddenly. The *Barca D'Amore* out of Los Angeles Harbor needed a piano man when the regular player suffered an appendicitis attack the night before the launch. Seven days and six nights at $200 per night, plus cabin and meals.

I grabbed the job, unaware that I would also be expected to do a great deal of glad-handing as well as prize-giving for the Ping-Pong and shuffleboard tournaments. They get you on deals like this, one-more-thinging you to death after the ship leaves the dock. They know it's tough to walk out on a job when you're a few miles out at sea.

It was what they call a "cruise to nowhere," meaning we'd stop for food and fuel but wouldn't be docking anywhere overnight. Most of the people on board were older than me by ten or fifteen years, and it wasn't until we were at sea a day or two that I noticed something weird.

There were no children on board. Kids were not allowed. This really was the Love Boat, a trip on which romances were rekindled, old promises renewed. There was a lot of hand holding, a lot of nose-to-nose conversations, and presumably a lot of Viagra-fueled midday humping.

What better sound track for such a sappy excursion than the piano-pounder who sang "Sweet Days"?

I played it twice a day—once at the early show, then again at the later one. The rest of my repertoire included songs by the Carpenters, Captain & Tennille, The Commodores . . . love songs, nothing but love songs, one more dreadful than the next.

It was what was known in the business as an Insulin Set. You needed an injection of the stuff at the end of the night to prevent a diabetic coma from all those sugary sounds.

Still, I tried to do a good job, and the people seemed pleased with what they were getting.

Except for one woman. Night after night she sat alone at a table for two, drinking scotch and sodas. Her table wasn't far from the piano and she was directly in my line of sight, absolutely expressionless as she stared my way. She was past her fortieth birthday and didn't want anyone to know it, especially herself, but everything she did to make herself seem younger backfired.

Her hair was dyed blond and cut short, but this only served to reveal a thickening neck that was starting to sag. She'd obviously spent time lying in the sun before the cruise, which highlighted nets of wrinkles around her eyes.

The eyes were her best feature. They were big and violet but impossibly sad, with the deep-down sorrows of a woman who'd always followed her heart to the wrong places.

The cruise director, a thin-lipped woman with her hair pulled up in a tight bun, filled me in on the mystery woman. She was supposed to have taken this trip with a man she'd been dating for nearly five years, but he dumped her when they reached the dock. At the dock! He told her it was all over, picked up his suitcase, got right back into the cab that had brought them to the harbor, and roared away.

He probably assumed she would do the same thing, but she didn't. She climbed the ramp and checked into her stateroom before joining the rest of the passengers at the rail, waving to strangers on the dock as the ship began its voyage to nowhere.

How could anyone take a trip under those circumstances? Maybe she couldn't bear the thought of returning to her apartment, with big bowls of dried cat food left for the tabby and the overwatered plants dripping on the floor. Maybe she harbored a wild hope of meeting somebody new on the cruise, but who? It was all couples. Everybody was taken.

Everybody but the lounge singer.

Each night it seemed she sat a little closer to the piano, the way a cat creeps up on a robin. By the fourth night out she was practically at my side.

I'd sing six or seven songs to start things off, take a break when dinner was served, and then come back with the sappiest songs in my repertoire to round off the evening. Of course a lot of couples asked me to play whatever happened to be "our song" during the second half. Usually they'd dance to it, on a small wooden floor beneath the twinkle of a spinning mirrored globe.

On the fifth night the sad-eyed woman finally spoke to me, just as I concluded the first half of the show.

"Sit here," she said.

It wasn't a request. It wasn't quite a demand, either. She didn't care enough to demand my presence. It was as if she just wanted to see if she could get her way.

And she could.

I sat across from her at a small round table for two. She had been drinking but her eyes were steady and clear, and up close they seemed to be lit from within, as if violet-flamed candles were burning behind each of them.

"Would you care to eat with me?"

I didn't even know if this was allowed. They don't like it when the help mingles with the customers, but this was an exceptional situation, and I wasn't about to ask the cruise director for permission to dine with a guest.

"Sure," I said, "that'd be nice."

"Want a drink?"

"I'd better not."

"Why not?"

"Well, I still have the rest of my show to do."

She cocked her head at me. "Are you saying you have to stay sharp for this drill?"

It was a terribly insulting thing to say. It was also accurate and hilarious, so I laughed out loud. I was still laughing when she extended a hand and said, "I'm Sharon Sherman."

"Mickey DeFalco."

"Yes, I know. I saw your name on the 'Appearing Nightly' poster."

Her handshake was firm and strong and she held my hand longer than she had to, breaking off when the waiter came by for our orders. She asked for a scotch and soda and I told him to make it two. We both ordered the roast chicken. When the waiter went away Sharon Sherman said, "What have you heard about me?"

"Nothing."

"Oh, don't bullshit me, please. It's a small boat. People talk."

"Well, the buzz around campus is that your boyfriend dumped you at the dock."

She wanted me to be straight with her, but maybe not that straight. "Yes, well. Such economy of language. I forgot for a moment that I was speaking with a lyricist."

"I'm sorry, Sharon."

"Don't be. You're absolutely right. That's exactly what happened."

The waiter brought our drinks. I took a sip, and it was the weakest alcoholic drink I'd ever tasted. The scotch was practically a rumor, and you'd need ten of them to get a decent buzz going.

Sharon took half her drink in one gulp and said, "He told me he didn't love me anymore."

"I'm sorry."

"No. Wait." She closed her eyes to help herself remember. "What he said exactly was, he still loves me, but he's not *in love* with me anymore. Like that makes a difference."

"It means he still cares."

"Oh, yeah. He cared enough to abandon me at the dock."

"I'm just saying—"

"Don't defend him!"

"I'm not!"

"You just did! You, of all people! The guy who wrote the all-time tearjerker about being dumped!"

"Take it easy, Sharon!"

"Ahh, it doesn't matter." She got to her feet, her legs surprisingly lean for the plump torso they were supporting. "I've got to go to the bathroom. Tell them to hurry up with the food, I need something in my stomach."

She left the table, staggering her way to the bathroom to murmurs from the crowd. I wondered how she could be drunk on such weak drinks, and then it hit me.

I took a sip from her glass. It had a kick like a mule. The watered-down drinks were for the entertainer, to make sure he was in shape for the after-dinner show. The cruise director had all situations covered.

I spotted her at the far side of the dining room, threw her a wave, hoisted my glass. She hurried over, smiling as falsely as a human being can smile.

"Be very careful, Mr. DeFalco."

"Miss Sherman invited me to dine."

"How wonderful. Please don't do anything to make her unhappy."

"I'd say she's already about as unhappy as anyone can be."

The cruise director's smile widened, in direct defiance of

what she was actually feeling. "Please remember that we are on a boat," she singsonged. "If this goes wrong, there's nowhere to go."

She wanted to say more, but just then Sharon Sherman returned to the table, so all she could do was pat me on the back and ask Sharon if everything was satisfactory. Sharon assured her that it was, and the cruise director walked away smiling.

Sharon sat down and said, "Is she afraid we're going to hump?"

I burst out laughing for the second time that night. I was trying to think of the last time a woman had made me laugh out loud twice in one night, or even once, for that matter.

"She's afraid of me making you unhappy," I explained.

"I'm already unhappy."

"That's what I told her."

"I don't remember a 'don't-hump-the-singer' clause in the cruise handbook. Did I miss that?"

Before I could answer, the waiter arrived with our chicken dinners. Sharon dug right in, with the appetite of a woman no longer worried about her weight. She ate everything on her plate and my baked potato as well.

"Don't worry, Mickey, nothing's going to happen between us," she said. "I only asked you to sit down because you looked as bored and lonely as me. Okay? Now finish your chicken. It's not bad, for cruise food. You'll need your strength for the second show. I'm going to be making a lot of requests. Can you play 'Push Push in the Bush'?"

I laughed so hard I spit a mouthful of chicken on the floor.

Sharon Sherman managed the office of an insurance company in Pasadena, a job she'd had for seventeen years. She could always tell when people were about to get divorced or married or thought they were soon to die because they shuffled their benefits and beneficiaries around. It was dull work until you took the time to figure out what people were up to. Then it became a fascinating study in the dark side of human behavior.

As far as Sharon Sherman was concerned, there was no bright side to human behavior, especially in the wake of what had just happened to her.

She was forty-two years old. She had never married, never lived with anyone. She had expected that her forty-nine-year-old boyfriend, Benny, would pop the question on this trip, but everybody knew what happened instead. It took a few days for the shock to pass, and when it did, Sharon had to admit something awful to herself—she was relieved.

We sat on adjoining chairs on the promenade deck, blankets over our legs, steaming cups of chicken broth in our hands. On the other side of the boat a shuffleboard tournament was in full swing, but Sharon had no interest in that. She was content to gaze out on the endless Pacific, where her thoughts could roam forever.

"If I'm honest, Mickey, it hit me as I watched him walk away. He walked like a duck, both feet sticking out, and it was like the end of a Charlie Chaplin movie, when the Little Tramp strolls off into the sunset. And I said to myself, how could I spend five years of my life with that clown? How?"

She stared at me, waiting for an answer. What could I say?

"You were in love," I ventured.

"The hell I was!"

"You must have felt something if you booked this Cruise to Nowhere."

She snorted. "What I actually had was a *life* to nowhere. You go on and on with somebody out of habit. You hang in there because there's always another event on the horizon—Christmas, or a birthday, or a vacation. And the years just . . . go by, you know?"

She sipped her broth, regarded me through half-closed eyes.

"You might not believe it to look at me, but I can actually be quite a difficult person."

"I'm shocked to hear that."

"Fuck you, DeFalco," she said sweetly.

A roar of cheers reached us from the other side of the ship.

"Somebody must have made a hell of a shuffleboard shot," I said.

"Yes, they do get excited about these little tournaments, don't they? Benny would have loved the competition. He actually enjoys shuffleboard." She took a sip of broth, shook her head in wonder. "How the hell could I have wasted my time with a man like that?"

"Well, they can be pretty charming, those shuffleboarders. And they've got good wrists."

Sharon gave my shoulder a playful punch. "Hey, Mickey. What do you say you and I go to the other side of this tub and throw all the shuffleboard disks overboard?" She giggled, thrilled by her own idea. "Come on. We'll wreak havoc!"

"I don't think it's such a good idea, Sharon."

"Why not?"

"Well, they'd probably bill you for the equipment, and they'd fire me."

"How could they fire you? We're in the middle of nowhere. The passengers would miss out on their last night of entertainment."

"Sharon—"

"Maybe they'd throw us in the brig! Think this ship has a brig?"

"I doubt it very much."

"You don't get rattled very easily, do you? I'm talking like a crazy woman, and you're perfectly calm."

"Something about the sea relaxes me."

"That's not it. You really don't care, do you?"

"About what?"

"About anything, ever since you had your heart broken."

I stared at her long and hard, the way you do when you've been recognized for what you really are and there's no place to hide, unless you jump overboard. I wasn't about to do that.

"I guess I don't, Sharon Sherman."

"Well, if you don't care, why don't you come with me now and help put an end to this shuffleboard madness once and for all?"

I looked past Sharon, to the far end of the deck. The cruise director stood there staring at me, nodding ever so slightly, just to let me know she was on the job.

Jesus Christ. That did it.

I sipped my broth, leaned close to Sharon. "Now's not the time. We'll do it tonight, after my last show, and really mess things up for them." I winked at her. "Tomorrow's supposed to be the tournament finals. We'll see about that."

Sharon's eyes sparkled with delight. I was beginning to see what Benny had seen in her, back when she had dreams.

The full moon shone so brightly that the two of us actually cast sharp shadows out there on the deck. It was past midnight, and just about everybody was in bed as the ship sped along on its senseless journey. The only sound was the hum of the engines and the burbling of water in the ship's wake.

We'd both been drinking but our mission kept us focused. They served me full-strength drinks when my last set was finished, so I had a nice load on.

The shuffleboard court was painted right onto the deck, enameled red paint on the wood grain. The poles and disks were in a tall wooden cabinet at the side of the court. Sharon opened the cabinet, picked up a pole, hoisted it like a javelin, took a few running steps toward the rail and let it fly. We couldn't see it but we heard it splash far below.

"That's one, Mickey."

There were half a dozen shuffleboard poles and we each chucked three over the side. I got much better distance on my throws than she did. I wondered if they'd sink or float. They were hollow metal tubes with wooden handles on one end and wooden half-moons on the other, to cradle the disks. Sharon let her last pole fly and flopped in a deck chair, winded by her efforts.

"You do the disks, Mickey, I'm too drunk."

There were a dozen disks, half red, half black, like giant checkers made from some stony composite. No way those babies could float. I got rid of them one at a time like a discus thrower, whirling my way to the rail and letting them fly. They hovered unseen in the night air for a few seconds before splashing down.

By the twelfth disk I was winded. Sweat soaked my shirt. Sharon Sherman put her hands on my shoulders.

"That was great!"

"Yeah, I enjoyed it, too."

"Can you imagine what they'll be like out here tomorrow morning? They'll be going crazy!"

"Crazy?"

"That's what I said, crazy. . . ."

She grabbed me by the cheeks, pulled my face to hers, and gave me a savage kiss. She kicked off her shoes and then shrugged her way out of her slacks and her underwear, still kissing me hard.

Then Sharon Sherman, naked from the waist down but buttoned up and proper from the waist up, began walking backwards until her hands found the deck rail at the prow of the ship. She reached behind to grab it and stood with her feet apart, like a surfer.

"Right here, Mickey," she said. "I'm on the pill, by the way."

I dropped my pants. She was ready for it. Our shuffleboard crime had served as all the foreplay we would need.

She leaned backwards against the rail, her back arched over

the top of it, head upside down, facing the waters we were plowing through. Her legs were scissored around me, locked at the ankles behind my back. I was humping her and keeping her from falling overboard at the same time.

She shuddered with a climax, keeping her back arched. She let her arms drop from my shoulders, stretched her hands to the sky, and cried, "I'm the Queen of the World!"

Then it was my turn to get there and I did, momentarily losing my balance in a spasm that could have sent both of us over the rail, which would have been a hell of a thing, as the ship would have plowed over us and chopped us to bits in its giant propeller.

But we didn't fall. I regained my balance and pulled Sharon all the way back on board, still inside her, her legs still straddling me. We held that position for a moment or two until Sharon loosened her grip, and as her feet touched the deck I slid out of her and she kissed me gently on the mouth.

"Good night," she said, but it sounded more like good-bye. It was a time to say nothing, so I said nothing, and I'm sure she appreciated it. This wasn't love, and it wasn't quite lust, either. It was a political act, an extension of the crime we'd just committed, something to do besides going crazy on a Cruise to Nowhere.

Sharon Sherman pulled on her panties and her slacks but carried her shoes in her hands as she made her barefooted way back to her cabin.

I didn't even get a backward glance.

I slept late, and would have slept even later if not for an urgent announcement over the public address system that nearly blasted me out my bed:

"Attention, all passengers! Anyone with information regarding the whereabouts of the shuffleboard equipment, please report to the cruise director's office."

I sat up in bed, laughing even as my head hammered with a

hangover. It hadn't been a dream! This crazy thing had really happened!

It was the big topic at breakfast, which was served buffet-style, and as I piled scrambled eggs onto my plate the cruise director was doing her best to placate a chubby guy with a comb-over. It seems he was in the shuffleboard finals, and what, he demanded to know, was going to happen now?

Meanwhile, the cruise director went to great lengths to try and resolve the shuffleboard snafu. She actually radioed a passing cruise ship to attempt to borrow their shuffleboard equipment, but the captain of that ship refused to stop and help.

And so it came to pass that I handed out "co-winner" trophies to the comb-over guy and his equally unhappy fellow finalist, a Hungarian with dyed red hair who wheezed like a harmonica with every breath he took. My contract called for me to play the piano and sing one last time, during a late lunch that was served an hour before the cruise came to an end in Los Angeles.

Sharon Sherman did not show up for breakfast or lunch. She must have stayed in her room until the ship reached the dock, and hurried off the boat as soon as the gangplank went down. I never saw her or heard from her again.

And the *Barca D'Amore* cruise director never hired me again. She must have suspected I had something to do with the shuffleboard fiasco.

That was really the beginning of the end for me in Los Angeles. If I'd made it as a cruise ship singer I probably would have stayed on the West Coast, and never returned to Little Neck, and never gotten the shocking news that awaited me the following day.

CHAPTER TEN

It happened innocently enough, when Flynn started busting poor Patrick's balls about his girlfriend, Scarlett, who worked the lunch counter at the local Kmart.

We were on our lunch break, sitting in the shade of a swamp maple. Patrick blushed and his ears went red as Flynn's barbs kept coming, one after another.

"How're you two gettin' along these days, Patrick? The guys get fresh with her at Kmart? Lotta young guys stop in there for lunch, ya know. . . . Patrick, Patrick, what's she gonna do in September, when you go away?"

That last one stung the kid pretty hard. He drained the last of his Gatorade and squeezed the empty bottle in his hands.

"She'll e-mail me," he said softly. "And we'll talk on the phone. We're in love, Mr. Flynn."

At that magical word the old Irishman relented at last and toasted Patrick with his coffee cup. "Good for you, Patrick. Love is a beautiful thing. Ask Mickey, here. Ain't love a beautiful thing?"

"That's what they say."

"Makes the world go 'round, am I right?"

"They say that, too."

"Well, Mick oughta know. He wrote the all-time love song, some say."

"I'd love to hear that song," Patrick said sincerely. "I couldn't find it on YouTube."

"Oh, Christ, Patrick, back in the day, it was the only thing you heard on the radio!"

There were only a few minutes left to the lunch break. Patrick moved closer to me.

"May I ask you something?"

"Sure, Patrick."

"Did you write your song for a girl?"

I was eating a peanut butter sandwich, which went gluey in my suddenly dry mouth.

"Yes," I managed to say.

"Lynn," Flynn helpfully added. "Lynn Mahoney."

"Lynn Ann Mahoney," I said, and it hit me for the first time that she had the perfect initials for a runaway: L.A.M.

Patrick's eyebrows went up. "Mahoney like the fireman family?"

"Same family," Flynn said. "She was the only girl. God help them. What a tragedy, huh? What . . . a . . . tragedy." Flynn sighed, then smiled. "Anyway, Mickey was nuts about that girl like you're nuts about Scarlett."

"That's true," I admitted. "And the boss-man here busted my chops about it just like he's busting yours."

Patrick's eyes were wide with wonder. "Whatever happened to her, Mickey?"

"She moved away a long time ago."

"Ran away," Flynn said. "I mean, I'm sorry, Mick, but that's what really happened."

I rolled my eyes. "All right, she ran away. She ran away and she never came back."

Flynn's eyebrows arched in surprise. "What are you talkin' about?"

"What do you mean, what am I talkin' about?"

"Mickey, you knucklehead . . . she's back."

My heart stopped, and then it started again at a gallop, and for a moment I thought I might faint. "What do you mean, she's back?"

"For Christ's sake, Mickey, she moved home with her mother a coupla months ago. You didn't know that? How could you not *know* that?"

Flynn didn't have a lot of details. Lynn's mother had suffered a stroke, and she could no longer live alone, so her daughter—her only child still living!—had moved back home to Little Neck to take care of her.

And according to Flynn, this had happened two months ago, which meant that Lynn had moved back to the old neighborhood even before I did.

I was numb for the rest of the workday, pushing my mower like a man possessed. It's a miracle I didn't run over every flower bed in Great Neck. For once, I was looking forward to the evening meal with the folks, which on that night happened to be tuna casserole, heavy on the noodles.

I waited until my mother had set all three plates down and settled herself into her chair before clearing my throat to calm myself. It didn't work. I was hotter than my lawn mower's motor at midday.

"How come you never told me that Lynn is back?"

My father's fork stopped halfway to his mouth, noodles dangling. "She is?"

"Come on, Dad. You knew."

"I swear to God, I didn't know."

I believed him. He was too wide-eyed to be bluffing. My mother, on the other hand, was keeping her eyes on her food.

"Mom. Why didn't you tell me?"

"What makes you think I knew?"

"Because you know *everything* that happens in this damn neighborhood."

"I don't know everything."

"You know everything that goes on in Little Neck. If Flynn knew it, *you* knew it. He probably found out from you!"

She lifted her eyes to look at me, thoroughly unintimidated at being caught in a lie. "Is it really such big news? Her mother's not well. She came home to take care of her, that's all."

"It was big news when she didn't show up to bury her father and her brothers! You couldn't wait to tell me about *that!*"

An iron grip around my left wrist, almost tight enough to cut off my circulation. All those years of working with heavy tools had given my old man powerful hands.

"Mickey. Take it easy."

"Dad, please let go of me."

"I will, but calm down."

He let my wrist go. I rubbed it, feeling the tingle of blood return to my fingers.

"I just think it's funny you didn't tell me, Mom," I began as calmly as I could. "We hear about every illness and every death at this table, every biopsy, every tumor, every shadow on every X-ray, but a piece of news like this just goes by the boards, somehow."

"What do *you* care if she's back?" she all but hissed.

I had to laugh. "How could I not care? I loved that girl!"

"She *ruined* you!"

A slap in the face couldn't have stunned me more than those three words. I flinched as if I'd actually been struck.

"Ruined me?"

"She broke your heart, Michael." She leaned closer to me, in danger of getting tuna casserole on her blouse. "Did you hear what I said? That girl broke your heart, but she did more than that. She broke something else that couldn't be fixed. She changed you forever."

I was shocked to see her eyes fill up with tears, tears of grief. My mother was mourning the loss of the boy I used to be. She dabbed at her eyes with a paper napkin, sighed, and came back strong, her eyes red but dry. She'd waited a long time to say these things, and the time had come at last.

"She wounded you. I can't forget that it happened. I remember the person you were before you knew her, and the person you became after. She took all the sweetness out of you." A wistful little smile tickled her lips. "Don't you think I remember the sweet boy you were?"

I swallowed, tasting bile. "Everybody gets their heart broken, Mom."

"Not like that, they don't. The way she just disappeared . . . there's something seriously wrong with that girl, Michael. No normal person does the things she's done. Running away like that. Missing those funerals."

"You can't make judgments about funerals. Some people just can't go through with it. You're different."

She turned to my father. "See how he turns things around?"

"She goes to ten funerals a week," I said to him. "To her it's like going to the movies. And the 'seriously sick' they pray for in church are like the coming attractions."

"Mickey. Don't make fun of your mother."

"No," she said, holding up a hand, "let him. Let him make fun of me. I'm an easy target. That's fine. And do you want to know *why* you feel free to do it, Michael? Because deep down, you know that I'll always love you, no matter what happens. I'll always be here for you. It's safe to take it out on me."

The hand in the air turned into a pointing finger, aimed at me. "When you had nowhere to turn, you came here. You didn't run to Lynn Mahoney. Remember that."

"I didn't know where she was."

"Well, now you know. She's back with her mother, just like you're back with your mother. She's also working as a teller at the Queens County Savings Bank. Actually, it's an HSBC now. All right? Now you know everything. Happy?"

"I don't remember the last time I was happy, Mom."

"And we know whose fault that is. Miss Free Spirit herself."

She got up. "Now I'm going to work. Yes, Michael, *another* funeral ceremony. Would you like to come with me? No? Well, then, I'll just clear the table before I go."

She picked up our three barely touched plates of food and tossed them in the sink, food and all. It was far and away the most reckless thing I'd ever seen her do, and even my father was shocked.

"Donna, for Christ's sake! What the hell's wrong with you?"

"That's right. Side with your son. I'm used to it."

She bolted out the back door, giving it a good slam. We sat still for a moment, and then I got up to inspect the noodly mess. Somehow, the dishes hadn't broken. Even when she was reckless, she was cautious. I started to clean it up.

"What the hell are you doing?"

"Cleaning up."

"No. Leave it. It's her mess. She'll clean it when she comes back. You and I are going out for a little while."

"Out?"

"Out."

"Dad, I've got to see Lynn, that's all there is to it."

"Not yet. You're all steamed up. You'll make the wrong move. Just come with me."

"Where?"

"Hey. I'm your father. Just do as I say."

It was an almost laughable command. I'd pretty much been on my own since I was eighteen, and here he was, twenty years later, giving me an order.

Funny thing was, I was happy to obey. I followed him to his car and we took off as if we'd just pulled a bank job.

* * *

We were out of the neighborhood before I dared to ask, "Where are we going?"

He shook a Camel into his mouth and lit it with the dashboard lighter. "Belmont."

"The racetrack?"

"I'm thinkin' you might like it."

I'd never been to the track with my old man before. I had zero interest in racehorses, or any other kind of gambling. I'd never even bought a lottery ticket. Gambling bored me, but my father was hooked. I'd grown up with the *Racing Form* around the house, and Steady Eddie would study it with pen in hand, making marks on the pages as if the words were revealing truths only he could perceive.

The worst possible thing had happened to him the first time he ever went to the track, according to my mother—he won big. He'd picked five winners. That was before I was born. He was apparently still trying to recapture that one glorious day. If it's easy the first time, why shouldn't it be just as easy every other time?

It suddenly hit me that I truly was his son, after all. My first song had been a breeze. We'd both failed to learn our lesson, him from the horses, me from my music. Success was a bitch who'd fucked each of us once and then vanished, without even leaving a note on the pillow.

"Do you remember that time you nearly hit that lamppost with your bike?"

My father's words jolted me. I needed a moment to figure out what he was talking about.

"You mean when you were teaching me to ride?"

"Yeah."

"Sure I remember. You saved me at the last instant. Grabbed the bicycle seat just in time."

He nodded, dragged on his cigarette. "Last night I had a dream that you hit that pole. I didn't get there in time."

"You dreamed this last night?"

"Funny, huh? You smashed your head. You weren't wearing a helmet. Nobody wore helmets in those days. Had to rush you to the hospital."

A shiver went through me, and then I tried to lighten it. "It was just a dream, Dad. Who knows what it means?"

"It means I should have looked out for you better when you were a kid out there in California, is what it means. Maybe I shouldn'ta let you go in the first place."

He was trying to apologize for the mess of my life. He had to do it while he was driving, so he could keep his eyes on the road, away from mine.

"Dad, it doesn't matter."

"It matters."

He turned to look at me. There was nothing to say, and the silence was excruciating.

Just then, some asshole driver cut him off on the highway. He jammed on the brakes and flung a protective arm across my chest.

"Did you see that dumb bastard, Mick? Talkin' on a cell phone. Always on their cell phones, these goddamn idiot drivers!"

"It's okay, Dad, it's okay."

"Cell phones! Goddamn cell phones! Why the hell do people have to stay in touch with each other twenty-four hours a day? What the fuck is that asshole talking about that's so fucking important?"

"Easy, Dad. . . ."

His arm was still across my chest, protecting me. He seemed to notice it for the first time and dropped it suddenly, seeming embarrassed.

"Dad. Thanks."

"For what?"

"For taking me in when I had no place to go."

He looked at me, rolled his window down, threw his cigarette away and turned his attention back to the road, on guard against further idiot drivers.

"You paid off the mortgage," he said to the windshield. "I should be thanking you."

At the racetrack I became his little boy again. He bought me a soft pretzel and a beer and if somebody had been selling teddy bears, he probably would have bought me one.

He touched the rim of his plastic beer cup against the rim of mine. "Cheers, Mick. We never had a beer together, did we? How fuckin' sad is that?"

"Better late than never, Dad."

I followed him around as if I were five years old, a kid visiting Daddy at his office. He led the way to the viewing area, a ring where the jockeys take the horses before a race. This gives the gamblers one last chance to eye the merchandise before laying down a bet. It was a serious business, almost somber, and deeply depressing. These magnificent animals, bred and fed and groomed to perfection, were being evaluated by a lot of slack-gutted guys with three-day growths of beard, scuffed shoes, and baggy pants buttoned below the belly.

One of them, a balding guy with an ear-to-ear comb-over, si-dled up to my father and asked him who he liked in the first race. My father shrugged, clutching his rolled-up *Racing Form.* He wasn't about to share.

"You're a real prick, Steady Eddie," the guy said without a trace of malice. He shuffled away and my father winked at me. I was startled and touched at the same time. I don't think he'd ever winked at me before. It was a hell of a time and place for my first wink.

He tapped my shoulder with the rolled-up *Racing Form,* jerked his chin toward a chestnut stallion and leaned close to my ear.

"That's the one," he whispered in my ear, and again I was startled, as this was the first time my father had ever whispered to me.

I didn't know what to say, and when at last I spoke my words couldn't have been more stupid.

"You sure, Dad?"

"Sure? Am I sure? That's very funny, Mick. If I were sure about this shit, we'd have a mansion in Kings Point."

"I mean—"

"Track's a little muddy. This one's good on mud." He pointed at the board. "He's goin' off at twelve to one. I'm gonna play him."

"What about that one? He any good?"

I pointed at a short gray horse with powerful-looking legs. To me the horse seemed to be brimming with energy, bright-eyed and strong. Also he wore the number three, my lucky number.

My father chuckled. "First of all, he's a she. A filly. And no, she's not much good. They probably just threw her in there to fill out the field."

"I like the look of her."

"She hasn't got a chance, Mick. Don't waste your money."

"Maybe just two bucks. Not to win, to come in third."

"We call that 'show.' "

"Yeah, to show. I'm gonna bet her to show. What the hell."

My father shook his head. "You're a real dreamer, aren't you?"

"Lynn used to call me that."

"You dream about her, don't you?"

I swallowed. "Every night for about twenty years."

He nodded, not surprised. "Well, let me tell you what I think. You get paid tomorrow, right? So you take your money and go to the bank and open an account. I hear they got one really nice teller. You go to her window, you see what happens."

I was too stunned to speak. I swallowed the rest of my beer as my father stared at me.

"You'da made an ass of yourself if you'd gone bangin' on her door tonight," he continued. "Gotta cool down before you make your move. Also, you don't want to meet her on her home turf. The bank's neutral ground. You got a better chance on neutral ground."

"Is that why you kidnapped me tonight?"

"Kidnapped? That's a little harsh."

"But that's why you brought me here, isn't it?"

"What do you mean?"

"This place. This is your turf, isn't it, Dad? You wanted to get your point across on your turf."

He fought to hide a smile. "I brought you here so we could win some money, kid. Come on, let's go to the window."

My father bet first. I was startled to hear him say, "Fifty on Mahogany Flash to win."

Fifty bucks! Did my mother have any idea that he bet this big? He answered my unspoken question by turning his head and muttering, "Don't mention this to your mother."

Still numb over the size of his bet, I slid two singles under the window and placed a bet on Merry Legs to show. Even the clerk seemed to be grinning at my foolishness. The horse was a 75-to-1 long shot. I was wasting two bucks—a subway ride I wouldn't be taking, a hot dog I wouldn't be eating.

At post time the odds on my horse had increased to 82 to 1, while a flurry of last-minute bets narrowed the odds on my father's horse to 10 to 1. If he won, he'd have five hundred bucks.

The race began. Everybody around me was on their feet and yelling, nobody louder than my father. It hit me that I had never before heard him express enthusiasm of any kind, and here he was, jumping up and down and screaming for a stupid animal to run fast.

I barely glanced at the track. I couldn't take my eyes off my father. He was alive. He looked twenty years younger, strong and passionate and hot-blooded.

I felt my eyes mist up. I was sorry that this was what he needed to feel this way. He'd been robbed. He'd never had a real passion. He did what he had to do, good old Steady Eddie, and he wasted his steam and his cream on the horses.

I was lucky, compared to him. At least I'd written my song, and tried to write others. His only thrills came from laying bets on overbred creatures who were put to death when they broke a leg. How had he ended up with such a life?

It was so sad that I wanted to run out of that place, but suddenly his arms were around me in a bear hug that hoisted me off my feet. Belmont Park exploded with noise, and his stubbly cheek scraped my face like sandpaper.

"We did it, Mick, we fuckin' did it!"

"We?"

He pointed to the board. Mahogany Flash had won, and who the hell should have come in third but a long-shot loser named Merry Legs.

My father had won five hundred bucks for his fifty, and I would pocket sixty-eight dollars for my deuce.

I was still locked in his embrace. It felt as if he might never let go.

"The DeFalcos rule!" he shouted to the sky. "Oh, baby, we *rule!*"

And for those few minutes, I guess he was right. If this was all he had, I wanted him to savor it.

We stayed for three more races. I didn't bet again. My father lost his next two bets but won on the third, so he was a few hundred bucks ahead on the night by the time we hit the road.

When we got home my mother was asleep, and the kitchen was spotlessly clean.

"Told you she'd clean it up, didn't I, Mick?" He patted my cheek. "You have fun tonight, or what?"

"It was good, Dad. Thanks."

"Tomorrow after work you go and see her, all calm and collected."

"Right."

"Be careful you don't daydream on the job, thinkin' about her. You work with power tools. Don't wanna lose a foot, or a finger. The girls don't go for maimed guys."

"Good night, Dad."

He went outside for his last smoke of the night.

I went to my room and lay in bed, thinking about the deposit I was going to make at Lynn's window the next day. It would be sixty-eight dollars more than it would have been, thanks to a long shot named Merry Legs.

But Merry Legs was a sure thing, compared to the long shot I was about to play.

CHAPTER ELEVEN

The bank was a sweet little place, a gingerbread house with bars on the windows, bars that hadn't been there when I was a kid. It was here that I'd made my very first schoolboy nickel-and-dime deposits in an envelope with a picture of the winking Wise Old Owl on it. *Save when you're young, no worries when you're old. . . .*

Whatever happened to that bank account? It was something to wonder about as I went up the path, past knee-high hedges and an immaculately trimmed little lawn.

Upon entering I felt the shock of the air-conditioning on my sweaty self. Hardly any customers were around. It was fifteen minutes to closing time.

And there she was.

She was seated at a barred teller window, as this bank lacked the suspicion and the sophistication to switch to bulletproof glass. She was busy going over the day's receipts and had not yet looked up. Her hair was pulled back in a ponytail, the same way she'd worn it when she was a kid.

Butterflies bumped around in the cavities formerly occupied

by my kneecaps. Somehow those legs of mine took me to her window. I stood at the bars like a man visiting his wife in prison.

"May I help you?" she asked, still not looking up.

That voice. If a brook could speak . . .

I pushed my pay envelope under the slot with a trembling hand.

"I'd like to open a savings account. Or maybe you could chuck this money in a wheelbarrow for me."

She looked up, and the sight of those sea-green eyes made me swallow a sob. Her eyes narrowed in puzzlement, widened in wonder, and finally settled into the same saucy green beams that haunted my dreams.

"Oh, my God, it's *you*."

"Hey, Lynn. Long time."

She sat up straight and shook her head. The ponytail flicked from shoulder to shoulder.

"That TV show of yours," she said, "was by far the worst program I've ever seen."

I was startled, stunned, amazed, and not surprised. Back in the day, I never knew what she was going to say, except that it was always going to be the truth. Nothing had changed.

I nodded. "That's why it only lasted three episodes."

"Three too many, if you ask me."

"Who's asking you?"

She smiled, then laughed. I was laughing, too, all the way from my soul. It's a funny sound, laughter in a bank, echoing off the walls and vaults, and neither of us could stop for what seemed like years.

But actually, it was only minutes. And speaking of minutes, there were only a few of them left until closing time, and Lynn Mahoney used them to open a savings account for me. She was all business as she slid a shiny green passbook under the bars, my deposit neatly recorded on its first page.

"Can I walk you home, Lynn?"

She nodded, her eyes shiny with sudden tears. "Sure, Mickey. Been a long time since anybody walked me home."

Elbows tight to my rib cage (the better to cover my stinking armpits), I walked along the streets of Little Neck with Lynn Mahoney for the first time since 1988. It was a walk I'd walked a million times in my dreams, a walk I'd never expected to make again.

Neil Armstrong's heart wasn't beating as fast as mine when he walked on the damn moon.

I was foolishly, ridiculously, breathlessly happy. Amazing, considering we hadn't so much as shaken hands. So far this felt like just another in an endless series of dreams. In those dreams I always ran to her and gathered her up in my arms, but in reality I was afraid to touch her, afraid that if I did she'd burst and vanish like a soap bubble.

She was even more beautiful than before, those chipmunk cheeks having melted away to reveal high cheekbones. I was delighted to see that her black pantsuit was bottomed off by a pair of black Reebok cross-trainers. She may have become a buttoned-down banker, but she was still ready to run.

What to say? My brain was a logjam of thoughts, and my mouth quivered as if I were about to burst into tears.

"I'm sorry about your brothers," I finally said. "And your father."

She nodded, did not falter or break stride. "I'm sure ol' Donna told you I wasn't there for the funerals."

"She might have mentioned it."

"Well," Lynn said, spreading her arms to indicate the limitless grandeur of Northern Boulevard, "I'm here now."

My heart sank. I'd never once heard her say anything even remotely sarcastic, until this remark.

"Yeah," I replied numbly. "Me too."

"I can't believe you're back with Mr. Flynn."

"He's the one who told me you were back."

"Yeah, well, nothing ever changes around here, especially the gossip. And as gossip goes, I'm pretty hot stuff, aren't I? The coldhearted bitch who ran off like a tramp, back home at last."

"Nobody's saying that."

"They're thinking it, Mickey. Can't say I blame them."

"They're also thinking about a one hit wonder who's back sleeping in his old room."

We walked two blocks in absolute silence. How was it possible there could be nothing more for us to say? I had to say something, *anything*, and suddenly I did.

"Did you ever get to Italy?"

Lynn seemed puzzled. "Italy?"

"When we were kids we used to talk about saving up to go to Italy. You wanted to see the museums. . . ."

"Oh God, I forgot about that!"

My heart sank. How could she have forgotten about Italy? It was part of the reason we'd fallen for each other!

"Florence and Rome and Venice," I persisted. "You were going to—"

She waved her hand, as if to erase an unpleasant memory. "Mickey. I remember now. No, I never made it to Italy. Never even got a passport."

"So where . . ."

I let the question tail off, realizing she didn't want to talk about the paths she'd taken after she ran off.

"Did *you* ever go to Italy?" Lynn asked.

"No, but believe it or not my song made it over there. '*Giorni Di Zucchero.*'"

"Is that 'Sweet Days' in Italian?"

"Actually, the literal translation is 'Days of Sugar.' They got some spaghetti-bender to croon it. Didn't sound half bad."

"It's a beautiful language, Mickey. Probably the most beautiful language in the world."

"Why'd you ditch me that way?"

I had to ask her like that, flat-out. She quickened her pace and I did the same to keep up.

"You gonna answer me, or what?"

"You got a pretty good song out of it, DeFalco."

"Fuck my song. Why'd you leave?"

"It had nothing to do with you."

"Oh, well, that's a relief."

"Mickey. Please. Be nice."

"Nice? You run off on me twenty years ago and now I'm supposed to be *nice*?"

We were practically jogging. Lynn refused to say anything.

"You know," I said, "every time I performed it, wherever I was, I looked for you in the audience."

She slowed down to a regular walk. It took her a moment to catch her breath.

"That's crazy."

"Maybe, but it's true. I had this stupid idea that you'd come to see me if I was anywhere near wherever the hell you were hiding, and drop in for a backstage visit."

"I wasn't hiding."

"Well, whatever you were doing, I always hoped you'd show up to hear me sing."

She shook her head. "I'm not a concert person."

"Funny, neither am I. But being the performer, I sort of had to be there, you know?"

She kicked a pebble. "Didn't have much luck with your other songs, did you?"

"Nah. They sucked. I only had one passion, so I only had one song."

"I guess Mick Jagger and Bruce Springsteen have a lot of passions, huh?"

"They're pros, Lynn. I'm just a guy who had his heart broken and poured it out in a song. It made me rich for a little while and famous for a few months but it didn't bring you back. Which I guess is what I hoped it would do."

It was the truth, a truth I was learning myself as I spoke it.

Lynn sighed. "You're amazing."

"Why?"

"The way you hang on."

"I was in love with you, Lynn."

She cocked a single eyebrow at me, the left one. I'd forgotten how she could do that.

"Correct me if I'm wrong, but didn't I hear that you got married?"

I felt myself blush, waved her words away as if they were so many pesky gnats. "That was a mistake."

"Uh-huh."

"Did *you* ever get married?"

"Mickey. Come on. I can barely stand to live with myself."

We headed down the street leading to the Mahoney house, a street I'd carefully avoided since my return to Little Neck. There were things I had to know before we reached that damn house.

"You're not going to tell me why you did what you did, are you, Lynn?"

Her shoulders sank. "Aw, Mickey, please. I can't explain it. I was a kid. I had a wild streak in me. I just had to get out there in the world."

"Come on. Something happened. Tell me what happened."

"Nothing *happened*. I got sick and tired of living in a house where my parents didn't even look at each other. The climate of misery gets to you after a while, you know? So I split."

"Where? Where did you go?" *Why did you leave me?*

She hesitated. "Lots of places," she finally said. "Maine. Seattle. San Francisco."

"How'd you get by?"

"I got by."

"You were going to teach art history."

She shut her eyes, shook her head. "Oh, God, I can't believe you remember that."

"I remember everything. So do you."

"Yeah. That's the problem. Be great if we could forget things, wouldn't it?"

"I don't *want* to forget what we had!"

"Mickey. Shh." She put a finger to her lips, as if I were an excited schoolboy who'd gotten too loud in class. She jerked a thumb over her shoulder. "You'll wake my mother."

We were in front of the Mahoney house, a huge, ugly redbrick structure fronted by a lawn where the Captain had knocked me on my ass that time. Now it was a garden of waist-high weeds, and the ramp the city had built on the stoop for the Captain's wheelchair was in a state of collapse, the lumber buckled and warped from the years and the weather.

"Christ, Lynn, this place needs a little work."

"Think so? I kinda like it like this."

"Why?"

"It annoys the neighbors." She smiled for an instant, a flash of the way she used to be, wonderfully naughty without malice.

We were standing at her front gate, the same place we used to stand to kiss each other good night, but now we weren't even touching each other. We were like two archaeologists visiting the ruins of an ancient love temple.

"How's your mother?" I managed to say.

She shrugged. "It was a pretty serious stroke." She looked at her watch. "I have to relieve the day nurse, Mickey. She gets cranky if she misses her bus."

She extended her hand for a formal shake, arm out all the way, fingers tight together like the slats of a spite fence. I could have cried. Then again, it was an opportunity to hold her hand.

So we shook like two lawyers, a bony and bloodless squeeze of two hands that used to lace fingers at the movies.

And then, just as my heart was about to break in a million pieces, she let go of my hand and hesitated before reaching up and poking my upper lip with her forefinger.

"Still refuses to behave, that lip of yours," she murmured.

I tingled where she'd touched me, allowed myself to feel a glimmer of hope. "I want to see you, Lynn."

"You will. I'm around for a while." *Until my mother dies. . . .* She managed a weak smile. "We're neighbors again, Mickey."

"That's not what I mean."

She sighed. "You know, even after all these years, you're still—"

"Stop. Shut up. If you tell me I'm still a nice boy I'll have to kill you."

She shrugged. "Then I won't. But you are."

"Ask Rosalind Pomer if I'm a nice boy. She'll set you straight."

"Who's Rosalind Pomer?"

"Nobody."

"Then I'd have a hell of a time asking her, wouldn't I?"

I could think of nothing more to say. She actually lifted her hand and waved to me, as if she were on a train that was pulling away.

"See you around, Mickey."

"Will I see you around? Do you mean that?"

"Mickey. There's a lot going on, understand? I'll call you when I'm ready, but please don't call me. Okay? Do we have a deal?"

Deals. I was making deals with her now.

"Will you really call me?"

"I will. I promise."

"Well then, it's a deal."

She opened the gate and walked up the mossy brick path toward the front door. I called out her name, as I should have called it out on that summer night so long ago. She stopped, turned to look at me.

"How the hell did someone like you become a banker?"

An easy question. She was so relieved she giggled. "I guess I just have one of those faces people can trust, huh?"

"I trusted it," I said, and that's the line that got to her. Her face went pale as she turned to rush inside. Moments later the day nurse came out, a skinny woman with gray, close-cropped hair who stared at me as she went around me. As she headed for Northern Boulevard she kept sneaking peeks at me over her shoulder. She probably thought I was some kind of a stalker. If she did, she wasn't too far off.

I stood and stared at the Mahoney house. It wasn't as if I expected Lynn to come running out and flying into my arms. I knew that wasn't going to happen.

I was remembering the last time I'd stood here, wishing Lynn would appear.

CHAPTER TWELVE

It was raining that day, a misty, almost greasy rain, the kind that comes late in November, when autumn hasn't quite made the turn into winter and water isn't quite ready to turn into ice. It was only around four o'clock in the afternoon but already darkness was falling.

Lynn had been gone for three months and I'd avoided her street ever since she'd disappeared, but on my way home from school I had this wild idea that maybe, *maybe* she'd be there.

She'd be there because it was my birthday, and all I wanted for my birthday was the return of my girlfriend.

It was a stupid, foolish dream, and I knew it even as I was walking toward the Mahoney house. It was all about hope, I guess. Even false hope was better than no hope.

The Mahoney yard was covered with big yellow leaves. The house was dark and looked almost abandoned, and then my heart soared at the sight of somebody moving at the end of the path. It fell just as fast when I recognized who it was. The Captain in his wheelchair, trying to roll himself up the ramp the city had built for him.

I was transfixed by the sight of him. In those few months since his fall down the basement steps, he'd lost a shocking amount of weight. His shoulders looked bony within the folds of a windbreaker that seemed way too big for him.

The rain had plastered his thick white hair to his skull, and his cold-reddened hands gripped the wheels of his chair. He was having a hell of a time of it. He rolled himself a few feet up the incline, groaned to a stop, and then rolled back down to where he'd started.

It was a shock to see this man in such a weakened condition. He actually had to rest and catch his breath after that little bit of effort. It was like watching a man die, but actually it was even worse than that. It was like watching a man who wanted to die unable to follow through with it, being deprived of that final step that would have put an end to his humiliation.

He must have heard me breathing. He turned his head to see me standing there stupidly in the rain. He squinted at me, and then his eyes widened in recognition before narrowing in suspicion.

"You," he said, and further words were barely necessary.

I wanted to run from him but I couldn't. I hated the man, but he needed me. He needed anybody, and there was only me on that rainy, rapidly darkening November afternoon.

By this time the rain had penetrated my school jacket. I shivered, but not from the cold. I made my way toward the Captain and stood before him like a bill collector.

He wouldn't lift his chin to look at me. He kept his head level and rolled his eyes upward to regard me, like an angry altar boy.

His legs seemed even skinnier than his arms, so skinny that the shoes on his feet looked enormous, a clown's shoes propped up on his wheelchair stirrups. The handles of his wheelchair seemed to protrude straight from his shoulder blades, like a pair of horns.

I cleared my throat. "Would you like a push, sir?"

"What the hell are you doin' here?"

"I was just . . . passing by."

"Bullshit."

"Would you like a push, sir, or not?"

He thought about it for a long moment. "The wheels are wet," he finally said. "Can't get a good grip on them."

That was a lie. The truth was that he lacked the strength to haul himself up that ramp. The Captain, who'd carried innumerable people out of burning buildings, was too weak to hoist his own weight. He could never admit that to himself, much less to me.

Now I saw that his hands gripped a brown paper bag, which was coming apart from the rain. He lifted the bag to his face and tilted it toward his mouth with a glugging sound. I smelled whiskey.

It was easy to figure out what had happened. In his condition, the Captain was totally dependent upon his wife for everything. She saw this as a perfect way to eliminate his drinking—she brought him food and beverages, but no booze.

Now she was out somewhere, and he'd taken it upon himself to roll his way to Little Neck Liquors. A perfect plan, except that he couldn't make it back up the ramp.

He still hadn't answered my question.

"Would you like a push, sir?"

"Just get me up this fucking ramp, already."

I got behind the chair and rolled him up the ramp. "That's enough," he said when we reached the flat part. "I got it from here."

"Okay, sir."

I opted for the steps on the way down, and when I reached the path he called to me.

"Hey, wait a minute, wait a minute."

I turned to face him. Now he could look down at me, just as he did in the old days. He stared at me in open contempt, as if

he were trying to figure out a way to avoid thanking me for getting him up the ramp. Then something else occurred to him.

"You don't live this way. What the hell are you doin' on my
street?"

His street. Jesus Christ.

"Like I said, I was just passing by."

"Bullshit, boy." He gulped whiskey for courage. I saw a shiver
catch him and travel right from his feet to his face, as if he'd
stepped on a live wire. He cleared his throat and hesitated before speaking.

"Is she coming home? Is that why you're here?"

"I don't know where she is, sir."

"If you did know, you wouldn't tell me, would you?"

"If I knew where she was, I'd be there with her."

"Guess she didn't love you the way you loved her, eh?"

He chuckled, the same cruel chuckle I remembered from the
day he'd invited me to box, or all those times he'd break his son
Brendan's chops for being a delicate boy. Maybe that nasty
chuckle was the only thing about this man that was as it had been
before he took that header down the cellar steps.

I climbed three of the five steps, so the Captain and I were eye
to eye. His eyes were glassy from booze but he was still as dangerous as a cornered rat. I thought hard of something to say that
would hurt him, and then it came to me.

"Would you like me to open the door for you, sir?"

"I can open the fucking door myself, thank you very much,
guinea-boy."

"All right, then. It was good to see you, Captain Mahoney."

"I'm not a captain anymore, I'm just a retired cripple."

For an instant I almost felt sorry for him, but I got over it fast.
"Well, enjoy your retirement," I said, which is just another way of
telling someone they don't have long to go.

I made my way back down the steps, deliberately smacking the soles of my shoes as I walked so the man could both see and hear this simple, precious action of which he was no longer capable.

"Mickey!"

He'd hardly ever called me by my name. I stopped and turned to face him. The tears on his face were mixed with rain, or maybe it was all rain, but either way the man was in hell. He swallowed and cleared his throat.

"You really don't know where she is, do you?"

I shook my head.

"She hasn't been in touch with you?"

"No."

He seemed to accept this as the truth. He turned his wheelchair toward the front door, dug into his windbreaker pocket for his key. I took his turn as a dismissal and continued walking, and then came the last words I ever would have expected from this man's mouth.

"If you hear from her, tell her . . ."

I stood staring at him, waiting for the rest of the sentence.

"Tell her to come home," he said in a quaking voice. "Tell her all is forgiven."

I'm sure that in his whole life the Captain had never, ever offered forgiveness to anyone, for any reason. Now, reduced to a skeletal cripple, he was finding compassion in his heart, a willingness to forgive his daughter for running away from home.

I cleared my throat before speaking. "Why'd she do it, sir?"

His jaws clenched. He began the answer by shaking his head.

"She's a crazy, crazy kid," the Captain said. "Not like my boys. My boys obeyed me. But that . . . girl . . ."

That was as far as he got, and it was clear he regretted the few words he'd spoken. He shut his mouth and ducked his head. I opened my mouth to speak, but just like that he was inside the house, shutting the door behind him with a thunderous boom.

At last I found my tongue.

"It's my birthday," I called to the empty front porch, and then I went home, toweled off, and changed into dry clothes in preparation for a spaghetti and meatballs dinner, to be followed by a Carvel ice cream cake we'd be having to celebrate the eighteenth anniversary of my arrival into this lonely, fucked-up world.

CHAPTER THIRTEEN

So now, I had a bargain with the great love of my life—don't call me, I'll call you. In other words, I'd been slapped with a restraining order.

I dropped the news on my parents at the dinner table that night. My mother's lips tightened but she said nothing. My father shrugged.

"All right, so you wait a while," he said. "It won't kill you."

Suddenly my mother spoke up, as if to remind me of something she'd already told me.

"Listen," she said, "you're singing at a birthday party tomorrow for Eileen Kavanagh's grandson, who's dying."

It was incredible. It sounded like some kind of sick joke, but I knew it wasn't. She said it the way a mother tells a child to take out the trash. We'd picked up where we'd left off when I went away. I was the world's oldest eighteen-year-old, just a kid being ordered to do something.

And what a fucking order this was!

"Mom. What are you talking about?"

"It's at three o'clock. You don't have plans, do you?"

"Plans? Apparently you're the one making all the plans!"

"Is it so much to ask," she said in an aggrieved voice, "to sing a song or two for a doomed boy?"

I literally gripped the sides of my head, as if to keep it from exploding.

"You're droppin' it on him kinda sudden-like, Donna," said my father.

She put a hand to her chest. "What could I do? Eileen asked me! She was in tears! The boy wants to hear you sing! Was I supposed to say no?"

"I can't sing, Mom. I'm too traumatized to perform, ever since the sinking of the *Barca D'Amore.*"

"Don't be fresh!"

"It would have been nice if you'd asked me, Mom."

"It would have been nice if you'd remembered that Eileen's husband died, Michael."

Oh Christ. "I'm sorry, Mom. I can't remember everybody who dies in Little Neck."

"I was mortified when Eileen told me you asked how her husband was. *Mortified.*"

My father chuckled, patted my back approvingly. "You did that? That's pretty funny."

"Oh, it's just *hilarious*, Eddie."

"Don't feel bad, Mick. That poor guy was dead years before they buried him."

I took my hands off my head. "What's this kid supposedly dying from?"

"*Supposedly?*"

"I'm sorry. You're right. Who would lie about a doomed child?" I cleared my throat to wipe the slate clean. "What's he dying of?"

"He's got leukemia. He's eleven."

"Jesus."

"Without a bone marrow transplant, he'll die. And so far, they can't find a match."

"And he wants to hear me sing."

"That's right."

I gave it a second for everything to settle in. I proceeded with caution, but I did proceed.

"If this kid's eleven, Mom," I said softly, "there's no way in hell he ever even heard of me."

"Michael!"

"It just doesn't make sense! I've been off the radar for twenty years! Why would he want me to sing for him? No way I'm on his Make-A-Wish list!"

"How can you sit there and make fun of a dying—"

"I'm *not* making fun of a dying kid! I'm just wondering what the hell is actually going on here!"

My mother held her hands up, palms out, and closed her eyes. "Michael, if it's too much trouble for you to take ten minutes out of your busy schedule—"

"How about this? How about if I have a test to see if my bone marrow is a match for his? Wouldn't that do him a lot more good than a song from a singer he's never even heard of?"

She just looked at me, the way mothers look at sons who have no respect or pity for the pain they've endured to bring us forth into the world.

"Okay, Mom, you win." I sighed. "I'll do it."

She pursed her lips and shook her head. "You certainly put me through the wringer first, didn't you?"

"I'm sorry. I just had to ask a few things."

"Nothing's changed, Michael. You're still full of questions."

"Questions are what separate us from the animals." I turned to leave. "After this, please don't volunteer me anymore."

With that, I went to my room and my father went outside to smoke, leaving my tearful mother to clean up the dinner mess.

I hated working birthday parties. That was the lowest rung of my musical career, and I swore to myself that I'd done it for the last time at the thirteenth birthday of a Los Angeles kid named

Eliott Weintraub, whose parents wanted to celebrate his bar mitzvah in grand style.

This was a year or two before my *Barca D'Amore* gig. It was one of those parties where the parents basically stuff a cannon full of money and fire it at the sky. A sculptor was hired to carve a refrigerator-sized block of ice into a statue of The Terminator, Eliott's favorite movie hero. There was a juggler, a fire-eater, and a magician. Three hundred guests wandered around the immaculately groomed grounds of Peter Weintraub, tax attorney extraordinaire to the rich and obscure.

Dom Perignon flowed for the adults, Shirley Temples for the children. Buffet tables groaned with enough food to feed a third world country. High in the sky, a blimp drifted overhead, flashing an electronic message in red lights:

HAPPY BIRTHDAY, ELIOTT. TODAY YOU ARE A MAN.

The wildest touch of all was the peacocks—two dozen of them strutting around the grounds, preening and pecking and spreading their glorious tails. The peacocks were the idea of the tax man's number one deduction—his wife, Eva Weintraub, who'd also thought to hire me. I sat at a huge white piano on a patio overlooking the grounds, tickling the ivories and singing for the crowd.

The bar mitzvah boy, a chubby kid with an angry face, barely gave me a glance. Now and then I'd overhear a guest or two talking about the piano player, the "Isn't-he-the-guy" kind of remarks I was getting used to hearing.

The best crack of the day came from a woman whose chocolate-dark tan was accentuated by the contrast of her freshly bleached teeth. It was as if Lena Horne had converted to Judaism.

"I hear they tried to get Elton," she said to a friend, "but he wouldn't wear the yarmulke."

Elton would be Elton John, of course.

Me, I gladly wore the yarmulke. The job was paying a thousand bucks, and I was so desperate that I probably would have worn a brown shirt if Eva Braun had been throwing this shindig instead of Eva Weintraub.

I couldn't help wondering how much money they'd offered to Elton. They probably saved enough on me to pay for the rest of the party.

The bar mitzvah was not a total success. As evening fell The Terminator was melting into a hunchback, the kids were totally sugared out, and nobody, absolutely nobody was listening to the piano player.

But the biggest problem was the peacocks. The birds were gorgeous to look at but they made an incredible mess. The Weintraub lawn was spattered with peacock droppings, big chalky globs of it all over the place. People were skidding on it, falling on the grass as if they were sliding into second base. One elderly aunt was taken away on a stretcher amid much hand-wringing. Eva Weintraub's elegant idea had literally turned to shit. You see this a lot at Los Angeles parties. Rich people shoot for *The Great Gatsby,* and they wind up with *Apocalypse Now.*

I'd been paid to play from two until six. At six P.M. Eva Weintraub, her eye makeup smeary from what could only have been a crying jag, handed me an envelope and thanked me for my time.

All the kids seemed to have vanished—off to smoke dope someplace, probably. The adult guests were gathered down on the lawn, where silver-haired Peter Weintraub, his paunch reined back by a pair of green suspenders, was holding court. He got to the punch line of his story and his buddies erupted in laughter.

"I don't remember the last time he made *me* laugh," said Eva. "I don't remember the last time he really looked at me."

I looked at her. She was holding up all right for a woman in her early forties. She might have turned heads in the Midwest but in Los Angeles, she wasn't even in the game. Hell, she wasn't even on the bench.

"Is it my fault that the peacocks made a mess on the lawn? Is it? Nobody told me they were such messy birds!"

"Mrs. Weintraub—"

"He's blaming me for this peacock fiasco!" she ranted. "Does that sound fair to you?"

"No, not at all."

Her eyes narrowed slightly as she whispered, "He's got girl-friends. Two that I know of."

She wiped her eyes, set her jaw. A fresh light came to her face. It was an amazing thing to see. Just like that, she was through feeling bad, one of those rare people who can actually decide to stop feeling bad and do something about it.

Eva Weintraub took me by the wrist. "Follow me," she said, though there wasn't really any choice in the matter as she dragged me into the house and up the stairs and into a bedroom over-looking the lawn party. She let go of my wrist, reached under her dress, removed her panties, tossed them aside, put her hands on the windowsill and spread her feet.

With all the emotion of a drive-in customer speaking her fast food order into the clown's mouth at McDonald's, she looked over her shoulder and said:

"If it's not too much trouble, I'd like you to fuck me from be-hind while I watch my husband as I'm betraying him."

I swear, those were her very words. It was as if she'd read them off a teleprompter. She even handed me a condom.

"Mrs. Weintraub, I don't think—"

"For God's sake, you're about to nail me doggie-style! Do you think you could call me Eva?"

"Eva . . . this isn't such a good idea. "

"If you don't do it, I'll scream 'rape.' Okay? Who are they going to believe, you or me?"

She meant it. She really meant it. And she was right. Who were they going to believe? The one with the better lawyer, that's who.

"Eva," I said, "this is crazy."

"I agree with you, but I'm very, very angry, and this is what I do when I'm angry."

"It's not what I do."

She laughed. "You followed me up here, didn't you? Where did you think we were going? What did you think we were going to do?"

"I'm leaving, Mrs. Weintraub. Thank you for—"

"Oh, we're back to Mrs. Weintraub, eh?"

She got that look in her eye, the look a woman gets when she's about to drive home the dagger.

"My husband didn't want you here. He said to me, and I quote: 'Get a real star for Eliott's party. Who remembers that loser?' "

She was good. She knew which buttons to push. She was the kind of woman who always got what she went after, but never what she wanted. There was a lot of that in the City of Angels.

"So," she crooned, "are you a loser, like my husband says?"

I let the words bite into my twisted soul, and then I rubbered up and rode her from behind while she stared out the window and fogged up the double-pane windows with her heaving breaths as she cried the words, "Oh, Peter, you sack of shit, he's bigger than you, he's *better* than you!"

She urged me to fuck her harder. I did as I was told, and it was certainly the angriest hump of my life, rougher and rowdier than anything she expected. She'd lit a fuse without expecting quite this big an explosion, knowing nothing of the rage I carried inside.

Her face bumped the glass. She turned to look at me, rubbing her forehead.

"Hey, cowboy!"

"Huh?"

"Take it down a notch. And put the yarmulke back on."

In my excitement I'd taken the yarmulke off my head and clenched it in my fist. I smoothed it out, put it back on, and finished the ride with a kosher flourish.

Given his sexual preferences, I'd guess that Elton couldn't have done what I'd done, could he?

Eva Weintraub stepped back into her panties while I zipped up and tucked in.

"Do I owe you for the additional service?" she asked, sounding serious.

I shook my head. I didn't even want to look at her. "We're square."

"I want you to see something before you go, Nicky."

"It's Mickey."

"Whatever."

She went to a closet and took out a rifle, which she seemed to handle like an expert. I froze at the sight of it.

"Jesus!"

"I take target practice twice a week. I'm actually quite a good shot." She chuckled. "Any crackhead who tries to break into my room is going to be one sorry *schvartze*."

She opened the windows wide. Sounds of the party drifted inside. I moved to grab the rifle but she was quick as a cat, turning to point it at my chest. I backed off, hands held high.

She turned to the window, pointed the gun toward the lawn and pulled the trigger. The boom shook the room. I expected to see her husband collapse, but instead a peacock fell over dead in an explosion of blue feathers.

Eva giggled. "He's upset because they're shitting all over the lawn, eh?" she said. "Well, I can fix that."

Another shot, another dead peacock. People were screaming, fleeing in all directions. The infamous Beverly Hills Peacock Massacre had begun.

"Mrs. Weintraub, stop!"

I moved to get the rifle once again, and this time she stunned me by belting me on the jaw with the butt of the gun, just like John Wayne in the movies. We were, after all, in Hollywood.

I went down, seeing stars. She continued firing out the window.

"Nothing but peacocks!" she cried, and she was good to her word. Not a single human being got shot.

I got to my feet, staggered down the stairs and out the front door. The shots continued to ring out, along with a wail of sirens in the distance—someone had called 911. I got my ass out of there as fast as I could.

I read all about it in the papers the next day. After I fled, Eva Weintraub apparently locked the bedroom door and continued to bring down one bird after another. One anonymous police source marveled at her marksmanship.

Peacocks are apparently pretty stupid. After the first few shots all the people had fled from the lawn but the birds continued to mill about, oblivious to the slaughter. Their wings had been clipped to keep them from flying away, making Eva's mission that much easier. By the time cops in riot gear broke down the bedroom door and subdued her she'd killed seventeen of the twenty-four hired birds.

BAR MITZVAH BLOODBATH, screamed one headline. Peter Weintraub issued a statement saying that his wife had been under "extreme emotional duress" of late and that the pressures of preparing for their son's bar mitzvah had taken a toll. There was nothing about his complaints regarding peacock shit all over the lawn, and how this had triggered his wife's bloody rampage.

On top of a substantial bird rental fee, the dead peacocks were valued at $500 apiece, costing Peter Weintraub an additional $8500. In a master stroke of chutzpah, Weintraub had the slain birds plucked, cleaned, roasted, and shipped to a soup kitchen in downtown L.A., where the homeless dined on what had to have been the most expensive poultry in history.

"I just couldn't bear the thought of it all going to waste," Peter Weintraub was quoted as saying.

TV crews were there to record it all, as people with hardly any teeth got their teeth into roasted peacock.

"It's a little gamey," commented one finicky bag lady.

By the time all the lawyering was done, Eva Weintraub pleaded guilty to charges of cruelty to animals in exchange for a suspended sentence and community service. About six months later Peter Weintraub was in the headlines for attempting to claim an $8500 charitable deduction on his income taxes for donating the roasted peacocks to the homeless shelter. The deduction was disallowed, and several months after that the Weintraubs quietly divorced.

My name never came up in any of the stories. I was both grateful and, in a funny way, disappointed. I think that's when I first realized my musical career was in serious decline. I was just the piano player, trying his best to earn an honest buck. From then on, I vowed to myself, I would never again play at a birthday party. It was a vow I was able to keep, until my mother went and volunteered me to sing at the party for the dying Kavanagh boy.

Eileen Kavanagh made a brisk living as Little Neck's top real estate agent. It wasn't easy to bully a person like my mother, but even she was intimidated by this powerhouse of a woman. Old Eileen organized blood drives and church picnics. She stopped people on the street to ask why she hadn't seen them at mass recently. She was an absolute pain in the ass, married to a shadow of a man whose hunched shoulders told the story of his life. He'd died six months earlier (as I'd learned when I first bumped into Eileen upon my return to Little Neck) and I imagine he hadn't struggled much to try and stay alive.

Eileen had a son named Eugene who was my age. I'd gone to

school with him but I'd barely known him. He'd been a straight-A student with his father's bland personality. Eugene had a successful dental practice, a house in Little Neck, a loyal wife, and a son who was dying of leukemia.

I actually wore a jacket and tie to the birthday party, as if I were attending the boy's funeral. It was clothing I hadn't worn since high school, but it fit me pretty well. I was losing weight fast, pushing that lawn mower.

Eugene answered the door. The years had been brutal to him. He had his father's hunched shoulders, a potbelly, and an almost totally bald head. There was a fringe of hair around his ears, but that was it. If his son got past his illness and lived, he'd probably have male pattern baldness to deal with.

What an ugly thought! A bolt of shame shot through me, and I actually shivered at my own cruelty. Eugene shook my hand awkwardly, the way you do when you've known someone your whole life without being their friend.

"Mickey. Long time no see."

"Hey, Eugene."

"Come in, come in."

The living room was crammed with people eating birthday cake off paper plates. "There he is!" exclaimed Eileen Kavanagh, chubby as a partridge in a snug green dress. She wore a trumpet lily corsage that got crushed as she hugged me, then dragged me to the other side of the room. I felt a lot of eyes on me, the eyes of the kids' mothers. Most of them were the right age to remember me. One doe-eyed woman stood before me in apparent awe. Eileen put an arm across her shoulders.

"This," she announced, "is my beautiful daughter-in-law, Karen, who somehow fell in love with my son over there."

She jerked her head toward poor Eugene, caught spooning cake into his mouth. He offered a goofy grin through a chocolate icing mustache.

I shook hands with Eugene's wife, who held on damply as she breathlessly managed to say, "I love your song."

Something funny was going on. I shook hands with more people as Eileen introduced me around ("I've known him since he could walk!"), and Eugene's wife couldn't take her eyes off me, but where the fuck was the sick kid? I figured he must have been up in his room, hooked up to various life support devices. Maybe I'd have to sing to him through a surgical mask. . . .

"Everybody!" said Eileen, clutching my wrist as if she feared I might otherwise fly away. "Listen up, please, listen up—the one and only Mickey DeFalco is here to wish our Steven a happy birthday!"

The mothers cheered, the husbands patted their hands together politely, and Eileen went to a sliding glass door that opened onto the backyard.

"Steven!" she bellowed like a drill sergeant. "Steven Kavanagh, front and center!"

I braced myself for the sight of a bony, bald-headed kid with haunted eyes tottering into the house. Instead, the healthiest-looking eleven-year-old I'd ever seen came bounding inside, red-faced and breathless. He'd obviously been interrupted mid-game and was eager to return to his friends, who were chucking a football around in the yard.

"Steven, say hello to Mr. DeFalco."

"Hello."

"Say it nicely."

"Hello."

I studied the boy for signs of impending death. There were dark circles under his eyes, but I could tell they were fading. His eyes were clear. He was well nourished, maybe even a little overweight. He was eager to get back to the game, but his grandmother had other ideas.

"Mr. DeFalco is going to sing to you for your birthday."

Steven rolled his eyes. "Now?"

"In a minute . . . oh, go on, go back to your game, I'll call you when it's time."

Steven dashed back outside, to much laughter all around. I used the commotion to pull Eileen aside.

"Is that the sick kid?"

"He's a lot better now, thank God." She crossed herself. "Would you like some cake?"

"No, thank you. . . ."

The mothers had gathered around the piano in the living room. They were waiting for me, and I noticed they had sheets of paper in their hands, with photographs of houses on them. I saw the words "Kavanagh Realty" at the tops of the pages.

Holy Christ. Good old Eileen was using her doomed grandson's birthday party to drum up a little business. That's why I was there, to help lure the suckers into the tent.

I was too stunned to be angry. Eileen grabbed my wrist again and tried to haul me to the piano, but I held my ground like a mule, then pulled her over to a corner.

"Mrs. Kavanagh, is your grandson actually dying?"

"Shhh! Lower your voice!"

I lowered my voice. "My mother told me he was dying of leukemia, and he wanted to hear me sing. Is that the way it is?"

Her nostrils flared. She took a deep breath and said, "Steven had a serious blood disease."

"Had?"

"He seems to have overcome it now."

"What's the disease?"

Eileen forced a cruel chuckle. "So many questions, Mickey! I wasn't aware that you'd been to medical school."

"As we both know, I'm a high school dropout. But that doesn't mean I'm an idiot. Please tell me what's wrong with Steven."

A sigh of surrender. "He had mono."

"Mono? You mean mononucleosis?"

"Yes, and it was touch-and-go for a while there."

Mononucleosis. Mono-fucking-nucleosis. The kissing disease. You stayed home from school for a few weeks reading comic books, and it went away.

This mess wasn't my mother's fault. This was all Eileen. I guess she was so used to bullshitting people to sell houses—exaggerating the square footage, lying about competitive bids that didn't even exist—that the habit spilled over into her personal life. She wanted to make a splash at her grandson's birthday party, and once she knew I was back in town, I became the splash.

So she did what she had to do to get me there. What was I going to do, walk out? She knew I wouldn't. She'd conned my mother, and she had me roped and tied.

The least I could do was try and loosen the ropes.

"Tell me something, Mrs. Kavanagh. Has anybody ever actually died of mono?"

"I can't answer that question, Mickey. If this is going to get unpleasant, I can offer you money for your musical efforts."

"Forget it, forget it. I overrreacted. I'm sorry." I gave her my best puppy-in-the-rain look. "I'd like to sing now, if that's all right."

She smiled at me, a smile rich with triumph. "You were always a good boy."

"Oh, well, you know. . . ."

I sat at the piano and flexed my fingers while Steven and his birthday guests were summoned from outside, a dozen hot, sweaty, hard-breathing kids eager to return to their game. Their mothers were in my face, at my back, at my elbows. I barely had room to play.

"Steven," I said, "I have a special song for you on your birthday, and I hope you enjoy it."

I cracked my knuckles, took a deep breath, and did what I had to do.

I sang "Happy Birthday." Badly.

The kid stared at me, sweat rolling down his cheeks. He looked at his friends. They all burst out laughing and ran back outside. I rose from the piano, took a bow, and headed for the door, amid a million murmurs.

Eileen caught up with me on the front porch.

"Mickey. What the hell was that?"

I shrugged in mock innocence. "I sang 'Happy Birthday' for his birthday. It *is* his birthday, isn't it? Or did you make up that part, too?"

"Come back and sing 'Sweet Days'!"

"I can't. I'm forbidden by law."

"*What?*"

"I sold the rights to my song years ago. I'm forbidden from performing it anywhere."

"Oh, come on!"

"It's the truth. I'm not allowed to sing it anymore."

The part about selling the rights was true, but the rest was bullshit, and she knew it. Her face darkened.

"You're full of shit," she hissed.

"Look who's talking."

Five minutes later I was home.

"How'd it go?" my mother wanted to know.

"Great."

"Didn't take very long, did it?"

"No, Mom, it didn't."

"And don't you feel good? Isn't it nice to do something special for a child in need?"

"It sure is, Mom."

I wondered if Eileen was going to tell my mother what had happened. I doubted it. If she told her what I had done, she'd also have to tell her what she had done to inspire my behavior. I couldn't help smiling. It was the perfect crime.

I went upstairs and changed into jeans and a T-shirt. The phone was ringing, and I had to marvel over Mrs. Kavanagh's brass balls—calling to complain about me after all, despite the scam she'd concocted to get me there.

I went downstairs, where my solemn mother awaited my arrival. She handed me a folded slip of paper.

"You just had a call from a girl," she said.

My heart soared. Lynn had come to her senses.

"Were you at least polite to her, Mom?"

She gave me an odd smile. "I'm always polite," she said over her shoulder as she walked away.

My hands shook as I unfolded the paper, expecting to see the one phone number I still knew by heart, but it was a number I didn't know, beneath a name that I did know, written in my mother's flawless Catholic school script: Rosalind Pomer.

I was disappointed and astounded at the same time. How the hell had she found me? And what the hell did she want?

She could only want one thing. I shoved the paper in my pocket and headed for the door.

"I don't know what time I'll be back!" I shouted to anyone who might have been listening.

CHAPTER FOURTEEN

I walked to the Little Neck railroad station and phoned Rosalind from there. She wanted to see me. I wanted to see anybody. I caught the train and reached Penn Station in half an hour.

From there I walked all the way to Rosalind's apartment, a glass and steel high-rise on Seventy-sixth Street and First Avenue. The doorman rang Rosalind's apartment and looked me up and down before telling me to take the elevator to the thirty-eighth floor.

Rosalind Pomer answered the door in a pink terrycloth bathrobe, seeming shorter and even wilder-haired than I'd remembered her, a pair of bifocals perched on the end of her nose. She dipped her head to regard me through the upper halves.

"Well, I never thought I'd see *you* again."

It was awkward for both of us. How do you greet a stranger you screwed in the sky? In the end we both went for the clumsy peck on the cheek, and then she gestured for me to come inside.

Piles of paperwork covered her living room table, and she'd

obviously been burrowing her way through it when I phoned. The ashtrays were full and the air was ripe with mentholated smoke. She led me by the hand to the kitchen.

"I'll make a fresh pot of coffee."

"I didn't know you smoked."

"How could you know? There's no smoking on planes."

"Right . . ."

"You lost weight. What'd you do, join a gym?"

I shook my head. "I'm pushing a lawn mower these days."

"For a living?"

"Well, I wouldn't call it a living. . . . How the hell did you find me?"

She shrugged. "I knew you weren't going to Manhattan from the airport, so I figured you'd be in Queens. You said you'd come back for a family situation, so I started calling DeFalcos in Queens. Got to you on my third try. Pretty simple, really."

I didn't like how easy it was for her to find me. I didn't like that even slightly. . . .

She cocked her head. "Were you ever going to call me?"

"I lost your card."

"Yeah, right," she replied, but she was smiling when she said it. "Who took that message from me?"

"That would be my mother."

"Not the friendliest person in the world, is she?"

"You caught her at a bad time. Not that there's ever a good time to catch her."

Rosalind poured boiling water through a deep cone filter into a clear glass coffeepot. It was black-as-dirt coffee, so different from the feeble stuff my mother percolated each morning, and then I noticed it had come from a Starbucks bag. Starbucks! My parents would have gone nuts!

She filled a small pitcher with milk, put two mugs and a sugar bowl on a tray and asked me to carry it to the bedroom.

I did as I was told. I set the tray down on the night table, and when I turned around she lay naked on the bed. The last thing she took off was her bifocals.

"Okay, superstar. Let's see if you're any good on the ground."

She crossed her legs, patted the bedspread. It was like a bad porno film, the rich bitch summoning the gardener in for a quickie.

"Can't I have my coffee first?"

She had to laugh. I had a swallow of coffee, damn good coffee, and then she put the lid on the pot and we got down to it. It was better in bed than it had been on top of the chemical toilet, and even though we climaxed at the same time, it was just a physical coincidence. The luck of the fuck, so to speak.

Filmed in sweat, Rosalind poured herself a cup of coffee and lit a Newport. "Hey, man, you're in some shape."

"Manual labor," I said, and then I noticed a framed photo of Rosalind with a good-looking guy on what had to be a California beach. They were cheek to cheek and they looked happy.

I pointed at the picture. "Your ex?"

"My current."

"Oh." Jesus Christ.

"Relax, he lives in L.A. We're doing the bicoastal thing."

The porn plot deepens. The rich bitch leading the dual life—a loyal partner on one coast, a roundheels on the other. And in midair.

"He know you do things like this?"

"I don't do things like this. Not normally."

"Yeah? Why now?"

She smiled, blushed, shrugged. "I'm really not sure. It goes against my better judgment."

We went at it again, slower and longer, and when we were through I really could have used a little nap, but she wanted to talk. She played with my chest hair in a way that was far too intimate for what we had going.

"So you're living with your parents."

"For the time being."

"What happened to you?"

"Rosalind. I'd have to know you a lot better to go into it."

She sat up straight, pulling the sheet up around herself. Her face had become all points—her cheekbones, her chin, her nose, even her eyes.

"You think you can just come here and fuck me, is that it?"

"I came here because I was lonely. The fucking was your idea, you might recall. I'd have been happy with a cup of coffee."

"Yeah, right."

"I mean that."

In a funny way, it was the truth. It was hard to be in Little Neck, knowing Lynn was just a few blocks away. This was a little escape for me, a vacation from obsession.

Funny thing is, it only magnified my obsession. What the hell was I doing with this woman when I'd finally found my one and only Lynn?

The phone rang. It was Rosalind's boyfriend, of course, so I pulled on my pants and went to the living room. You get a hell of a view from the thirty-eighth floor, but something was funny about this place, and then it hit me. I put my hand over my head and touched the ceiling without even getting on my tiptoes. That's how they did it with the new buildings—dazzle 'em with the view, and squeeze in as many floors as you can. An architectural trick that even a crafty lawyer could fall for. . . .

Rosalind came out in the bathrobe cinched tightly around her waist. "Sit down a minute, Mickey."

I did as I was told, on a deep, fluffy couch the color of blood. She stayed on her feet, so I knew a lecture was coming.

"I'm not a whore, you know."

"Never said you were."

"Do you . . . like me?"

"You're good in bed. You're good on toilet, too."

You can be a little cruel when you're famous, or even when you're a has-been. People sort of expect it, and people like Rosalind even like it a little bit.

She covered her face with her hands. "I'm feeling all guilty about David now."

"So why'd you invite me up?"

She hesitated. "David can't hit it the way you can."

"Oh."

"He's sweet, he tries, but . . ."

She came to the couch and sat beside me. "It's a structural problem, strictly structural. It has nothing to do with the way we feel about each other."

"Gotcha."

I couldn't stifle a yawn. Rosalind smiled. "You're tired. Go take a little nap while I get some work done. When you wake up, we'll order in Chinese."

I went along with the plan. I conked out for a while and awoke with absolutely no idea of where I was. The bed was near the window, so the first thing I saw when I opened my eyes was the blaze of the nighttime Manhattan skyline, far below. I dimly wondered if maybe I'd died and ascended to heaven.

But Lynn wasn't with me, so it couldn't have been heaven. Then reality came crashing down as Rosalind appeared with a sack of Chinese food, a bottle of cold white wine and two glasses.

We ate General Tso's chicken and sipped the wine as we half-watched a CNN report about the chances of another terrorist attack in Manhattan. The anchorman mentioned the possibility of terrorists renting apartments in high-rises so they could blow them up, and that made Rosalind nervous, so she turned down the sound on the TV and pounced on me, determined to get in one last screw in the event that bombs were ticking in the basement of her building. We were back to the rough-and-ready stuff, which was okay by me, and when it was over I was exhausted, ready to sleep again, this time right through the night, if she'd let me.

But she wanted to talk.

"Hey, Mickey. What's it like?"

"What's what like?"

"To sing and hear all those girls screaming for you."

"Come on, Rosalind."

"I really want to know."

"Why?"

"Because I was one of them."

I sighed, sat up. "It's . . . overwhelming."

"What else?"

"Scary."

"What else?"

"Lonely."

"Lonely?"

"I was all alone up there. No band. Just me and the piano."

"But isn't it a rush, hearing all those screams?"

"You don't really hear it. Mostly I was trying not to screw up out there. That takes a lot of concentration."

"Hey, Mickey."

"I'm still here."

She sat up in bed. "Sing it for me, will you?"

"Huh?"

"Sing 'Sweet Days.' "

She was as wide-eyed as a child awaiting a bedtime story, and she was dead serious. For the second time that day, I'd been asked to sing my damn song.

"I left my piano at home."

"Come on. Please."

"I forget the words."

"Very funny. Come on, just this once."

"Roz, if there's one sure thing in my life, it's that I will never, ever sing that fucking song again."

"You don't have to get hostile!"

"I'm sorry. I just . . ."

I was out of words, out of hope, out of everything. Rosalind left the bed and went to the kitchen with the leftover Chinese food and the plates. I'd deal with her rage when she came back. I was spent, totally spent. I actually dozed off and probably would have slept through the night, except that she woke me with the loudest shriek I'd ever heard.

I ran to the kitchen to find Rosalind standing on a chair, pointing at the sink with a quaking finger.

"Oh my God, oh my God, oh my *God!*"

"What the hell happened?"

She shut her eyes. Her nostrils widened with a deep, closed-mouth breath. "He's in the sink. A mouse."

"A mouse?"

"Or maybe it's a rat. My God, could I have a rat in here? Holy shit, I'm going to have to move!"

"Calm down, Roz."

She pointed a shaking finger. "He's under the dishes. Unless he went down the drain. . . . Can they go down drains?"

"How the hell should I know? Maybe he came up through the drain."

She clapped her hands over her face. "Get him out of here, Mickey. Please, get him out of here."

I crept to the sink. The plates we'd eaten off were in there, smeared with lo mein noodles. But one of the noodles was twitching, and it was pink. It was the tail of a tiny rodent, hiding beneath the dishes.

I turned to Rosalind. "I'm guessing it's a baby mouse."

"A baby?"

"I can see the tail."

A shiver went through her. "Can you catch it?"

I looked around the kitchen. An empty Häagen-Dazs ice cream

container was in the garbage, the lid still on it. I grabbed it and removed the lid.

"What the hell are you doing?"

"I'm going to try and catch him in this container."

"And then what?"

"One thing at a time. . . ."

Container in my left hand, lid in the right, I hovered over the sink, trying to figure my next move. I could no longer see the twitching tail. Had he gone down the drain?

I set down the lid and the container, gingerly removed the top plate. Then the one beneath it. There was just one plate to go. He had to be under it.

Rosalind's sink had a hose attachment with a spray nozzle. I tested it in the adjacent sink.

"Mickey, what the hell are you doing?"

"I'm gonna soak him so he can't jump."

"Ohh, Jesus . . ."

Hose in hand, I lifted the last plate and soaked the sink. At first I thought there was nothing there, but sure enough, a tiny gray blob was struggling in the drain. A baby mouse. He shook the water off his marble-sized head and blinked his shining eyes at me.

I grabbed the ice cream container and the lid. The mouse struggled up past the lip of the drain, and it was easy to coax him into the container. I clapped the lid on top, and that was that.

Rosalind was still standing on the chair. "Did you get him?"

"I got him." I could feel the little guy hopping around in the ice cream container.

Rosalind stepped off the chair and sat down on it. She hugged herself as if a winter wind was blowing through the kitchen.

"I don't understand it," she said through chattering teeth. "This is a brand-new building. We're thirty-eight stories up. How could a mouse get in here?"

"Nature finds a way, you know?"

"Kill him."

"What?"

"Kill him. Squash the container."

"I can't kill him!"

"Why not?"

"Because we're both named Mickey."

"Oh, that is just hilarious."

"I'll take him outside and turn him loose."

"Loose?"

Container in hand, I went to the bedroom and put my clothes on. Roz was waiting for me at the front door.

"At least take him a block or two away, or he'll come back to my sink."

I couldn't help laughing. "Yeah, right. He's got a little homing device in his brain."

"Well, if he did, it wouldn't bring him *here,* I can tell you that much."

Her voice had changed. She was angry, despite my heroics, glowering at me through narrowed eyes.

"Got something you want to say to me, Roz?"

She hesitated, then spat it out.

"This is *your* fault. You brought him here."

"How the fuck did I do that?"

"On your clothes. He was hiding in your pants, or something. It's the only way he could have gotten in."

The porn plot thickens: the filthy gardener fouling the palace of the princess, high in the sky. Carrying vermin, along with his substantial tool.

I was giggling. I couldn't help it. I didn't want to help it.

"I brought him here from Little Neck. Is that what you're saying?"

"I don't know where he came from, but you brought him in. It's the only way." She shivered. "The only way," she repeated.

I almost felt sorry for her, but not sorry enough to be nice.

"You're a snob, Roz, you know that?"

"If I were a snob, would I be fucking you?"

It was a good point, and she made it well, as a good lawyer should.

Little Mickey was bouncing around in the Häagen-Dazs container. I was tempted to let him out, but stopped myself. I didn't want him to die. So instead, I kissed Rosalind on the forehead.

"Maybe you're right, Roz. Maybe I did bring him with me, some way, somehow. But if I didn't, remember this—he's just a baby. That means he's part of a litter. And mice have big litters."

I waited for it to register on her terrified face, then left the apartment. Suddenly I was out on the street, looking for a place to free my little friend. Who, by the way, had probably arrived with the Chinese food. Hopped into the bag in that greasy restaurant kitchen just before the illegal alien delivery boy from Hong Kong stapled the bag shut, slung it into his bicycle basket, and rode the wrong way up First Avenue to Roz's building.

Even at three A.M. there were cars and buses all over the streets. I didn't want little Mickey to get squashed. The world seemed like an incredibly dangerous place for such a little life. There was only one thing to do.

I started walking west, toward Central Park. I figured he'd stand a chance in there. I crossed Fifth Avenue and leaned over the park wall, ice cream container in hand.

"Good luck, little guy."

I popped off the lid. He dropped to the ground and vanished with a hop into the foliage. Then I began the long trip back to Little Neck.

CHAPTER FIFTEEN

The sun was rising and birds were chirping as I made my way to my bedroom, where I collapsed until Sunday afternoon. I staggered down the stairs to the kitchen, where my mother was salting a roast beef in a pan full of chopped onions. The kitchen reeked with the smell of them.

"Well. Look who's alive."

"Barely . . . where's Dad?"

"Watching the ball game."

I was puzzled. I couldn't hear the TV set.

"At the Little Neck Inn," she added.

I could barely believe what I'd just heard. "Dad's at a bar?"

She nodded, shook pepper on the roast.

"He never went to bars!"

"Things change, Michael. And no, you didn't."

"I didn't what?"

"You didn't get any more phone calls last night."

She knew just how to stick it to me. I headed for the door.

"Where are you off to now?"

"Taking a walk."

"Well, walk to the bar and tell your father we're eating at four."

The Little Neck Inn wasn't what I had in mind as a destination, but orders are orders.

I'd never been there before. I'd moved to L.A. before I'd reached the legal drinking age, so I'd never partaken of the charms of the neighborhood's most popular gin mill.

The Little Neck Inn was a little bit like a funeral parlor without the corpse, the bar lined with men who hunched over their drinks like mourners. The place reeked of beer that had probably been spilled during the Eisenhower administration. My eyes needed a moment to adjust to the darkness before I spotted my father on a stool at the end of the bar, watching the Yankee game on a TV set high on the wall.

The sound was off so people could hear the jukebox, which seemed to have been stocked with oldies. It was truly a relic, filled with rotating 45 disks that played at the touch of a needle. Bobby Darin was tearing up "Beyond the Sea" as my father turned his head and did a double take at the sight of me.

"What the hell are you doin' here?"

"Got a message from Mom. We're eating at four."

He rolled his eyes. "We've eaten at four every Sunday since fire was discovered. Why the hell would she need to remind me?"

"I don't know, Dad."

"Sit down. Have a beer."

A balloon-bellied bartender came to us, a dark-haired, light-skinned guy who moved with the cocky strut of a prizefighter.

"Sully, meet my son, Mickey."

We shook hands. He had a hard grip that would have popped my knuckles a few weeks earlier, but the yardwork I'd been doing made it possible for me to return the squeeze, volt for volt.

"You're the singer." A lilting voice, straight from Dublin.

"If you say so."

"Pleasure to meet you." He turned to my father. "Couple of longnecks?"

"Good idea, Sully."

"If the guys who drink here had long necks, they could do to themselves what they can't seem to convince their women to do for them."

"Poetry, Sully, pure poetry."

"Just a thought." He set a pair of long-necked bottles of Budweiser in front of us before strolling away.

We clinked bottles. It was hard for me to figure how a guy who made a stink over a $3 latte at Starbucks was willing to shell out $5 for a bottle of beer. It was even harder for me to believe I was actually sitting with my father in a saloon. We were both a little shy about it, as if we were a couple of guys waiting for our turns at a whorehouse.

"Well," said my father, "what do you think of the place?"

"They do a lot here with the color brown, huh? Brown walls, brown floors, brown bar."

"They don't go in for the hanging plants, if that's what you mean. Anyway, I've been comin' here once in a while since your mother got goin' at Eruzione's."

"Mom have anything to say about this?"

"Ahh, she made a little stink in the beginning about me comin' home smellin' like a brewery. But I pointed out that she comes home smellin' of formaldehyde, and which is worse?"

I laughed out loud—man, when was the last time I'd done that?—and then my old man dropped the hammer.

"Got laid last night, didn't you?"

It was shocking to hear such words from my father, who kept his eyes on the ball game.

"Yeah," I told the television, "but not with the one I want."

"Mickey."

We turned to look each other in the eye. He hesitated, like a kid trying to remember his lines in a school play.

"Be true to your heart," he finally said, as if these were the last words he'd ever be speaking to me. I let them sink in.

"I'll try, Dad."

"Don't try. Just do it."

Right then I noticed a guy about my age standing at my side, eyeing me like I owed him money, tottering like he might topple at any second. He wore soiled coveralls and he smelled like rotting vegetables. His pug nose was wrinkled in recognition.

"Hey," he began, "I went to school with you, didn't I?"

"Are you Frankie McElhenny?" I asked, but I wasn't asking. I knew.

"Yeah. Yeah, and you're Mickey, ain't you?"

"Good to see you, Frankie," I lied.

We shook hands for no good reason. "What are you doin' here, man?"

"Just havin' a brew."

His heavy mouth-breathing was unmistakable. Back at St. Anastasia's school I used to feel it on the back of my neck all day long, and I think the only reason Frankie McElhenny got through grammar school is because I kept my elbow high to give him an unobstructed view of my test papers. He dropped out of school even before I did and got a job in private sanitation. Apparently, he still had it.

He gave my back a swat. "I don't believe I'm seein' you here, man!"

"Long time."

"How's the music? Got another song comin' out?"

"Working on it."

I could get away with an answer like that with a guy like Frankie. The passage of twenty years between songs wouldn't seem strange to him. After all, what was time? Merely the thing you endured between the closing of the Little Neck Inn at four A.M. and its reopening the following night. If only Einstein could have seen it that way. . . .

And then it happened, right after Elvis finished "Don't Be Cruel," which by the way was written by the vastly underappreciated Mr. Otis Blackwell (I always like to note the songwriter, as he/she is usually the person who takes such a screwing when it's time to dole out the credit and the money). At first I thought I was imagining it, but that plaintive piano was unmistakable coming from that ancient jukebox, followed by my rather angelic voice piercing the beery air of the Little Neck Inn.

I looked at the grinning Sully, who snapped his hand to his forehead in a half-mocking, half-serious salute.

"I forgot to tell you," my father said sheepishly. "They got your song on the jukebox here."

"I wonder who could have provided it to them."

Frankie McElhenny whacked me on the back as if he were trying to dislodge a bone from my throat. "Hey!" he shouted to nobody and everybody. "This is the guy! *This is the guy!* I went to school with this guy, here!"

And so with my back being pounded by a drunken grammar school classmate I sat and listened to myself sing. Those were the longest two minutes and forty-six seconds of my life.

When the song ended, my father and I decided to have one more beer, and then one more on top of that. Things were looking pretty good, all of a sudden.

We got home two hours late. The roast beef was overdone and the chopped onions were scorched to cinders. My mother was fuming.

"I'd like to propose a new rule," she said through tight teeth as she sawed through the bloodless meat. "If you're going to stay out all night, I must be told. Otherwise, I wait up and worry all night. Is that fair?"

I let the words sink in. I was about to say something, but my father beat me to it.

"Who you talkin' to, Donna, Mickey or me?"

I burst out laughing. I couldn't help it. Then my father was laughing, and then my mother, bless her heart, was smiling, though she fought it hard.

"This meat is like shoe leather," she said as she set down our plates.

My father took a friendly swat at her ass. "Hey, that's great, Donna! I need new shoes!"

CHAPTER SIXTEEN

I was afraid that Flynn was going to bust my chops with a lot of questions about Lynn, but I caught a break. There was bigger news than our reunion, much bigger news.

Patrick Wagner, the all-American boy, had gotten a tattoo over the weekend.

It was a green barbed wire thing around his right upper arm. It had been Scarlett's idea. She had gotten the same tattoo. Flynn thought Scarlett was too wild a soul for Patrick, and here was his proof.

"Jesus Christ, Patrick, are you nuts or somethin'?"

He flexed his muscle, making the barbed wire bulge. "Don't you like it, Mr. Flynn?"

"What'd that thing cost you?"

"A hundred."

"Christ!"

"Scarlett says the tattoos are better than rings, because they'll never come off. They're there for eternity."

"Like your love for Scarlett, huh?"

"That's right."

"Bet your parents were thrilled."

"Ahh, they'll get over it."

We were in the truck, rolling down Northern Boulevard to-ward Great Neck. Flynn pointed out the window at the tattoo parlor, a grubby-looking place.

"You better hope they used clean needles, boy."

"They did."

"If that thing gets infected, I ain't payin' you disability."

We got in half a day's work before huge black rain clouds rolled in behind our heads, turning day to night, and suddenly drops of rain the size of robin eggs were pelting down.

We scrambled like mad to get the equipment back up on the trailer and covered with burlap to keep it from rusting away, then roared back to Flynn's garage. The workday was over.

It was strange to go home late in the morning of a weekday. The rain hadn't let up a bit, so I burst through the door as wet as a seal.

"Don't move!"

My mother's voice startled me. She held a hand up, palm out. "Just stay there a second."

I obeyed, dripping on the mat inside the door, and a few sec-onds later she returned, handing me a towel. I dried myself off as best I could.

She stared at me in a panicky way, and that was understand-able. I'd upset her rhythm. Normally she had this time of day and the house all to herself, and here I was in her midst, chased home by a whim of the weather.

I hadn't even thought about it. If I had, I would have gone to the movies and sat through whatever was playing, twice, just to get home at my normal time.

But it was too late. We were together in the house, and that was it.

When I got myself as dry as I could I passed the towel back. "Thanks, Mom."

"I'll get you a dry T-shirt."

"This one's all right."

She didn't seem convinced. "Did you eat your lunch?"

"I guess I left it on the truck."

"Come on, I'll make you a sandwich."

"I'm not hungry, Mom. . . . What's that smell?"

The air was sharp with the odor of a cleanser I recognized without being able to immediately identify. She didn't answer but led the way to the kitchen, where dozens of knives, forks, and spoons covered the kitchen table, atop a protective layer of newspaper. Half were tarnished, half were shiny. A blackened rag lay beside an open jar of chalky silver polish. She'd been in the middle of the job when she heard me at the door and came running.

"It's Silver Day!" I exclaimed.

She was surprised. "That's what we called it when you were a little boy."

"Yeah, I remember. Let me help you."

"You don't have to."

"Mom, I want to help."

"It's a messy job, and it's got to be done just so."

"I did it when I was seven. Think I can't do it as well now as I did when I was seven?"

"You didn't do it very well when you were seven. You always left polish between the fork tines."

"I never knew that."

"I didn't want to hurt your feelings."

"Give me a chance to get it right. Please."

She hesitated. "I'll get another rag."

It was elegant silverware, a set of knives, forks and spoons— forty pieces in all, a total of eight settings with a rosebud pattern on each handle.

It had been a wedding gift to my parents from my father's mother, a brooding, suspicious widow who died when I was five years old. I remembered her black dresses and her frightening face, like an old catcher's mitt with chin whiskers, and the way she stared at me as if she meant to melt me into a puddle with her gaze.

Apparently the old girl thought her son and daughter-in-law would be doing a great deal of entertaining, but in my memory the only time the silverware ever came out was one Thanksgiving when Grandma DeFalco herself came over to eat with us. She took one look at the four fancy place settings and announced it wasn't necessary to get the good stuff out for her. Over great protests from my father and tears from my mother, the good stuff went back into the cherrywood box and we ate the bird with the bent-tined forks we used every day.

And since that day, that cherrywood box with its recessed compartments in the shapes of each utensil was taken out from its place under the stairwell every six months or so, its contents emptied, polished, and replaced in an event my mother used to call "Silver Day."

Now I remembered that it was usually raining on Silver Day. It was the kind of task a woman like my mother found for herself to salvage an otherwise wasted morning, when you couldn't wash windows or hang laundry on the line.

"Not too much polish on the rag," she warned, handing me a tattered bit of one of my father's old undershirts. "A little goes a long way."

"All right, Mom."

For a few minutes there was nothing but the sound of our blackening rags rubbing the tarnished silver back to a low luster. Finally, she broke the silence.

"Did you have a good time in the city?"

"It was all right."

"Who'd you see?"

"Somebody I knew from L.A."

"A girl."

"A woman."

We were quiet for a moment, busy with the rags and the polish. It was easier being together this way, watching our hands instead of looking into each other's eyes.

She opened her mouth, closed it, thought things over, and suddenly said, "Your sex life is none of my business, Michael. Whatever you do, you do. I know you have . . . needs. You're your father's son."

I felt myself blush, and took a moment to gather myself. "Thanks, Mom," I finally said. "I've always felt that your sex life was none of my business, either."

A pink flush rose to her cheeks, then receded. We were even. We'd made each other blush. It was a standoff.

Now what?

Luckily for both of us thunder rumbled, and it was just the sound to change subjects upon.

"Had quite a time with your father at the Little Neck Inn, didn't you?"

"It was okay. You ought to come with us next time."

"I think I'll pass on that offer, thank you very much."

"I mean it, Mom."

"Oh, I spent enough time in saloons when I was a child, looking for my father."

I was shocked. She had rarely spoken to me about her childhood, which I knew to have been rough: a hard-drinking father who ran off, a mother who died young trying to keep the family going. The little bit I knew, I'd learned from my father, not her, nuggets of information he'd shared with me when I was a teenager who wondered why his mother sometimes had sudden crying jags for no apparent reason. As it turned out, these jags happened twice a year—once on the date that would have been her father's birthday, once on the date that would have been her mother's.

I rubbed a soup spoon with my rag, buffed it clean, and

looked at the reflection of my upside-down face in its bowl. "You actually went from saloon to saloon?"

She nodded, eyes steady on her hardworking hands. "And me no more than twelve at the time."

"Jesus, Mom."

"It wasn't pleasant. He cut quite a swath in his time, your grandfather."

Funny, but I'd never thought of this man who died before I was born as my grandfather. I'd never known a grandfather, or aunts and uncles, as each of my parents were only children. Besides my parents the only relative I'd ever known was Grandma DeFalco, whose spirit, if it existed, was certainly snickering over the cruel curse of her enduring legacy, the gift of The Silver That Was Too Good to Use. . . .

"What was he like?"

"Who?"

"Your father."

She made a funny sound, half laugh, half snort. "Good-looking, charming, and lazy. A deadly combination."

"Pretty rough for your mother."

"Yes, Michael, it was." She finished shining a knife and picked up another. "That T-shirt of yours is still wet. I'll get you a dry one."

"I'm fine, Mom."

She wanted to get away, but I wasn't about to let that happen. I put a hand to her shoulder, eased her back into her chair.

"Look, when you do the forks, don't leave any polish between the tines."

"I won't."

"Because it hardens up like a rock if you don't get it all off. Work the rag between the tines. It's the only way to do it."

"I will. What was she like?"

"Who?"

"Your mother."

She sat back in her chair and stared at me. Rain lashed at the windows, and just then my mother's eyes went wet, as if with the rain.

"Michael, she never got one break. Not one."

I put down my rag and made what might have been the bravest move of my life as I reached my smudged hand across the table to take hold of hers. It was a lot smaller than mine, like a child's hand, if you ignored the roughness. I gave it a squeeze.

"I'm sorry, Mom."

She squeezed back. "She tried, Michael. Until the day she died she made sure I had my music lessons. I was good, you know."

"I'm sure you were."

"If there hadn't been so many distractions at home, I might have become . . ."

She hesitated, not sure she wanted to tell me what came next. Then she drew a long breath, and I knew it was on the way.

"When I was in fifth grade I could play Chopin. Really. They had me play in the auditorium, in front of the whole school."

"Wow."

"Yes, well, in the middle of it my father staggered in drunk and collapsed in the center aisle for all to see."

"Jesus!"

"It broke my concentration, I promise you that. I just sat there on the stage with my hands in my lap, staring at my father flopped on the floor. It didn't even seem real. Like I was watching some horrible movie, all about my own life."

A shiver went through me. My mother shook her head and sighed.

"I don't know how she did it, little thing that she was, but my mother got him to his feet and dragged him out of there. He was no lightweight, my father. I can still see him draped over her shoulder like a six-foot eel, feet dragging the floor as she went off with him."

I let out a long, jagged breath. My mother seemed to be in a trance as she continued the story.

"She gets him up on her shoulder, and I can hear people giggling and snickering away, and before she heads out she turns to me up there on the stage. Know what she said? She said, 'Donna, play.' That's all. Then she marched off."

I was tingling. "You played?"

"I did. Picked up where I'd left off when he hit the floor."

She leaned toward me. "Michael, I know you've heard cheering in your time, but I think I can say with certainty that even you never heard applause like I heard that day in the little auditorium at the School of the Most Precious Blood."

She let her head fall, and I was glad for that, because my own eyes had misted up. "You see why I took your music so seriously?" she asked the table. "All those annoying lessons I made you take? I knew the talent was there in the family. It was just a question of nurturing it the right way."

She looked up again, the both of us trembling.

"I wanted the best for you, Michael. I know I was overprotective. I know I drove you crazy. It's just that I know firsthand what happens to families where things get . . . careless."

"You were never careless, Mom."

"Yes, I was. We let you go too young. That was our big mistake."

"That was my choice."

"It shouldn't have been. We should have kept you here."

"I would have run away."

"Just like . . ."

She couldn't finish the sentence, couldn't bring herself to say the name aloud. So I did it for her.

"Just like Lynn," I said.

She nodded, swallowed a sob, composed herself, took a jagged breath. "Michael. Why did things go so wrong for you?"

"Mom, it's like what they say at the Vatican. You know what they say at the Vatican, don't you?"

"What's that?"

"Shit happens."

It was a risky joke to crack, but she actually giggled. I got up and went around to her side of the table and embraced her from behind. The strength in her shoulders was startling, all tense and taut like a jockey in the homestretch. But suddenly she relaxed, as if the horse she'd been riding since the day I was born had finally, *finally* crossed that damn finish line.

"I think I would have liked your mother."

"She had balls, Michael. I've got them, too."

I laughed out loud. She reached back to stroke my hair.

"Whatever it is you want with your life, Michael, I'll try to help you get it."

This was as close as she could come to a blessing for me and Lynn, and it took all of her considerable courage to say it.

"Thanks, Mom."

Another rumble of thunder. I gave her one last squeeze before breaking the embrace and returning to my side of the table.

"Hey," she said. "We finished the silver."

"Yeah, it looks good."

"There's leftover macaroni I can heat up. Let's put the silver away and I'll make us some lunch."

"No."

"No? You're not hungry?"

"No, I mean, let's *not* put the silver away." I plucked out two full settings and handed them to her. "I'll pack up the rest of it while you give these a rinse, Mom. What do you say we eat our lunch with a little style today, huh?"

She beamed, she shined. "I'd say that was a fine idea, Michael."

And that's how we ate our lunch that day, reheated (and

slightly crusty) macaroni and cheese. All we really needed was one fork, but there was something so soothing about the sight of those other utensils, like sparkling soldiers eager to serve, that it just might have been the greatest meal of my life.

"Who's better than us, huh, Mom?"

"Not a soul, Michael. Not a blessed soul."

Of course, those utensils all went right back into the cherry-wood box after the meal, and as I set the box under the staircase it occurred to me that my mother would probably like it if I didn't tell my father what we'd done that day.

Not that he'd be mad. Quite the opposite. It's just that it would be our little secret, our first little secret, a memory to treasure and protect like the silverware itself.

CHAPTER SEVENTEEN

Two nights after the silverware experience the phone rang at our house, and it was for me. My father was grinning and mouthed the words "It's her" as he passed me the phone.

"Lynn?"

"Mickey. Could you come over right away?"

"I'm on my way."

I flew out of the house without a word to anyone, my heart hammering with every step. My patience had paid off. She'd sounded desperate and lonely. She'd come to her senses at last, all because I'd given her the light and the air to realize how much she missed me.

I was out of breath and all but quaking with joy when I reached the Mahoney door, which opened before I had a chance to knock on it. Lynn stood there, ashen-faced and trembling.

"My mother fell out of bed and I can't lift her."

I was stunned. I needed a moment to shift gears emotionally, from passion to emergency.

"All right. I'm here."

"Mickey, thank you."

"Take me to her."

For the first time since old man Mahoney had banned me from this house I crossed the threshold into a place I remembered for its gloom. Now it was even worse. The carpets were worn, the furniture sagged, and God knows when the walls had last tasted paint. Leaks in the ceilings had left bubbly, rust-colored patches. It seemed more like an abandoned hunter's lodge than a house inhabited by a widow and her daughter on the edge of Queens. I remembered that the Captain had liked making fires, roaring fires, and the rug in front of the fireplace had the burn holes to prove it.

The air was tart with a medicinal smell, a blend of Vicks and rubbing alcohol. A coughing sound jolted me. Lynn led me to the next room, which I'd remembered as a dining room in which I'd never been invited to dine, but now it had been sensibly converted into Mrs. Mahoney's bedroom to avoid all those stairs.

She was on the floor in a tangle of sheets and blankets, lying on her side. A skinny white foot protruded from the tangle, and coils of gray hair starfished out from her head. Her eyes were wide open and serene, staring blankly at the baseboard directly in the line of her gaze.

In the middle of the room was the bed she'd fallen from, a hospital-issue number with cage doors on each side. The side of the bed she'd rolled off had its door down.

I turned to Lynn. "How do we do this?"

"Let me talk to her first."

She knelt at her mother's side like a priest preparing to administer last rites.

"Mom, Mickey is here. Remember my friend Mickey?"

Friend. That stung a little. Mrs. Mahoney took a deep breath in response and blinked her eyes.

"Yeah, he's here to help us. Okay? We're going to get you back in bed now."

The toes of her protruding foot curled up as if with a spasm, then relaxed. Lynn turned to me.

"Come on over now, Mickey," she said in a chirpy, singsong voice. "Let's get my mom back in bed."

I squatted beside Lynn to size up the situation. Mrs. Mahoney continued to stare at the baseboard with an eerie serenity, a serenity she'd never exhibited back when she was hauling all those loads of laundry up and down the cellar steps. Or maybe she was just numb from it all, this life in which she'd buried a husband and four sons and seen her runaway daughter return home for the final act. . . .

"How should we do this, Mickey?"

"Let me do it by myself."

"You can't lift her all by yourself!"

"What's she weigh, eighty pounds?"

Lynn shook her head. "Not even."

"All right, then, let me do it. You get the bed ready."

As Lynn smoothed out the one sheet left on the bed I slid my arms beneath Mrs. Mahoney who, incredibly, had fallen asleep during the past few moments. I braced myself for the initial hoist, but there was no need. The woman was as light as a bird, and lifted off the floor as easily as a saint's ascent to heaven.

I set her down snoring—snoring!—in the same position she'd occupied on the floor. Lynn straightened out the bedding around her body, tucking here and there until it was just right. I half expected her to slip a teddy bear under her arm.

"We keep her down here because of the stairs."

"I figured."

"I could have sworn I closed the gate on her side."

"You probably did."

"Well, I'm in big trouble if she found a way to get the gate down." She might have been talking about a clever pet she had to outwit. She yanked up the gate, which locked with a metallic click. Instinctively, and without waking, Mrs. Mahoney reached out a hand and gripped one of the aluminum bars that held her prisoner. Lynn sighed, turned to me.

"All day long she tries to get out of bed."

"Can she walk?"

"Not without help."

"Talk?"

"Couple of words a day. She says 'laundry.' I bet she wanted to get out of bed so she could do the laundry. Maybe she dreams that this house is still full of people."

She shivered, shuddered to rid herself of such a horrible thought. "Thank you for this, Mickey. You are sweet."

I was sick of being told how sweet I was. "You going to buy me a drink?"

"A drink?"

"Yeah. That's my fee for picking ex-girlfriends' mothers up off the floor at a moment's notice. One beer."

She shook her head. "No beer in the house."

"What've you got?"

"There may be some whiskey."

"Whiskey it is."

Lynn stared at me. "And then you'll leave, won't you, Mickey? No funny stuff?"

"I'll drink my whiskey and I'll leave. I've got work tomorrow."

"So do I."

I followed her back into the living room, where she told me to wait while she got the drinks. I was stunned by the sight of the fireplace mantel, which I'd somehow missed on the way through earlier.

It was a shrine to the Mahoney boys, framed photographs of each of them in full-dress formal fireman's attire, backdropped by the American flag. Identical poses, identical camera angles— the fire department must have taken such pictures of all its members so they'd have something to give the newspapers in the event of disaster.

The center photo was larger than the rest, a glossy of the Captain himself, staring grimly at the camera as if the photographer had just cracked a joke about the Irish. There were piles of gold braid on his shoulders and a lot of scrambled eggs on the peak of his cap. The smirk on his lips made it clear that he'd risked his own life countless times to save the lives of people who weren't good enough to lick his boots.

And of course there was the framed Pulitzer Prize–winning photo of him as the Burning Angel, emerging from that blaze with the child in his arms.

Lynn returned with two glasses and a half-empty bottle of Jack Daniel's. She'd answered the door wearing loose jeans and a too-big gray T-shirt, but only now did I notice she was barefoot, a detail that delighted me. Not since our last time at Jones Beach had I seen those feet, long and narrow and straight-toed. She plunked herself down on a corner of the couch facing the mantel.

"Come on, John Wayne, have your drink and then hit the trail."

She reached out a hand to pat the cushion farthest from hers. I put my ass exactly where her hand left an indentation. She set the glasses on the coffee table and poured out two generous shots. This, I realized, was the last of the late Captain's booze supply.

"This will be our first alcoholic beverage together, Lynn."

"I guess that's true."

I held my glass out, and after hesitating she did clink with me.

I was never much of a whiskey man. The first sip numbed my tongue and made my teeth feel loose. Lynn sipped her drink and pursed her lips as if the stuff were burning a hole in her belly, only if that's what was happening, why did she down the rest of it in a gulp and again fill her glass?

"Jesus, Lynn, take it easy!"

"What do you think of the shrine?"

"Huh?"

She gestured at the mantel without looking at it. "All the dead Mahoneys. Wasn't there a rock group called the Dead Mahoneys?"

I swallowed. She was turning tough on me, lifting her shield into place.

"Come on, Mickey, you were a musician! Wasn't that the name of a band?"

"I think they were called the Dead Kennedys."

"You're right, you're right. . . . Can you name them all?"

"Can I *what?*"

She waved a hand toward the mantel. "Name all my dead brothers, and I'll pour you another drink."

The horror of it was, she meant it.

"Are you serious? You think I don't remember your brothers' names?"

"I'm waiting."

I got off the couch and went to the mantel, forefinger and thumb cocked like a pistol as I ticked them off. "Frank. Jimmy. Thomas. Brendan."

"Very good, DeFalco. Hold out your glass."

"And this big guy in the middle is Walter."

She finished pouring, set the bottle on the coffee table. "Didn't ask you for *his* name, did I?"

"No, but it's kind of hard to forget the name of the man who kicked me out of this house forever."

Lynn chuckled. "Ahh, Mickey. You showed him in the end, didn't you? Little could the Captain have suspected you'd outlive him and one day return to lift his widow back onto her sickbed."

"Knock it off, Lynn!"

I'd never spoken to her so harshly before, but she didn't get angry. She knew she'd been out of line. She sighed, ran a hand through her hair.

"Mickey, I'm sorry. I'm just kind of stressed with my mother and everything."

"I understand."

She looked at the photos, took a sip of whiskey. "I miss Brendan the most," she said softly. "He was special. Do you remember him?"

"Remember him? Are you kidding? I remember what you did to make him feel better that time."

"What time?"

"That time at the ballfield."

Lynn seemed shocked. She stared at me. "My God. I can't believe you remember that time at the ballfield."

I felt myself smile. "I can't remember what I had for breakfast, Lynn, but I remember that time at the ballfield."

Brendan Mahoney was the the baby of the family, a sensitive kid with an artistic side that must have been hell to hide in the midst of all that macho Mahoney manhood. Lynn was convinced he had great artistic talent, and bought him a set of watercolor paints and a small easel for his seventh birthday.

But from the moment he was born the fire department was his destiny, like it or not, and the Captain also forced him to play Little League baseball, a game at which his three brothers had excelled.

Brendan was no ballplayer. We were all there to watch him strike out with the bases loaded in the bottom of the ninth inning one Saturday afternoon, ending the ball game and his team's hopes for a championship.

"What a pansy," the Captain muttered as Brendan, poor Brendan remained standing at home plate as if he meant to die there, a willowy ten-year-old weeping big tears that disappeared in the dust as kids from the other team did a victory dance all around him.

Lynn turned to me, fighting back tears of her own. "Do you mind if we don't go to the movies tonight?"

"What do you want to do?"

"I want to take Brendan out."

And that's just what we did. It was a balmy June evening, the sky all rosy and purple with the coming of night. Lynn had packed a picnic basket, so I knew whatever she had in mind would be taking place outdoors. But where? It was Brendan, still wet-haired from the shower and dark-eyed from defeat, who asked where we were going.

"The ballfield!" Lynn chirped.

He stopped and looked at her as if she'd just smacked his face.

"I don't want to go there, sis!"

"Lynn," I said, "this doesn't seem like the greatest idea in the world."

She set the picnic basket down and grabbed the two of us in a tight hug.

"You're going to have to trust me, guys."

And so we did. By the time we got to the ballfield, the league games were long over. A giggly teenage girl stood in the outfield with her boyfriend, a goofy-looking kid with curly hair and eyeglasses, who knelt in the grass as he fiddled about with the tail of a huge kite.

Lynn pointed at them. "This is going to be good," she promised. "Come on, we'll set up the picnic in the outfield."

For the next hour we sat on the grass, ate bologna sandwiches, and laughed our asses off at the sight of that poor kid trying to get his kite aloft. He'd run with it, trip and fall, then get up and try it again, only to get tangled up in the string. His girlfriend tried to help, and they both got tangled in the string.

Brendan was laughing so hard I thought he was going to rupture himself. Only Lynn could have figured out that this was the way to heal him—take him to the very spot where he'd failed so miserably, and show him how life goes on.

Soon a sliver of a summer moon appeared, and with it came a fresh breeze that was enough to lift the kite into the sky. The three of us cheered and ran over to congratulate the kite boy, who was nice enough to give Brendan a turn handling the kite.

"Just don't yank it," the kite boy warned. "I don't want to lose it."

Brendan obeyed, his hands steady on the string, feeding it out an inch at a time as if he meant for the kite to reach the moon, which now shined as brightly as Brendan's eyes. . . .

Lynn sat there on the couch, staring at me through dewy eyes.

"That was a magical night at the ballfield," I said. "You healed Brendan that night."

"You think?"

"I know."

She smiled. "Maybe you're right, Mickey. But do you remember another night that wasn't so magical?"

"Which night?"

"The night of the flaming ropes."

Her face darkened. My own face felt numb. Maybe I'd made a mistake, playing the memory game with Lynn. For every kite-at-the-ballfield story, there was a flaming ropes story.

I finished my drink, poured myself another. Lynn didn't try to stop me.

"Remember the flaming ropes, Mickey?"

I gulped my drink like a cowboy, waited for a shiver to go through me like a gust of evil wind.

"Yeah, I remember," I said softly. "Be pretty hard to forget the flaming ropes."

CHAPTER EIGHTEEN

It happened shortly before the Captain banned me from the Mahoney house. It was a Saturday, well past midnight. We'd been to a dance in the gym at my high school and Lynn wanted to make us hot chocolate.

"Don't worry," she said, "everybody'll be asleep."

The smart thing would have been to kiss her at the door and go home, but when you're crazy in love you don't always do the smart thing. Besides, something else was going on.

We'd been close all night, without even having to talk. I suspected this was the night it might happen between Lynn and me, as naturally as the sun sets and the moon rises. I had a three-pack of Trojans in my jacket pocket, just in case. I'd bought them at a pharmacy near my school, miles from home. I was conflicted about the rubbers, and it wasn't a moral issue. I just didn't want to use them. They would be putting a layer between Lynn and me, and there were no layers between Lynn and me. In a funny way, I feared that the act meant to bring us even closer might actually push us apart. . . .

We went into the house and closed the door behind us as quietly as we could, but before we could take a step toward the kitchen we noticed a glow from the fireplace. That wasn't particularly unusual—the Captain loved fires and often built them when the weather turned cold. He'd probably built this one and gone up to sleep when the flames burned down, but then I noticed that the screen hadn't been placed in front of the fire, a big no-no under the Captain's rules.

There was little time to ponder this oversight because suddenly, a five-foot horizontal flame leapt straight from the coals, right toward the couch. It winked out so fast it was almost like a mirage, except we'd both seen it.

We heard the Captain's throaty chuckle before we saw him seated there on the couch in his boxer shorts and a sleeveless undershirt, clutching a rectangular can that turned out to contain lighter fluid, the stuff you use to get a barbecue started.

"Oh God, I hate when he does this," Lynn breathed, and then he did it again, squeezing a line of lighter fluid toward the coals and laughing at the rope of fire that leapt at him and vanished as suddenly as it had appeared.

He laughed out loud, clutching the can as he turned and saw us.

"Well, hello there, kids!"

He was bombed out of his skull, so totally out of it that he actually seemed happy to see me. But I was about to find out why he was so cheerful.

"Dad. Are you all right?"

He seemed offended by the question. With his other hand he picked up a bottle of Jack Daniel's from the floor and took a long, gurgly slug.

" 'Course I'm all right! What could be wrong? I'm makin' flaming ropes!"

Lynn was paralyzed with fear and embarrassment. The Captain offered me the lighter fluid can.

"What do you say, Mick? Wanna make a flaming rope?"

"Please go to bed, Daddy."

"I'm not tired. Here." He patted the couch cushion. "Sit here. Works better if you sit."

"Daddy, I—"

"Sit down here, Mickey!"

His voice rocked the rafters. I obeyed him and sat down, if only to keep him from shouting again. I waited for his wife to come running, or any of his sons, but nobody did. It seemed impossible that they could have slept through a sound like that. Maybe they heard it and were too petrified to come downstairs. . . .

The Captain held the can up to my face and shook it so I could hear the syrupy fluid slosh around.

"See this stuff? Very dangerous. You're supposed to squirt it on charcoal, let it sink in, and then light it." He belched. "But that's no fun. Squirting it on fires is fun! Watch!"

He squeezed another line of fluid at the coals. The flame leapt toward him like an enraged snake, but at the last instant he tilted the can upward to break the connection.

The air was ripe with the reek of oil smoke. The Captain chuckled, well pleased.

"See that? See what I did there? Gotta be quick about it, or the can'll explode in your face."

He handed me the can.

"Your turn, Mick. And try not to blow up the house."

A deadly challenge, from the man who hated me most. Jesus Christ Almighty.

"I'd rather not, sir."

"Pussy."

"Daddy!"

He ignored his daughter. "Do it like I showed you and you won't get hurt."

"Daddy, what's the point of this?"

"The point is, I want to see this little guinea grow some balls."

The boxing fiasco was nothing compared to this. This was absolute lunacy. I had no idea things were this bad. I always knew the guy was an asshole, but until now I never thought he was a psychopath.

And a calm psychopath, at that. This was his element, the climate of fear and danger. He could see how terrified I was, and it pleased him. It made him more of a man than me. He was so much of a man that he was willing to sit beside me at the risk of getting his own ass blown to Kingdom Come, just to see me suffer. That's how much he hated me.

He put a hand on the back of my neck and gave it a squeeze, such a hard squeeze that I felt a tingle of nerves down my back and all the way to my heels.

"You gonna do it, or you gonna chicken out?"

Lynn had left the room. It was me and the Captain. The can felt slippery in my hand, from my own sweat and the greasy residue of the lighter fluid. I held the can upright, gave it a gentle experimental squeeze. It was about half full.

Fuck the Captain. I was going to do it. If it went wrong, at least I'd be taking him with me.

I rehearsed it in my head—aim, squeeze, then tilt the can upward to keep from blowing myself up. The bed of coals crackled, glowing as red as a pile of rubies.

"Aim for the middle," the Captain advised. "That's where it's hottest."

I was hyperventilating. I felt dizzy. Holding the can in both hands, I pointed it toward the fire, willing myself to give it a squeeze. I wasn't the type to pray but I might have knocked off a quick Hail Mary right then, a prayer to keep me from fucking up, and as I clenched my teeth and urged my hands to do it Lynn came rushing back to the room, moving awkwardly because she was carrying a huge spaghetti pot by its two big handles, a pot so full of water that it lapped over the edges, and then it seemed as if the pot became a wild animal Lynn was struggling to subdue as it tipped over the coals and drenched them in a roaring hiss of steaming smoke.

Black water sloshed out from the fireplace, soaking the floor in front of it. Lynn kicked chunks of blackened embers back into the fireplace and stood there in defiance of her father, who'd staggered to his feet.

"Jeez, Lynn," he mock-pouted, "you wrecked the game!"

"The game is over, Daddy. Go to bed."

The Captain stared at her, then at me. He brought the whiskey bottle to his lips and took a long sip, draining it. Then, ignoring the puddle of black water, he put the screen in front of the dead fire, turned to me and held up an instructive forefinger. I stood to face him.

"Safety first, Mick. All it takes is one spark, and this house could go up like . . ."

He strained for a comparison, and suddenly his eyes closed. He turned and collapsed face-first on the couch, as if he'd been shot.

Even as he came crashing down he managed to hang on to the empty whiskey bottle. He rolled onto his back and cradled the bottle as if it were a newborn. Then he was snoring, his big feet hanging over the arms of the couch.

Lynn set the spaghetti pot on the floor, then found a quilt to cover her father. I could feel my hands pulsing, looked at them and saw that I was still clutching the can of lighter fluid.

I set it on the mantel and reached out to hold Lynn, but she was mortified by what had happened, and she didn't want to be touched.

I let my arms fall. "I'll help you clean up, baby."

She shook her head. "I can handle it," she whispered.

"I'll get some paper towels. They'll soak up—"

A jarring sound from the couch—the Captain had begun snoring. Even asleep, the fucker was a loudmouth. Lynn stood guard over him, as if fearing he had one last move to make, one last scheme to humiliate me.

"Mickey," she said over her shoulder, "go home."

"You sure that's what you want?"

"Please. Go."

And that's what I did. I'd expected to make love to my girl that night. Instead, I left her house without even touching her.

I didn't start crying until I was outside, halfway down the Mahoney path. As the Captain slumbered, his one and only daughter cleaned up the ravages of his latest escapade. There was nothing I could do to help her, nothing she would let me do to help her.

The night had turned cold and I pulled my jacket tight around myself, feeling the bump of the Trojan box in my pocket. So close, and yet so fucked up.

Now, all these years later, we were seated on that same couch. Lynn gulped the rest of her drink and shuddered, holding herself by the elbows as she got to her feet.

"You'd better go now, Mickey."

"I will. But I have to tell you something about that night."

She looked at me without saying anything. I cleared my throat, actually felt my face reddening.

"I thought we were going to do it that night."

"Do what?"

"You know. The thing we never quite got around to doing."

A tickle of a smile came to her lips, just a tickle, but at least it wasn't a frown.

"I had a three-pack of Trojans in my pocket. I was afraid you'd feel the bump when we were dancing."

"I did."

"You did? You never said anything!"

"I didn't want to embarrass you." The smile grew. "We would have, that night."

"You think?"

She nodded without shame. "I was ready."

"So was I."

I stood up and looked at her, stared at her, willed her to love me. The words came from my heart, not my brain.

"Please come back," I begged. "Come back to who you were."

She buried her face in her hands, and when she took her hands away her eyes seemed dark and hollow. "There's no way back."

"You love me. I *know* you love me."

"I can't say that I do."

"Well then, *I'll* say it. I know it. You could have gotten your mother back into bed all by yourself. That's not why you called me tonight."

"It's not?"

"It was like lifting a laundry bag. You could have done it alone, but you wanted me here. Let's quit fooling around."

I stretched my arms toward her. "Lynn, hold me. All I'm asking is for you to hold me."

I kept my arms out, but did not approach her. Days seemed to pass, but it was actually only seconds before she moved to me and fell into my arms.

I buried my face in her shoulder and wrapped myself around her. She quivered as if a current were running through her, but at last that stopped, as if it had been calmed by my embrace. She let out a jagged sigh and pulled back to look at me, her hands on my cheeks, eyes wide and green and shining.

"I saw you, Mickey."

"Saw me where?"

"In concert."

I was staggered. "You told me you never saw me perform!"

"I lied."

"Where?"

"Seattle."

I remembered the Seattle concerts. I was the one-song opening act for the Rolling Stones, believe it or not, performing in a one-piece black zip-up suit smothered in sequins. The zipper only went as high as the middle of my sternum, the better to display my generous forest of chest hair. I left the stage to the somewhat disturbing sound of hysterical teenage females, and that's when Mick Jagger spoke his one and only sentence to me.

"Mate," he said, "I wish I could be Italian for just one night."

Lynn was giggling. "I loved that black suit you wore."

"You should have come backstage."

"It would have been awkward."

"Why?"

"I . . . wasn't alone."

A great green dagger of envy cut my heart in half, as if the fucker had just joined us in bed.

"Who was this person?"

"Just a guy."

"Did you tell him about me? Did you tell him the song was about you?"

"No. Funny thing is, going to the concert was his idea. All his life, he wanted to see the Stones in concert."

"Oh, swell. So even when you went to see me, you weren't really going to see me. I just happened to be the opening act."

"Don't be like that, Mickey."

"You fucked him, didn't you?"

"Oh, Mickey—"

"So you must have been in love with him."

"Wrong. I fucked him because I *wasn't* in love with him." She hesitated. "I fucked *all* of them because I wasn't in love with them."

All of them. A population.

"I'm sorry, Mickey," she said, "but you pretty much did the same thing, didn't you?"

"Yeah, but only because you left me."

"I'm so sorry."

She was killing me, and she knew it.

"Let's not talk about that concert anymore, Lynn."

"Okay. But there's just one thing I have to ask you, about that thing you did when you finished your song."

"What thing? You mean blowing a kiss to the crowd?"

"You didn't blow a kiss to the crowd."

"Excuse me, but I always blew a kiss to the crowd. My agent made me do that. He thought it was cute."

"You didn't do it the night I was there."

"What did I do?"

"You got up, walked to the edge of the stage, spread your arms and yelled, 'Bring back my angel!' "

"Bring back my angel?"

"Your exact words. It was like . . . a plea to the heavens."

"Jesus, I don't remember doing that. If I did do that, it was the only time."

"I'm sure it was."

"What makes you so sure?"

"Because it was the only time *I* was ever in the audience. Somehow, you must have sensed that."

Son of a bitch. She was still a believer, after all.

"Maybe you're right," I allowed.

Mrs. Mahoney let out a long, low moan, all vowel sounds. It was time for me to go. We both knew it.

"Wait," Lynn said, "I want you to have something." She ran upstairs and came back with a rolled-up paper with a rubber band around it. "Don't look at it now. Open it when you get home."

Lynn held my hand as we walked to the front door.

"Can I see you tomorrow?" I asked.

"No. Not on a school night."

"Funny."

"You get paid on Friday, right?"

"Uh-huh."

"Come by my window and make a deposit, and we'll . . . take it from there."

"Okay." She let me kiss her on the forehead. "Friday."

My parents were asleep. I crept quietly to my room and unrolled the paper. It was a faded watercolor painting of a little boy flying a kite in a big green field, with a teenage couple cheering him on. A sliver of yellow moon gleamed in the sky. It was signed simply "brendan" in pencil, all lowercase letters. I taped it up on the wall, next to my framed record cover.

CHAPTER NINETEEN

Patrick Wagner was having a hell of a day. He couldn't stop yawning, and seemed to be tripping over his own feet. Flynn was worried.

"Jeez, Patrick, you all right?"

"I'm fine."

"Hell happened to you?"

He rubbed his sweaty face with both hands, leaving dirt streaks. "Scarlett made me go to the movies in the city. Didn't get back until midnight."

"Holy Jesus, this girl's gonna kill ya, Patrick."

Patrick was about to offer a mild, polite objection when his sleepy face suddenly came alive. He turned to me.

"Hey, I almost forgot. I heard your song in this movie last night!"

I thought he was fucking with me, but quickly realized that Patrick never fucked with anybody. He suddenly looked like an Indian in war paint, the skin of his face burning red with excitement behind the dirt streaks.

"You heard my song in a movie?"

"Yeah!"

"It can't be."

" 'Sweet Days,' right? Something about it feeling like a haze?"

I swallowed. "Yeah, that's my song, all right."

Flynn whacked me on the back. "That's great! They gotta pay you for that, right?"

I shook my head. "I sold the rights to that song a long time ago."

"Aw, jeez! What'd you do that for?"

"Needed the money. Tell me about this movie, Patrick."

It was a love story, he said, about a summer romance that comes to an end when the girl meets a rich guy and dumps her boyfriend, a housepainter.

"Typical," Flynn sneered.

"In the end she doesn't want either of them," Patrick added.

"What's the name of this movie?"

"Uhhh . . . give me a sec, I'll think of it."

"Where'd you see it?"

"Somewhere on the West Side."

Flynn jerked a thumb over his shoulder. "I got the *Post* in the truck. Go get it, Patrick, look it up."

Patrick fetched the paper and pawed his way to the movie section. "Here! Here it is. Movie's called *Don't Push Me*. Pretty good, I have to say. For once Scarlett and I both liked the same movie."

I took the *Post* from his hands and tore out the movie page. Flynn chuckled.

"So now you're gonna go see this movie tonight, ain't you?"

"I have to."

"Try to catch an early show, would you, Mick? If the both of you are tired tomorrow, I might have to get behind a lawn mower myself and do some real work, God forbid."

I was lucky with the trains, and it wasn't even six o'clock as I settled into a seat at a movie theater on West Eighty-sixth Street to see *Don't Push Me*.

What a jolt it was to hear the first few notes of my song, just as the opening credits began! Behind me I heard a guy whisper, "I remember this song!" I sneaked a look back and wasn't surprised to see that he was chubby and balding.

Anyway, the song tailed off after the second stanza as the movie began. It was pretty much the way Patrick described it— poor boy meets girl, poor boy loses girl to a rich guy, girl dumps rich guy and decides to go it alone. There was a funky, offbeat quality to the whole thing that made it work. The housepainter was a little bit of a prick, the rich guy wasn't a complete asshole, and the girl wasn't a sap or a gold-digger. They were all just people. The actors were unknowns, and the director was an Australian making his first film in America.

At the end of the movie the girl takes off by herself, and you see both guys getting on with their lives—the rich guy yelling at some poor slob in his office, the housepainter squatting on a dropcloth, stirring a can of paint. In the final image of the film he sheds a tear into the paint, which he stirs into the mix. As he does this the screen fades to black and my song comes up again, its final stanzas playing over the closing credits.

> Sweet days are gone
> But I will go on
> Knowing somehow, you care . . .
> Even though you're not there. . . .
> I'll shed a tear and be through . . .
> Knowing I have lost you . . .
> Babe, I'm caught in a maze . . .
> And there's just one . . . way . . . out . . .
> Sweet days!

I waited for it, through credits for assistant directors and key grips and sound technicians and even the damn catering service, and at last there it was, in white letters over black: "Sweet

Days," written and performed by Mickey DeFalco, courtesy of the motherfucking record company that robbed me when I owed money in seventeen different directions and would have sold my soul for a hundred bucks.

Funny thing was, nobody left the theater until the credits and the song were over. The house lights came up and revealed that most of the women were weeping. I sat very still for a little while, aware that my heart was pounding away. It was as if I'd just visited my own grave and found that the people who'd deemed me dead may have been slightly mistaken.

On the way out I was caught in the funnel of people trying to wedge through the exit doors and happened to get shoved up against the guy who'd been sitting behind me. He was arm in arm with a hefty woman who obviously was his wife.

"'Sweet Days'!" he said, giving her an affectionate squeeze. "Man oh man, that's the song we were listening to when Kevin was conceived, eh, Amanda?"

To which she delivered a playful sock to his rib cage, then held him even closer than before. Thanks to me there was a kid named Kevin in the world, squeezing zits on his chin and bugging his parents for a bigger allowance.

"Mickey DeFalco!" the guy's wife said. "My God! Wonder whatever happened to him?"

You just stepped on his foot, lady.

My father looked at me in wonder, took a pull from his longneck Bud and pursed his lips.

"They can just use your song like that?"

"It's not my song anymore. That's the point."

"Bastards."

We were elbow to elbow at the Little Neck Inn, which was pretty crowded for a weeknight.

My father patted my shoulder. "It's a lousy break."

"There's nothing I can do."

My father shook his head, then shook a Camel into his mouth. He was just about to light it when Sully snatched it from his mouth.

"Not in here, Steady Eddie. You know the law."

"Jesus Christ, Sully, it's a stupid fucking law. Beer and a cigarette! They go together like Adam and Eve!"

"I agree, but we must comply, mustn't we?"

My father snatched the cigarette back from Sully and walked outside to smoke it, leaning against the wall of the inn. I stood by his side, watching him savor that butt like a lifer in the prison yard.

"If anybody ever told me a day would come when I couldn't smoke in a bar, I'd have laughed in his face, Mick."

He took a deep drag, held the smoke, reluctantly let it go with a long, slow breath. "You good with Lynn?"

"I'm seeing her on Friday."

"Not before?"

"She doesn't want to see me until Friday."

He took a last drag, snapped the cigarette toward the curb.

"Women calling the shots, and no smoking in bars. Jesus Christ." He jerked his thumb toward the bar. "One for the road?"

"I don't see why not."

The pay envelope was short on Friday. I'd forgotten that Flynn stopped the clock whenever it rained, so that half a day I'd lost to the storm hit me in the pocket.

But there was still enough for me to make a small deposit, so I hurried to the bank and went straight to Lynn's window, my passbook and cash in hand.

She gave me a strange stare, and I figured I'd messed everything up by not phoning her. Had she really wanted me to stay away until Friday?

"Lynn? You mad at me?"

"Why would I be mad?"

"Because I didn't call."

"I'd be mad if you *had* called."

She pressed her forehead to the bars of the teller cage and I did the same, so that our skins touched.

"Will you come over tonight?"

My heart flooded with sweet relief. "Of course I will."

"Can you sleep over?"

My God. The words I'd waited twenty years to hear.

"I'll ask my mom."

"Don't kid about it, Mickey."

"I always kid around when I'm nervous. You know that. I'm sorry. The answer is yes, yes, yes, yes, yes, *yes,* I can sleep over."

She smiled. "Well, only if you're sure."

She pulled back from the bars and became all business again, probably because somebody was waiting to be served behind me. But she still had a strange look on her face, and I found out why.

"The weirdest thing happened, Mickey."

"What's that?"

She took my money, made the deposit, and slid the passbook back to me.

"Right after you left the other morning?"

"Yeah?"

"I heard your song on the radio."

It cooled off that evening. A sweet, cold gust of wind swept down from Canada in the middle of the walk from my parents' house to the Mahoney place, the kind of thing that made you feel all alive again.

My overnight bag—a plastic sack from the supermarket—contained a fresh T-shirt, clean underwear, a toothbrush, my razor, and a three-pack of Trojans, just in case. I had just finished packing it when my mother appeared at my doorway.

She held me by the cheeks. "Be careful, Michael."

"I'm always careful, Mom."

"And things still happen. So be very careful."

And just before I left the house my old man pressed a hard piece of paper into my palm that nearly cut me. It turned out to be a twenty-dollar bill, folded many times.

"Maybe you want to take her to the movies," he said.

But that wasn't what Lynn had in mind. We ordered in a pizza and listened to an oldies radio program while Mrs. Mahoney slumbered away in the next room.

"This is the station that played your song," Lynn said. "Maybe they'll play it again."

"I'm sure they will."

She looked at me in surprise. "Pretty cocky for a guy who's been off the charts for twenty years!"

"You don't get it, Lynn. Something happened."

I told her all about the movie sound track, and how it had obviously rekindled some interest in the song.

"You don't get anything out of it?"

"Not a dime."

She sighed, and with God as my witness it was just then that "Sweet Days" began to play on the radio. Lynn's eyes widened, either at the sound of the music or at the sight of me standing before her with my hand out.

"May I have this dance?"

She laughed out loud. "This isn't a dance song!"

"I wrote the damn thing. It's whatever I say it is."

She took my hand. I pulled her to her feet and began a clumsy close dance, putting all my concentration into not stepping on her feet as we moved around on the kitchen floor.

She held me closer, let her chin rest on my shoulder. I kissed the side of her face, tasting tears. The song came to an end, but we continued to hold each other.

"Man, did we ever have to wipe some dust off that one!" the deejay chuckled. "Mickey DeFalco's one and only hit song, 'Sweet Days,' getting new life these days in the low-budget hit movie *Don't Push Me!* Hey, whatever happened to Mickey De-Falco? Talk about your teen stars who vanish without a trace! He cooled off faster than today's temperature, which, by the way, dropped an amazing twenty-two degrees in less than one hour's time—"

Lynn clicked off the radio. "What do you say we go to bed?"

She just said it, as if we'd been married for twenty years and had fallen asleep watching a black-and-white movie on TV.

"You sure?"

"Yes. Go on, go upstairs ahead of me. I've got to get my mother settled."

I hadn't been in Lynn's room since we were kids. She still had that same sagging brass bed, facing a window overlooking the backyard. The walls were covered with Brendan's watercolor paintings, held up with bits of tape. It occurred to me that I should have them framed for her, as well as the one she'd given me.

I stripped down and looked at myself in her bedroom mirror, really looked at myself for the first time in ages. My face and forearms were tanned almost black, while the rest of me was fish-belly white. My hair was just starting to get touches of gray, and there were shadows under my eyes I'd never noticed before.

Desperation personified. I looked like a deeply mortgaged farmer who's just been told that a hailstorm is heading toward his crops.

Right then Lynn appeared at the doorway, fully clothed, her face whiter than milk.

"Get dressed, Mickey. We've got to get my mother to the hospital."

CHAPTER TWENTY

Lynn's mother had gone into some kind of a seizure. The white of her right eye had turned red. She was shaking so much that the bed rattled like a tambourine as she lay there, with Lynn struggling to pin her down by her shoulders.

"Mickey! Hold her down while I call an ambulance!"

I did as I was told, and through the horror and the panic it did occur to me that this was the closest I'd ever come to hugging Mrs. Mahoney.

A sudden surge of power—she wanted to get up off that bed! I had to lean all my weight against her bony shoulders to keep her down. It was as if she'd left some crucial thing undone, and couldn't allow herself to die until she did it. Lynn rushed back to the bed, replacing my hands with hers against her mother's shoulders.

"Go out and wave down the ambulance, Mickey."

It was there in minutes. Two crew-cut guys in snug uniform shirts with Little Neck Ambulance Corp patches on their chests jumped out and jogged to the house, carrying a stretcher. Suddenly Mrs. Mahoney was putting up no resistance, as if some primal instinct detected that these were uniformed men, capable men, men to be feared and obeyed. They strapped her to the stretcher and carried her out, gently and efficiently.

Lynn and I rode in the back. She held the hand of her mother, who regarded me with her one clear and wide-awake eye. She startled me by making a sound, two sounds in fact. To my ears it came out "I" and "Oy."

Lynn patted her hand. "He sure is, Mom."

I didn't get it. "I sure am? What did she say?"

"She said you're a nice boy."

My scalp tingled. It was the very thing Mrs. Mahoney used to say about me, before her husband banned me from the house.

Then her eyes closed, and she did not awaken for the rest of the short ride.

And so from the rich promise of Lynn's bed the weekend suddenly shifted to a semiprivate room at a local hospital, overlooking the Long Island Expressway.

An enthusiastic young doctor who looked as if his skin had cleared up just last week told Lynn that something had "worsened" in her mother's condition, and that she may have brought it upon herself by refusing to rest properly. The struggles to get out of bed, the restlessness . . . all of it served to further weaken the already damaged blood vessels in her head.

Lynn cut right to it. "Is she going to die?"

The doctor cleared his throat. "I'd say it could go either way."

"Depending on what?"

"Depending on how she responds to what she's done to herself."

Lynn rubbed her face, limp with exhaustion. "You make it sound like she's trying to commit suicide."

"Well, in effect—"

"In effect, you guys are scared to death that I'll try to sue you for something. Let me put your mind at ease, Doctor. I would never do that. My mother has had a terrible life. All I want to do is make sure she doesn't have a terrible death."

The doctor swallowed hard. "That's reasonable." He adjusted his glasses, cleared his throat, and resumed speaking in a calmer, deeper tone, clearly the voice he used when he wanted people to believe he was telling the truth.

"It's touch-and-go. What's going on inside her head is not knowable until something happens. She could die in an hour or she could live another fifteen years."

Lynn nodded, then startled the doctor by grabbing him in a grateful embrace.

"Thanks for being straight with me," she said over his shoulder. "I truly appreciate that."

I doubt very much that he'd ever been touched by anyone as beautiful as Lynn. His face was still burning a bright red as Lynn released him, and suddenly he remembered that he had other patients to look after and staggered away, his white coat flapping.

We sat in adjoining chairs at Mrs. Mahoney's bedside and held hands, watching the rise and fall of her abdomen. With her eyes closed the horror of that lone red eye was hidden, and she seemed to be sleeping peacefully. Some kind of monitor had been wrapped around her upper arm, and intravenous fluid dripped into the other arm.

In a bed on the other side of the room lay an enormously fat woman whose gentle moaning never stopped. A janitor who came in to empty the waste baskets cheerfully informed us that she'd just had her gallbladder removed.

"Too many pork chops!" he giggled on his way out.

I looked at the clock on the wall. It was eight-thirty. Less than an hour earlier I'd been lying in Lynn's bed, awaiting her arrival. Now I was fully clothed, on a death watch for her mother.

My life was often disappointing but rarely dull.

I went down the hall and returned to Mrs. Mahoney's bedside with two wretched cups of coffee from a machine and two packages of Hostess cupcakes from another machine. The coffee tasted of the pipes that dispensed it, but we drank it anyway and ate the cupcakes.

Lynn reached out to stroke her mother's hand, which did not respond to her touch.

"He crushed her spirit," Lynn suddenly said, as if she were in the middle of a story, and she didn't have to tell me who "he" was. "It got to the point where she didn't even *say* anything, unless it was to answer a question from him, or respond to a demand. She dished up the food and washed the clothes. He sat there waiting to be served, like the king he thought he was. She waited too long to stand up to his bullshit. By the time she did . . ."

Lynn's voice trailed off. She looked at me. "Your mother's lucky. Your father is decent."

"Yeah, but it's hardly a marriage made—"

"Steady Eddie never hit your mother, did he?"

I was shocked by the question. "Of course not! What are you saying here?"

Lynn's eyes brimmed with angry tears. "Remember the day you and I met? That day you were collecting for all those weeks of newspapers?"

"Of course."

"Know why my mother wasn't around to pay you all those weeks?" Lynn pointed to the floor. "She was here. In this hospital. He'd fractured her skull. With one punch."

I had to sit. I fought an urge to puke, willed my stomach to calm itself. Lynn wasn't quite finished.

"Usually he was clever about hitting her," she continued. "Bruises, maybe a few contusions. Nothing on the face, where people could see them. But that one time, he lost control."

"Jesus Christ Almighty."

"He told the doctors she'd fallen down the cellar stairs. And she played along. I begged her to tell the doctors the truth, report him to the cops, but she . . . played along."

"Why?"

Lynn sighed, squeezed her mother's hand. "Because she was just a shell of a person by that time. She'd disappeared. Disappeared without going anywhere. Ever watch a person disappear? It's worse than watching them die. Much worse. And there was nothing I could do about it."

"You tried."

"Not hard enough. But it's funny, isn't it? After I ran away, he fell down those same cellar steps he'd lied about to the doctors. Got himself paralyzed, and she had to spend all those years wheeling him around, wiping his ass. She wasn't free until he died, free at last, and look at what happened—she had a stroke, just a few months later." She made a snorting sound. "I'd say God's got a little bit of a mean streak, Mickey, wouldn't you?"

It was starting to jell. Lynn feared that a man, *any* man, even me, would one day crush the life out of her. I could understand that. I didn't like it, but I could understand it. All I had to do was show her I was different, an exceptional, wonderfully wise male. Piece of cake, right?

Suddenly she narrowed one eye at me, as if she didn't like what I was thinking.

"Remember how I asked you to name my brothers the other night? Well, now I'm going to ask you a much tougher question. What's my mother's name?"

I opened my mouth, closed it, gulped like a goldfish.

"This is embarrassing."

"Don't be embarrassed. It makes perfect sense. How could you remember her name? He took it away from her, along with everything else."

"Maybe I never knew it. She's always been Mrs. Mahoney to me."

"You knew it, all right, but you forgot it. My mother's name is Ruth. Ruth Brady. That was her maiden name."

As if in response to the sound of her name, Mrs. Mahoney let out a little moan. Lynn squeezed her hand.

"You'll be all right, Ruthie girl."

A nurse appeared in the doorway and said we had to leave. I got to my feet but Lynn stayed put, holding her mother's hand, as if she hadn't heard a word.

The nurse came into the room, a wide-nostriled, heavy-breathing young woman with the bullying air so common and necessary to the members of her profession. Her calves were cannonballs, stretching those sections of her white stockings into fishnet patterns.

"Excuse me," she said. "You have to leave now."

Lynn turned her face to look at the nurse, smiling the same sweetly false smile she used on rude people when we were teenagers.

"I'll be staying here the night," she said, not in challenge or defiance, but as a simple statement of fact, like a science teacher informing schoolchildren that the earth is round.

The nurse's eyes widened in disbelief. She wasn't used to this.

"Miss. You have to leave."

"I have to stay here with my mother."

"Sorry, it's against the rules."

"You don't look sorry."

"Lynn," I began, but she held up a hand to silence me, the other hand still grasping her mother's. Then she turned to the nurse.

"Here's the deal," Lynn began, calm as a priest doling out penance. "This could be the last night of her life. So if she starts to die and she wakes up and I'm not here to say good-bye . . . well, that'd be a crummy way to go out, wouldn't you say?"

The nurse stood as still as a statue.

"I don't want to get you in trouble. Please, feel free to call security and let them know I'm here, refusing to budge. And if they decide I have to go, well, my man here will sling my mother over his shoulder and carry her home. Because the only sure thing is, she can't be by herself in the homestretch."

At last the nurse blinked, folded her arms across her chest and jerked a head in my direction. "Is he staying here, too?"

She'd won. My baby had won. Lynn shook her head.

"No. It'll just be me."

The nurse nodded, tilting her head to show Lynn some chin and nostril, a little touch to make it clear she didn't fear Lynn in any way and was going along with the plan because she wanted to.

"Well," the nurse said, eager to claim her little victory, "he's gotta shove off right now."

"He will. I'll say good night and he'll go."

The nurse lumbered off. I took Lynn's free hand in both of mine. "What can I do?"

"Nothing, baby. Go back to my bed."

"I'll come back first thing in the morning. I'll bring you breakfast."

Out in the hallway a night worker pushed a circular floor polisher, nudging it just over the room's door saddle before retreating to the hall. A sweet odor of wax wafted into the room, oddly reminiscent of church smells. Lynn put her hands over her face as if to rub away a yawn, but when she took them away she was crying.

"Rough world, ain't it, Ruth?"

I got behind the chair and held Lynn from behind, squeezed her, crushed her, tried to melt her body into mine.

"I love you, Lynn."

I wanted her to tell me she loved me. She squeezed my forearms, drew a long breath to speak. Here it comes. . . .

"Pancakes."

"Huh?"

"My breakfast. You said you were going to bring me my breakfast. I want pancakes from the International House of Pancakes, with banana walnut syrup on the side."

"Okay."

"On the *side,* DeFalco. Don't let them pour it on. By the time you get here they'll be soaked through."

"I heard you."

"And black coffee with three sugars."

"Jesus, banana walnut syrup and three sugars. Good thing we're in a place with lots of insulin."

"Come here."

I came around to face her. She stood and took me in her arms, and then came my first real kiss from Lynn Mahoney since we were kids, a no-bullshit kiss—no shields, no fences, no caution.

The big nurse reappeared in the doorway and unlike Lynn, I *was* afraid of her. We kissed again, a peck on the lips this time, and I left the hospital walking on air.

Not so much because of the kiss. That was part of it, but the main thing was what Lynn had called me during her battle with the nurse.

My man.

I phoned my parents to let them know about all that had happened, and that I was sleeping at the Mahoney house. I had to walk about a mile to get there, and as I approached it I was struck by a bizarre sound that grew louder with each step, an urgent, insistent knocking noise high in a maple tree just outside the hedge.

It was a woodpecker, pounding away on a rotted branch that should have been pruned years before. Here it was, nearly midnight, but on that sleepy street in Little Neck, chances are that the only two creatures still awake were me and a bird whose body clock had gone mad. It was as if the spirit of Captain Walter Mahoney had seized the soul of the bird to hammer out a warning: *Stay away from my house, stay away from my house. . . .*

I went to Lynn's room and got into her big bed, still able to hear that crazy bird's hammering.

"Fuck you, Walter," I said to the bird. It felt good to say it. And I slept.

CHAPTER TWENTY-ONE

At the International House of Pancakes a fat waitress took my takeout order. She brought me a cup of coffee to drink while I waited at the counter, and suddenly my song started playing over the restaurant's loudspeakers.

The waitress topped off my coffee cup.

"Must feel funny for you, huh?"

For the first time I really did look at the woman who was serving me. She had a moonlike face framed by hair dyed a wild shade of red and pulled back into a tight bun. I peered at the face and mentally peeled away the flesh and the years to realize this was Rosie Gambardello, the first woman I'd ever been with. I could only hope she didn't sense the shock I felt at the sight of her.

"Rosie! Jesus! Hello."

"Heard you were back, Mick! How ya doin'?"

I shrugged. "Same stuff."

Same stuff? The same as what? The last time I'd said good-bye to her was when I'd tumbled out of her car half dressed, fully loaded and minus a load, and oh so sorry that this precious thing had been shared with her and not Lynn.

She looked like a circus clown in her powder-blue uniform dress. There could not have been a worse color for the body she had. Her life had obviously gone horribly, horribly wrong.

But she was smiling. In a way, that made it even worse.

"Pretty wild that they'd be playin' your song while you're in here, huh?"

"Pretty wild, yeah."

"I'm hearin' it all the time lately. Maybe 'cause this is an oldies station, huh?"

"I guess."

Obviously she didn't know about the movie, and I wasn't about to tell her. My song came to an end, dipping seamlessly into the first few notes of "Chances Are," the Johnny Mathis classic. Unfortunately for me there were no other customers at the counter, so Rosie was all mine.

Jesus Christ, how long did it take to make an order of pancakes to go?

"You got any kids, Mick?"

"No."

"All those women you've had, and no kids? I got a kid."

Out came her wallet. She flapped it open like a cop showing a badge, revealing a shot of a chubby grinning boy with blond bangs, seated before an ocean-blue backdrop. He wore a white shirt and tie with the letters SAS embroidered on it.

Somewhere in my mother's house was a picture of me just like it. It was the official St. Anastasia school photo. Same tie, same backdrop, different face.

"Tony Saputo."

"Who?"

"My kid. That's my kid's name. Remember Petey Saputo?"

"No . . ."

"Well, that's his father. He was an asshole. Still is."

She flapped the wallet shut and pocketed it, then stared at me like a girl you bump into after a one-night stand who wants to know why you haven't called. Only this was happening twenty years later.

"So," I said at last, "you're sending him to St. A's, huh?"

She seemed insulted by the question. "Whuddaya think, I'd send him to public school? It's all Chinks and Koreans around here now! I send him to P.S. 94, he'll wind up doin' his math on a friggin' abacus!" She sighed, shook her head. "But it ain't cheap, Mick. Three grand a year now, at St. A's. Can you believe that? Three grand, for fourth grade. What was it when we went there, a hundred? Two hundred?"

A bell rang, which meant two things—an angel had earned his wings, and my damn pancakes were finally ready. Rosie brought them to me in a Styrofoam shell, along with the coffee and the banana walnut syrup. I paid her at the register, and when she handed me change she grasped my fingertips and pulled me close.

"I was your first, wasn't I?"

"Yes, you were, Rosie."

"The first of thousands."

If that's what she had to believe, I was going to let her. In some weird way, it made her feel important. I was dying for this conversation to come to an end, and there was no end in sight.

"God." She giggled. "You were nervous with me."

"I was drunk on your father's wine."

I shouldn't have said that. Her eyes narrowed, as if she'd just felt the flick of a whip. "Not too drunk to remember," she said bitterly.

"Rosie. Is there something you want from me?"

She shook her head, shrugged. Her eyes brightened with angry tears, which she easily blinked back. "I just didn't want you to forget that it happened."

I put a clumsy hand on top of her chubby one. "I remember, Rosie."

"I'm thinkin' that maybe . . . I dunno . . . we could get together."
I took my hand off hers. "It's not that time anymore."
"All right."
"But I'm flattered."
"Yeah, yeah, you look flattered."

I picked up my bag and turned to leave, wondering if I should have left a tip, wondering if that would have added insult to injury, when suddenly Rosie's question caught me like a dart between the shoulder blades.

"Who're the pancakes for?"

I hesitated, turned back to face her, felt my face redden. She knew. I was an idiot to think she wouldn't.

"Want some advice, Mick? Stay away from her. There's somethin' seriously wrong with that girl. I mean, she always thought she was better than everybody, but now . . ."

"Now what?"

Rosie's lips quivered. "She'll break your heart all over again."

It sounded like both a threat and a warning. I couldn't let it go at that.

"Rosie," I all but whispered, "you don't know her. I'm the only one who really knows her."

She shook her head sadly, grabbed a damp cloth, and wiped the counter between us.

"You don't know shit, Mickey DeFalco. Guess you'll find out the hard way."

I didn't tell Lynn about Rosie. She was delighted to get the pancakes and ate them with ravenous pleasure while her mother slumbered away. The doctor said that Mrs. Mahoney was in stable condition, and should stay in the hospital for a few days for observation.

Things were looking up. Lynn was willing to come home, at least for a little while.

We would have the house to ourselves.

We held hands as we walked back to the Mahoney house. It was a gorgeous day, clear and dry and sunny, and suddenly the world was a big, juicy ripe apple, and I was about to bite into it.

Except the apple turned around and bit me.

A cop car pulled up in front of us and parked at a hard angle to the curb. Two young cops, one skinny and the other muscular, jumped out of the car and hurried toward me.

"Hey," the skinny one said, "are you Mickey DeFalco?"

A film of sweat broke out all over my body. It actually made Lynn's hand feel slippery in mine.

"Yes, I am," I said, fearing the worst, both happy and sad that at least I was with the woman I loved when it all came crashing down.

The cops stood there with their hands on their hips. Then, almost shyly, the skinny cop put out his hand.

"Just wanted to say that's a killer song you wrote," he said. "Been hearin' it on the radio all the time lately."

I shook hands with both of them.

"They don't write 'em like that anymore," said the muscular cop. He thumped himself on the chest. "Real heart, man."

"Well, thanks."

I introduced them to Lynn without telling them she was the inspiration for the song. They touched the brims of their caps and nodded, then drove away.

I had to sit down on the curb. I was soaked in sweat. I was hyperventilating. Lynn sat beside me and rubbed my shoulders.

"Hey, Mickey, what's this all about?"

I looked at her. I loved her—God, how I loved her!—even more than when I was a kid. But it had to be perfect, and that meant she had to know everything about me that mattered, and that meant it was time at last for the secret truth that had been burning a hole in my soul ever since my return to Little Neck.

"Lynn, listen to me," I began. "You're the only person in the world who ever knew me inside out. I always liked that, liked that there was one person in the world who really knew me."

She couldn't help chuckling. "Mickey. We've been apart for twenty years. There are going to be some gaps in what we know about each other, you know?"

"I'm not talking about who we slept with, or any of that bullshit. I'm talking about crucial stuff. You and I have to know each other's crucial stuff if this is going to work."

"Mickey. Just tell me."

"It could change the way you feel about me."

"I doubt that."

I took a deep breath, inspected the cloudless sky. Lynn's hand massaged the back of my neck. It was just the nudge I needed to get the words moving.

"It happened just before I moved back," I began. "See, I'd been homeless for about two weeks in Los Angeles, and things were really bad."

She stared at me in shock. "Homeless? You mean literally homeless, out on the street?"

I shrugged. "Actually, I was on a beach," I began, and then I told her everything, absolutely everything that mattered.

CHAPTER TWENTY-TWO

When you're homeless the wind has a way of finding you at night, especially in a place like Los Angeles, when the desert breezes come to life after sunset. They persist like bill collectors, nagging, chilling reminders that you are not welcome anywhere indoors, except for places like cafeterias and public libraries, and even then you can't let your chin fall to your chest and nod off or they throw you out on your ass.

I'd found a good spot to crash. It was an abandoned shed off the beach in Venice, a place that had once been used to store tools. It was surrounded by tall, thorny weeds and had a splintered wooden door that slid open, and if I got inside and closed it all the way I was fully protected from the wind.

It was like an oversized coffin but I knew I was lucky to have found it, lucky that another down-and-outer hadn't claimed it already. I'd recently checked out of the shitty rooming house I'd called home and this crummy little box was going to have to do me for a while. My few worldly goods were in a storage locker at a bus station. There was a public toilet on the beach they unlocked at seven A.M. I could shave and brush my teeth in there and when the sun was high, I could keep relatively clean by swimming in the Pacific.

The key was to avoid bringing soap to the water's edge. That's how they nail you for vagrancy, if they catch you lathering up in the surf.

I never allowed myself to believe I was actually living in that abandoned shed. I told myself it was where I went to rest, to collect my thoughts, to figure out my next move.

But a few nights became a week, and then two weeks, and then one morning I slept past dawn and awoke to the persistent nudging of a shoe to my rib cage, a well-shined shoe that was laced on the foot of a tall, pot-bellied man with a cap and a badge.

"Let's go, buddy," he said, not sounding angry or cruel, just bored by this task he'd certainly performed a thousand times before. Cops have that foot nudge down pat. It's not a kick, so you can't cry brutality, but they dig in between the ribs and leave marks that bloom into bruises the next day.

I blinked at him, not yet fully awake.

"Hey, come on, get up. *Up*. You can't live here."

I think it was the word "live" that got to me.

"I don't live here," I said. "I just passed out last night."

"Yeah? Where were you last night?"

"At a party."

"A party where?"

The problem with lying to cops is that you've got to keep the lies coming. I just didn't have the steam for it.

I slowly rose to a sitting position. "I can't remember."

The cop slid the door open all the way, and it was horrible to see it all in the early morning dazzle of the California sun. Cupcake wrappers littered the floor around me. I was covered by a burlap sack I'd found on the beach and pressed into service as my blanket. My rolled-up jeans were my pillow, and on a tiny cement shelf I'd placed my bar of soap, toothbrush, toothpaste, and disposable razor. An empty Gallo wine jug completed this stark picture of solitary domesticity.

There were no two ways about it. I was a homeless man, a bum, a wino, and this was my pathetic attempt at creating a home.

"A party, huh?" The cop chuckled. "Looks to me like the party was in here."

I was still sitting. I looked at the cop, a heavyset guy who seemed to be my age, maybe slightly older, a little too old for a beat cop but safe and secure with a pension to come and a second career in private security, as long as he could avoid getting killed on the job. He probably had a kid, maybe two of them, and a wife in stretch pants who played the lottery once or twice a week, just for the hell of it. And they had a house. Walls, floors, ceilings, maybe even a yard. The screen door squeaked. She was on his ass to oil it. He kept meaning to do it. . . .

I was overcome with envy for that cop. It was the first time in my life I'd ever felt jealous of another man's worldly goods, and it was so overwhelming that I put my face in my hands and burst into tears.

This startled the cop. Now he wasn't just giving a guy the bum's rush, he was dealing with a basket case. He squatted, put a seemingly friendly hand on my shoulder.

"Hey, buddy, calm down."

"I'm sorry."

"Lemme see some I.D."

"Am I under arrest?"

"Hell, no. You got any I.D.?"

I was thinking about saying I didn't have any I.D., but figured I'd seem like more of a citizen if I could show him something of mine with a former address on it. I unrolled my pants, dug my wallet out of the back pocket and passed him my driver's license, which I kept up to date even though my car had been repossessed years earlier. It was made out to DeFalco, Michael A., and when the cop's eyebrows went up, I knew I'd been made.

"Holy Mother of God, are you Mickey DeFalco?"

I shrugged. "Some people call me Mickey."

"Are you the guy with the song?"

I struggled into my jeans without standing up. How well he had put it. The song, singular.

"Yeah. That's me."

The cop's face was bright with wonder, his eyes shining like two brown suns. His name plate said O'Brien, but for the moment, he'd forgotten all about being a cop. He was a fan.

"Man, I love 'Sweet Days'! Shit, that's what was playin' on the radio when I proposed to my wife!"

"No kidding."

"Yeah, champagne, red roses, and you!" He chuckled. "Later on she told me she'd only said yes because of the song!"

This wasn't a particularly stunning thing to hear. Sappy songs inspire a lot of foolish behavior.

I hesitated before asking, "You still together?"

"Oh, yeah. Nineteen years now. Still in love, like a coupla kids."

"I'm glad for you."

The wonder of it was wearing off. The squatting cop shifted his weight, shifted his mood. "Jesus, man," he said, as if I'd just been in a train wreck, "what the hell happened to you?"

"Am I under arrest?" I asked again. I'd never been arrested. It was one of the few things I had left to be proud of.

He looked at me as if I were insane. He rose to his feet, the handcuffs on his belt clinking as he did.

"Arrest? You think I'd arrest *Mickey DeFalco*?"

"Well . . ."

"Come on, man, I wouldn't do that!"

I'd caught a break. Officer O'Brien's hair was thinning in

front and his belly was lapping over his belt buckle, but his face glowed like that of a child on Christmas morning.

I was his youth, his hope, a reminder of all the good things that ever happened to him back when his hair was full and his belly was flat. A younger cop might have run me in and grabbed himself a bit of fame for arresting a one hit wonder who'd hit the skids, but Officer O'Brien, I was beginning to realize, was not just a fan of mine.

He was a disciple. And that's not always a good thing.

He watched me put my shoes on, one at a time, like any mere mortal. I snapped a shoelace and had to make do with the longer piece, pulling it out and rethreading it through half the holes. Then I folded the burlap sack and set it in a corner of the shed, put my meager toiletries in a plastic sack and crumpled the cupcake wrappers up in my fist. I picked up the wine bottle, and my work was done. I may have been a skel, but I was a damn neat skel. I emerged from that thing with my head held high, as if I'd just checked out of a five-star hotel.

"I'll get out of here now, Officer O'Brien."

"Billy. Call me Billy."

"Okay, Billy."

He loved hearing me say his name. "Listen, Mickey . . . Can I call you Mickey?"

"Why not?"

"You need a ride anywhere, Mickey?"

"I don't exactly have anywhere to go."

"Can I walk with you?"

A cop, asking permission to walk with me.

"Sure, Billy. I'm just going to throw this stuff in the trash."

We walked together in the sand. It was not yet seven A.M., which meant the public bathroom was still locked. We were the only ones around, save the occasional jogger. I threw the cupcake wrappers and the wine bottle into a wire trash basket. Now that I had a free hand, the cop held his hand out to shake with me.

"I can't believe I'm walkin' with Mickey DeFalco!"

"I can't believe I'm walking, period."

"Feelin' stiff?"

"Yeah."

"What the hell do you expect, sleepin' on a cement floor at your age? Hey, are you hungry?"

I hesitated. I figured he was going to offer to take me to some greasy spoon cop diner, where I'd wolf down eggs and dough-nuts while he asked questions about my life. I was hungry, all right, but not that hungry.

"I'm not really hungry," I lied. "But if you're going downtown, I'll take a ride."

"I'm not going downtown."

"Hey, no sweat."

"My shift's just about up. I'm goin' home. You want to come home with me? I'd like the wife to meet you."

I laughed out loud. I couldn't help it. The whole thing was so freaking absurd. The laugh was almost painful, because the laugh muscles in my throat had atrophied.

"What's so funny, Mickey?"

"You want your wife to meet me?"

"She's a huge fan! You think I'm actin' goofy . . . man, she is your Numero Uno! Whaddaya say? Please?"

I didn't want to do it, but I didn't care for the rest of my op-tions, either. I couldn't bear the thought of sitting in a public li-brary, reading a newspaper on a stick. I didn't want to sit on the beach and look at the waves. I didn't want to wander.

I wanted to be some place where I was wanted, even by strangers.

I cleared my throat. "Do I look all right?"

Officer O'Brien was almost gleeful. "You look fine, just fine!" He clapped me on the back. "Oh, man, this is going to be *great!*"

We got to the cop car and I hesitated, not knowing whether to get in the front or the back. Officer O'Brien opened the front door for me. The back was for suspects, the front was for flashes-in-the-pan.

It was nice to be sitting on something soft. I checked myself in the rearview mirror. I needed a shave, but that was to be expected. I tilted my chin back, checking my neck for those ridges of dirt you always see on bums. I seemed pretty clean, though maybe a little briny from all those Pacific Ocean baths.

"Hey, Billy. Mind if I brush my teeth?"

"You mean now, in the car?"

"I got a system. I won't make a mess."

He nodded and watched as I squeezed a bit of toothpaste onto my toothbrush and went to work, sucking hard the whole time to avoid leakage. I rolled the passenger window down.

"Spit hard," he said. "I don't want toothpaste on the door."

I did as I was told, my head and shoulders all the way outside the car window. Then I wiped my mouth with the back of my hand, and I was as ready as I'd ever be to meet the cop's wife.

The O'Brien residence was a weatherbeaten little salt box of a house surrounded by a cyclone fence and shaded by a solitary palm tree. I expected to see toys and bikes in the front yard but it was bare of everything except a yellowing cover of rough desert crabgrass, the kind you didn't have to bother mowing since it grew outward and flat, but not up. Weeds grew up and through the links of the fence, clinging like the fingers of a desperate old lady.

We entered the house through the kitchen. Two parakeets were singing in a cage, and on the windowsill was a bowl with two small turtles.

Billy's wife was at the stove, a tall, angular woman straight out of the West Coast beauty guidebook. She looked as if she'd been born on a beach, a mermaid doing her best to conform to life on land. Strawberry-blond hair tumbled over her shoulders. Her eyes were as blue as the summer sky, and they had a perpetually sleepy look, maybe because her husband worked odd hours, maybe because of her nature. She wore a red silk robe and nothing else as she poured hot water through a coffee filter. The robe swished when she moved. Her feet were long and flawless— straight toes, and her toenails shined like mother-of-pearl.

This was the natural state of her toenails. She wore no polish or makeup of any kind.

"Hey, Robin," said Billy. "Got a surprise for you. Say hello to—"

"I know who he is." She closed her eyes and was silent for a few moments, as if to thank the forces of the universe for bringing me to her door. "Oh my God, this is just too hard to believe!"

She extended a hand. I took it in my own and she held it for a long time, as if to confirm the reality of my presence.

And a funny feeling went through me, a tickle of a warning saying I didn't belong here, I didn't need anybody's charity, and who the hell were these people?

But the kitchen was warm, the coffee smelled heavenly, bread was toasting and oh, good God Almighty, how sweet it was to be out of the wind!

"Mickey DeFalco, in *my* home," said Robin, holding my hand in both of hers, like a fortune teller. She was obviously an aging hippie, a flower child only now starting to wilt, with a smoky voice and rings on almost all her fingers. In her day she'd attended antiwar rallies, been tear-gassed, marched on Washington. Not your typical "Sweet Days" fan, but a fan she was, right to the core.

"Well," she added breathlessly, "this is one to make the gods sit up and pay attention."

Billy stood by, grinning like crazy as he unbuckled his gun belt and slung it over the back of a chair. Suddenly I saw that he was a man who existed in a state of apology, typical of schlubby guys who marry beautiful women. He was sorry that he was just a beat cop, sorry that they lived in such a small house, sorry he'd had the audacity to fall in love with a woman so far out of his league.

But not today. Today Billy O'Brien wasn't such a mug, after all. He was the greatest husband in the world, because he'd delivered Mickey DeFalco to his wife.

"I was tellin' Mickey here that his song was playing when I proposed to you," Billy said.

Robin nodded. "It certainly was. To what do we owe the honor of your presence?"

She was still holding my hand in both of hers. I broke the grasp, and didn't sugarcoat it. "Your husband found me asleep at the beach. Instead of dragging me in for vagrancy, he took pity and gave me a break."

Robin stared at me in disbelief. "You have no home?"

"I've, ah, had a little bad luck lately."

"Stay here."

The words came from Billy O'Brien, who seemed as surprised to have spoken them as I was to hear them. I had known this man for less than an hour, and his wife for less than five minutes, and here I was, being invited for—well, for what? An overnight stay? To live there? It was too much to process.

I felt dizzy. I had not eaten properly in days. My jeans hung low on my hips. I tugged at my belt loops to keep from stepping on my cuffs. Before I could say anything Billy O'Brien turned to his earth mother of a wife.

"I mean, if it's okay with you, Robin."

She seemed surprised by his question, as if he'd just asked her if she thought the earth was round. "Well, of course it's okay! We've got the room."

Billy sighed with relief. He put a strong hand on my shoulder, gave it a squeeze. "You're staying, and that's all there is to it. Come on, let's have breakfast."

I asked to use the bathroom first. The soap was scented, some kind of wildflower mix. I was careful to wash all the grime off my hands and face before using the fluffy hand towel, and then I had to force myself not to gulp the coffee or wolf down the scrambled eggs.

It was an unbelievable situation. I was in a cop's house, eating and relaxing and being treated like a king because of a song I'd sung twenty years earlier, three thousand miles from this sanctified kitchen.

My imagination didn't carry me past the conclusion of breakfast. I wasn't really considering Billy O'Brien's invitation to stay. I knew the hot food and coffee would give me that same rush of optimism I'd seen on the faces of countless homeless guys braving the light of day with bellies full of soup kitchen slop.

Today's the day, you tell yourself. *Today's the day my luck is going to turn around.*

But it doesn't. It never does. You pound the same streets all day long, and hope to hide from the wind at night.

I was tired of it. I was happy to be at the O'Brien breakfast table, happy to listen to Billy tell me about drug raids in East L.A. and hear Robin talk about the yoga classes she taught at the local Y.W.C.A. They were only two or three years older than me but they behaved as if they were my parents, and that suited me fine. I could use some parenting. I hadn't been a kid in a long, long time.

So I stayed. Billy drove me to the bus station where I had my stuff in a locker. I picked it up and brought it back to the O'Brien household, and just like that, I was one of the family.

I got sick almost immediately, with a raging fever that lasted for two days. My immune system was probably all messed up by those weeks of living in that tool shed. It was as if my body had waited until I was in a safe place to go into a complete collapse, and that sweet, soft mattress in the O'Brien guest room was that place. I stayed in bed, where Robin and Billy took turns bringing me cups of broth, saltine crackers, and ginger ale. By the third day I was strong again, sheepish about my weakness and feeling like a freeloader.

Robin sat on the edge of the bed and stroked the hair away from my forehead, the way my mother used to. "You've been living hard, Mickey. You needed time to heal."

"I'm okay now."

"You just take it easy. Let us take care of you."

"I'd like to do something for you. I mean, if you've got any work around the house that needs doing . . ."

Billy came into the room, unbuttoning his uniform shirt. It was morning. His shift had just ended. "How you feelin', pal?"

"I was just saying how I'd like to do something for you and Robin."

"Want to paint the house?"

"Billy!" Robin scolded.

"Hey, I was only kiddin'."

Robin turned to me, rolled her eyes. "He's been meaning to paint the house for about two years now."

"Ahh, I'll get around to it."

I sat up in bed. "Let me do it," I said. "Please. I'd be delighted. I've got the time, believe me."

They looked at each other. I put a pouting look on my face.

"Come on, Mom and Dad," I begged, "I promise I won't spill any."

They both laughed out loud, and then Robin shut her eyes, clasped her hands together.

"Mickey DeFalco is actually going to paint my house," she said, in what appeared to be a prayer of thanks. "Oh, my goodness, this is just too much."

We all had breakfast together, then Billy took me out to the garage and showed me where the supplies were—half a dozen cans of white exterior latex paint, drop cloths, rollers, and brushes. He wished me luck, went to his bedroom, pulled the shades and went to sleep. If nobody disturbed him he'd sleep until about six in the evening. He told me that this was his pattern, ever since they'd put him on the midnight-to-eight shift a few months earlier.

I got to work right after breakfast. It was a big job that was going to take three or four days, but I didn't mind. At least I didn't feel like a freeloader anymore. The O'Briens were getting something in return for room and board besides the charming company of a one hit wonder.

The house was pretty far inland, and at midday there wasn't so much as a breath of a breeze. I was up on a ladder, sweltering as I rolled the paint onto those faded shingles. Robin kept bringing me lemonade while Billy slumbered away in his air-conditioned bedroom.

"Mickey," Robin said, "why don't you take a break?"

"I'm all right."

"I have to teach a yoga class but I can cancel it if you're feeling sick again."

"No, no, I'm fine, Robin."

"Here, put this on so the sun doesn't burn you alive."

She handed me a wide-brimmed straw hat, torn and battered but still serviceable. I clapped it on my head.

She smiled at me. "You look like Vincent Van Gogh."

"I guess that's a compliment."

"Oh it is, it *is*. Your intensity. It's the same as Van Gogh's."

"Wasn't he insane?"

"What great artist isn't?"

"Robin, he painted masterpieces. I'm painting a house."

She refilled my lemonade glass and passed it back to me. "You'd be surprised. Sometimes mindless tasks inspire creativity."

"They do?"

"Certainly. I'll bet you're writing songs without even knowing it."

"I am?"

"Subconsciously, sure. Just let your thoughts flow, Mickey. It'll come."

I gulped the lemonade. I didn't like the way this was going. Suddenly there were expectations of me beyond a freshly painted house.

The next day, while bringing me lemonade, Robin brought up the songwriting thing again. This time I couldn't just let it go.

"Robin, it's been a long time since I wrote a song, or even thought about writing a song," I said gently. "Those days are gone."

"Yes, but new days are beginning, Mickey." She ventured a conspiratorial smile. "A second flowering, so to speak. Ever hear of that? It's the rarest thing in the plant world. Once in a while, for reasons no one can explain, a flower that's supposed to bloom once a year gives a second bloom."

"Too bad I'm not a plant."

"It works on spiritual levels as well. A second flowering. That's what I see for you, Mickey."

She looked left and right. "For *us,*" she added. She winked at me, went to her battered red VW bug and drove off to teach a yoga class.

Slightly crazy people are far more dangerous than the totally insane. You don't see them coming and by the time you do, they're already in your life.

I didn't like being compared to an insane artist, and I didn't like being part of an "us" I knew nothing about. Did Robin want to write the tunes to go with my lyrics, or the lyrics to go with my tunes? What other "us" could she have been referring to?

That's how far out of it I was. That's how badly I wanted to believe that Billy and Robin O'Brien were my surrogate parents, who only wanted the best for me.

I told myself that Robin was only trying to push me so I'd be as good as I once was, dipped my roller in the paint pan and resumed the job.

On the third day of the job, I had to stop kidding myself when Robin crept up behind me, reached between my legs and gave my balls a gentle squeeze. I leapt away from her.

"*Jesus,* Robin!"

She put a finger to her lips. "Quiet!" she hissed. "You'll wake Billy!"

"Robin. What the hell are you *doing?*"

She was scarlet with what appeared to be shame and confusion. She shook her head and whispered, "I'm so sorry, Mickey. I was really just kidding around. I had no right."

"That's right! You didn't!"

"It won't happen again. I just . . . look, I have to teach a yoga class. We'll talk about it later."

She ran to her car and took off. I was shaking so much I had to sit in the shade for twenty minutes to calm down. Under normal circumstances I'd have been out of there like a shot, but I had a paint job to complete, and I didn't want to run off and just leave it. It would have been hard for Robin to explain my disappearance to Billy, and I didn't want to mess up what had appeared to me to be a good marriage.

That was the toughest part of all. They were an affectionate couple, the real deal, or so it seemed to me. They held hands, they kissed, they nuzzled.

Why would she grab my nuts like that? Could she have been just kidding around, like she said?

It almost didn't matter. Either way, I had to get out of there, and the only way to do that was to finish the paint job. I got to my feet and went back to work, but I was rushing, so of course I fucked up. I knocked over half a can of paint and lost an hour cleaning it from the front path. As night fell I still hadn't done the window frames. It wasn't a big deal, but it was a day's work, so I had one more night as the guest of a dedicated cop and his erotic, flaky wife.

Billy came outside with Robin to take a look, all yawny from his daylong sleep. He rubbed his eyes, looked at the house and smiled.

"Oh, *man!* Great job, Mickey." He slipped his arm around his wife's waist. "What do you think, Rob?"

"Yeah, it's looking good."

I cleared my throat. "Well, I want to get it finished by tomorrow."

Robin's face darkened. "Tomorrow?" she asked. "What's the rush?"

I hesitated, made up the wildest story I could think of. "I'm going to see my parents back in New York."

Robin's eyes widened in shock but Billy was grinning with what appeared to be genuine happiness for me.

"Yeah," I continued, making it up as I went along, "been a long time since I've seen them. Being here with you guys makes me realize how much I miss the whole family thing, you know?"

"Buddy," Billy asked gently, "how you gonna pay for the plane ticket?"

I swallowed. "I have an emergency fund with about a grand in it. My last money in the world, you know?"

This was a lie. I had nothing. But Billy believed me, socking me on the arm. "You sneaky son of a bitch! Listen, let me pay you something for this amazing paint job."

"No, man, we are square."

"How long you stayin' in New York?"

"I'm not sure yet. Gonna play it by ear."

"Well, when you come back you got your old room waiting, if you want it."

"Thanks, Billy."

Robin stood staring at me, her arms folded tightly across her chest. She was not happy. Billy turned to her and she forced a smile, just in time.

"Dinner ready yet, or what?"

Billy managed to put away three portions of Robin's vegetarian lasagne. I struggled to finish one portion and Robin barely touched hers, choosing instead to smoke an herbal cigarette that smelled a lot like a reefer as she stared at me through half-lidded eyes.

Billy did all the talking. He was excited because this was the night they were going to pull a raid on a drug den in South Central. He was starting his shift early, which meant he'd be leaving the house at around eight o'clock.

"Be careful out there, man," I said, and it occurred to me that his wife should have been saying this. He laughed, patted my shoulder, kissed Robin on the cheek and was out the door, and suddenly it was just Robin and me in all that excruciating silence.

She stubbed her cigarette out. "He takes such a childish pleasure in his work."

"I wouldn't say that."

"Can I talk to you about what happened today, Mickey? I mean, now that you're leaving us and everything?"

"We don't have to talk about it, Robin. I probably over-reacted."

She drew a deep breath. "I had no right to touch you as I did. It was wrong. I'm truly sorry."

"Let's just forget it."

"Do you mean that? Can we wipe the slate clean?"

I knew that once I left this house, I'd never be back. Wiping the slate clean would be easy.

"Yeah, we can wipe it clean."

She smiled. "Thank you, Mickey. I don't want you to think ill of me. Let's have some wine."

Before I could object she poured two big glasses of California red. We clinked glasses and sipped.

"I'm leaving Billy," she said abruptly.

The wine went sour in my mouth. I set my glass down and saw that my hand was trembling.

"This has nothing to do with you," Robin said. "It's been building for a very long time."

She stared at me, seeking a response from my eyes. Finally I spoke.

"I'm stunned. You two seem good together."

"You think so?"

"You seem very . . . affectionate."

"Oh, I like Billy. He did the same thing for me that he did for you."

"I don't understand."

Robin chuckled in a sinister way. "I was pretty much homeless when he found me living on the beach. He took me in. It's what he does. It's his pattern. Notice his pets?"

She gestured toward the parakeets and the turtles. "He'd never have a dog, or a cat. Nothing that could run free. He likes bowls and cages. Trapping things, in the name of love. Birds. Turtles. Me." She sucked air through clenched teeth. "I've been in a cage for twenty years. I think that's long enough, don't you, Mickey?"

She lit another herbal cigarette, took a long drag and held the smoke for so long that her exhalation was nearly clear, and brimming with words that shocked me.

"Every time he goes to work, I pray that he won't come back."

"Jesus, Robin!"

"It's true. I know it's terrible, but it's true. Like tonight, with this drug raid. Maybe he'll finally catch a bullet, and I'll be free."

What the hell could I say to *that?* I had to say something. "He's a good man, Robin."

"You think so?" She leaned closer to me. "If he's such a good man, what's he doing taking payoffs?"

I was stunned. "Payoffs?"

"Oh, yeah. He doesn't even know that I know. Care to see?"

She rose from the table, went to the kitchen cupboard and

took a Maxwell House coffee can from the back of the top shelf. She removed the lid and held it under my nose, as if she wanted me to sniff it.

It wasn't coffee. It was cash—wads of it, rubber-banded into tight rolls.

"Jesus Christ."

"There's almost six thousand dollars in here. Tonight he'll come back with more. How good a man do you think he is now?"

I was exhausted. More than anything in the world I wanted to take a shower, collapse in bed, and conk out. But Robin wanted an answer.

"He probably wants good things for you, so he bends a few rules."

"Bends a few rules, eh? That sounds lovely."

"Robin, he cut me a break and he helped me out. I can't diss the guy."

"Loyal to the end, huh?"

"Something like that." I got to my feet. I was dizzy and wobbly. "I don't feel so good."

Robin's expression turned from miserable wife to concerned mother. She put the lid on the coffee can and put it back in the cupboard.

"You might be dehydrated, Mickey. All those hours in the sun."

"I think you're right."

"Take a nice cool shower and go right to bed. Drink some water before you fall asleep, or you'll have a terrible headache tomorrow."

"I will."

She got up and hugged me, a friend embracing a friend. "Mickey, I'm sorry I unloaded all my baggage on you. Truth is, I'm a little isolated here. Don't get to speak with many people."

"I understand."

She waved a loose hand in the air, an erasing gesture. "Don't listen to what I said. It's the wine. . . . Billy and I, we're all right. Just have to work some things out, that's all."

"Well, I think that'd be for the best."

"I'm going to zone out and watch TV for a while. You shower and flop." She gave my cheek a chaste kiss. "Good night, Mickey."

"Good night, Robin."

I was proud of the way I'd worked a truly tricky situation. I'd stuck up for the man who'd rescued me and expressed sympathy for his troubled wife.

I went to the bathroom, stripped down and stepped into the shower. The cool spray on my face was a wonderful relief, like a fire being extinguished on my forehead. I began to feel optimistic. I'd regained my strength, here at the O'Brien house. If I ever got back on my feet and had a place of my own, maybe I could invite them over for dinner, and we'd laugh over the funky way our lives had intersected, a cop rousting a skel from an abandoned tool shed.

Robin and I could keep that testicle grab to ourselves. She was confused, desperate, isolated. She hadn't meant anything by it. We could both bury it, forget it, never mention it again. It'd be as if it never happened.

Sure.

Naked except for her many rings, Robin stepped into the shower as if she had an appointment to be there.

"Jesus Christ!"

"Just relax, Mickey." She grinned at me, showing teeth I was noticing were crooked for the first time. No orthodonture for this woman, and that made sense, because what homeless person ever had good dental work?

The water flattened her hair against her skull, and the true length of all those wavy locks was startling, touching halfway down her back. Her breasts were small but beautifully rounded, with large nipples the color of red wine. She smoothed back her hair, put her hands on my shoulders, and there was no place to hide my hard-on.

"I *knew* it," she said. "You couldn't fool me."

"Robin—"

"Nothing's going to happen tonight, Mickey," she said, with the eerie calmness of the truly insane. "We'll just shower together, get acquainted."

I was quaking. My teeth were chattering. "Please get out."

She put a hand to my cheek, with the eerie calmness of the truly insane. "Mickey. Stop panicking. Stop fighting it." She shut her eyes, the better to dream. "This was meant to be. This is the rarest of all things, a second flowering for both of us."

She reached for my cock. I twisted away from her, my back to the tiled wall. The only way out was to push past her, and I didn't want to touch her.

I was breathing hard, scared and panicked and, believe it or not, lonely. There wasn't a person in the world I could reach out to for help, and I was at the mercy of a crazy lady. I actually started to cry.

"Billy is my *friend!*" I all but wailed.

She laughed out loud, opened her eyes wide. "Really? Well, he's my husband, but I'm not sure he's my friend."

"We can't do this!"

She slapped my face. "Stop making it complicated." She shut her eyes again and turned her face to the shower spray, like a farmer giving thanks for the rain. "Look at me!" she shouted to whatever god she believed in. "I'm taking a shower with Mickey DeFalco!"

She turned and hugged me with a strength that was almost shocking. Her mouth sought mine, but I twisted away, and that's when I heard the front door open, then footsteps, then a pounding on the bathroom door.

"Robin! Hey, Rob, you in there?"

Robin and I froze in place, gripping each other by the elbows.

Billy barged into the bathroom, and I could hear him breathing hard on the other side of the shower curtain. The man was actually chuckling.

"You believe this, Rob? I go on a raid to the shittiest part of town, and I forget my friggin' vest! Got time for a kiss?"

He ripped aside the shower curtain. At the sight of us a shudder went through his body, but then suddenly he was as still as Mount Rushmore, regarding the two of us from a face turned to stone.

I looked in Billy's eyes and saw his entire life collapse. Everything he thought he knew, everything he believed in, everything that mattered to him had just been brought down like the Twin Towers.

Robin turned and faced Billy, her bony back to me. Billy was breathing hard now. He looked as if he might pass out but some cop instinct kept him on his feet, alert, on the job.

"Billy," Robin said in a matter-of-fact voice, "nothing's happening here. We're just showering."

It was the typical flaky hippie-dippy sort of thing she'd been saying all her marriage, and getting away with, but not this time. Billy's eyes widened in pure heartache.

"Oh, that's great," he breathed. "Just showering, huh?"

"That's right."

His eyes brimmed with tears and his lower lip quivered like a little boy's. "Jesus Christ, Robin. The meter man was one thing. But Mickey? *Mickey DeFalco?* You hadda go and fuck Mickey De-Falco?"

Robin sighed. She seemed almost bored. "Oh, we haven't fucked. *Yet.*"

I think it was that last word that cost Robin O'Brien her life. With an almost weary look on his face Billy lifted his gun and shot his wife twice in the chest.

I caught her in my arms and nearly went down myself, but somehow I managed to stay on my feet. Blood gushed from between her breasts and flooded down her flat belly, mixing with the running water and swirling down the drain like an endless red ribbon. That crazy old hippie girl was dead.

I set her down in a sitting position. She toppled sideways, her cheek on the shower drain. Sensibly, Billy nudged her head off the drain with his foot so the shower wouldn't overflow. It was the same foot he'd used to roust me from the tool shed.

I stood before him, not bothering to figleaf my hands over my now limp cock. He was whimpering as he breathed, a sound that was louder than the water streaming from the shower head.

"Mickey," Billy moaned. "Aw, Mickey. *You?*"

I spread my hands. "Billy. It wasn't my idea. She just came in here."

He nodded. He seemed calmer. "I know, Mickey. I shoulda seen it comin.' I know what she does."

"You know?"

"Shit, I've always known. . . ."

I had minutes to live, and what went through my mind was not the end of my life, but how rough the headlines would be on my poor parents. JEALOUS COP SHOOTS WIFE, ONE HIT WONDER IN SHOWER. . . . SOUR ENDING FOR "SWEET DAYS" SINGER . . .

My God, the story had so many good angles! Lust, faded fame, homelessness, vengeance, wasted promise, nudity, adultery—I could see the TV crew from *E! True Hollywood Story* showing up at my parents' house, pounding on the door, begging for sound bites. . . . What a finish, what a fitting fucking finish for a blue-collar boy from Queens who'd hit it big and then lost his way. . . .

Billy knelt down, the bulletproof vest he'd come home to get jutting up to his chin. If only he'd remembered to take that vest in the first place! How the fuck can a cop forget his bulletproof vest?

Or *did* he forget it? Had he left it behind on purpose, obeying some blind cop instinct that told him his wife was up to no good?

He actually put his fingers on Robin's neck to feel for a pulse.

Then he started to sob. He staggered to his feet, like a drunk trying to get back his dignity, and then he looked at his dead wife as
if he'd just come upon her in an alley. It hit him all at once.

"Oh my God, I shot my wife!"

He put his hands over his face, still holding the gun. I suddenly realized that the water was still running. It was a loud
shower, the floor all hollow and tinny. It seemed important to do
something about that, so I shut the water off.

The sudden silence was jarring. Billy took his hands away from
his face. Snot bubbled from his nose. He wiped it with the back
of his gun hand and managed an awkward smile.

"Know what I regret, Mick? I regret that you never did sing
'Sweet Days' for her. Her birthday is next week, and I was gonna
ask you to serenade her. That woulda been a hell of a birthday
present, don't you think?"

I was shaking with fear. My knees were literally knocking together.

"I'd have done it," I said softly.

Billy smiled at me. "I know you would have. You're a nice guy."

"I could sing it now, if you want."

I couldn't believe I said that. The words just jumped out of
me. It was a survival instinct. I wanted Billy to put the gun down,
and I knew my song had been a seminal thing in his life, and I
guess I thought the sound of it coming from me, standing naked
over his dead wife, would drain him of further homicidal im-
pulses.

A faint smile came to his face. He looked down at Robin, back
at me.

"Go ahead," he said. "Sing."

I cleared my throat. I wasn't even sure I knew all the words
anymore. "Sweet days . . . feel like a haze . . ."

I was rusty. I was out of tune. I was petrified. After the first few words Billy put up his bare hand, made a face as if he'd just gotten a bad clam.

"Never mind, Mick. Don't bother. I'd rather remember it the way it was."

I shut my mouth. He raised his gun and pointed it at my face. I heard a watery sound. I looked down. I'd lost control of my bladder and was pissing on Robin's body.

Billy raised the gun again, pointed it at my face. Then he sighed, lowered the gun.

"I got a better idea," he said, more to himself than to me.

He stuck the barrel under his chin and blew his brains all over the ceiling.

The air went red-misty with blood and brain matter, which gave off a metallic smell I knew came from the iron in the red blood cells. I remembered this from my high school chemistry class, one of the last courses I took before dropping out and pursuing this crazy life that had brought me here, to the blood-soaked bathroom of a corrupt L.A. cop and his crazy wife, both now quite dead.

I don't know how long I stood there. I became aware of a stickiness on my face and hair, and knew it had to be Billy's brain matter. With Robin at my feet I lathered and rinsed myself twice, dried off, stepped out of the shower and over Billy's body and went on autopilot, doing the things that had to be done.

I went to my room and put on fresh clothes. I packed up all my stuff and returned to the bathroom for a last look at my two dead friends, the people who had taken care of me in my most desperate time of need.

Their eyes were open, the two of them. They'd be found with their eyes open, unless I closed them. Which I didn't. That would have involved getting close to them, and since I'd stepped out of the shower, the floor around Billy's head had flooded with

an astonishing amount of blood, and I knew it was important not
to leave footprints anywhere.

And now the big question was obvious—who, if anyone, knew
that I'd come into their lives? Who had they told?

They were isolated people. I hadn't been introduced to any of
their neighbors. Robin had her yoga classes, but it wasn't likely
she'd told any of her students about me, or was it?

And what about Billy? Might he have told any of his fellow
cops that he was sheltering Mickey DeFalco, the legendary one
hit wonder? It would be a pretty tough secret for an ordinary
man to hold, but Billy was not ordinary. Robin was right about
him. He was a control freak, and control freaks are cagey about
information.

It was possible, very possible that I could walk away clean from
this ungodly mess.

I was jolted by the sound of a human voice. They were the
words of an irritated black man, coming from the walkie-talkie
on Billy's hip:

"Hey, O'Brien, where you at? You comin' on this raid with us,
or what? Please respond. . . ."

It was one of his fellow cops. They were waiting for Billy, and
when he didn't show, I knew they would come looking for him.

I had to move fast. I went from room to room, checking to
make sure I'd left nothing behind.

A surge of fear—what about my fingerprints? They were all
over the house, and all over the outside of the house, and all
over the painting equipment!

But I'd never committed a crime, never been arrested, never
been fingerprinted. So what if my prints were all over the place?
They might not even look for a third person. The evidence was
clear-cut—for whatever reason, Officer O'Brien had killed his
wife in the shower before turning the gun on himself. Cops flip
out all the time. A damn shame, but it happens.

Then, for the first and only time in my life, I broke the law. I went to the cupboard and grabbed the Maxwell House coffee can.

The money couldn't do Billy and Robin any good, and they had no children, and what would happen if I left it behind? Maybe nobody would find it, and it would be chucked out with the rest of the groceries in a big careless cleanup. Or maybe some other crooked cop would take it.

"I'll make it right," I vowed to myself, zipping the can into my bag.

The parakeets were restless in their cage, fluttering from perch to perch. Robin normally fed the birds and the turtles at this time of night, and I was going to do it, but the wail of a distant siren changed my mind. It was time to go. The cops who'd soon be swarming the place could feed the animals.

I forced myself to be calm as I stood at the front door. I took a final deep breath before stepping outside and walking, not running, toward the sidewalk.

At the sidewalk I turned right and continued walking, my duffel bag high on my shoulder. I had no idea of where I was going, but I was on my way. Each stride I took was a step farther from the pit of hell. I gobbled up the long suburban blocks—five, six, seven of them before a police car passed me, going in the opposite direction. I forced myself not to hurry, not to give those cops any reason at all to pull me aside and shine a light in my face.

A plane soared overhead, low and loud. I wasn't far from LAX. Suddenly, I knew what I had to do. That crazy lie I'd told Billy about going to visit my parents was morphing into the truth. This was an excellent time to put three thousand miles of distance between myself and the horrible thing that had just happened.

Believe it or not, I happened to come upon a bus stop just as a bus bound for the airport pulled up. When I got there I went straight to United Airlines and bought a one-way ticket for their next flight to JFK for $268, paying for it with fourteen twenty-dollar bills from the coffee-can cash. The friendly woman at the counter informed me that a round-trip ticket would cost just $328, but I told her I wasn't sure when I'd be coming back.

Which was an outright lie. I knew that I would never again be setting foot in the City of Angels.

The plane lifted off just twenty minutes later, less than two hours after Police Officer William O'Brien had taken the life of his wife before turning the gun on himself.

CHAPTER TWENTY-THREE

She knew it all. She knew everything. Lynn's face was pale as she put a hand to my damp cheek, gave it a gentle pat.

"Jesus, Mickey. You got mixed up with some crazy people."

"That's about the size of it."

"So it just went down in the record books as a murder-suicide?"

"I really don't know. I don't *want* to know. I ran away and never looked back. But every time I see a cop car, I shit my pants."

She stroked my hair. "You didn't do anything wrong, Mickey."

"Yeah? Why didn't I get out of that shower faster? If I'd run out as soon as she came in, he'd never have caught us."

"You were in shock. You were paralyzed."

"I don't know about that."

"Give yourself a break, Mickey. You tried to be decent."

"The point is, if I hadn't come into their lives, they'd both still be alive, you know?"

Lynn's eyes welled with tears. "No, Mickey. The point is, if *I* hadn't come into your life, they'd both be alive. If I hadn't run away, you wouldn't have written the song, you'd never have gone to Los Angeles . . . see what I'm saying?"

She put a hand to her chest. "It all connects to me."

What a Catholic. I was an amateur by comparison. Lynn fell sobbing into my arms.

"I'm sorry, Mickey. I'm so sorry!"

"Lynn, come on! It's not your fault!"

"It's not your fault."

"It's *nobody's* fault," I said, realizing that I meant every word of what I'd just said. I pulled back from her, looked into her shining eyes. An idea leapt into my mind, and a heartbeat later I was voicing it.

"What do you say we both decide to believe that it was nobody's fault, and that we're both decent people, and that we deserve a freaking break here?"

She nodded, wiped her nose. "Think that'll work?"

"I'll give it a shot if you will."

"All right, Mick."

She was helping me. I was helping her. We could make each other well again. It was amazing. It was like magic, but it was better than magic. It was the healing power of love, like the love that I'd sung about without fully understanding, but I certainly understood it now.

Lynn managed a crooked grin, sighed, and said, "Not to bring up a touchy subject, but where's all that cash you took? I know it's not in the bank."

"I stashed it in my closet. There's this high spot over the door my mother can't reach."

"The broken bricks, where you used to hide *Playboy* magazines?"

I felt my face turn red. "Jesus, did I tell you about that?"

"You used to tell me everything, Mickey."

"Well, anyway, that's where it's been since I got home. I know I can't keep it, but I don't know what to do with it."

"I do."

"You do?"

"Sure." She took my hand the way a faith healer might reach for a nonbeliever. "We'll take it to the city and give it away."

"Who are we giving it to?"

"Whoever needs it. Come on, let's get moving."

"*Now?*"

"Yeah, Mickey, now. I think it will be better if we do this thing first."

It. We both knew what "it" was. And she was right. I wanted to come to her clean, as clean as I could be.

"Go get that money," she said. "Meet me at my house in half an hour."

I did as I was told. Luckily for me, nobody was home, so I got the coffee can and slipped out without being seen. When I picked Lynn up she'd showered and changed into jeans and a T-shirt, pretty much the same outfit I was wearing. On our way down the steps of her front stoop we saw that several slats of the wooden ramp had collapsed to the ground.

"I've got to get rid of that thing," Lynn murmured.

"I can do that for you." I hesitated. "You know, I pushed him up that ramp once."

"*You?*"

I told her about my rainy birthday, all those years ago, and how I'd hoped that she'd come back to see me, and how the Captain wasn't able to get himself up the ramp without my help.

"Did you talk to him?"

"Not much."

"What did he say?"

"He wanted to know if I'd heard from you. He wanted me to tell you to come home, that all was forgiven."

Her eyes widened, then softened with sadness. "Forgiven," she echoed. "Well. That's nice to know."

"He was pretty drunk, Lynn."

"Yeah? What else is new? Come on, let's move, let's do this thing."

We caught a train to Penn Station and after the conductor took our tickets and moved away, we were the only ones left in the car.

"Let me see it, Mick."

I handed her the coffee can. She peeled off the lid and looked inside. She handled money all day at the bank, so the sight of all those bills did not startle her.

"How much?"

"Almost six thousand. . . . How are we going to do this?"

"We'll just give it to the homeless."

"How?"

"We hand it to them."

"Just like that?"

"Why not?"

"How much per person?"

She shrugged. "A hundred, two hundred. Whatever you like."

"Lynn, let's say we give them a hundred apiece. That's almost sixty people. Think we can do that in one day?"

She grinned, kissed my cheek. "Piece o' cake."

It was a crazy, nutty, wonderful plan, and I knew she was doing it to save my soul. This was my penance, a more useful penance than I'd ever been granted by any priest. My ears popped as the train rolled into the tunnel beneath the East River. Next stop, Penn Station.

"Think this'll get us into heaven, Lynn?"

She shrugged, even managed a laugh. "I don't know about getting into heaven. I'm just hoping to stay out of hell."

In Penn Station a thin, bearded man was squatting with his back against a tiled wall, a grimy paper coffee cup clutched in his hand. He was too weary to shake it, too tired to bother getting a musical sound out of the few coins in his cup.

I pointed at the guy. "Him?"

"Why not?"

I took five twenties from the can, folded them in half, breezed toward the guy, dumped the bills in his cup and kept moving. By the time his grimy fingers reached for the bills I was back at Lynn's side. She took me by the elbow and led me away.

"We can't hang around for thanks or small talk," she said. "We'll try to find beggars with cups. That way we just drop the money and go."

"Have you done this before?"

"No, but I handle money all day long, and I know how it can make people crazy."

As we made our way up to the street we heard a cry of astonishment behind us.

"Don't look back," Lynn said. "He might want more."

It went a lot faster than I might have imagined. We walked the city streets with no destination, seeking out the homeless. They were everywhere, stooped and round-shouldered in the midst of all those square-shouldered assholes bellowing into their cell phones for all the world to hear.

Lynn gave a hundred to a young man with a greasy ponytail who sat with a sad-looking mutt in front of a cardboard sign that said HUNGRY, HOMELESS. His mouth fell open at the sight of the bills but he did not make a sound.

I was suspicious of that one. "He could be a faker," I said. "He looked well nourished, and he has a pet."

"What the hell, Mickey, even if he's a faker, the dog is for real."

We made our way north and east, giving out hundreds all the way, jogging away from the people who got the cash as if we'd just left burning firecrackers in their grimy paper cups.

It was great. It was unbelievable. I felt like a hot-air balloonist dropping sandbags, soaring higher with each drop. Lynn was right. This mission wasn't going to take long at all.

We entered Grand Central Terminal, and the glory of the

place hit me just as hard as it hit me when I was a kid seeing it for the first time, all that marble and all those windows, and shiny brass clocks from a time gone by. . . .

We were both hungry. We got big salty pretzels and Cokes and sat on the hard-polished floor, eating and drinking and watching the mobs crisscross the floor. I checked the coffee can and saw that more than half the money was gone.

Then I saw him.

He looked as if he might have played professional football, an enormous black man in a torn overcoat, ridiculously loud plaid pants, and laceless, greasy sneakers that looked to be a few sizes too small and may have accounted for the pained look on his face. Atop his head was a big, puffy, graying Afro that tilted like a condemned building.

He took long, regal strides across the wide floor, obviously caught up in the bum's dilemma—no place to go, and no place to rest without being harassed by a cop.

I didn't dare step in front of him—he'd have knocked me down like the night train. So I fell into stride beside him, nearly jogging to keep up. He was a head taller than me. It was like looking up at a statue.

He was ignoring me, or maybe his peripheral vision was no good. I held five twenties in front of his face.

"Here, sir. That's for you."

He stopped walking, took the bills and studied them as if he'd never seen currency before. With his other hand he grabbed me by the shoulder with a strength that was astonishing. My collarbone felt as if it might snap. I opened my mouth to cry out but my vocal cords seemed paralyzed.

The giant was staring into my eyes. His eyes were oddly serene, though reddened by who knows how many restless nights, or years. I couldn't break free of his grasp and I couldn't find my voice to call for help, though in truth the last thing I needed now was a cop.

What if a warrant for my arrest had been issued from coast to coast? That would have been the ultimate irony—getting nabbed for the L.A. thing while giving dirty money away to the homeless in New York!

The giant licked dry lips and attempted a grin. "Now listen, little man, and tell me—why did you give me this money?"

His voice was as deep as a kettle drum. I waited for its rumble to die down before replying, "I'm trying to be a good guy."

What a lame-ass thing to say! He maintained his grip on my shoulder, looked at the bills, looked at me. He shook his head as if he'd been handed pieces to a puzzle that didn't fit.

"Why?" he demanded.

"I don't know. I guess I want to . . . pay for my sins?"

He startled me by laughing, revealing brown teeth that seemed as jagged as a wolf's. He released my shoulder and shook the bills in my face.

"Pay for your sins with real money, is that it?"

"I guess."

"Kinda literal, ain't it?"

"Yeah. Yeah, you're right about that."

He cackled, pocketed the bills, thumped my shoulder twice with his hand, and was gone.

I returned to Lynn. "I thought that guy was going to kill me."

"Easy, baby. I'll take you to a nice place."

"Where?"

"It's a surprise."

We left the terminal and headed eastward and downtown, dropping hundreds all the way.

I had six hundred bucks left in the coffee can when we reached Lynn's destination—Gramercy Park, the only park in Manhattan where you need a key to get inside. Only the people who live along the park's borders get keys.

"I love this park," Lynn said. "Even though we can't get inside, I wanted to see it."

It looked glorious in the late afternoon sunshine—tall trees, immaculately maintained footpaths, black nannies in white outfits pushing strollers containing Caucasian babies. A piece of old New York that had somehow survived.

We started walking the perimeter of the park, and there she was when we turned the corner, sitting on the sidewalk with her back against the wrought-iron fence—a bag lady with her worldly possessions jammed into a two-wheeled cart. Clothes, deposit cans, and even a cruddy old black telephone with a rotary dial. Why would anyone keep such a thing? Maybe it was the last phone she'd ever owned, from the last place she'd ever lived in.

She was street-grimy, tinted dark by the exhaust fumes of a million buses, but there was a weird dignity to her. Her thick brown-gray hair seemed cleaner than the rest of her, swept back behind her ears—she must have had a hairbrush or a comb tucked away somewhere in that junk. Snug inside a red cloth coat, she leaned against the fence as if it were a beach chair, with her face tilted toward the sun. In her mind, she could have been on the shore in East Hampton, waiting for the ringing of the lunch bell from a seaside mansion. . . .

When we stood in front of her we put her in sudden shadow and she opened her eyes, which turned out to be remarkably blue and clear.

"How am I supposed to acquire a tan if you stand in my sunshine?"

Her voice stunned me. She sounded as if she'd grown up in a finishing school. Her teeth were yellow but there were no gaps in her smile, which she beamed at me in a way that was both friendly and menacing.

"What can I do for you?" she asked, as if she were seated at the customer service desk at Bloomingdale's. I looked at Lynn. She seemed fascinated and frightened. In a strange way this woman was much scarier than the giant at Grand Central. I reached into the can and took out a hundred bucks.

"That's for you," I said. She took the bills without counting them and casually tucked them inside her coat. You'd have thought strangers gave her a hundred bucks every day.

"Take care," I said as we turned to leave.

"Wait!"

We turned back to face her. She pointed with a filthy finger at a building directly across the street. It was a magnificent brownstone with potted flowers on the stoop, red geraniums that glistened from a recent watering.

"Do you see how those geraniums have been watered? Can you see that they're wet?"

"Yes, ma'am."

"That's the wrong way to do it when a plant is in direct sunlight. You burn up the petals that way. The right thing to do is to water them at the roots."

I could think of nothing to say in response to this impromptu gardening lesson. Why had she told me this? Could she tell from looking at me that I was a gardener? Did she have mystical powers?

She smiled at me and pointed at the house again. "I was born there, you see, so I do take an interest in these things."

I swallowed. My heart was hammering. My brain told me she could have been a crazy, delusional old lady, but my heart told me she had to be telling the truth.

She raised her finger slightly, to indicate a higher target. "Third floor, facing the gardens out back. That was my nursery. Light blue wallpaper with angels on it. I'd fall asleep counting the angels. . . . A midwife delivered me. Do you know what a midwife is?"

"Yes, I do."

"Anyway, that was my home until I left for college. I was very happy there, very happy indeed."

She seemed happy now, remembering it. Somewhere along the way, her life had gone horribly, unimaginably wrong, and now here she was, sixty- or seventy-something years later, back where she started. Twenty yards from the door, and a million miles from home.

Why wasn't she angry? Maybe the wisdom of her years told her she was lucky to have ever had it at all. Or maybe she was nuts. It amounted to the same thing.

Lynn spoke up. I'd almost forgotten she was with me.

"Did you play in the park when you were little?"

The old lady's face brightened. "Oh, yes! Let me show you something."

She dug into her coat pocket. Moments later she pulled out an ancient brass key that was green with tarnish and handed it to Lynn as if it were the Holy Grail. It was a large, heavy thing with a loop at one end, the kind of key that looked as if it could open a castle door.

"Do you know what that is?"

"Yes," said Lynn. "It's the key to the park, isn't it?"

"Right you are, child. Sadly, the locks have been changed many times since we lived here, but I like keeping it for—oh, I don't know—old times' sake, I suppose."

She took the key from Lynn, put it back in her pocket and shifted her back against the fence, in search of a more comfortable position.

"How," I began, and it came out like a cry, and that was as far as I got. The question was just too terrible to actually put into words. The old lady knew what I wanted to know, though.

"It's hard to get things," she said, "and it's easy to lose them." She narrowed her eyes at us. "But I have a feeling you people already know that."

Lynn's lips were trembling. She pulled me aside, out of the old lady's earshot.

"Give her the can."

"What?"

"Give her the rest of the money."

"You do it, Lynn."

She took the can from me and squatted at the old lady's side. "This is for you," she said, handing it over. The old lady peeled off the lid and peeked inside at the bills. She didn't even raise her eyebrows. Then she took the hundred I'd given her, put it in the can, put the lid back on, and stuck the can inside the many folds of her coat.

"That's quite a bit of money," Lynn said gently. "You can get a room tonight."

The old lady smiled. "I live *here*," she replied simply, as if she were stating the obvious to a child.

It was a dismissal. We both knew it. Lynn put her arm across my shoulders as we began the walk back to Penn Station. Neither of us looked back at the old lady with six hundred bucks in a coffee can, the last of the shakedown money from a corrupt Los Angeles cop. Our glorious mission had come to a bizarre end.

"That should last her a long time," Lynn said.

"Unless somebody mugs her."

"Who would mug a homeless person?"

"Another homeless person."

"Mickey. Maybe we should go back and open a bank account for her."

"What?"

"I can do it for her. It'll take ten minutes. We'll bring her to an HSBC and get her a checking account. You can guard her stuff outside the bank while I do it. As long as she's coherent enough to know her name—"

"Lynn, Lynn. Turn around."

She did, and the two of us looked back to the fence where that old lady had been. She was gone, gone, gone.

"Oh, Mickey. Hold my hand."

We were close, Lynn and I, almost as close as we'd been in the old days, and that's when I thought of one more thing to do, with my own damn money.

"Hey, baby. You ever been up the Empire State Building?"

"Never."

We looked up at it in the waning light of day, the once-tallest building in the city that lost its title when the Twin Towers went up and regained it when they came down.

"I've never been up there either. Should we go?"

"Now?"

"It's right here. What the hell. Let's do it."

I paid for admission tickets and we took a series of elevators to the observation deck, eighty-six stories in the sky.

The view was astounding, truly a thing to take your breath away. The sun had just set and lights were coming on throughout the city below us, which sprawled in all directions, embraced by two rivers.

The spikes atop the gates surrounding the observation deck curved inward and down, ending in sharp points to discourage jumpers. Far below, dozens of wretched lives had been brightened by what Lynn and I had done that day.

The air was chilly with the coming of autumn, and I was overwhelmed with hope as I embraced Lynn from behind, a deed that coaxed gentle words from her mouth, words I had to ask her to repeat.

"I said, I've been here before."

That surprised me. "I thought you said—"

"I didn't think I had been here, but now it's coming back to me . . . this view . . . oh, God . . ."

She was trembling, and not from the cold or the wind. I tightened my embrace, and she did nothing to try and break it.

"Lynn? You okay?"

She nodded, not looking at me, and hesitated before saying, "I was here with my dad."

I was stunned. "Your father brought you up here?"

"Uh-huh. I must have been five years old, maybe six. I think he had to attend some conference about fire prevention in skyscrapers, and for some reason he took me along. I guess there was no school that day. . . ."

I broke my hold on Lynn, who walked to the edge of the deck and put her head against the fence, facing Ground Zero.

"Yeah, I remember this view," she said to the wind. "There's no other view like it in the world, so I must have been here."

She turned to look at me. "It was just the two of us. I don't know where my mother could have been, or my brothers . . . home, I guess."

Her eyes shined with sudden tears. "He said, 'Look all around you, Princess. This is the world, and it's all for you, every bit of it.' "

She lowered her head and put her face in her hands. It was hard for me to imagine the man I had known ever saying anything like that to anyone.

"I guess he loved me, in some crazy way," she said to her hands.

"I'm sure he did."

"This was before . . ."

She stopped speaking, lowered her hands. Her eyes widened and narrowed in one continuous motion that told me she'd caught herself in the nick of time, stopped herself from revealing something she'd kept locked up her entire life and now, giddy from the heights and the sights, she'd nearly let out of the bag.

"Before what?" I asked as gently as I could. She forced a smile and shrugged.

"Before he turned into a complete asshole. Come on, DeFalco, take me home, it's been quite a day."

There was more to know. She knew my secret and I had a feeling this was hers. Lynn had given me a glimpse of it, a flash of lightning that lit the landscape for an instant, but the image was gone as fast as it had appeared.

We rode the elevators back down and were seized by a weird

depression at street level. It was a blowy night. Paper cups and sheets of newspaper whirled around on the sidewalks, like ghosts with no place to go. We only had to wait a few minutes for a train to Little Neck.

"You okay, Lynn?"

She hesitated. "Will you stay with me tonight? If you stay with me tonight, I think I'll be okay."

"Of course I'll stay with you. I already said I would."

"What I mean is, I'd like to make love with you, if that's okay."

If it's okay.

"Yeah. Yeah, that'd be . . . really good."

"You sure? If you need time to think about it—"

"Lynn, I've been thinking about it since 1987. I don't want to think about it anymore. I'd like to do it more than I'd like to do anything else in the world."

She held me tightly all the way home.

Lynn checked in with the hospital while I took a shower. Her mother was still in stable condition, still unconscious. I got into the bed while she took a shower.

Unless the world came to an end it was about to happen, this thing I'd come to believe would never happen.

I checked under the bed, and there they were where I'd left them—a three-pack of lubricated Trojans, with an expiration date of May 2014. Was anyone really expected to carry them around for that long?

The door creaked and she entered, her hair hanging damp, a blue terrycloth robe covering her body. I lay there on my back, my cock tent-poling the sheet. She jutted her chin toward it.

"Are you naked under there?"

"Yeah."

"Can I have a look?"

I pulled the blanket away like a magician revealing a rabbit-in-a-hat trick, but there was no trick, just the way I felt about her, hard and true. Then she let the robe fall to the floor, and at last I saw what I'd been dreaming about for so many years.

It was a paradoxical body, a baffling blend of generous curves and sharp angles that made me wonder how it was possible to be so lean and so voluptuous at the same time. It really was not so different from the body I'd gazed upon at Jones Beach, except for the dark webs of wrinkles just below her eyes. I stared and stared, and only a growing sense of light-headedness made me realize I'd been holding my breath. I let it out, resumed breathing with a gasp. Lynn smiled at me.

"So. Do I meet with your approval?"

"You're more beautiful than ever."

She got under the blanket with me and we rolled into each other's arms, just like that. As we kissed I felt a quiver running through her, or maybe it was going through me. She bit my ear with playful restraint, took my face in her hands.

"You all right?" she asked.

"Yeah. You?"

"So far."

"Long time coming."

"Yeah, but your persistence paid off."

"So you're *glad* this is happening, right?"

"For God's sake, Mickey, we're naked in bed together after twenty years of mental foreplay. Of *course* I'm glad this is happening."

Something was off. I probably knew less about women than any man in the world but I did know this woman, and I knew that something was off.

I cleared my throat to talk about it but before I could she slipped down and took me in her mouth. The pleasure was gentle and thorough and maddening, so that I had to twist around and do her without breaking the connection, and after sixty-nining each other for what felt like forever it was at last time to see how well we did or did not fit.

I slid my arm under the bed and pulled out the Trojans.

"It's okay, Mickey, you don't need those."

"I don't?"

"You look clean to me. Are you clean?"

"So far as I know."

"All right, then. I'm clean, too. Let's trust each other on that."

My God, sex without a condom! Lynn and I were going to christen this voyage by going skin to skin!

It was too much. Suddenly there wasn't enough air in the room. I got up to open the windows as wide as they could go, and the curtains puffed back and forth with cool breezes. Lynn lay on her back, her hair spilling all over the sheets in a blond cornucopia. I knelt before her, as if to confess my sins, but I'd already done that. She took my cock in hand and stroked it.

"Now."

I let her guide it, seemingly a centimeter at a time. This was what I'd dreamed of, what I'd given up for lost. The sensation was as startling as it should have been pleasurable, and so why wasn't it pleasurable?

Because Lynn lay there as if she were undergoing a surgical procedure. I was breathing hard, afraid of hurting her, afraid of doing it wrong, afraid of failing to satisfy her, and mostly, *mostly,* afraid of her tight-shut eyes and that sudden snarl on her lips. . . .

"Why are you out of breath?" she asked through tight teeth.

"I was just wondering . . ."

"Wondering what?"

I had to say it. "What have you got, a diaphragm?"

"Oh for God's sake!"

She brought her knees together and I was out of her. She rolled to her side and popped up into a sitting position, clutching the sheet to her chest. I covered myself with the other half of the sheet and gazed at her face. The green flecks in her eyes seemed to be swimming like maddened tropical fish, and this, I remembered, only happened when she was enraged.

I tried to swallow, but my mouth was cotton. "I think it's a fair question."

"I'm *not* wearing a diaphragm, Mickey."

"All right, so you're not wearing a diaphragm. It's all right with me, Lynn. I'll have a kid with you, if that's what you want."

I couldn't believe I'd said it. Here I was, barely able to take care of myself, offering to reproduce with Lynn on our very first time together. It was crazy, it was insane, and I meant every word of it.

"I love you, baby. Let's make more people like you."

Her eyes filmed with tears, giving the fish more room to swim, only now they weren't swimming as fast. Her anger was dying.

"Mickey . . . Jesus, you're a sweet boy."

"I'll pay you to stop saying that. All I mean is, I'd love to be the father of any kid of yours."

"That's impossible."

"Well, it'd be tough, but I wouldn't say—"

"Mickey. Don't you get it? I can't have kids."

It was as if I'd had the wind knocked out of me. I held my breath, had to tell myself to start breathing again.

"What do you mean, you can't have kids?"

"Something happened to me. I can't get pregnant."

It didn't immediately register. *Something happened?* What did that mean? An accident? An infection? A pregnancy that went wrong and destroyed the reproductive structures? As with most males the female anatomy was a mystery to me, but somewhere in my head I heard the sound of a vault door slamming shut forever.

It wasn't that I was child-crazy. I had no particular feeling about kids either way, but I had feelings about Lynn, and the concept that Lynn would end with Lynn hit me harder than I ever could have imagined.

"Since I was twenty-one," she added in response to the question I hadn't yet asked.

Now my eyes went wet, and why was that? A million reasons, maybe, but most likely over the death of a dream I never even realized I'd been carrying. You don't just want the woman when you're crazy in love. You want the whole thing, and all the possibilities that come with it.

"I'm sorry," I finally said.

She chuckled. "Sorry for me, or for you?"

"Just . . . sorry."

"Well, Mick, it you were planning on future generations of DeFalcos, they won't be happening through me."

I felt myself shiver. She pulled the sheets up around herself in sudden modesty, Eve tasting shame for the first time.

"I guess you feel differently now, huh, Mick?"

I shook my head. "I'm just sad, Lynn."

"Well, be sad somewhere else. This house has had enough sadness to last five centuries." Tears ran down her cheeks. She pointed at the door. "Just go, Mickey. I'm so sorry I disappointed you. Please, please go."

I dressed and left without saying another word. Dead men can't talk, and I was a dead man.

CHAPTER TWENTY-FOUR

No death is as painful as the death of a dream, and suddenly I realized just how elaborate my dream of the way it was going to be with Lynn Mahoney had been. A lifetime's worth of wishing and wondering, blown away like a feather in a hurricane.

Ever since she'd run away, teams of night laborers had been toiling away in my dreams to build a castle in the air, the castle I would one day gallop toward aboard my white horse with Lynn seated behind me, her arms tight around my waist.

It was a nice castle. I didn't know it was there until it was gone, and that went for the muscular steed that evaporated between my legs, and those arms around my waist that suddenly lost their grip. . . .

I was standing on the sidewalk outside Lynn's house. No, I was in the middle of the street, and a car was honking to get me out of the way.

How had I gotten out here? Had I walked down the stairs of the Mahoney house, opened a door? I must have, but I had no memory of it. I moved to the sidewalk, staring in wonder at the sullen, goateed kid behind the wheel of the car, who flipped me the bird before roaring away.

"Asshole!"

The crickets were loud, and it almost sounded as if they were scolding me as I began walking home.

Home? Did I say I was walking home? Bad plan. Very bad. Back home I could only disappoint my parents with tales of how horribly wrong things had gone, and my mother would want to help me, somehow, but you can't have a funeral service for the death of a dream, can you?

No, you can't. What you *can* do, though, is head to the Little Neck Inn, where the elite are known to meet on Saturday nights.

I shouldered my way to the bar, hoping my father would be there. Maybe I could talk to him about what had just happened, but Sully shook his head when I asked if Steady Eddie was around.

"Here and gone. Came in with a bit of an attitude tonight and left when I wouldn't let him smoke."

"What was he upset about?"

"Tell you the truth, son, he wasn't in a chatty mood, though he did mumble a few choice phrases about slow horses on his fifth or sixth lager. Are you drinkin' tonight? Because if you're not, you're takin' up a prime piece o' real estate."

I slapped the bar. "Beer and a shot, my good man."

"We call that a boilermaker around here."

"All right, a boilermaker."

He hesitated before putting a longneck on the bar, then filling a shot glass.

"That's eight bucks."

"And well worth it." I threw a twenty on the bar, downed the whiskey, and chased it with a swallow of beer. Sully made change and slapped the bills down hard to get my attention.

"Let's take it easy, now, Mick."

I pressed my hands to my chest. "Am I causing a problem?"

"You've got a look in your eye. I know that look. Nine times out of ten it leads to broken furniture."

"Sully. I just want to get drunk."

Sully sighed. "All right, all right. Here's a speech I've made a million times, so once more won't hurt."

He leaned over the mahogany, the bar halving his balloon belly. "Whoever she is, she's not worth it. You're better off without her. No matter what you do, you'll never make her happy. Nobody knows how to please them, especially us. Now drink up, go home, and pull your pud."

"I will. But first, another shot, please."

"Comin' up."

Sully poured with a deft hand. The world was starting to lose its hard edges. I downed the second shot, chased it with a swallow of beer, motioned for a third shot. Sully poured it and set a fresh longneck on the bar.

"You ain't drivin', are you, Junior?"

"I haven't owned a car in years. And lay off the Junior stuff."

"Sorry. Merely my awkward attempt to indicate how youthful a person you appear to be, despite your advanced years." He went to the other end of the bar, and just then a heavy arm fell across my shoulders.

"Hey, pal!"

It was my old back-pounding classmate Frankie McElhenny, redolent of sweat and garbage. I actually put my arm around him and pulled him close, like a long-lost friend.

"Frankie! Good to see you!"

I meant it. I was starved for a distraction, any distraction. Frankie seemed puzzled, almost startled.

"Really?"

"Absolutely. Let me buy you a drink." I stood on the rungs of my bar stool, like a man on horseback standing in the stirrups. "Sully! The usual for my good friend!"

Sully brought Frankie a dripping mug of draft beer, the cheapest drink they sold. "The rungs of that stool ain't what they used to be, Mickey. Kindly be seated."

I obeyed. Then I clinked my bottle against Frankie's mug, he settled down on the stool beside me, and we were on our way.

It's hard to remember what Frankie was talking about after he first sat down, but I do remember that the word "suck" came up a lot. His boss sucked, the people whose garbage he hauled sucked, his ex-girlfriends sucked. . . . Every swallow of beer seemed to raise another one of his enemies above the tree line. I put another twenty on my money pile and wouldn't let Frankie pay for a drink. He had no problem with that.

Suddenly he whacked my shoulder, nearly knocking me off my stool.

"Hey. You ain't gonna believe what I heard. Know that song you wrote? I hear it's in some new movie."

"I know."

Frankie's eyes narrowed. "You *know?*"

"I saw the movie."

"I heard it sucks."

"That's not true. It's a pretty good movie."

His nostrils widened. "All of a sudden you're the big movie critic, huh?"

For the first time, I sensed that there could be trouble, the kind of trouble Sully's antennae had picked up the moment I'd entered the bar.

"All I'm saying is, it's not bad."

I could hear his breathing, almost a growling sound, like a guard dog slowly getting angry. "You always thought you were better than everybody else. You and your shitty little song."

The world was whirling. I was in no shape for a fight. But I was also angry enough not to care about whatever happened next.

Stupidly, defiantly, suicidally, I got to my feet.

"I'm not better than everybody else, man." I poked his chest. "But let's face it. If I hadn't lifted my elbow to show you the answers, you'd still be in eighth grade."

It took a while to get to Frankie, as if my words were being delivered by a carrier pigeon fighting a hard wind. But the bird got there at last, and the flame burned hot in Frankie's eyes as he lunged for me.

His fist found my left eye, luckily for me a glancing blow, or he would have caved my skull in. I countered with a shot to his chin, and then he wrapped his arms around me and the two of us crashed to the floor.

He was a lot stronger than me, and all the rage of his wretched life went into a bear hug that crushed my rib cage. I couldn't breathe, couldn't break his embrace. The world was going dark when suddenly he let out a cry and his grip went loose. I saw Sully, billy club in hand, drag him to his feet and set his ass down on a bar stool, so that Frankie looked like nothing more than a passed-out drunk.

Then Sully pulled me to my feet with astonishing strength. He was still gripping the club. I thought he was going to clock me one, but I was wrong. He put his lips to my ear to deliver the message, urgent and angry.

"Get your ass over to Starbucks, Junior. I'm hearin' that your old man's got himself into a bad situation."

I was still woozy. "Starbucks?"

He pushed me through the crowd and out the door. "Just get goin', man, get goin'!"

CHAPTER TWENTY-FIVE

The walk and the air helped sober me up, and the sight of my father in the front window of Starbucks hit me like a pail of ice water. He sat alone at a small round table in the middle of the place, leaning back, legs crossed. He seemed to be in a trance as he lifted a cup of coffee for a sip, which he followed with a drag from a Camel. It was a long drag, a get-the-smoke-all-the-way-down-to-your-ankles drag, and he held the smoke for a good five seconds before slowly letting it go in a long, puffy plume.

I went inside. The other customers were huddled by the cash register, clutching their cappuccinos and their laptops and staring in disbelief at that atrocity in their midst—an indoor smoker!

A frantic kid in a green apron and a Starbucks baseball cap came up to me and said, "Do you know this man?"

"He's my father."

"We can't get him to stop smoking. He's on his third cigarette! The manager wants to call the cops."

"The *cops?*"

"Please, just get him out of here."

I crossed the highly polished floor and sat in a chair across from my father, directly in the line of his smoke stream.

"Dad? *Dad!*"

He blinked his way out of a daydream and looked at me. A smile lit up his stubbly face, then a frown.

"Hey, Mick, what happened to your eye?"

"Little fight at the inn."

"Yeah? Hope you got in a good punch or two."

I could tell from the glaze over his eyes that he'd downed at least half a dozen beers. He was speaking softly, though. This was an unusual thing about my father. He was blustery when sober, quiet when drunk.

His eyes drifted as he took another drag. I patted his hand to get his attention. My own buzz was fading fast, in the midst of this crazy crisis.

"What are you doing here, Dad?"

He sighed. "Oh . . . guess I just wanted to see what a two-dollar cup o' coffee tasted like." He leaned forward, looked left and right before adding, "It's nothin' special, I can tell you that much. Your mother's instant is as good as this stuff. Guess what they're sellin' here is . . ." He hesitated, sought the right word . . .

"Ambience."

He chuckled, sat back, took a last drag from his Camel, dropped it on the floor, and squashed it under his toe, where he'd mashed two other butts on the otherwise immaculate floor.

He shook another cigarette into his mouth and lit up.

"Dad. What do you say we get out of here?"

"In a minute. I still ain't finished my two-dollar coffee."

"You can't smoke in here, Dad. You're upsetting these people."

He arched his eyebrows in mock surprise. "They're really upset?"

"Yeah."

"Fuck 'em."

"Dad—"

"Look at this." He pulled a ticket from his pocket. It was from the local off-track betting parlor. "See this? This is a trifecta bet. Know what a trifecta is, Mick?"

I knew. "You have to pick the first three horses in a row."

"In a row, that's right. Look at this ticket."

He handed it to me. I saw that he'd placed a twenty-dollar bet on the L, M, and N horses, in that order.

He cleared his throat. "As you can see, I played L, M, N. Wanna know what the winning combo was? L, N, M. The M horse got nosed out by the N horse. *Nosed out!* I'da had it, Mick. Woulda paid *six grand* for my twenty. Six thousand bucks. My fucking luck."

Six grand. Just about the same amount Lynn and I had given away.

My father suddenly jabbed a finger toward the floor.

"Know what used to be here? *Right here,* on this spot? Julius Bernstein's candy store. You old enough to remember him? Fat Jewish guy, always had a big cigar jammed in his mouth?"

"I remember."

"Nice guy. He had a soda fountain. Stools that swiveled." He twirled his finger in midair. "You could sit there and swivel and read the paper and drink an egg cream and have a cigarette, without anybody botherin' you. And now . . ."

He couldn't finish the thought. He waved his hand around the place to indicate the pompous prints on the walls, the ridiculous coffee bean displays, the dribble of toothless jazz from unseen speakers.

"I just wanted to sit where I used to sit and smoke where I used to smoke."

"Let's go home, Dad."

"Yeah, yeah. Soon's I finish this butt."

A red strobe light cut across the Starbucks walls. A cop car had pulled up in front of the place. The asshole manager had actu-

ally called the cops. My father's smoking was now a police matter. Somewhere else in Queens some old lady was being clubbed
over the head for her handbag, but she'd have to wait her turn
as New York's Finest dealt with this emergency—a deranged
nicotine junkie.

"Dad. The police are here."

He didn't seem to hear me. "I'da bought something nice for
your mother with that money, Mick. I'da shared it with you, too,
so you could do somethin' nice with Lynn."

"Lynn and I are all through, Dad."

Those words got to him, pierced his buzz. I could see it in his
suddenly focused eyes.

"You had a fight?"

"I don't know what we had, but this thing isn't going to work.
We both know it."

His shoulders sagged. Just like that, he was sober, or damn close
to it. "Aww, Mick. It happened to you all over again. Goddamn."

A big-bellied cop strolled in, followed by a skinny cop and a
weedy little guy who turned out to be the manager, the knucklehead who'd called the police. Both cops were young. Their
name tags read Esposito and DeNinno. The big one, Esposito,
seemed amused by the whole thing. He pushed the bill of his hat
up a notch with a forefinger, just like cops in the movies do when
they find themselves in an absurd situation. He seemed confident that he could Hey Pal his way out of this one.

"Hey pal, whaddaya say you put out that cigarette, okay?"

My father looked at the cop. "I'm not your pal."

The cop turned to me. "He with you?"

"He's my father. He's having a rough night."

"Get him outta here."

"I'm trying, Officer." I got to my feet. "Dad, please, let's go."

My father remained seated, slumped back even deeper in his
chair. He took a drag from his butt and blew a stream of smoke
straight at the cop's bulging belly.

"Don't you guys have real criminals to chase?"

Jesus Christ. Esposito, no longer amused, pulled his cap down snug. "That's it. Get up."

My father obeyed, rising slowly to his feet. I felt a flood of relief. He knew he'd taken it as far as he could, and wisely chose to pull his horns in, except he took one last drag from his beloved Camel, exhaled through his nostrils like an enraged bull, and flicked the butt as hard as he could at the cop's chest.

Sparks flew. Esposito grabbed my father and pushed him face up against the wall, where DeNinno cuffed his hands behind his back.

It happened as fast as a snake bite. Through it all was my father's laughter, which continued even as they frog-marched him to the police car and threw him into the backseat.

I begged them to let me ride with them to the 111th Precinct, and they gave in. I sat next to my father and pondered the possible charges. Endangering the lungs of others? Assault with a deadly cigarette butt?

As the car pulled away I looked back at Starbucks. The geeks were back at their tables, and the kid in the green apron was sweeping up the butts and the ashes with the world's faggiest little broom-and-shovel set.

Esposito drove, while DeNinno got on the police radio to let headquarters know they were bringing in a suspect. We roared down Northern Boulevard. For a moment I thought they were going to turn on the siren.

The cops didn't even look at us. We got nothing but the backs of their necks.

My father's handcuffs clinked as he leaned forward.

"Hey, fellows. Either of you guys got a cigarette?"

My father's demeanor had changed by the time we reached the 111th Precinct in Bayside. He knew he was in trouble, knew he'd be taking all kinds of hell from my mother over this ridiculous situation and the court appearance he'd have to make. He hung his head as we were guided into the station.

"I fucked up, Mick."

"Don't worry about it, Dad."

The place was a zoo. Shouts of outrage from the nearby holding pen echoed off the tiled walls. It was a Saturday night roundup, drunks and junkies and wife-beaters tossed in there to cool off.

Esposito led my father to the desk sergeant, a jowly man with bushy eyebrows who was writing something in a ledger. He didn't even look up from his paperwork as he asked, "Another D and D?"

That's cop-speak for Drunk and Disorderly. Esposito nodded. "Yeah, and this one assaulted me."

At last the desk sergeant looked up at my father. "What'd he do?"

"Suspect was smoking a cigarette in a Starbucks. When asked to leave the premises, he refused, then flicked a cigarette at my chest."

The bushy eyebrows steepled in surprise. "A cigarette? He was smoking a cigarette in a friggin' Starbucks? That's *it*?"

Esposito swallowed. "Well . . . he flicked it pretty hard at my chest."

"Ooh, a cigarette butt, huh? Good thing you were wearin' your vest, eh, Espo?"

Esposito blushed. A funny look came to the sergeant's eyes. He was trying to look at my father's face, but my father was hanging his head like a reluctant penitent.

"Hey. Look at me, buddy."

My father sighed, obeyed. The sergeant studied his face.

"I know you, don't I?"

"Don't think so."

"You sure about that?"

My father shrugged. "I don't know any cops."

"What do you do for a living?"

"Auto mechanic."

It took a moment, and then it hit the sergeant. His face softened, then hardened as he turned to Esposito.

"Uncuff this man."

"But—"

"Just do it, and get back out on patrol!"

Esposito did as he was told. My father brought his hands forward, rubbed his wrists. He looked in wonder at the desk sergeant.

"You work right over here on Bell Boulevard, right? Gandolfini's Garage?"

"Yeah . . ."

The sergeant nodded. "You fixed the transmission on my Chevy, 'bout two years ago. Another guy said the whole thing was shot, two grand he wanted, but you did it for twenty-five. You found one little burned-out wire, and you replaced it for twenty-five bucks. Remember?"

My father shook his head. "I fix a lot o' transmissions. Don't remember yours."

"Well, I remember, 'cause it's the first time I didn't get robbed by a mechanic. Hey, they had a nickname for you at the garage. What the hell was it?"

"Steady Eddie," I said.

The sergeant seemed to notice me for the first time.

"He's my dad," I explained. "Steady Eddie DeFalco. Never missed a day's work in his life."

"Well, be proud of your father, because they don't make 'em like this anymore."

It was an oddly touching moment. For once, my father was the celebrity, and *I* was basking in *his* glow.

The desk sergeant shook hands with my father, then with me. "I'm sorry about this stupid mess. I'll get someone to run you home."

"We'll walk," my father said. "We need the air."

"You take care, Steady Eddie."

We left the police station and began the two-mile walk to Little Neck.

"You okay, Dad?"

He shrugged, rubbed his wrists. "Little sore. They cuff you pretty tight."

I wanted to put my arm across his shoulders, but that's not what I did. I was proud of him, sorry for him, sorry for myself, sorry for Lynn, sorry for the whole fucking world and its billions of inhabitants, bumping into each other and hurting each other and making an everlasting mess out of whatever gifts they had.

We were in the midst of a long, steep stretch of road between Bayside and Douglaston, a stretch with no traffic lights and no homes, just shuttered shops and weedy vacant lots. Hardly anybody ever walked this length of sidewalk. It was creepy in the moonlight.

"I gotta take a piss, Mick."

"Me too."

We had a back-to-back father-son piss in the weeds.

A car roared past, full of drunken kids who laughed and shouted obscenities at us. I finished pissing and quickly zipped up but my father calmly kept going, like a cherub in a Roman fountain.

"Mick."

"Yeah, Dad?"

At last he finished, zipped up and turned to me. "Thanks."

"Sure."

"Let's try not to wake your mother when we get home."

"I'm all for that."

We walked a mile or so in silence, passing a run-over raccoon in the middle of the street, his teeth bared in a final grimace of agony.

"It's really a shame," my father murmured.

"Driver probably never even saw him."

"No, not the damn raccoon. You. You and Lynn." His eyes brimmed with tears but his voice was steady.

"Nobody should lose the girl of his dreams twice, Mickey. Once is enough to kill you. It just ain't fair."

CHAPTER TWENTY-SIX

Sunday morning breakfast. My mother always went to the seven o'clock mass and came home with a bag of bagels, a container of Philadelphia cream cheese, and the *New York Post*. You served yourself on Sunday morning. It was a good system for my father and me. It didn't matter what time we staggered downstairs.

On this Sunday it was almost noon before I made it down. From the look of my father, he'd only gotten there a few minutes earlier. My mother was at the stove, making fresh coffee. She brought the pot to the table and poured cups for me and my old man.

"What happened to your wrists, Eddie?"

There were reddish rings around my father's wrists, bruises where the handcuffs had been. He looked at them in false wonder.

"I don't know."

"You don't know."

"I was workin' on a foreign car. No goddamn room under the hood. Musta scratched 'em tryin' to reach the fan belt."

"Both wrists, all the way around."

"Looks like."

She knew she wasn't going to get anything more out of him. He was a rock. He'd have made a great criminal. He wasn't even nervous.

She gave up and turned to me. "And you. What happened to your eye?"

I wasn't even going to try and bluff it. "Got into a little fight at the inn with Frankie McElhenny."

"Oh my God."

"It's nothing. He just clipped me."

"Why?"

"We were both drunk."

"Why were you drunk?"

"Because Lynn dumped me."

That froze her in place. She closed her eyes, shook her head.

"Easy, Mom."

"She breaks your heart the first time. This time she almost gets you *killed!*"

"He didn't almost get *killed,*" said my father, strengthened by the coffee. "For Christ's sake, Donna, don't turn everything into an opera."

My mother almost sputtered with frustration. "I'm calling Frankie's mother!" she blurted. "She should know what he did to our son!"

My father and I burst out laughing. We couldn't help it. It was just so ridiculous.

"We're grown men, Mom! What's Mrs. McElhenny going to do, make Frankie stand in the corner?"

My mother wasn't laughing. She'd had enough of us. She took the *New York Post* and tossed it on the table.

"I have to go to work," she said calmly. "You guys just keep laughing. Meanwhile, take a look at page sixty-eight and see how funny you think *that* is. Put the cream cheese in the refrigerator when you're finished."

She left the house. My father grabbed the *Post* and flipped to page sixty-eight.

"Oh, boy, Mick. . . ."

It was a half-page story with a publicity photo of me from back in the day, under a headline reading WHERE IS MICKEY DEFALCO?

It was one of those whatever-happened-to yarns, a story generated by the popularity of *Don't Push Me*. As far as the writer of the article knew, I was last seen somewhere in Los Angeles.

My father tapped the page with contempt.

"Look at this. The guy says you 'fell off the face of the earth.' How can he write something like that? Just because he doesn't know where you are, you fell off the face of the earth?"

"It's just a dramatic touch."

"Yeah? And where does he come off callin' you a flash in the pan?"

"I *was* a flash in the pan, Dad."

"Well, that's more than *he* ever was."

His shoulders sagged. He was still tired. He went upstairs to grab some more sleep.

The phone rang. I was going to ignore it, but on the zillion-to-one chance that it could have been Lynn, I grabbed it on the second ring.

It was Mrs. Kavanagh, calling to see if we'd seen the article in the *Post*. I assured her we had and hung up.

It rang again. This time it was Flynn, calling about the same thing.

"Jeez, you're a star again, Mick!"

It rang a third time. I was going to ignore it but I just couldn't.

"Is this my all-time favorite mouse-catcher?"

This wasn't too surprising. Rosalind Pomer was the textbook starfucker. All it took was a surge of publicity, good or bad, to dampen her drawers.

"How are you, Roz?"

"Pissed that you never came back that night. Happy that your song is a hit again."

"How's your rodent problem?"

"I figured out what happened. That little mouse came in with the Chinese food. He sneaked in with the delivery!"

"I guess you're suing the restaurant for damages, huh? Trauma and all that bullshit?"

"I thought about it, but you took the evidence away."

"Sorry about that. . . . Did you like the story?"

"What story?"

"Come on, Roz. Today's *Post*. You're not calling me because of the story about me in the *Post*?"

"I'm a nice liberal Jewish girl. My family would disinherit me if they ever caught me reading the *Post*."

"There's an article about me in there."

"Really?"

"I thought that's why you were calling."

"Listen, Mickey, come to town."

"Now?"

"Yes, now. I've got a surprise for you. Been working on it for a while, and it came together suddenly. . . . Are you busy?"

"I'm the least busy man you'll ever know."

"Not for long. Come on, come to town. Don't even think about it. Just do it."

I hung up the phone and just did it.

She gasped at the sight of my eye.

"Little fight in a bar," I explained.

"My God! You're a brawler!"

"Why are you all dressed up?"

She was wearing black pants, a black top, a black leather jacket, and spike heels.

"We're invited to a party."

We?

"A party? You want to take me to a party?"

"I thought it might be a nice change of pace."

"Your friends aren't supposed to know about me."

"These are my downtown friends. None of them know David."

She had uptown friends, she had downtown friends. Me, I'd just lost the only friend I'd ever had.

I gestured at my clothes, a T-shirt and jeans that probably still reeked of the beery floor at the Little Neck Inn. I also needed a shave. "I'm not exactly dressed for a party, Roz."

"That's all right. It's in SoHo. Lots of artsy-fartsy people."

I followed her down to the street and got into a cab that took us on an eighteen-dollar ride to North Moore Street. All the way there she was going on and on about what a thrill it must be for me to have my song in a movie.

"I don't get a nickel for that."

She was shocked. "That's ridiculous!"

"I signed away the song rights a long time ago."

"I can look into that if you like. I am a lawyer, as you know. I'd like to expand into entertainment law."

Here we go. No wonder she called me. It was almost a relief to know she was working an angle. It took away any guilt I might feel about bad behavior, past or future.

"Thanks anyway, Roz," I said, "but a deal's a deal."

"Hey, are you okay, man?"

I took a deep breath, smelled a trace of Lynn on myself. "I'm just upset about the song," I lied.

"Who wouldn't be?"

It was horrible, absolutely horrible to be with the wrong person at a time like this, and I knew it. But the only thing worse was the thought of being alone. Or so I thought at the time.

So here I was in SoHo, going to a party with a woman I did not really like, much less love, and to make matters worse she was being affectionate, stroking my cheek with her blunt little hand as the cab reached North Moore Street. She took my hand, laced her fingers with mine, and even this tiny thing was wrong, all wrong. Her fingers were short and stubby. It was like holding five little cigars.

"Let's just try and have a good time, okay, Mickey?"

A good time.

The loft was a converted factory space of some kind, with wooden beams high overhead and rough brick walls painted white. Music boomed from speakers in the corners, and dozens of white wine drinkers were shoulder to shoulder, eating pita bread sandwiches and raw vegetables off paper plates.

Rosalind introduced me to the hostess, a tall, spooky redhead named Marion. She had a pasty complexion and dark areas under her eyes, as if she hadn't slept in days.

"You haven't changed much," Marion said, which is a funny thing to hear from someone you're meeting for the first time. "I love, and I mean *love* your song."

"Thank you."

"It's perfect in the film."

"We haven't seen the film yet," Rosalind chirped, speaking incorrectly on my behalf. She had her arm around my waist and nervously gulped white wine from a plastic cup.

I stuck to what I'd been drinking the night before, Jack Daniel's. Marion pulled my cup toward her face, took a whiff, and smiled.

"Ahh, you're a whiskey man."

"I never saw him drink whiskey until today," Rosalind said.

"Hmmm," said Marion, who peered into my eyes before turning and gliding away from us.

"Be nice to her," Rosalind said. "Her boyfriend just left her. For another *guy*, would you believe."

"Great time to throw a party."

"It happened after the invitations went out. Hey, slow down, Mickey, that's powerful stuff."

"I know what I'm doing. What's this surprise you have for me?"

"It's coming, it's coming. . . ."

I broke her embrace and went to the bar for a refill. I could feel myself being watched. The word had obviously gotten around about the has-been singer in the shitty clothes.

Rosalind stayed right where I'd left her, having an animated conversation with a group of people. I worked my way through the crowd and sat down on a windowsill.

A slim black man with a shaved head and a pierced ear sashayed to my side and pointed out the window with a flamboyant finger.

"He lived right there, you know."

"Who?"

"Kennedy. John-John Kennedy. That's where he lived with his wife, right until the day they died."

"Oh."

"The paparazzi used to drive us *crazy*. That's the only good thing, since the tragedy. No more damn paparazzi, night and day."

"Uh-huh."

"By the way, I'm Deron, from upstairs," he said, extending his hand.

"Mickey, from Queens."

"But not a queen, I take it?"

"Not yet, Deron, but I'm giving it some serious thought, the way my heterosexual life's been going lately."

He giggled. "I know who you are. *Everybody* knows who you are. We've got a bit of a surprise for you, a little later."

Because of the drinking I'd done the night before I was suddenly drunk, seriously drunk. Deron chirped on about his love for music while I continued to sip Mister Jack.

"So," he said, "no new music from you?"

"Nah. I'm done with it." I pointed to my wounded eye. "I'm a prizefighter now."

"Get *out!* No offense, but aren't you a little *old* for that?"

"I'm nearing the end of my career."

"And then?"

"And then, Deron, I have no fucking idea, to be honest with you."

Rosalind appeared and gave Deron a kiss on each cheek.

"I'm trying to steal him from you." Deron giggled.

"Sorry, Deron, he doesn't play for your team."

"Not yet, he doesn't." He winked at me, put a hand to his lean throat and slinked away.

Rosalind stared into my eyes. "You're drunk."

"Extremely."

"Let's get some food into you."

She dragged me to the pita bread and the raw vegetables, not exactly the stuff you crave to fight off alcohol. I grabbed a few pieces of pita and shoved them into my mouth, chewing like a dog.

"Mickey. You're embarrassing me." She pulled a bit of stray pita from my mouth. "Come on, man, don't be like this!"

I finished chewing and swallowing. "I'm not some fucking show pony."

"Excuse me?"

"My song pops up in a movie, and all of a sudden you want to trot me around?"

Rosalind wanted to say something but suddenly the music stopped and Deron was standing on a chair in the middle of the loft, calling for everybody's attention. He spotted me and pointed my way.

"We have with us today the one and only Mickey DeFalco," he announced. "Mickey, we're pleased to have you here as we proudly present TFN—Three Fat Niggahs!"

Three young, enormously overweight black men in shiny

black warm-up suits suddenly appeared and climbed onto a makeshift platform, waddling from side to side in a menacing shuffle. They wore unlaced sneakers, gold chains, and backwards baseball caps. Suddenly rap music was bellowing from giant speakers, rap music with a familiar beat.

It was my song. It was "Sweet Days," gone gangsta.

Amazingly it worked, in a weird way. The lyrics had always been deceptively angry and these guys conveyed it masterfully, with a lot of finger-pointing and groin-grabbing. The crowd clapped in time with the thudding percussion, and when it was over, the loft exploded in applause. The biggest, fattest member of TFN came to the front of the platform and scanned the room.

"Yo, yo, where dat Mickey DeFalco at? Get your ass up here, white boy!"

In the commotion that followed I grabbed Roz by the elbow, hauled her into a small bedroom and slammed the door behind us.

"That's the surprise, huh?"

"Didn't you like it? They're friends of Deron's! Aren't they great?"

"What the hell do you want me to say?"

She pointed toward the loft. "Do you realize how *big* those guys are? TFN is on the rise, Mickey! I know their agent and I suggested your song to them! Aren't you the *least* bit excited?"

"It doesn't *matter* what I think! None of this does me any good! It's not my song anymore!"

"Let me work on that."

"I don't want you to work on anything."

She stared at me, sized me up, shook her head. "You know, man, you've got a real attitude. It's like you *want* to fail."

"Don't analyze me."

"You are the poster child for denial."

I stepped toward her. She suddenly seemed terrified. "Rosalind, why are we kidding ourselves? Why are we out on a date?

We don't date, we *fuck*. Want to get down to it? Huh? What do you say we stop this bullshit and get back on familiar turf?"

I grabbed her arms and pulled her down to the mattress. She let out a howl and gave me a knee in the balls that made my ears ring. She raced from the room, slamming the door behind her.

I had to wait a minute or two to let the pain recede. When I was able to get to my feet I noticed that the bedroom window led to a fire escape, and that's how I left the party, zigzagging my way down three flights of rusty ladders as TFN launched into another song, loud enough to loosen the bricks from the mortar.

The walk to the subway sobered me up. I had no idea of what was going to happen next. I only knew that I'd started weeping, and I couldn't stop all the way back to Little Neck.

CHAPTER TWENTY-SEVEN

It couldn't go on like this. I was going to have to go somewhere, *anywhere*, just to be by myself, but my funds were limited, to say the least.

They were limited because I'd given away all my dirty money with Lynn. Her big idea! All I had left was the money I'd put in the bank, those few minuscule deposits I'd made at Lynn's window.

I got up to go to work as usual on Monday morning, trying to ignore the big freeze emanating from my mother at the breakfast table. My father had already left for work.

"You're very quiet lately," she said.

The unspoken part of that sentence was "and I'm very worried about you, and I cannot live like this for much longer."

She was right. I couldn't pull this kind of crap while I was living under her roof. I gulped my eggs and rushed to work.

Despite my stupor, I was stunned by one thing—for the first time, I got to the garage before Patrick, the perpetual early bird. Without Patrick around, Flynn had nobody's balls to bust but mine.

"So, Mick, how goes the latest chapter in Little Neck's all-time love story?"

"It's actually the last chapter. She dumped me."

Flynn's eyes widened. "Jeez, I thought it was goin' good."

"That makes two of us."

Minutes later Patrick came trudging along, lunch bag in hand.

"Latest you've ever been," Flynn remarked. "Why you mopin', Patrick?"

"I'm not moping!"

"It's in your face, kid."

Patrick studied his shoes and sighed deeply. "I might not be going to Purdue."

"Get adda here!"

Patrick looked the boss in the eye. "I mean it, Mr. Flynn. All of a sudden it just . . . doesn't feel right."

"Ahh, get in the truck, both of you."

We sat as we always did—Flynn driving, me at the passenger window, Patrick between us. Flynn shifted the loose, grinding gears as we approached a hill.

"This is all about Scarlett, ain't it?"

Patrick wouldn't answer, but his moist eyes and tight lips told the story.

"Hah! I knew it!"

"Lay off, Mr. Flynn."

"What do your parents say?"

"They don't know. Yet."

"They'll pop a gut if you bail out."

"Maybe."

"Mickey, talk to him."

I shrugged. "What can I say? I didn't even finish high school. If he doesn't want to go, he doesn't want to go."

Flynn rolled his eyes, threw his cigarette out the window.

"Patrick, Patrick, listen to me. Where you gonna go to school? Huh?"

"I thought maybe the community college."

"That's a joke! They don't even have a football team!"

"Fuck football."

Flynn hit the brake, nearly sending Patrick and me against the windshield. A car honked behind us. Slowly, not believing what he'd just heard, Flynn put the truck back into gear.

"What are you sayin'? All of a sudden you don't like football?"

His voice broke as he said, "I don't like the idea of being away from my girl."

Flynn rolled his eyes, gripped the wheel like a getaway driver.

"You guys," he muttered. "I don't know about you guys anymore. The two best guys I've ever had, and look at you. *Look* at you! Done in by your so-called better halves!"

One thing he could count on from both of us was hard work, no matter how we felt. Patrick and I really threw ourselves into it that day, and as we were loading up the lawn mowers after our first job he grabbed my elbow.

"You understand, don't you, Mick?"

I sighed. "Look, man, if you're doing this for the girl, it could be a mistake. You're young. You're both young."

"*You're* still in love with *your* first girl."

"She doesn't want anything to do with me anymore, Patrick."

"If you really love her, it's not over."

"Stop listening to the songs, kid, and hear the news. Love *doesn't* conquer all."

"But you understand how I feel, don't you?"

"Yeah, Patrick, I understand."

And I also understood that this man-child named Patrick could develop and harden every muscle in his body except his heart. He startled me by grabbing me in an embrace even more powerful than Frankie McElhenny's, an embrace my still-tender ribs could have done without.

"You're the only one who gets it," he murmured in a quaking voice before releasing me. "Know what? When I say my prayers tonight, I'm going to pray for you and Lynn."

"You pray at night?"

"Sure do."

"On your knees?"

"Yup. The more you suffer, the better God listens."

This strange, strange day was about to get even stranger.

At lunchtime Flynn always tuned his transistor radio to a station that played golden oldies. The noontime deejay was a highly caffeinated guy named Jimmy Pack, a.k.a. Jimmy ("The Rat") Pack. He called his listeners "pack rats," and he loved hosting contests on the air. On this day, he rolled out one hell of a contest.

"Hey, pack rats, it's hot out there at high noon (bing-bong chimes for the stroke of noon) and speaking of hot—have we got a contest for you! Jimmy needs your help on this one, my friends—we need you to help us choose the sappiest, and I mean the *sappiest* love song of all time! The one that made you lose your lunch, run out and get an insulin shot!

"Are you ready, pack rats? Here, in no particular order, are the five candidates!"

(Soundup: "We had joy, we had fun, we had seasons in the sun . . .")

"Terry Jacks, 'Seasons in the Sun'! Oh, baby! Hang a bucket on that one and you'll get enough sap to make a barrel of maple syrup!"

(Soundup: "Feelings . . . nothing more than feelings . . .")

"Morris Albert, 'Feelings'! Funny how a song about feelings can leave you so numb, isn't it? I got a *feeling* this one could be the sappiest song of all time!"

(Soundup: "All by myself . . . don't wanna be all by myself. . . .")

"Eric Carmen, All By Himself! Boo-friggin'-hoo! Can you be-lieve this song was a hit? They should play it when they put peo-ple on 'hold' at Masturbators Anonymous!"

(Soundup: "Some people wanna fill the world with silly love songs. . . .")

"Paul McCartney, 'Silly Love Songs'! He wrote that one for Linda. . . . Hey, Paul, what did you sing to that second wife of yours—'Peg O' My Heart'? Ooh, I'll do some time in Purgatory for *that* one, pack rats! And last but not least . . ."

(Soundup: "Sweet Days . . . feel like a haze . . . a summertime craze . . . but it ain't just a phase . . .")

"Mickey DeFalco, 'Sweet Days'! Well, Mick, it turns out you *were* just a phase, but if you win the sappiest song contest, you'll be right back on top! On top of *what*, I don't actually know. . . ."

I stopped chewing my sandwich. Patrick sat there open-mouthed before breaking into applause. Flynn laughed out loud as Jimmy Pack went on about the numbers to dial to vote for the sappiest song. It was seventy-five cents per call, and the winner would be announced at lunch tomorrow.

Patrick stood up and reached into his pocket to count his change.

"Patrick," Flynn said, "what the hell you doin'?"

He pointed to a pay phone down the street. "I'm gonna vote for Mick."

Flynn rolled his eyes. "Patrick. Do you understand what's goin' on, here? Mickey doesn't *want* to win. That would be embarrass-ing."

Patrick swallowed. "Oh, yeah." He turned to me. "Sorry, Mick."

"Don't worry about it, Patrick. You go ahead and vote for me if you like."

"No, no, Mr. Flynn is right."

Patrick resumed eating his sandwich. Flynn turned to me and spoke in a whisper.

"Nice kid, but sometimes I get the feelin' he didn't always remember to wear his helmet out there on the field, ya know what I'm sayin', Mick?"

Lunch was almost over when a long, lean guy in jeans and a wrinkled denim shirt came walking our way, a cigarette in his mouth, a scowl on his face. He was about my age and he had one of those deliberate three-day growths of beard, shaved along the edges. A contradictory face, a bum with a butler.

There was a manic determination to his stride, as if he were both in a hurry to get somewhere and hopelessly lost. But when he saw me sitting there on the sidewalk with my peanut butter and jelly sandwich, his face lit up.

"Are you Mickey DeFalco?"

He said it like a cop, and for an instant I thought I was at long last being nailed for the L.A. thing. Then I realized I could have been in trouble for what had happened the night before with Rosalind. Could she have filed an assault charge against me, for the way I'd dragged her down on that bed in SoHo? Attempted rape? It wasn't impossible.

I finished chewing and swallowing. "Actually, my proper name is Michael DeFalco."

He clenched a fist in triumph. "Man, have I been lookin' for you!" He extended his hand. "I'm Joel Schmitter."

I shook his hand without getting up. Flynn and Patrick eyed the guy like a couple of bodyguards. Schmitter was still holding my hand when he added, "I'm a producer with *Hollywood Howl.*"

"Oh for Christ's sakes," Flynn muttered.

Schmitter chuckled. "Hey, I know, I know, it's not the greatest TV show in the world. But man, am I glad we found *you!*"

"We?"

He jerked a thumb over his shoulder. "My crew's in that blue van across the street. Relax, we're real discreet. Plain van. We could be anybody."

"What do you want from me?"

"Could we talk in private?"

"I have nothing to say to you."

"Just walk around the block with me, please. No cameras, no mikes. All right? Come on, I've come a long way for this."

I turned to Flynn and Patrick, who regarded Schmitter through narrowed eyes. "I'm going to walk around the block with this guy."

Flynn nodded. "If the waiter comes back while you're gone, do you want dessert?"

"Yeah, the apricot soufflé."

"You got it."

I got up and walked with Schmitter, who waved to the guys in the van, a wave that told them to stay put, but be ready.

"Your boss is a real comedian, huh?"

"He has his moments."

"You know why we're here."

"Yeah, I'm not an idiot."

"Quite a story, your comeback, wouldn't you say?"

I had to laugh. "I didn't come back. A movie came out with my song in it, that's all."

"A hit movie, man. And you didn't get paid shit."

"How do you know that?"

"Checked it out. I'm good at my job. Listen, man, the whole friggin' country's wondering what the hell happened to you. That's why I flew three thousand miles."

"How'd you find me?"

"Ha! You wouldn't believe what I went through! Called all over L.A., nobody knew where you'd gone. I mean, *nobody*. So I ask myself, where does a nice Italian kid from New York go when he's down on his luck? And the answer is, he goes home. Home is always home for you spaghetti-benders, am I right?"

"I'm half Irish."

"I figured. Your mother doesn't look Italian."

I stopped walking. "You saw my mother?"

"Unless it was the maid. Knocked on the door, asked her where you were. She shut the door in my face."

"We don't have a maid."

"Well, then, it musta been your dear old mother."

We resumed walking. "Why didn't you phone first?"

"It's not my style."

"Just in our brief time together, Schmitter, it seems to me you don't have much of a style."

"Hey, I found you, didn't I? Tracked you down on a job that moves all over the place."

"How'd you know I was cutting lawns?"

"Hey. I don't divulge my sources." He smiled, showing nico-tine-stained teeth. "Come on, give me a little credit."

"All right, I give you credit. But listen to me when I tell you that if there was a door between us, I'd be shutting it."

"Like mother, like son, huh?"

"We're not a terribly friendly family."

He kicked a pebble, like a frustrated child. "Come on, *talk* to me. Give me a few sound bites so I can get out of your life forever."

"Sound bites about what?"

He gripped his chest as if he were having a heart attack. "Come *on,* man! You had a number one song when you were just a kid, and now you're a middle-aged man pushin' a friggin *lawn mower!*"

"Thirty-eight is middle aged?"

"Close enough. Hey, excuse me for having an opinion, but that is a big story!"

"If it's such a *big* story, how come they didn't send a reporter with you?"

He couldn't help laughing, and this time it sounded real. "My man knows the game, doesn't he?"

"This isn't the first time I've dealt with TV interviews. I knew I was in decline when they stopped sending reporters."

"What do you want from me? It's summertime. Lots of reporters on vacation. This is the best we can do. But listen, you're better off with me handlin' it, Mickey. I promise there won't be any stupid questions from some dumb meat puppet tryin' to sound like a journalist."

"Schmitter, I'm not talking to you, and that's it. Tell your boss you tried your best."

He hesitated, bit his lower lip. "We'll pay you."

That stunned me. "You pay for interviews?"

"When we have to. Three thousand bucks."

I looked him in the eye. He wasn't kidding. He was offering me the same money I'd be getting for a whole summer sweating behind a lawn mower, just for answering a few questions on camera.

Three thousand bucks. With that kind of money I could take off someplace for a month, get out of my parents' faces, get out of my own skull.

"Cash?"

"Well, no, not cash. Come on, we're a legitimate business! Gotta account for expenditures!"

"Uh-huh."

"Listen, man, I'm not an accountant or anything, but I'm guessin' that in your current tax bracket, you'd get to keep most of it. No offense, but it's true."

"Uh-huh."

"So, what do you say? I got a contract right here." He pulled a folded white paper from his back pocket. "You sign it, and we're on our way."

"If you're offering three, you've been authorized to go as high as five."

Schmitter gulped. "Smart guy, aren't you?"

"Not particularly. But when you get fucked over enough times, you have to be an idiot not to detect the pattern."

"Would you do it for five?" He pulled out a cell phone. "Lemme call my boss, we'll make it happen—"

"No, no. No deal. I just didn't want you to go away thinking I was an idiot."

"I'm not going away."

"Well, I am."

We turned the final corner on the block. Patrick and Flynn were finishing their lunch. Schmitter lit up a fresh cigarette with nervous hands, like a gambler down to his last few chips.

"Tell me one thing," he begged. "All those chicks, just throwin' themselves at you. What was that like?"

"Repetitive."

"Oh, Jesus, see what I mean? That's a fuckin' *great* sound bite! Why won't you talk to me?"

"Because . . ."

It was a great question, actually. Why wouldn't I do it and grab the easy check? I didn't have to exploit anyone for the money, it wasn't drug money, and God, did I ever need it. . . .

Schmitter was waiting, a drop of sweat rolling slowly toward the point of his Adam's apple. I cleared my throat.

"Because the past is precious," I finally said. It might have been the truest thing I'd ever said.

Schmitter rolled his eyes, as if I'd just read him something out of a fortune cookie.

"All right, man, now I'm gonna tell you something I *don't* have to tell you. This story airs tomorrow night, with or without you. We got other people talkin' about you, see?"

"Who?"

He grinned at my sudden vulnerability. "You wanna know who we got, and what they had to say, you gotta give me the interview. Otherwise, tune in tomorrow night and see if *they* think the past is precious."

"I'll tune in tomorrow night."

"You'll wish you'd talked to me."

"Whatever." I extended my hand, which he grudgingly shook. "I think you're an asshole, Schmitter, but I do admire your persistence."

"All right, Mickey. Now there's one other thing, and you don't have a choice in the matter. We're gonna shoot some footage of you cuttin' this lawn." He held his hands up, palms out. "Long as we're out on the street, on public property, you can't do anything about it."

"Get my good side."

His face sagged. "Come on, *talk* to me. Don't make me take the fuckin' red-eye home with nothin' but this bullshit Home and Garden b-roll and a few lame-ass sound bites from people in this neighborhood."

People in this neighborhood. Jesus Christ, could he have approached Lynn? *"Excuse me, Miss Mahoney, I'm Joel Schmitter from the sleaziest show on television. How'd you like to tell the whole world about you and Mickey DeFalco, and how your doomed romance inspired his one and only hit song?"*

No way she would talk to him, no way in the world. She was too private, had too much class, too much dignity. But those qualities eluded a lot of other Little Neckers.

I tried to act nonchalant. "You talked to people in Little Neck?"

Schmitter shrugged. "Maybe one or two. How do you think I found out where you work?"

"What'd they say?"

"Nothing exciting. The kind of shit you only use when you don't get the sound bites you want. See, if you talk to me, we won't even use those other sound bites."

He had a bottomless bag of tricks. The only thing to do was to walk away without another word to him, which is what I did. Patrick and I got the mowers off the trailer while Flynn gathered up the lunch junk.

"Everything all right, Mick?"

"Yeah. Might want to comb your hair, though. These guys are going to shoot us cutting this lawn."

Flynn looked over at the van. Already the short, ponytailed cameraman had his camera on a tripod, while an exasperated Schmitter was telling him exactly what he wanted with a lot of flamboyant hand gestures.

"Well," said Flynn, "I might have to show 'em what I can do."

To the astonishment of Patrick and me, Flynn gripped his belt buckle and proceeded to dance an Irish jig on the sidewalk, his big belly jiggling, his feet amazingly deft and light despite his old war injury. The cameraman and Schmitter could only look at each other and wonder why they'd ever gotten into such a line of work.

Schmitter was good to his word. The crew stayed on the street while the camera rolled. It was pretty dull stuff, following me going back and forth on the lawn, but it was all they were going to get. Once I looked over and saw Schmitter on his cell phone, having a heated conversation with somebody who had to be his boss back in California, busting his chops over the interview that never happened.

It was a pretty big lawn, so they had plenty of footage of that, and then of course came the truly thrilling footage of Patrick and me loading up the machines on the trailer. Schmitter held up the contract and wagged it like bait. I ignored it.

He had just one move left, and here it came, just as I was getting the tailgate locked up. I heard footsteps, and there they were in my face for the ambush interview, the soundman hovering a fuzzy microphone on a stick over my head.

"Mr. DeFalco," Schmitter said, as if we'd never met, "we're here from *Hollywood Howl*. Could we have a minute of your time?"

I looked at Schmitter, who clearly both loved and hated what he was doing for a living. The cameraman stood calm and steady, rolling on whatever it was I was going to do.

And then I did it. It was stupid, but I did it. I looked right into the lens and gave it the finger. A three-thousand-dollar shot, and they had it for nothing.

"All right?" I said softly. "You guys happy now?"

I got into the truck, where Patrick and Flynn were waiting. Flynn put it in gear and we roared away as if we'd just knocked over a bank.

CHAPTER TWENTY-EIGHT

The next night, nearly seven P.M., just minutes until *Hollywood Howl* airs. I pick up the kitchen phone, dial four digits, hang up. Pick it up again, dial six digits, hang up. Pick it up a third time, dial seven digits, hear it ring once, hang up.

What a fucking idiot I am. "Just do it," I say out loud.

So I dial Lynn's number once again and feel my heart pounding away. I actually have a sheet of paper with notes on it, to guide me in case a brain freeze hits. It's the same thing I used to do when we were first dating.

"Hello?"

Showtime.

"Lynn, it's me."

The jagged sound of her breathing.

"I just wanted to see if you're okay."

"I'm okay."

A flat-out lie, but I let it ride. "How's your mother?"

"Still in the hospital. I'm just leaving now to see her."

"Want me to come with you?"

"Mickey. What are you doing?"

"Lynn, I apologize."

"For what?"

"For the way I reacted."

She actually giggled, or maybe it was a swallowed sob. "Mickey, you can't apologize for a reaction. It's like apologizing for having brown eyes. You were shocked by what you heard. Anybody would be."

"Baby—"

"You feel how you feel. I respect it."

"Whoa, whoa—"

"I'd be wasting your time, Mickey. Rock bottom, that's the deal. And maybe that's the worst sin there is in this world, wasting somebody's time."

"Let's go to Italy."

"Oh, my *God*."

"What do you say, a trip to Italy? You up for it, baby?"

It just came out of me, this crazy idea from a man who could barely afford bus tickets to Hoboken. Lynn said nothing, but I could hear her crying.

"We'll go to Venice," I continued. "We'll ride a gondola. We'll go to every museum on the boot. Italy's boot-shaped, isn't it?"

I could no longer hear her crying. She'd hung up.

I looked at my notes: "Ask if okay. If needs anything. Say you love her." I crumpled up the paper and threw it in the garbage.

"Michael, it's starting!" my mother called from Planet Earth, and then I gathered myself and joined my parents in the living room to watch *Hollywood Howl*.

I was the top story of the night, introduced by the anchorman as a "musical mystery." On the screen behind him was a giant publicity photo of me from my heyday, grinning like a jerk.

"Mickey DeFalco seemed to have it all—and then suddenly, he vanished," the anchorman said. "Now his one hit song is fast becoming a hit all over again, and the world is wondering: Whatever happened to Mickey DeFalco? *Hollywood Howl* found out."

The segment started with washed-out footage of me in a corny old music video, singing "Sweet Days" as I walked along a beach, the very beach, in fact, where Lynn and I went for our last date. Long shots of me walking and singing. None of that quick-cut bullshit they do now, two-second shots, thirty to a minute, rat-a-tat-tat, tailored to the all but extinct American attention span.

"Back in 1988, it was sweet days indeed for young Mickey DeFalco with a love song that rocketed to the top of the charts," the narrator began. Then the music video footage dissolved to crystal-clear footage of me from the day before, pushing the roaring lawn mower.

"But now, it's *'sweat'* days for DeFalco, who at age thirty-eight toils as a gardener for hire back in his hometown of Little Neck, New York."

I had to chuckle at that one.

"That was nasty," my father murmured. "They go out of their way to be nasty."

"They call it being edgy, Dad."

"Edgy, my ass."

"Eddie!"

There was a sudden cut to a woman identified as a "celebrity journalist," who said my rise and fall was one of the most baffling in the history of the music business.

"Who the hell is *that?*" my father demanded.

"An expert on my life, Dad."

"What the hell does *she* know?"

"Nothing. They probably threw her a few hundred for the interview."

"Shh!" my mother said. "We're missing the whole thing!"

They cut to a clip of me and Lois from our TV pilot.

"Oh, my God," I said, "where'd they dig *that* up?"

"DeFalco starred in a TV show named after his song," the narrator continued. "It was dropped after just a few episodes. He married his costar, the former Lois Butler."

And suddenly there was the surprisingly chubby face of my ex-wife, and these were the first words from her mouth: "He was always a mystery to me."

There was footage of Lois splashing around with a couple of kids in a giant swimming pool, as the narrator explained that even though Lois was happy now as a mother of three and the wife of a TV producer, she was still "haunted" by her short-lived marriage to DeFalco.

Haunted.

"He had so much anger," Lois said. "He'd had his heart broken when he was a kid, and he never got over it. As much as I loved him, it was a relief to walk away from him."

"With a quarter of a million dollars!" my mother exclaimed. "I'll bet *that* was a relief!"

Oh, it got worse. They even had a publicity photo of me opening a "Sweet Days" ice cream parlor, cutting a ribbon with a giant pair of scissors. They went on about how that venture went belly-up, and that I pretty much "disappeared" after that.

They dissolved from that photo back to me cutting grass. "So here he is now, back where he started," the narrator said. "According to his ex-wife, he's a heartbroken man. The question is . . . who broke his heart?"

Cut to Rosie Gambardello serving up a Western omelette to somebody at the International House of Pancakes.

"Mother of God," my mother said. "Tell me I'm not seeing this."

"Rosemary Gambardello is a divorced single mom, working as a waitress at the International House of Pancakes in Little Neck," the narrator said. "She says she and DeFalco were once sweethearts."

"I was his first girlfriend," Rosie said with a straight face. "You know, puppy love. It didn't work out. Just one of those things. Next thing you know, he writes this great song."

Back to footage of Rosie on the job, as the narrator says: "So is this the great love of Mickey DeFalco's life, the one who inspired the song that continues to delight us now, all these years later? Well, we tried to get an answer to that and many other questions . . . without much luck."

Cut to the camera approaching me as I'm putting up the tailgate on the trailer. You hear Joel Schmitter say who he is and where he's from, asking if he could have a minute of my time.

"That's the man who came to the door!" my mother cried.

And then I give him the finger, a gesture the technicians at *Hollywood Howl* blurred so it could air in prime time.

I can hear my mother's hands as they slap against her cheeks.

"That's tellin' him!" my father yells.

"All right?" I ask Schmitter. "You guys happy now?"

"The question," the narrator says, "is not if *we're* happy . . . but if *you* are happy, Mickey DeFalco."

Back to Lois: "I don't know if he'll ever be happy. He was a troubled, troubled boy. And now, he's a troubled man."

Back to Rosie: "I'll always remember him the way he was, not the way he is."

And the piece ends, of course, with me moving in slow motion, once again flipping the blurred bird to the camera. The shot freezes, there's a dramatic music sting and at last, it's over.

"Well," I said as they went to a commercial, "you are now the proud parents of America's favorite psychotic."

"I really, *really* don't like that particular gesture," my mother said.

"Do you know what it means, Mom?"

"Oh, I know what it means, all right. It means fuck you."

My father and I couldn't have been more shocked if the pope had suddenly appeared in the living room and pissed on the rug. I had never heard her utter that word before.

"Jesus, Donna," Eddie said. Her lips were curled into a Mona

Lisa smile, which she turned toward me. Yes, the smile said, I'm a woman of the world, I know things you never thought I knew, so please, *please* don't treat me like a crazy, sheltered Catholic.

I managed to say, "I rarely use that gesture. I was provoked."

"Oh, I know. I saw what happened. But in the future, Michael, don't let other people diminish you with their crudity. That's my advice."

The phone was ringing. My father rose to answer it but my mother told him to sit.

"We are *not* answering the phone tonight," she announced. She got up and pulled the plug on the phone, mid-ring.

"Mom. I'm sorry I got rude with that TV crew."

"I know you are."

"They're lucky he didn't throw a punch," my father said.

"No, Eddie. *We're* lucky he didn't throw a punch. They could sue."

"What could they get from him?"

"Not him, *us*. He lives here now. We're responsible for him. They could take our house."

They started to argue about whether that was legally possible when I interrupted by yelling, "For Christ's sake, I didn't throw a punch!"

Silence. We sat looking at each other as *Hollywood Howl* continued with a story about Britney Spears's sudden weight gain.

"Is it true about you and Rosie?" my mother asked.

"Of course not! You *know* the song's not about her!"

"Did you date her?"

"We sort of went out for a little while."

"Went out? I don't remember that!"

"Mom—"

"Tell me! I have a right to know!"

I rolled my eyes. "I screwed her in a car. Once."

She looked at my father. "Nice, huh?"

Eddie spread his hands. "You asked for it, Donna. He told you."

She sagged back in her chair. "The things I don't *know* about your life," she said in a voice of wonder. "Eddie, did you know about Rosie?"

"I found out from the TV, just like you."

She pointed at me. "Whoever watched that tonight is going to think you have a thing for fat girls. My God, Lois certainly let herself go! I always knew she would."

She got up and left the room. My father grabbed the remote control.

"Let's see if there's a Yankee game on. Get the taste of that garbage out of our mouths."

I didn't need a baseball game. I needed my woman back. And suddenly, I realized that I needed another woman's help to get that done.

I headed for town, not even phoning first to see if Rosalind was home. The night doorman at her building was a menacing-looking Puerto Rican who seemed ashamed of the frilly gold-braided jacket they forced him to wear. He told me she wasn't home.

"Do you know where she went?"

A sly grin crossed his face. "I can't tell you that."

"So you *do* know."

He shrugged noncommittally.

I pulled out a ten-dollar bill. "I missed your last birthday. Been meaning to give this to you."

He took the bill, slipped it into his pocket, looked away from me and said, "She's at her gym. Eightieth and Lex, I think."

"The gym? At this hour?"

He chuckled. "She never stops, man, never stops. . . ."

I ran there to find an all-female ground-floor gym called Power Babes, with floor-to-ceiling windows looking out on the avenue. It was past ten o'clock but the place was in full swing, with dozens of highly paid white women on exercise mats, treadmills and stationary bikes.

On the bike closest to the window sat Roz in sweatpants and a snug tank top, furiously pedaling away while reading the *Wall Street Journal* on the machine's handlebars.

I tapped on the window. She looked up from the newspaper, scowled at me, and began pedaling even faster, as if to put distance between us. Tough thing to accomplish on a stationary bike.

I entered the place, told the receptionist I had an urgent message for Ms. Pomer and went straight to Roz, still pedaling like mad.

"Did Pedro tell you I was here?" she gasped. "I'm going to have his ass fired!"

"Look, I'm really sorry about what happened in SoHo."

"What you did was the worst thing that ever happened to me. The *worst*."

"I know. I was an asshole."

"We're all finished, Mickey. You and I are through."

At last she stopped pedaling and let her head fall forward. Drops of sweat soaked the *Wall Street Journal*.

"Hand me a towel, would you?"

I meekly obeyed her.

"By the way, Mickey, you fucked things up royally with TFN. They wanted to meet you, but you dissed them by ditching the party. Now they don't want to record your song."

"Like I said, it's not my song anymore."

She rubbed her face with the towel. "So what's this all about? You wanted to end it like a gentleman, face-to-face?"

"Well, there's that. Plus . . . can I ask you something?"

"I'm listening."

I took a deep breath. "My old girlfriend told me she can't have kids, but she won't tell me why."

She cocked her head, narrowed her eyes. "Excuse me?"

"My old girlfriend. Something's wrong with her body, and she can't have kids, and when she told me about it . . . well, I guess I didn't react very well."

"This is the one you wrote the song about."

"Uh-huh."

"And you're asking *my* advice on how you can make things right with *her*."

When she put it that way, it did sound pretty outrageous. I swallowed, nodded.

"Jesus Christ, Mickey." She stared at me for what seemed like weeks. "What did you do when she broke the news to you?"

I shrugged. "I told her . . . I was sad."

Roz rolled her eyes and shook her head.

"God Almighty, you really are a child, do you know that?"

"A child?"

"Yeah. It's all about how it affects you."

She slapped my face with a sweaty hand. "For God's sake, Mickey, *grow the fuck up*, already!"

Heads turned to stare at me, the only male in the place. Even the personal trainers were all women, muscular mamas with whistles around their necks and fury in their eyes. I stood as still as a statue, not wanting to give anyone an excuse to pounce. I let the sting recede from my cheek before speaking.

"You think I'm not a grown-up?"

"You're not. You're spoiled. You got too used to getting things. Like me. I was just a toy to you."

"Wasn't I a toy to you?"

"Well, I tried to change that on our last date, and look what happened."

"You're right, you're right."

Her anger was spent. She couldn't fight if I didn't fight back. She reached out, patted the cheek she'd just slapped.

"Look, I'm a little tense, okay? I'm doing some mental house-cleaning. Just broke up with David. Realized he couldn't really mean much to me if I was carrying on the way I did with you."

She wiped her face with the towel again. "I let myself go crazy with you. I'm the girl you screwed in the sky. How could you take me seriously?"

Roz reset some buttons on the exercise bike's console. She was ready to resume her workout.

"You really care about this girl, don't you, Mickey?"

"Yeah."

"Then love her like a man, not a boy. Get out of your own skin and think about how *she* must feel."

"I don't even know what happened to her!"

"Find out, shithead. Find out! Be *aggressive*. Be willing to be humiliated. Lose your damn pride. Don't just let things happen. Make it work."

It was the kind of bullshit bootstrap advice you hear from grinning idiot psychologists trying to sell their latest self-help books on morning TV shows.

But it was also right on the money.

I sighed. "She doesn't want to have anything to do with me."

"It's really pretty simple, superstar. If you deserve her, you'll find a way to her heart. If you don't, you won't. I've got to start up again before my legs stiffen."

She began pedaling. I was dismissed. I started to leave the gym, but before I got to the door Roz called me back.

"This special woman of yours. It wasn't that fat waitress on *Hollywood Howl* tonight, was it?"

"No. She's just somebody I screwed once."

"Oh. Kind of like me, huh?"

"We screwed *twice*, Roz. On the plane, and on mouse night.

Don't you remember? How could you not remember? That really hurts. I'm not just a piece of meat, you know."

I ventured a smile. She didn't want to smile back, but she couldn't help it.

"Believe it or not, DeFalco, there are things about you that I'm going to miss."

She lowered her head, clenched her teeth, shut her eyes, and began pedaling as if she meant to take off and fly to the moon.

CHAPTER TWENTY-NINE

It was madness the next day at work. Flynn had watched *Holly-wood Howl* and announced that he'd never seen such a crock of horseshit in his life. Drivers beeped their horns and shouted my name as they drove past the lawns we were cutting. A female customer actually asked for my autograph on the back of a Con Ed bill. I gave it to her, and then she asked me to please pull the dandelions growing along her back path.

I was a star again, or the shell of a star, which is maybe the same thing. If anybody was looking for me, they were going to find me.

It didn't take long.

I was walking home from work when suddenly a man jumped out of a black sedan parked in front of our house. He walked toward me as if I owed him money.

"Mickey DeFalco?"

"Yes . . ."

He looked to be in his early fifties, lean and serious inside a baggy blue suit. He flapped open a billfold with identification I didn't even look at. "I've come from Los Angeles to see you on a matter of some importance."

I knew it would happen. It was almost a relief.

"I know what you want," I said.

He seemed surprised. "You do?"

"Yeah, I won't give you any trouble. Look, do you mind if we go to the diner around the corner? I don't want my mother to hear this."

I also didn't want her to look out the window and see her only begotten son being handcuffed, in case that was on the agenda. That would have finished her off.

The man managed a smile. "That'd be fine with me, Mr. De-Falco."

"Mickey, please. Call me Mickey." I led the way to the Scobee Grill diner, wondering if he kept his gun in a shoulder holster or an ankle holster, wondering if he'd put a bullet between my shoulders if I broke into a run.

I didn't want to run. At that moment, all I wanted was coffee.

The man's name was Belachek. He had that intense, birdlike look across the eyes that all determined people seem to have. We got a booth and ordered coffee.

He could tell I was not a flight risk. The way things were going, I didn't much care about whatever happened to me next. The worst thing of all would be the follow-up story on *Hollywood Howl*. They'd have footage of me being remanded to Los Angeles, standing in a courtroom in an orange prison jumpsuit as some court-appointed lawyer entered a "Not Guilty" plea on my behalf. Joel Schmitter would gloat about being the one who'd tracked me down, helped the cops bring me to justice for my part in the deaths of Officer William O'Brien and his wife, Robin. He'd probably get a raise.

Schmitter's raise bugged me more than anything. That's how fucked up I was.

Maybe Belachek would believe me when I told him I hadn't done anything wrong, except for swiping that coffee can full of money. Maybe he'd be impressed that I'd given it away to the needy.

Or maybe he didn't give a shit either way. Belachek had worked long and hard to find me, and the fact that he'd been beaten by a tabloid TV show certainly must have galled him.

He sipped his coffee and his eyes scrunched up. "Jesus, that's strong."

"That's how the Greeks like it."

"Is this place run by Greeks?"

"Is there a diner in New York that isn't?"

Belachek chuckled. "I may need a muffin to absorb the caffeine."

He ordered a corn muffin and bit into it plain, no butter, no jelly. No wonder he was thin.

"So am I under arrest, or what?"

Belachek was stunned. He shook his head, sipped coffee to help get the muffin down.

"I'm not a cop, Mr. DeFalco."

"You're not?"

"I'm a private investigator. Why would anyone want to arrest you?"

"You've come all the way from Los Angeles to see me, so the news can't be good."

He forced a smile. "Maybe it is, maybe it isn't. It's all in how you look at it."

"For God's sake, man, what the fuck do you want?"

He clapped his hands clean of crumbs before reaching into his inside jacket pocket, removing a snapshot and passing it to me. It was a publicity photo of the *Barca D'Amore*.

What the fuck was this all about?

"Do you recognize this ship?"

"Sure I do. It sank a few weeks ago."

"Yes, it did. You were once employed aboard this ship, were

you not? And your employers were less than delighted with your services, weren't they?"

Where was this going? Was I a suspect in the still-unsolved sinking of the *Barca D'Amore*?

"Whoa, whoa, Mr. Belachek, I happen to have an alibi. I was here in Little Neck with my parents when it happened. We watched it on the news, and then we had dinner. Chicken pot pie, as I recall, but I could be wrong about that."

He ignored my smart-ass attitude and passed me another snapshot.

"Do you recognize this woman?"

I stared into the eyes of the woman in the photo, big and sad and smoky. I didn't have to tell Belachek that I recognized Sharon Sherman. He could tell from the shift in my breathing.

"Met her on the ship," I said.

"Yes, Mr. DeFalco, that's right. You met her on the ship. I'm glad you remember that. I'm glad you acknowledge that."

"Acknowledge" is a bad word in a situation like this. It implies a confession. Belachek creamed and sugared his coffee and took another sip. "Ahh, that's better. Takes the voltage out of the coffee, doesn't it?"

"Why are you here, Mr. Belachek? Why would anyone give a shit about a stupid cruise I worked on . . . what was it, two years ago?"

"Eighteen months, actually."

"Whatever. But who gives a shit?"

"Look, I've come a good long way to find you, Mr. DeFalco." He tapped the snapshot with a bony finger. "Could we just please talk about the cruise, and your relationship with this woman?"

I couldn't imagine why this man should be giving me the third degree about that cruise. But if I gave him a hard time, he could chase me with subpoenas and whatever other paperwork he could think to fling at me, and he probably had friends in the

Los Angeles Police Department he could bring into it, and that I definitely did not need.

So I sat back, sipped my coffee and began telling him all about the cruise, and about the way we sabotaged the stupid shuffleboard tournament by chucking all the equipment overboard, and how we capped off this act of rebellion by having sex on the rail overlooking the ship's prow.

Belachek took it all in without seeming surprised. He and I had each downed three cups of coffee by the end of my tale.

"So," he said. "You never got caught for the shuffleboard thing, huh?"

"No. We got away with it, unless that's what you're here for. What happened? The shuffleboard sticks washed ashore? My prints were on them? The cruise ship company wants me to make good for them?"

Belachek chuckled. "That's funny. That's really funny."

"Well, if that's not it, then what? Who sent you to find me, Sharon Sherman?"

Belachek's face darkened. "Sharon didn't send me, Mr. DeFalco. Sharon is dead."

I swallowed. My stomach dropped. It's an eerie thing to learn that someone you've been with has died, no matter how fleeting a union it might have been.

"Jesus, that's awful. . . . When?"

"Two weeks ago. A cerebral hemorrhage. Fell sick and died on the same day. She was forty-four. Never sick a day in her life, until the last day."

We were both quiet for a moment. I was thinking about how fragile everything is, and at the same time thinking that Sharon's death hadn't been so bad, as deaths go. Splendid health, and then sudden death. No middle ground. It sounded good to me.

But what the fuck was going on? Had Sharon put me in her will? Why else would Belachek have been looking for me?

The waitress came by with the coffeepot. We both shielded our cups with our hands.

"Not to pry here or anything, Mr. Belachek, but who sent you to find me, and why?"

He sighed, sat back in the booth. "Sharon's lawyer sent me, actually."

"Her lawyer?"

He nodded, reached into his jacket pocket and pulled out another photograph. He looked at it before passing it to me gently, as if it were a loaded gun on a hair trigger. It was a shot of a beautiful green-eyed baby with jet-black hair.

"This is Sharon's son, Aaron," Belachek informed me. "And according to Sharon's will, you are his father."

The air in the diner suddenly went warm, and seemed to contain no oxygen. I took deep breaths, but that didn't help. My hands were actually damp with sweat. I didn't want to damage the photograph, so I set it down on the Formica tabletop, locked my hands behind my back and leaned forward to study the picture as if it were a priceless museum piece. I needed a moment to take it all in. I'd just been informed that I was a father, by a private eye in a booth in a Greek diner.

"My *son?*"

"According to Sharon's will, yes."

Was there a resemblance to me? Nothing I could detect. Also, the kid seemed happy, and that didn't seem like the kind of kid I'd be likely to sire.

I looked up at Belachek, felt a drop of sweat roll to the bottom of my chin. He passed me a napkin. I wiped my chin.

"Stunning thing to come out of the blue, huh, kid? Sorry about that. No easy way to break it to you."

Me and my "always use a condom" rule. This was the exception that proved the rule.

"She told me she was on the pill."

"Nothing's a hundred percent, kid."

"Do you think he looks like me?"

"I didn't travel three thousand miles to give an opinion. I came here to find you."

"What about Sharon's boyfriend, that Benny guy, the one who dumped her at the dock? Maybe he's the one. Maybe—"

"Benny is sterile. I have a medical document attesting to that fact. Seems Benny contracted the mumps when he was thirty-two. Wiped out his swimmers for good. I can show you the document, if you like."

"I'll take your word for it." I looked again at the photo of that beautiful, beautiful child. "Who's taking care of this kid?"

"For the time being, he's in the hands of Sharon's only living relative, a cousin in Massachusetts. A small town outside Boston. That's where Sharon's from, originally."

"The cousin wants money," I ventured.

Belachek shook his head. "She wants you to take the child."

"Take him?"

"Yes."

"You mean adopt him?"

"Mr. DeFalco, you cannot adopt your own child. If he's yours, he's yours. You simply take him."

I sat back in the booth, raw and numb. I had expected to be arrested and thrown in jail in connection with a murder/suicide, but instead I was learning that I might be a father.

"How old is this . . . Aaron?"

"He's nine months old. Born nine months after the cruise, almost to the day."

"How's he . . . what I mean is, is he . . . you know . . . healthy?"

"Perfectly healthy, as far as I know."

I rubbed my eyes, kept my hands over my face. Life. Fucking life. It just keeps coming at you.

"Jesus Christ. *Jesus Christ* . . ."

Belachek reached across the table, gave my shoulder a friendly squeeze. "I know it's a lot to absorb all at once."

"Absorb? Who's absorbing anything? I'm in shock, here!"

"Look, Sharon Sherman never meant for this to be a burden to you. If she'd lived, you never would have known about Aaron. She was perfectly content to raise the child by herself. It's exactly what she was doing when she dropped dead."

Belachek held up a finger. "But she was an extremely precise person. Working in life insurance, she knew as well as anyone how suddenly things can happen, and how messy things can get for the living when a loved one dies. She was determined to take care of her son, no matter what happened."

He pulled out a document in a book report–type binder that turned out to be Sharon's will. "Everything she had goes to Aaron. Her estate was worth almost half a million dollars. There's a trust fund for the child's education. It's all hammered down—no ambiguity, no confusion. Until the final lines of her last will and testament."

Belachek put on his reading glasses and flipped to the last page. "Finally," he read, "I wish to reveal the identity of my son's father. He is Mickey DeFalco, the singer. I have never shared this information with anyone. Mickey DeFalco himself is unaware that he is Aaron's father. I leave it to my surviving family members to either inform Mr. DeFalco, or continue keeping it a secret."

He took off his glasses, put them in his shirt pocket. "Obviously, Sharon's cousin didn't want to keep it a secret. And Sharon, true to form, provided the funds for a private investigator to track you down." He grinned. "That'd be me."

I wanted to speak but my mouth was dry. I signaled to the waitress for a glass of water. She brought it over and I downed it in a gulp. It tasted of chlorine and plumbing. It chilled me so deeply that I actually shivered, though maybe I was shivering for other reasons.

"Lucky for you I was on *Hollywood Howl*," I said.

Belachek didn't like hearing that. "I'd have found you without that," he replied calmly. "It was only a matter of time."

I nodded. I shouldn't have been breaking his balls. He was only doing his job.

"What's next?"

"Well, a DNA test is in order, wouldn't you say? Would you have a problem with that?"

"No, I . . . no, of course not."

"Good. That simplifies things."

I expected him to offer me a time and a place for the test, but instead he took a small rubber-stoppered lab bottle from his pocket, containing what appeared to be a miniature toothbrush.

"Here," he said. "Take out the toothbrush and rub it around inside your mouth."

"Now?"

"You got something better to do? Go on, do it, fill up those bristles with cheek cells."

I did as I was told. It took about ten seconds. I stuck the toothbrush back inside the bottle, sealed it, and returned it to Belachek, who took out a pen and wrote "DeFalco" on the label. He stuck it in an envelope, sealed the envelope and stashed it in his jacket pocket. Then he sat back to finish his corn muffin, with the relaxed look of a man whose tricky task has been successfully completed.

"You seem like a nice guy," he said. "Then again, in my line of work, anybody who isn't spitting in my face is a nice guy."

"How long's the DNA thing going to take?"

"We'll know in a week. Maybe less. I'll call you, or you can call me." He gave me his card.

"So my . . . this kid's in Massachusetts? Where exactly—"

"Don't even ask, Mr. DeFalco. I can't tell you more than that right now."

Aaron Sherman . . . or was it Aaron DeFalco? The child, my

maybe-probably son, was only 250 miles away. A train ride. A five-hour drive. I could be there before midnight, if I knew where I was going. . . .

Belachek picked up the tab and left the waitress a three-dollar tip. He reached over to pick up the photo of the child, but I grabbed it first.

"Can't I keep it? I'm sure you have copies."

He thought about it, shrugged, let me keep it. We left the diner together. I walked him to his car.

"Can I say somethin' to you, kid?"

"Do I have a choice?"

"No, you don't. Listen. I like you, so I'm gonna tell you something."

"I'm listening."

He gripped me by the shoulders, the way a school guidance counselor might grab a gifted but lazy student.

"Life takes funny turns," he said. "Try to turn with them. Otherwise, you hit walls."

"I'll remember that. Can I ask you one thing?"

He released my shoulders. "Name it."

"I already asked you, but I'm asking again—do you think this kid looks like me?"

Belachek took the picture and held it beside my face. He looked from one to the other, squinting one eye.

"Let me put it this way. If this kid were frowning? Hell, he'd be a dead ringer for you. A dead ringer."

We were sitting around the kitchen table, finishing our meal. It was lasagne left over from the night before. My mother was urging my father to have the last spoonful, because otherwise she was going to have to throw it away.

"Take it, Eddie."

"For Christ's sake, I don't want it!" He cobwebbed his hands over his plate, fingers spread wide. The spoon came my way, and

I covered my plate as well. My mother stood there like a pilot in the fog, with no place to land. She sighed, shook her head, dumped the spoonful back into the pan.

"It's a sin."

"Gluttony is a sin, too," my father said. "If I'd forced it down, I would have sinned."

"Oh, Eddie—"

"I have something to show you," I blurted, a lot louder than I meant to say it. I took the photo of Aaron from my shirt pocket and passed it to my father, who looked at it quizzically before passing it to my mother. She studied it for a few moments before guessing, "Is this Mikey Gallo's son?"

Mikey Gallo was a bus driver and an usher at the seven o'clock mass every Sunday. What the fuck would I be doing with a picture of Mikey Gallo's son?

"No, Mom, that's not who it is."

"He looks a lot like Mikey Gallo's son, doesn't he, Eddie?"

"Who the hell is Mikey Gallo?"

"He's an usher at St. Anastasia's . . . oh, that's right, you don't go to church, do you?"

"You go enough for the two of us. I figure I'm covered."

"That's not the way it works, Eddie, we each have to—"

"This boy is your grandson. Maybe."

I don't know why I said it that way, instead of saying he was my son, maybe. I guess I wanted to connect the baby to my parents as directly as I could.

My mother went pale. My father got up and stood behind her. He shook a Camel into his mouth and lit up, sensing quite correctly that if ever he was going to get away with smoking in the house, this was the time. Surprisingly, my father spoke first.

"Good-lookin' boy," he said softly.

"Oh my dear sweet God in heaven," my mother said to the ceiling. It wasn't a cry for help, or mercy. It was a call for order, some semblance of order in her son's crazy, crazy life.

She turned to me, trembling. "Are you sure he's yours?"

"Pretty sure, Mom. I'll know for certain in about a week."

"Jeez, Mickey, you been ridin' bareback, or what?"

"I know, Dad, I know."

"When'd you find out about this?"

"About two hours ago. A private eye from Los Angeles tracked me down."

He put a hand on my shoulder, as if to share the burden of the weight of the world with me. My mother put the photo down on the table and rubbed her eyes.

"How old is this child?"

"Nine months."

"And his mother waited all this time—"

"His mother just died. She was a very private person who was happy to raise the kid all by herself. Never told anybody I was the father. It was revealed in her will."

"Her will?"

I nodded. "If she hadn't died, I never would have known about little Aaron, here."

My mother's face softened. Hearing the boy's name made it all real to her. "Aaron? That's a biblical name!"

"I guess it is."

"Was this woman a Catholic?"

"You know, Mom, I have no idea."

"Well, how did you meet her?"

I was too tired to sugarcoat it, or smooth the edges.

"She was on that cruise ship I worked on, the one that sank a few weeks ago. We had a one-night fling. That's all. It just kind of . . . happened."

My mother shut her eyes over the carelessness of her only begotten son, the kind of person who could have sex with a woman without knowing about her religious beliefs, not to mention her educational background, her father's line of work, whether the family owned or rented. . . .

She opened her eyes and studied the photo again. "This poor child has no mother."

"He's with a cousin right now, someplace near Boston. The cousin wants me to take him. There's a big trust fund. That's a good thing, right?"

My mother shook her head, chuckled in a sad way. "Michael. Your *life*."

I braced myself for the worst. "What about my life, Mom?"

Her next words really did surprise me. "You never got away with anything," she said softly. "Whatever you did, you paid for it, and then some. Ever since you were a kid. You never . . . caught a break."

She spoke the words the way you'd deliver a eulogy. I actually shivered at the sound of them. It was more like something my father would have said, with a few "shits" and "fucks" thrown in.

"Hey, Donna, take it easy," my father said. "What about his song? Didn't he get a break with his song?"

She chuckled again, the same way. "You think so, Eddie? I think that song was the biggest curse of all. Look at where it's gotten him. Look."

They looked at me, their shipwreck of a son. My father tipped his ashes into his cupped palm. My mother had apparently gotten rid of all the ashtrays.

"Well," my father said, "let's not get too excited just yet. Let's wait for the test to come back, and figure out what's next."

I had to admire them. They were pretty calm, considering what was happening. For twenty years it had been just the two of them in the house, and then I returned out of the blue, and suddenly here they were, one lab test away from becoming a three-generation family under one small roof.

My mother wiped sudden tears from her eyes. Grandmother-hood is supposed to be something you dream about and antici-pate and grow into. It's not supposed to land in your lap like a football. She'd been cheated out of something precious.

My father put his arm across her shoulders. "You know, I think we still have the crib in the attic." The crib that had held me!

My mother sniffed, cleared her throat. "No, Eddie, don't you remember? We gave it to the Lamberts when their daughter was born."

"Oh that's right, that's right."

"I suppose we could get it back. That child must be ten, eleven years old by now."

"Unless they gave it away to somebody. . . ."

They were amazing. They'd gotten over the initial shock and gone straight to the practical matters ahead. They were a good team, my parents. I guess that's why they'd lasted, and would continue to last. They were totally different people who gave each other all kinds of bullshit, but when it came to the big-ticket issues they pulled their oars in the same direction.

But they were also getting old, and they did not need this latest mess of mine.

"Listen," I said, "this is *my* problem. No matter how it goes, I'll handle it."

They looked at me the way parents look at their little boy in a space suit who's just announced that he's going to fly his cardboard rocket ship to the moon. My mother reached across the kitchen table, clasped my hands in hers and held on as if I were a lifeline.

"Michael, tell me one thing."

"Anything, Mom."

Her eyes brightened with hope. "Did you at least *like* the mother of this child?"

I nodded. "She was nice, Mom. She was really nice. We kind of . . . connected."

"Evidently."

She let go of my hands, slid back in her chair, tucked her hands between her knees. "Well, that's something, anyway. That's something. It's good to know she was a nice person. Isn't that a good thing, Eddie?"

He kissed her on the forehead. "Well, it ain't a bad thing."

"Take that cigarette outside, please."

I went to sleep early, and it wasn't until the middle of the night that I sat bolt upright in bed and realized that this jarring turn of events might just be the solution to my problems.

CHAPTER THIRTY

It was so simple. Lynn would raise little Aaron with me! We'd ride up to Massachusetts, pick up my child, and begin our lives anew. Together we would shape this little life, restore old bonds, heal old wounds.

Would she want to raise another woman's child? Of course she would, if the child was mine! All I had to do was get Lynn to forgive me. Piece of cake, or so I hoped and prayed.

I didn't need a DNA test to tell me what my heart already knew. I was the one. Little Aaron was mine. I was eager to get this thing going. I wanted Lynn and I to meet him before he took his first step. That would be a hell of a thing to miss.

I didn't fall back to sleep for hours. I was yawny and tired when I reached Flynn's garage the next morning, and he stunned me with the words, "You lost."

I had no idea of what he was talking about. The DNA test? My mind? What?

"The radio contest," Flynn continued with a smile. "'Feelings' was voted the sappiest song. 'All by Myself' was second. You were third."

"I demand a recount."

In the midst of it all was Patrick, poor heartbroken Patrick.

He'd talked it over with his parents and agreed to stick to the plan and play football for Purdue University. Then he'd gone to see Scarlett and told her they'd make it work, that she could come and visit him, that he'd be home for Thanksgiving, but that didn't keep the two of them from having an all-night fight over his imminent departure. The undeniable truth was that his athletic gifts were taking him away from the most important thing in his life for the next four years. At his age, the time did not pass swiftly.

At the lunch break Patrick's normally voracious appetite was gone. He barely touched his food and stared off at the sky, as if he were imagining that maybe there was a gentler planet somewhere out there in the galaxy where life would work out better for a guy like him.

Flynn's voice was kind. "Come on, Patrick, eat up. You'll faint out here if you don't eat."

"I'm not hungry."

"You got some time before you go to Purdue. Try and enjoy it."

He shook his head. "I have to be at football camp in ten days."

"Well, that's better than nine days, ain't it?"

Patrick turned his gaze toward me. "Mickey understands. Mickey's the only one."

"Tell him, Mick," Flynn said. "He ain't listenin' to me."

I patted his rock-hard shoulder, tried to give it a squeeze. "First things first, Patrick. Finish your lunch. You're going to need it."

I meant what I said. We were at the Haffner house, the toughest lawn of the week, a place we simply called "the hill." It was a slope of green that was more like the side of a mountain than a lawn in Great Neck.

But Patrick ignored my advice and rose to his feet. "I'm going back to work."

"Patrick, buddy, don't do the hill by yourself. Sit. Eat."

"You got another fifteen minutes," Flynn added, but Patrick ignored him, too. He pushed his mower to the top of the hill and pulled the rip cord.

"Lucky you, Mick," Flynn said. "By the time we finish lunch Patrick'll have the hill all done."

He cut the flat part at the top of the lawn first, the easy part, and then the hill was all his.

"He'll love Purdue," Flynn said. "You watch. He'll go and he'll love it."

We sat and watched him work. Something funny was going on. You had to stand at the top of the hill and work your way down on the sides of your feet, holding on tightly to the lawn mower so it wouldn't get away from you. If the grass was even slightly wet, you slipped and fell on your ass.

Patrick was handling it fine, but he was moving too fast. The muscles in his arms were bulging and ropy, and his eyes burned with concentration. Soon he had half of the hill cut.

Flynn looked at his watch. "Five minutes left for lunch," he chuckled. "Looks like you're off the hook, Mick."

And then Patrick looked at me, the way you'd look at someone you know you're seeing for the last time. Suddenly he lost his footing, and his lawn mower plunged toward the street.

He should have just let it go, but this was a kid who never let anything go. Clutching the handle, he strained in vain to stop the mower while his legs raced down the hill, picking up speed with each stride.

"Let go!" Flynn shouted.

An oil truck was approaching. Patrick and his mower were heading straight into its path. I jumped to my feet and raced toward Patrick. I dove at him, wrapping my arms around his waist. The two of us tumbled and hit the sidewalk as the lawn mower rolled into the street and was smashed to pieces by the truck.

Flynn hop-limped toward us as the oil truck screeched to a halt. Patrick's heavy breaths were like cloth being ripped. He was facedown on the sidewalk, and I was on top of him. He turned his head to look at me, his nose bleeding profusely.

"Jesus Christ, Patrick!"

"You okay, Mickey?"

"Elbow hurts. . . . You?"

He put a hand to his face, brought it away wet with blood.

"I think my nose might be broken," he said calmly, as if he were delivering a weather report. Then he fainted dead away.

We had to carry Patrick to the truck. He regained consciousness halfway through the ride to the emergency room and insisted that he was fine and wanted to go back to work.

"Shut up, Patrick," Flynn said. "Just shut up."

All I had was a scraped elbow, but Patrick's nose was broken and he'd suffered a mild concussion. He was stretched out on a cot that wasn't quite long enough for him. They wanted him to rest for an hour or so before heading home. Flynn had to go back to the Haffner place to pick up all the equipment we'd left behind. I told him I'd stay with Patrick.

Flynn shook hands with both of us.

"I'm sorry I broke the mower, Mr. Flynn," Patrick said.

"Hey. Forget about that. Rest, okay? The two o' you, rest. Day off tomorrow."

He left the emergency room. Five minutes later Scarlett showed up, and suddenly I knew what Patrick's torment was all about.

She was stunning, an absolute jaw-dropper, with sky-blue eyes and long brown hair. She wore a sleeveless Kmart smock that showed off the barbed-wire tattoo on her bare upper arm.

She took one look at the bandage over Patrick's nose and the dark circles under his eyes and burst into tears.

"Ohh, baby, *baby!*"

He rose from the cot on unsteady feet. Scarlett fell into his arms.

"I'm okay, Scarlett, I'm okay."

"Your nose! Is it busted?"

"Yeah." He chuckled. "I'm not gonna be as handsome as I used to be."

"What happened?"

He told her how he'd been cutting the steep lawn and lost his balance, and how I'd tackled him just before he would have gone into the street with the lawn mower.

Scarlett was puzzled. "Why didn't you just let go of the mower?"

"I don't know. Somehow I couldn't." He gestured at me. "Mickey here saved my life."

"I also broke his nose," I couldn't help adding.

Scarlett turned to me. We'd never been properly introduced and here she was now, leaping into my arms and hugging me as if I'd just pulled her aboard a life raft.

"Oh, God, Mickey, thank you, thank you!"

"You're welcome."

"By the way, I love how you flipped the bird to that asshole from *Hollywood Howl*." She looked at her watch. "I have to get back to Kmart. Believe it or not, my stupid boss wouldn't give me the afternoon off, even after I told him what happened."

She gave Patrick a gentle kiss on the lips, eased him back down onto the cot.

"See you later, baby. Love you."

"Love you, too."

And just like that she was gone, with so much energy and spirit I half expected her to fly out the window like Tinker Bell.

Patrick watched her go with a childlike smile on his lips.

"See that, Mickey?" he said. "See how special she is? See why I can't go to Purdue?"

My bandaged elbow was throbbing. I'd refused a painkiller and now I was sorry I'd done that. I gestured for Patrick to move his feet so I could sit on the end of the cot. I wanted to be close to him for what I had to say.

"You asshole," I began.

Chapter Thirty-one

Patrick was stunned by my words. I'd never spoken to him that way before.

"Mickey?"

"Don't fuck with me, Patrick. I know what you did."

He spread his hands. "What did I do?"

"You didn't really lose your balance. You went down that hill on purpose."

"Oh, yeah, right!"

"Patrick. This is me. Come on. No bullshit, now. What the fuck happened on the hill?"

He tried to stare me down, but I was better at it than he was. I held my gaze until his eyes got shiny with tears. He covered his face with his hands.

"I'm all fucked up, Mickey," he wailed through his fingers.

I put a hand on his shoulder. He was quaking.

"*You* should understand," he said. "You of all people. I love that girl. I *can't* leave her. I won't."

"That's up to you."

"Yeah?" He sniffed back snot. "Sometimes it seems to me like it's up to everybody else. My parents. Mr. Flynn. My coach."

"Scarlett," I added. "Don't forget Scarlett."

His eyebrows went up. "What do you mean?"

"She's trying to run your life, too, isn't she?"

His face went as white as the bandage. "Hang on, hang on. We are *totally* in love, Mick."

"I know you are. But sometimes love makes you do crazy things."

"You think I *wanted* to get hit by that truck?"

"In some deep-down, crazy way . . . yeah, Patrick. That's what I think. You figured that if you hurt yourself, maybe got your knee racked up, you wouldn't be able to play football. Right? You wouldn't have to make a tough decision. You could just stay here in Little Neck, a fucking cripple."

He pointed a thick finger right at my face. "What do *you* know?"

"Hey, you're right. Who am I to be giving advice? Look at me. Look at how fucked up my life is. I made a fortune, and I lost it. I'm living with my parents, still moanin' over a girl I lost twenty years ago."

"So you know how I feel!"

"Yeah, Patrick, I know how you feel. You burn hot, just like I did. I lost the girl, and I fell apart. It happened. I can't change that."

I was surprised to feel tears in my eyes, which I took a moment to blink back.

"But I did one good thing, Patrick—I sang my song. I wrote it and I sang it and it's all mine, and it always will be, no matter who owns it. I'm a loser, but I did do that one good thing, and only I could have done it."

"It's a beautiful song," Patrick said, almost fervently.

I nodded, licked my lips. "Thing is, I got this feeling that football is *your* song. It's what makes you special. So I guess what I'm saying here is, don't you want to sing your song? And how are you going to feel if you don't even try?"

Patrick stared at me, long and hard.

"Scarlett won't run away like my girl did," I said. "If it's real, she'll hang in there. Look, you're going to make up your own mind about this, but I just wanted you to know what I thought."

Patrick embraced me, almost hard enough to puncture a lung.

"You are *not* a loser," he whispered.

"Yeah, well, some might disagree. Ease up, Patrick, I'm about to black out, here."

Just then Patrick's parents arrived, and I was shocked to see that they weren't much older than me. Patrick's father was a thickset six-footer with thinning blond hair and a hard hand-shake that told me he'd probably played some football himself.

I was surprised to see that Patrick's mother was short and dark, and I thought she didn't resemble her boy at all until I noticed the way her ears stuck out.

"My boy!" she kept crying as she embraced him. "Ohh, my *boy!*"

"I'm all right, Mom," Patrick said, but she just wouldn't believe him. While his parents smothered him with hugs, I waved good-bye to Patrick and slipped out of the emergency room and into the parking lot.

I needed air. I needed a painkiller. I needed Lynn.

And suddenly it hit me that here I was, right at the place where they'd brought her mother.

I went around to the front of the hospital and walked straight past the front desk, as if I were late for an appointment. Nobody stopped me. I kept going, all the way to Mrs. Mahoney's room.

And if ever I was to believe that God has a strange sense of humor, this was the time, because just as I entered the room, they were stripping the bed where she had lain.

An exhausted-looking Lynn, tears streaming down her face, sat almost primly in the chair she'd spent so many hours in over the past few days, filling out a form on a clipboard.

There's a bit of paperwork involved when your mother dies.

CHAPTER THIRTY-TWO

We fell into each other's arms. Even if she didn't want me, Lynn Mahoney had nobody else. My arms would have to do.

She felt frail and feverish, and quaked like a newly hatched chick.

"I'm so sorry, Lynn."

"Thanks."

"Come on. Let's go home."

"Your home?"

"Yeah."

"Good ol' Donna, huh?"

"Lynn, I hate to say it, but this is her specialty. She knows just what to do."

"Do?"

"The body. The funeral."

"Oh. . . ."

We left the hospital and began the walk to Glenwood Street, holding hands. She noticed my bandage.

"What happened to your elbow, Mickey?"

"Hurt it on the job. No big deal."

We were still holding hands when we entered the kitchen, where my mother stood peeling carrots at the sink. She turned to face us and then put the peeler down, as if to show Lynn that she meant her no harm.

I didn't allow any time for awkward silences.

"Mom, Mrs. Mahoney just died."

My mother put a hand to her throat. "Oh, my God. Lynn. I'm so sorry."

"Me too, Mrs. DeFalco."

She came to us and spread her arms for a double embrace.

"Lynn . . . Michael . . ."

She took us both, one in each arm, and startled me by planting a gentle kiss on Lynn's cheek.

"Do you still hate me, Mrs. DeFalco?"

My mother hesitated. For a moment I thought she was going to deny that she'd ever hated her, but it was a time for truths.

"Not anymore."

"Why not?"

My mother shrugged. "What would it help?"

Lynn swallowed. "That's pretty big of you."

"No, it isn't. It's the right thing. Sooner or later I get around to doing the right thing. Usually later."

"Thank you, Mrs. DeFalco."

"Call me Donna. I'm not that much older than you anymore."

She was right. We were all adults now. We all knew what it was like to get knocked down, and how hard it was to get up.

But you do get up, don't you? What else can you do?

My mother pressed her hands gently against Lynn's cheeks. "I'm sorry about your mother. She was a good lady."

Lynn put her face to my mother's shoulder and wept. My mother stroked her hair.

"It's all right, dear. I'm going to take care of everything."

Most people are paralyzed when a loved one dies. What do you do? How does it all work? My mother knew how it all worked. She was the one who made it work, the grease that kept the cogs spinning in the intricate machinery of mourning. She made Lynn lie down on the living room couch, pulled off her shoes, covered her with a light quilt and then said she needed me in the kitchen.

"Finish peeling those carrots for me, would you, Michael?"

I did as I was told while she worked the phone like a stockbroker, arranging everything from the coffin to the headstone in a rat-a-tat-tat manner. It wouldn't cost Lynn a dime, she told me on the sly, because she was going to make sure it all fell within the insurance budget allowed for firemen's widows.

"Don't you worry," she said with a wink. "I'll take good care of your girl."

My girl.

By the time I'd finished the carrots Lynn was fast asleep, like a kindergarten child at naptime. I sat on the arm of the couch and stroked her hair, gently enough not to wake her. In the kitchen I could hear my mother say, "You can do better than that," and I knew she was dealing with the local florist, knocking down his price for a mixed-color carnation display for the final farewell to Mrs. Mahoney.

In the midst of this madness was a baby somewhere in Massachusetts, a baby whose mother was dead and whose father might have been me.

I couldn't tell Lynn about that. Not yet. Not yet.

Soon.

The wake.

Ruth Brady Mahoney lay in the coffin, wearing a plain gray dress, her face set in a smile I never saw when she was alive. There weren't a lot of visitors, and the people who did show up to pay their final respects came and went as if they were double-parked. Truth was, Mrs. Mahoney was a little bit of a curiosity. The obituary in the local paper identified her as the widow of the legendary Burning Angel and the mother of four firefighters who'd died in the same dreadful blaze.

And so-near strangers dropped in to get a glance at this human reservoir for grief and suffering, the way people slow down to gawk at a good car wreck.

Lynn sat before the coffin just as she'd sat by her mother's hospital bedside. She seemed strangely calm, and I wondered if she might have taken a tranquilizer.

I sat down next to her. At that moment we were the only two in the room, not counting the body.

"Can I get you anything?"

She shook her head, turned to look at me. "Nice suit."

I was wearing a charcoal-gray suit that I'd last worn in high school. The pants were a little short, until my mother adjusted the cuffs.

I shot my jacket cuffs, the way a gangster would. "You really like this suit?"

"Looks damn good on you."

"I was going to take you to the junior prom in this suit."

Her eyes widened. "It's that old?"

"Can't you smell the mothballs?"

"Who did you take to the prom?"

"Lynn, I never went to any prom."

"Neither did I."

"Well, I'm sure we didn't miss much."

She turned her gaze toward the coffin. "Weird, isn't it? None of my brothers ever got married. My mother had no daughters-in-law, no son-in-law, no grandchildren. I'm it, Mickey. The last of the Mohican-honeys."

She stroked my cheek. "Let me be by myself for a minute, would you, Mickey?"

I did as I was told, bumping into Carmine Eruzione in the hallway. "Mickey!" A ghastly, ghostly smile lit up his face. "Long time no see!"

Eruzione was as lean as a greyhound. His eyes were like yellowed Ping-Pong balls deep in their bony sockets, and his cheeks had the sucked-in, sour look of a man who expects the worst from people. The few strands of gray hair left on the sides of his skull were slicked straight back. He could have been sixty, and he could have been ninety.

You'd look at him and swear he had a week to live, except that this was how he'd looked for the past twenty-five years. Death, it seemed, was going to leave this undertaker alone. Professional courtesy.

He put out his hand to shake and it was all bones, like reaching into a bag of clothespins. I hoped he couldn't feel me shudder.

"How are you, son?"

"I'm doing all right, Mr. Eruzione," I lied.

My voice quaked. I couldn't help it. Even now, he scared the shit out of me. His odors enveloped me like a fog—a rich, fruity cologne and the peppermint reek of his breath fresheners. As bad as he looked was as good as he smelled. He put a hand on my shoulder.

"What a shame, huh?"

"Yeah, it's a shame."

"Ah, well. We all gotta die sometime, am I right?"

"You would know."

"Hey, you wanna hear somethin' funny? Not ha-ha funny, but, like, odd?"

"Sure."

"She died on the same date her sons got killed. Eleven years later, to the day. Remember when they got killed, those four firemen? *Madonna*, that was crazy. Place was jammed. I had to rent extra chairs. TV crews all over the place . . . You weren't here for that one, were you, Mickey?"

He might have been talking about a memorable ball game.

"Missed it," I said.

"Anyway, it's just one of those ironic things."

"Don't mention it to Lynn, if you haven't already."

"Don't worry. I only noticed 'cause I checked the family records. I won't say a word."

He made a zipping motion across his lips, gave me a horrible wink, and smiled so broadly that I could see how far his gums had receded from his long, horsey teeth. Then he glided off, and I was sort of surprised that he wasn't wearing a cape or carrying a sickle. He'd buried six Mahoneys, and there was just one to go. Christ!

I walked off blindly, bumping straight into my mother.

All night long she'd been doing everything—carrying cups of water to mourners, slipping Kleenex to the weepers, adjusting floral arrangements. . . .

"Mom. How do you *do* this?"

She cocked her head in puzzlement. "What do you mean?"

I gestured at the black pressboard sign with white letters she'd pressed into place earlier in the day, letters spelling MAHONEY, with a little white arrow pointing the way to the corpse.

"*This,* day in and day out. Doesn't it get to you?"

"Of course it gets to me."

"Then why do you do it?"

"Because I can, and most people can't."

I stared at her. She was either brilliant or insane, cold as a fish or warmhearted beyond the limits of my comprehension, a soldier who kept marching, no matter what. But beyond all that, she was my mother. I'd come out of her, like it or not, and I might as well like it.

"Go see Lynn," my mother said. "She needs you."

I went to the room and saw Lynn from behind, resting her head against the shoulder of a man who had his arm around her. I felt a stab of jealousy until I realized the man was my father.

Steady Eddie looked smart and handsome in his jacket and

tie, but he was uptight. This was his wife's turf, and he was just a reluctant visitor.

He stuck a finger inside his collar, gave it a tug. "This tie is killing me," he told Lynn. "How do people wear ties?"

"I don't know, Mr. DeFalco."

"Eddie. Call me Eddie, for Christ's sake."

"Okay, Eddie. I don't know how people wear ties."

"It's a noose, I swear to God. I can't see any point in wearing a tie. Guess that's why I never made it at the executive level."

Lynn actually giggled, nuzzled against his chest. I knew what was going on. She felt safe with my father. He was making her laugh, distracting her from this dreadful thing we were all going through.

He was doing the things I should have been doing, the stuff I should have been smart enough to do. He was being a man.

Suddenly there was a hand at my elbow, and my mother was leading me to a corner of the room, near the visitors' register.

"Is it almost over, Mom?"

"Almost."

"Does a priest say a prayer or something?"

"Not tonight. You're going to sing your song instead."

She said it as if it were the most sensible, logical thing in the world.

"Mom. Are you nuts?"

"Did I ever tell you how much I liked your song, Michael?"

It was a hell of a question. In all those years she'd never actually ventured an opinion about "Sweet Days." She'd talked around it, saying I'd inherited my musical talent from her side of the family and things like that, but she'd never actually said anything good about the song itself.

"Come to think of it, Mom, you never did."

"Well, that was wrong of me, Michael. Your song is wonderful. It's tender and touching and it speaks for loss far better than any old priest could." She touched my cheek. "So sing it. Sing your heart out."

"I can't."

"Yes, you can. You've got your heart back, now, so use it. *Sing.*"

"Mom—"

"Trust me. Just trust me."

"There's no music."

"I think it will work a capella. The lyrics are almost a prayer. What do you think, Michael?"

I wasn't thinking at all, anymore. I was just being. My mother corralled the mourners into a common area, a sort of chapel-shaped space near the funeral parlor's entrance. She raised her hands to silence the murmurs.

"Normally, we end these evenings with a prayer," she began. "But tonight, we do it with a song from my son."

She beckoned for me to join her there in front of the crowd. She took me by the shoulders to position me just right, like a school photographer setting a timid student in place for the camera, and then she was gone.

They were waiting. I cleared my throat and began to sing the song I'd refused to sing for Rosalind Pomer, the song I'd refused to sing for Eileen Kavanagh's "dying" grandson, the song that made and destroyed me.

My voice was deeper and hoarser with the years, and for the first time ever I wasn't afraid that I'd forget the words. How could I? The words were me.

Everybody stared. Just then Patrick Wagner arrived in a jacket and tie, hand in hand with Scarlett. John Flynn showed up, too, with his arm around Charlotte. And Eileen Kavanagh was there as well, taking it all in with her apprasing eye. It was as if my singing voice had summoned them all, just in time for the final farewell. . . .

And who were those two men, both oddly familiar? Why, it was Sully the bartender and Frankie McElhenny, who was barely recognizable in a state of relative cleanliness. It seemed hard to imagine them existing outside the walls of the Little Neck Inn, but there they were, and it occurred to me that this was the first time I'd ever seen Sully's stubby little legs, always hidden behind the mahogany.

My father had his arm across Lynn's shoulders. Tears rolled down the face of Steady Eddie, and though Lynn's eyes brimmed with tears they did not spill over. She was looking at me, in me, through me. . . .

When I finished singing I just stood there, looking at them all. For a horrifying moment I feared there might be applause, but there wasn't. There was silence, and I mean super-silence—no coughs, no throat clearings, nothing. After a few seconds I let my head fall and shut my eyes, and they all took it as a signal to disperse.

Two pats on my back. I turned to see Sully.

"Well done, lad," he said. He wanted to say more but was too choked up to speak. Frankie McElhenny shook my hand, murmured an apology for our barroom brawl, and left.

Eileen Kavanagh gave me a peck on the cheek and couldn't resist saying, "I hope you don't get in trouble for this."

"I took a chance, Mrs. Kavanagh. Figured it was worth it."

She glared at me, then left in a hurry.

My father patted my back, and then Lynn said the oddest, rightest thing of all.

"You're all grown up now, aren't you?"

"I guess so, Lynn."

"Thank you, Mickey. That meant a lot to me."

I introduced Lynn to Patrick and Scarlett. Patrick had a smaller bandage on his nose but his black eyes were darker than they'd been the day before. He looked like a raccoon on steroids, big and strong and a little bit woozy, in the wake of his concussion.

"I'm sorry for your loss," he said to Lynn, words he'd obviously rehearsed on the way to Eruzione's.

John Flynn expressed his condolences to Lynn, then took her in a farewell hug before telling me and Patrick that we had to talk in private. He led us to the men's room, an immaculately clean place of porcelain and white and black checkerboard tiles. His hand went to his pocket, and out came two wads of cash with rubber bands around them.

"Your money, guys."

It was Friday, payday. We hadn't been to work that day but Flynn wanted to take care of business.

It struck me as a crude thing to do at a wake, but what was even more jarring was the size of the bankrolls. They were way too thick. The man's emotions had him too mixed up to count right.

"This is too much," I said.

"Yeah, Mr. Flynn, it's double the usual pay," Patrick added, thumbing through the bills.

Flynn cleared his throat. "It's a week's severance on top of what I owe you guys."

"Severance?"

Flynn nodded, his hangdog cheeks jiggling like a bulldog's. "It's all over, guys. Called all my customers today and told them I was through with the business. Growing season's just about over, anyway."

It took a moment to hit me. I was out of work, once again.

"Why?"

"Ahh, I'm tired, Mick. I know I don't do much, but I'm tired o' listenin' to the customers complain, tired o' chasin' the money, tired o' people tellin' me the check's in the mail. . . . I don't know." He rubbed Patrick's hair. "It hit me yesterday when I thought this knucklehead was gonna get killed. Life's too short. Me and Charlotte are headin' for Florida, soon's we sell the house."

All Patrick and I could do was stare at Flynn. Then Patrick held out his hand, the one clutching the wad of money.

"I owe you for the lawn mower I wrecked, Mr. Flynn."

Flynn ignored the money, cocked an eyebrow at Patrick. "You goin' to Purdue, or what?"

Patrick took a deep breath, squared his shoulders like a Marine. "Yes, sir, I am."

"Good. Then I won't have to kill you."

He turned and pointed at me the way a cop would. "Make somethin' happen in your life, Mick. Hear me? Get the hell out of Little Neck."

"I will."

"You damn well better, or I'll be all over your ass."

He hugged Patrick, then he hugged me. "By the way," he said, "that song was the most beautiful thing I've ever heard."

On those words, Flynn was gone. Patrick pocketed his money, then turned to me red-faced.

"No more work for us, huh, Mick?"

"Guess not."

"So this is it, huh?"

"Guess so."

He extended his hand for a shake. "Been great workin' with you. . . . Will you write me?"

I shook his hand, then pulled him close for a hug. "Good luck, little brother. You go out there and show those Indiana jokers how the game is played."

I kissed his cheek. He broke the embrace and left the men's room, stifling sobs.

I went to the sink, threw cold water on my face and realized that a funeral parlor is as good a place as any to find out that your job is dead. The lights in the bathroom flickered on and off, a signal that the place was about to close.

I went outside and saw my parents standing with Lynn at the edge of the parking lot.

"Well, Michael," my mother said, "I'd say the song worked out."

"Uh-huh."

She was rolling. She was calling the shots. She turned to my father. "Eddie, get the car. Michael, you're staying at Lynn's house tonight. She shouldn't be alone."

Lynn did not object to this plan. Me, I had no problem with it. I only hoped my mother's instincts about the living were as good as her instincts regarding the dead.

CHAPTER THIRTY-THREE

Eddie and Donna say good night as if they're dropping us off at the prom. We watch them drive off before going into the house.

"Drink, Mickey?"

"Great idea."

Out comes the whiskey bottle. We sit together on the living room couch. I loosen my tie, take a tiny sip of whiskey, barely enough to wet my lips. My whole life is riding on this night, and I'm going to need all the brain cells I have.

Lynn sips some whiskey and holds it in her mouth before swallowing. I'm gathering my strength and my courage to pitch my plan for happily ever after, you and me and baby makes three, but she beats me to the punch with words of her own.

"I'm leaving in a few days. For good."

I'm shocked, but I shouldn't be. Lynn has been leaving ever since she'd arrived. "Where are you going?"

"Far from Little Neck."

"What about this house?"

"As of tonight, it's officially on the market." She passes a business card to me. "Got this little souvenir from one of the so-called mourners. Remember her?"

EILEEN KAVANAGH REALTY. Yes indeed, I do remember her.

"Jesus, that's a pretty crude thing to do."

Lynn shrugs. "A wake itself is pretty crude. People gathering around a corpse, talking about where they're going to eat later."

"Why'd you go through with it?"

She shrugs. "I don't know. Your mother just kind of took over, and I let it happen. Guess it was nice to be taken care of, for a change. Been a long time since anyone . . ."

She can't finish the sentence. She sips more whiskey, blinks back tears. "She's all right, your mother."

"You're right about that. Took me my whole life to realize it."

"You're lucky. Most people never find out.'"

I spread my arms across the back of the couch, hoping Lynn will lean against me. She does not. She leans away. I look away from her, look around the room. It's a cluttered house, a very cluttered house.

"Lot of stuff to pack up."

"Nope. Everything stays, except for my clothing. That's the deal I made with Eileen Kavanagh. It's all her problem."

"She'll hold a yard sale."

"Actually . . . no."

"No *what?*"

Her face darkens with an odd look, almost an evil look. A storm is gathering in her soul. She starts nodding, as if in agreement with words being whispered into her ear by an invisible demon.

"I changed my mind," she says. "There won't be a yard sale. There won't be any kind of sale."

"What the hell are you talking about, Lynn?"

She looks at me, as if deciding whether or not I can be trusted with what's coming next.

"I've got a better idea," she says.

She goes out the back door and returns a minute later with a big red can, a two-gallon can. She struggles under the weight of it, sets it on the floor, and unscrews the cap. Then she lifts the can and starts sloshing its contents along the baseboards.

It is gasoline, of course.

"Jesus Christ, Lynn, are you *nuts?*"

"Let me do this thing, Mickey!"

I wrestle the can from her hands. She tries to get it back.

"Everybody's gone now!" she cries. "Let me burn down this *fucking mausoleum!*"

She can't get the can from me, so she gives up and slaps my face once, twice, three times, losing strength with each slap. Then she collapses on the couch, defeated. The room reeks of whiskey and gasoline. Already the stuff is evaporating on the floor.

I screw the cap back on the gas can, carry it to the back door, and throw it as far as I can into the jungle of the backyard. Then I return to the living room and open all the windows.

"You're not setting this house on fire," I say, as calmly as I can. "There have been enough fires."

"I'll do it when you leave."

"I'm not leaving."

"Yes, you are."

"Actually, you're right. I *am* leaving. But here's the big news, baby. You're coming with me."

Her eyes are red and raw. It's clear that the last of her strength is gone.

"Give up, Mickey, *please.* For both our sakes, give up. It's just too late."

"Just listen to me, baby. Listen to me this one last time. . . ."

I have the photo of little Aaron right there in my shirt pocket, and I'm dying to show it to her, just hand it to her without a word, but before I can bring my maybe-son into the mix, I have to deal with Lynn and me, and the words I choose for this are pretty simple.

"Lynn. I want to be with you, right to the end of the line."

She shuts her eyes tightly and shakes her head. "Let go, Mickey," she says, oh so gently. "For your own sake, let go."

But I can't, any more than I can will myself to stop breathing.

"Listen to me. Flynn's out of business. I'm free. See? We're *both* free to go. This is meant to be."

"You don't even know where I'm going!"

"Anyplace away from Little Neck is all right by me."

"Mickey. Please stop dreaming."

"That's exactly what I'm trying to do. I'm tired of *dreaming* about you. I want the real thing. We're so close now, Lynn."

She's staring off into space, as if at a distant, dangerous star my eyes aren't strong enough to detect.

"Lynn, look at me. I really couldn't take it if you ran away from me again."

She turns her gaze at me and continues staring, long and hard. Whatever it is she's never told me no longer has a place to hide.

The distant, mournful whistle of a Long Island Rail Road train bound for Manhattan pierces the silence. Whenever you hear the train whistle that clearly, it means that the clouds are low, that rain is on the way, and sure enough the rain begins to fall, a gentle, almost crackly sound on the overgrown Mahoney lawn. It's just the nudge Lynn needs to tell me what she's been holding all these years.

"Mickey," she begins, "did it ever occur to you that I was trying to spare you?"

"From what?"

"From a mess you didn't deserve. A mess you couldn't handle."

"What I couldn't handle was you taking off like I never existed."

She's trembling. "I'm sorry."

"So am I, but we can get past that."

She shakes her head, and the tears that had been brimming in her eyes splash down her face.

"Remember when you were saying how we had to know the crucial stuff about each other? Well, you don't know my crucial stuff."

I dare to stroke her hair. She does not bite.

"Just tell me, Lynn. This is the night. This is the time. Talk to me as if the world is going to end in the morning, okay? Because if I lose you again, that's exactly what'll happen to me."

She stares at me, then pinches her nostrils. "I can't take the stink in here. Let's go outside. Take the whiskey and the glasses."

We sit out on the front stoop, just like we used to. The rain has already stopped. Lynn pours herself more whiskey. She looks sort of like an actress from a 1940s movie, tough as nails, Bette Davis about to let somebody have a cold, hard truth right between the eyes.

That's how she looks, but it's not how she sounds. She speaks softly but clearly. Her voice is like a voice in a dream, a voice in a nightmare.

It's the voice of a child in the dark.

Sometimes the ugliest things in the world begin almost casually. They don't happen so much as they appear, reveal themselves, and there you are, trying to remember what life was like before it became a horror show.

By the time she was fifteen years old Lynn Mahoney had come to despise her father for the way he treated three of the most important people in her life—her mother, her brother Brendan, and me.

Walter Mahoney was not your everyday fireman, hoping to put in his twenty years and draw a pension without getting killed along the way. He had ambition. He'd parlayed his fame as the Burning Angel into a sterling career with the fire department. That prize-winning photo of him carrying that small black child to safety while his own body was on fire had been reproduced in publications around the world.

He rose fast through the ranks and was made captain when he was barely thirty years old. When feature stories were written about the Burning Angel, he always surrounded himself with his wife and children for the photo spreads. He was a big stand-by-the-wife guy, at least in print.

"While I'm putting out the fires," he said, "she's back here, keeping the home fires burning."

It was great copy. Clever lines like that were second nature to him. Everybody loved it. And it was complete bullshit, from start to finish.

The Captain was an abusive husband, a borderline alcoholic and the kind of father who expected his children to do what they were told when they were told to do it, if not sooner.

His wife was there for meals, laundry, and sex, not necessarily in that order. They were the classic case of high school sweethearts who got married because there was no real reason not to get married. Walter spoke to his wife as if she were a lowly civil servant who could not be fired. And in a way, that's exactly what she'd become.

Walter Mahoney was not happy, but he thought of himself as a good Catholic, so divorce was absolutely out of the question. Ruth had borne him five strong, healthy children. He was sticking with her, no matter what.

What never occurred to him was the idea that Ruth might not stick by him.

You had to admire her, a woman in her forties suddenly deciding she'd endured enough misery. She had a high school diploma and no marketable skills, but Ruth Brady Mahoney was ready to leave, willing to step out into the Great Unknown rather than grit her teeth through the rest of her time on earth with the Burning Angel. She'd taken one beating too many, physically and emotionally.

She actually packed her bags one night and was about to catch a bus to her sister's house in Scranton, Pennsylvania, to begin her new life. By this time her three oldest sons were firemen and had moved into their own apartment not far from the Bronx firehouse where they were stationed. Lynn and Brendan, the two youngest, were the only children left at home. Once she found her feet in Scranton she'd come back and get them—a week or two, at most.

She was not kidding, and the Captain knew it. That's when he put on the greatest performance of his life. He begged her to stay—not forever, but just until his next promotion came through. Walter Mahoney was aiming high. He intended to land the top job, Fire Commissioner for the City of New York.

He wasn't just after the glory of the promotion. He also wanted the money. It would be a huge hike in pay, which would result in a pension that would be enough to carry them through their separate lives after they split.

But they'd never give such a high-profile job to a man in the middle of a divorce. Until the promotion happened, they had to stay together just to keep up appearances.

Ruth agreed to the deal, but she had a condition of her own—one that was totally non-negotiable. The Captain would no longer share her bed. She'd cook and clean as usual, but sex was one part of the charade she would not be able to manage.

The Captain agreed. What else could he do? He set himself up in the basement with a cot, a battered bureau and a reading lamp. He could have taken one of his boys' empty rooms but he didn't want his three grown sons to know what was going on, in case they dropped by for dinner. They idolized the man and never saw his faults.

Only Lynn and Brendan knew what was going on. Lynn felt the old bastard was getting exactly what he deserved, but Brendan couldn't help feeling sorry for his dad despite the years of torment he'd endured for being a reluctant boxer, a terrible baseball player, and an overall disappointment as a son.

"My other daughter," the Captain would occasionally sneer when referring to Brendan.

Brendan remained as loyal as a collie, despite the Captain's cruelty. When the Captain first moved down to the basement Brendan would go down at night to see if he needed anything, but Walter had usually whiskeyed himself into an early sleep. He was drinking more heavily than ever, showing up at work with hangovers that sometimes left him all but incoherent.

Walter Mahoney was not yet fifty years old, in splendid health except for whatever damage his drinking was inflicting. Another man painted into such a corner would have sought a girlfriend, but this was not even a possibility for Walter. No matter how careful he was, the word would get around. He'd be found out. He'd never make fire commissioner, not a man with a mistress on the side.

No, the Burning Angel was going to have to find another way to satisfy his burning needs, a way that would not jeopardize his career in any way, a way the world would never know about.

He would have to keep it within the walls of his house, the place where he thought of himself as more than a captain, or even a commissioner.

He was king.

It began after he moved into the basement. Lynn first sensed it through his long, prolonged stares. She told herself she was imagining things.

Then one night the Captain came up from the basement to have a chat in the kitchen with his only daughter, moments after I'd dropped her off after a date.

"Hey there, Princess."

His words shocked her. He was trying to speak with Lynn as if they had a close relationship. She'd have been more comfortable with the approach of a stranger in a bus station.

"Dad. What are you doing up?"

"Couldn't sleep. . . ."

Her mother and Brendan were sound asleep. It was past midnight. She smelled whiskey on her father's breath but he didn't seem drunk, standing at the top of the basement steps in his stocking feet, red suspenders off his shoulders and dangling down to his knees. He always wore red suspenders, on or off duty.

"So. How's the DeFalco kid?"

Lynn was wary. "Since when do you care about Mickey, Dad?"

"I care about you. That's why I ask."

Lynn could have laughed out loud when he said he cared about her, but she didn't.

"We're doing fine, thanks," Lynn finally said.

"Main thing is that you're being careful. You *are* being careful, aren't you?"

"Dad. I don't want to talk about this."

"Just please tell your poor old gray-haired father that you're being careful, so I can sleep soundly."

Lynn thought about it. We hadn't had sex (thanks largely to the night of the flaming ropes), so caution wasn't an issue. But if she told him there was nothing to be careful about, he probably wouldn't believe it, and he'd badger her for more information. Lynn decided to take the easy way out.

"Yes, Dad." She sighed. "We're being careful."

A relieved look came to his glazed eyes, and a faint smile came to his lips.

"Young people are different today," he said. "In my day you didn't have sex until you got married."

"Dad. Please."

"All right, we won't talk about it. What do you want to talk about?"

"With you? Nothing."

"All right, then, I'll talk. I'm going to tell you a story about the Burning Angel, but you can't tell a soul. Wait here, I'll be right back."

He went down to the basement and came back with the framed Pulitzer Prize–winning photograph of himself carrying that small black child to safety. It truly was an extraordinary photograph, the child's mouth wide open in a wail of terror, Mahoney's wide-open eyes blazing with hope and determination. And of course, the flames that licked at his shoulders and coatsleeves. . . .

"Some picture, ain't it?"

"Yes, Dad."

"There's an amazing story behind this photo."

"What's that?"

The Captain chuckled. "It's a setup."

Lynn was stunned. "What are you talking about?"

"Oh, I saved the kid, all right. It was a good rescue. But we kinda helped that picture along, if you know what I mean."

"I don't know what you mean."

The Captain sighed. "I was good friends with that photographer. Saw him outside the building before I went in. Told him I had a feelin' I was gonna make a good rescue that night."

"Dad, don't tell me—"

"Just listen. Lotta times when a colored guy's house is on fire, the kitchen is fulla grease. They like their greasy food, the colored, you know? So you got all these little grease fires going."

The Captain seemed to blush, either with shame or covert pride. "I smeared a little burning grease on my shoulders before I grabbed that kid. Knew it'd make a good picture." He muffled a laugh. "Didn't know it'd make *that* good a picture, though."

Lynn couldn't believe what she was hearing. "Daddy. Good God!"

The Captain's face softened. "Don't be mad at me, sweetie. I was young and I was ambitious. Also, the guy who took the picture won a Pulitzer Prize for it. A goddamn Pulitzer!"

Lynn stood and stared at him, amazed, appalled, and almost nauseated. Her father had wasted precious seconds inside a burning home to phony himself up for a photograph! What if those seconds had cost that kid his life?

It was as if she'd spoken the question aloud.

"I knew what I was doing, Lynn," the Captain said. "Nobody got hurt, and a hero was born." He chuckled. "World needs heroes, doesn't it? So I figured, why not me?"

Lynn said nothing. She stood rock-still, waiting for her father to go away. But he lingered, as if he were even prouder of his scam than he would have been over the real thing.

"Anyway, the photographer just died, so now you're the only one who knows, besides me. Just you and me. Even your mother doesn't know."

"Dad. Why are you telling me this?"

"Why?" He chuckled as he approached Lynn and stroked her cheek. "Because I want us to be close. Very close. As close as a man and a woman can be. Not tonight, but soon. *Very* soon. Do you know what I'm saying, baby?"

All she could do was stare at him in disbelief.

He kissed her on the forehead. "Your mother's going away next weekend. 'Night, sweetheart. " He winked at her, and then he receded down the cellar steps like a vampire at the first rays of dawn.

Where was Lynn supposed to turn? Her three older brothers were out of the question. They wouldn't have believed her. She couldn't tell her mother. She couldn't tell me. She couldn't tell Brendan.

She could barely tell herself it was happening even as it was happening, in the broad daylight of a beautiful morning in August, the day Lynn and I went to Jones Beach together for the very last time.

Lynn was getting her beach stuff together in the kitchen when the Captain sidled up and embraced her from behind. She felt his hardness against her back. She turned and shoved him away, an act that seemed to amuse him.

"Daddy!"

He spread his hands, innocence personified. "I'm just hugging my daughter! Can't I be nice to my own daughter?"

"Daddy, don't *do* that!"

"You don't understand, Princess."

"I think I do."

They had squared off against each other. The Captain—neatly dressed in his uniform, clean-shaven, doused with a sharp cologne—was the very picture of a leader, an important man among men. He casually poured himself a cup of coffee from the pot his wife had made before leaving for an overnight trip to her sister's in Scranton.

The only other person in the house was twelve-year-old Brendan, sound asleep in his room. The Captain had timed it just right.

Lynn made a gun of her hand and pointed her index finger straight at her father's heart. "Don't you ever, *ever* touch me again. Do you hear me?"

He sipped his coffee, shrugged, shook his head. "Is that any way to talk to your father?"

"Did you hear what I said?"

The Captain gulped the rest of his coffee, rinsed the cup, and set it in the drying rack.

"Princess—"

"And do not call me 'Princess.' I never could stand that."

He seemed genuinely surprised. "Really? Even when you were a little girl, riding up on my shoulders?"

Lynn grabbed her beach bag and headed for the door. The Captain blocked the way. She smacked his face. He grabbed her by the wrists. The beach bag fell to the floor as the Captain dragged his daughter to the kitchen table and forced her to sit. Then he eased himself into the chair directly across from Lynn, still gripping her wrists.

"Let go of me!"

"Will you sit still if I do? *Will* you?"

She nodded. He released her wrists. She remained seated.

"I want you to stay with me in the basement tonight."

"Jesus, Daddy. *Jesus!*"

"Take it easy. I'm not a bad man. I'm human, like everybody else."

A Good Humor ice cream truck went down the block, bells jingling. Lynn felt dizzy. It seemed impossible that sweet, gooey ice cream sandwiches and fathers who wanted to fuck their daughters could exist in the same world, on the same street.

The Captain leaned across the table.

"I can't be alone down there tonight. I just . . . can't."

Lynn hugged herself, as if the temperature in the kitchen had plummeted to the freezing point.

"Dad. Listen to me. I cannot do this thing. *Please* don't ask me to do this thing."

"You do it with that DeFalco boy."

"No, I don't."

"Oh, come on, now. Don't lie to your father."

"It's *not* a lie!"

He pulled out his pocket watch, checked the time, slipped it back into its pocket.

"Listen, I've got to get to work. I'll see you later."

As if they'd been having an ordinary, everyday conversation!

"You will not see me later."

"Yes, Lynn, I will." His sudden smile was chilling. "Because if it isn't you, it'll be Brendan."

For an instant, she didn't understand. Then it hit her like a meteor from the farthest reaches of space. She looked into his blazing eyes and at last saw the full scope of his plan, the dark brilliance that made him the man he was.

Firefighters make the best arsonists. Walter Mahoney understood that if he set fires in three corners of a room, whoever was hiding in there would have to run to that fourth corner . . . right into his arms. It was all about giving a person no other choice.

Walter Mahoney had a dark genius for giving people no other choice.

At last Lynn was crying, something she'd vowed she would never do in front of this man. She hung her head, shut her eyes, wished it all to be a bad dream, *willed* it all to be a bad dream. She felt his hand stroking her hair, as gently as if she were a kitten.

"Don't cry, baby girl."

She lifted her head, opened her eyes and stared into the eerily calm face of her father.

"Dad. You don't mean it."

"I mean everything I say. You know that."

"Daddy, *please* . . ."

"Brendan is practically a girl anyway, isn't he?" The Captain chuckled. "I'll just do it, no problems. He's not like you. He's not a fighter."

He winked at Lynn again, smiling as broadly as he'd ever smiled. "What the hell, the little fairy would probably enjoy it. I'll be home late. Have a good time at the beach, Princess."

He left the house whistling.

That was what Lynn Mahoney was carrying around on our very last day together at Jones Beach, the day that inspired my song. I was wondering if she'd stopped loving me, and she was wondering whether or not to let her father fuck her so he'd keep his hands off her kid brother.

Was he bluffing about Brendan, or would he actually go through with it if she didn't give in to him?

She had a good long time to think it through at the beach. She could report him to the police, but then what? They probably wouldn't believe her. It would be the word of a hormone-ridden teenage girl against that of the greatest hero in the history of the New York City Fire Department. She'd probably wind up being sent to a shrink.

She already knew that telling anyone in her family was out—but what about me? Lynn and I told each other everything, but this was different. Knowing something like this would change me forever, the way it had already changed her forever. She could never feel the same way about herself, knowing her own father wanted her. Her innocence was gone, a precious thing to lose so early in life.

And she didn't want me to lose mine.

So she kept it all to herself, knowing that the lower the sun sank on the horizon, the closer she was coming to the biggest, darkest decision of her life. She didn't know what she was going to do, but one thing she did know—that bastard wasn't going to get his hands on Brendan.

She phoned Brendan from a pay phone at the beach and told him to see if he could stay the night at the house of his good friend, a kid named Jeffrey. As it turned out, Brendan had already been invited to Jeffrey's for the night, so it was all set.

The only two people in the house that night would be Lynn and the Captain.

The Captain did not get home until nearly midnight. There had been an all-day conference in Manhattan about cutting-edge firefighting techniques, followed by a banquet at a hotel attended by top fire officials from the tristate area.

Lynn sat waiting for him in the kitchen. She wore jeans and a sweater, though the night was warm. The Captain entered the house quietly, as he always did, even when he'd been boozing.

"Hello, Princess."

She could smell the whiskey on his breath. He smiled at her almost shyly as he loosened his tie.

"Brendan asleep?"

"He's at Jeffrey's for the night."

She saw the gleam of triumph in his eyes. It was working out just as he'd planned it. He held out his hand, like a boy at a party asking a girl to dance.

"Ready?"

"Yes, Daddy."

And she meant it. She was going to have sex with her father, to spare her brother. She'd get through it somehow. She'd shut her eyes and grit her teeth and pretend it wasn't happening.

Would he wear a condom? This was what she was thinking as she took his hand and allowed herself to be pulled to her feet.

"I won't hurt you, Princess. I promise."

She nodded. What bullshit. Whatever happened next, the worst of the hurting had already happened.

He led the way to the door leading to the basement. Lynn hadn't been down there in years. Even when she was a little girl, the place frightened her. It was as if she'd always known this day was coming.

The Captain opened the door and pulled the light cord, illuminating the bare cinder block walls within.

And that's when Lynn's plan changed, in the blink of an eye.

"You watch these steps, baby girl, they're steep."

They were the last words she ever heard him speak. Lynn pulled her hand free from his before shoving her father down the stairs with every ounce of strength she had.

They were indeed steep steps, twenty wooden rungs that led sharply down to a cement floor, pretty much at the same angle a firefighter would lean his ladder against a burning building. The

Captain actually completed the better part of a flip in midair before his back slammed against the bottom few steps with a crash that shook the house. But he made no sound as he rolled onto the floor and lay on his back, gazing blindly at the ceiling.

Lynn's heart was pounding as she studied him from up at the doorway. He wasn't moving. He might have been dead, but she couldn't be sure. And she wasn't about to descend the steps and find out.

Bad things live in cellars. Spiders. Mice. Ghosts. And fathers who want to fuck their daughters.

She took a last look at her father, pulled the light cord, and went up to her room, where she rapidly packed her bags. Then Lynn Mahoney vanished into the night for what she was sure would be the rest of her life, believing herself to be a murderer on the run.

But she wasn't.

Lynn's mother got home late the next morning. She heard the moans of pain the Captain had been making since he'd regained consciousness sometime in the middle of the night. She called for an ambulance and within minutes they were there, strapping the Captain to a gurney after first immobilizing his neck to prevent spinal damage.

It was too late for that. Several of the vertebrae in his lower back had shattered. He would never walk again.

But he was able to talk all right, and the story he stuck to was a simple one—he'd had too much to drink, lost his balance, and fallen down the stairs. Everybody who'd ever known Walter Mahoney found that a little hard to believe. The man had the balance of a cat. Nobody had ever seen him stumble or trip.

"I lost my balance," he insisted. The only other person who knew the truth was on a Greyhound bus headed far, far from home.

It was nearly nightfall before anyone noticed that Lynn was

nowhere to be found. She wasn't at work and she wasn't with me. These were the only places anyone thought to look. She wasn't a worldly person. She was a small-town girl who'd suddenly vanished like a puff of smoke. A runaway, for no damn good reason.

The Captain never got his promotion. The city would sooner have embraced an adulterous fire commissioner than a paraplegic one.

But it was a big story in the papers (FALLEN ANGEL was the headline in the *New York Post*). And the city did build him that ramp to the door of his house, and wished him the very best in a well-earned retirement.

Little Brendan never knew what his father would have been willing to do to him, never knew why his sister had taken off like that. He promised his father that when he grew up he'd become a fireman, just like all the other Mahoney males. It was a promise that got him killed in that Bronx blaze, along with his three brothers.

Lynn lived her life from city to city, state to state. She rarely stayed anywhere longer than a year. She had glancing relationships with men that never lasted more than a few months.

She was a moving target, both physically and emotionally.

When she was twenty-one she had her tubes tied. She did not want to bring any of that man's grandchildren into the world, ever. A bloodline like that had to be stopped, or so she told herself.

Lost in the decision was the fact that her father had also sired Brendan, the sweetest child she'd ever known. She was only twenty-one, all alone in the world, making a choice propelled by grief and despair. She was sorry about it later, but what was done was done.

Lynn never got in touch with anybody in the family. While the Captain was breathing, it just could not happen. She was living outside Boston when she read about the death of the Burning Angel in a local newspaper.

At long last, it was time to come home. And by the time she got there, her mother had suffered a debilitating stroke.

No wonder that old prick never wanted me around. No wonder poor old Ruth never had a relaxed moment in her life. No wonder every fucking thing in the whole wide world.

By the end of the tale the whiskey bottle is empty.

"Some story, huh, Mick?"

I'm shivering. My teeth are actually chattering.

"Forgiveness!" Lynn cries to the sky. "Remember how he told you he forgave me, that time you pushed him up the ramp? Wonder if he meant for running away, or shoving him down the stairs."

"He didn't say."

"The hell with him, either way." Her eyes narrow. "I'm having my mother cremated. She's not lying next to that bastard through eternity."

The fog I've lived in for all these years has burned away at last, and now I have to ask myself how I like the light, because what it reveals is the only woman I've ever loved, curled hard upon herself on that stoop, like one of those armored bugs that rolls up into a ball when you touch it. Lynn's forehead touches her knees and she's hugging her legs, like a child about to do a cannonball off a diving board.

"You did the right thing, Lynn," I say. "You did the only thing you could do."

"No, I didn't. I meant to kill him. It would have worked out a lot better if I'd killed him. I didn't mean to trap my mother behind his wheelchair for nineteen years."

"Did she know what you did?"

"Only you know, Mickey. Only you will ever know."

I try to swallow, but my throat is dry. "At least he never . . . you know . . ."

"Mickey, it's not about penetration. It's about my own father wanting me that way. My *daddy . . .*"

Now, at last, I know everything about the woman I love, and suddenly the words of a woman I never loved leap to my mind. It's advice from Rosalind Pomer, who told me just what to do in the situation I find myself in now.

Love her like a man, not a boy.

What would a man do? He'd fight to make things right. I'm ready to try.

"Lynn. You are *not* destroyed."

I'm not sure she even hears me. I slide over and wrap my arms around her. She allows it but continues to hug herself, and now she's shivering, too, a violent shiver. It's like she's being electrocuted.

"I tried to kill my father."

"He deserved it."

"But I messed up. Instead I destroyed what was left of my mother's life, and my own."

"You are *not* destroyed! I won't allow it. You hear me? I will *not* allow it!"

She lifts her head to look at me as if I'm on a lifeboat she hasn't got the strength to climb aboard. Her eyes are wide, wide open, hiding nothing, as they were the very first time I ever saw her, when she opened the front door to pay the nervous newspaper boy.

"You should have kids, Mickey," she whispers. "You'd be a good father, just like Eddie. I can't give you that."

"Well, it's funny you should say that, Lynn. Very funny."

The time has come. I show her the photo of Aaron. In the light of the outdoor porch lamp she studies it in wonder. I tell her all about him, and his mother, and my wild, crazy plan for the three of us. Or maybe I'm wrong. Maybe it's not such a wild, crazy thing to do. Maybe it's the *only* thing to do.

Lynn takes in the whole story, and by the time I finish I see that there's a spark in her eye. She's coming back to life. She's going to be okay. *We* are going to be okay.

"Lynn? You with me, baby?"

"Are you sure you want me to be . . . you know . . ."

"His mother? Of course I do."

She stares at the photo for what seems like weeks. Then she shakes her head.

"Know what's funny, Mickey?"

"What's that?"

She swallows, chokes back a sob. "He has my eyes."

She collapses in my arms exhausted, relieved, spent. There are no more secrets to carry, no more mysteries. Despite all that's happened, it's going to be all right. *I* believe it. *She* believes it.

And anybody with a reason not to believe it is dead.

We go back into the house. The living room is really chilly now, with a night wind blowing straight through from window to window. The stink of gasoline is gone. Lynn shivers with the cold.

"Mickey. We have to make a fire."

My heart sinks. "Lynn. Please. We can't torch this house."

"No, no. We're going to sell this house, and use the money for the things we're going to do." She swallows, shudders with a final fear.

"But we've got to burn that ramp. Can we do that? Can we burn it all up tonight, and forget about it forever?"

We can sure as hell try.

I go back outside and start pulling it apart. The ancient nails have dissolved into rust lines and the rotted planks break easily over my knee. Back in the house Lynn crumples up sheets of newspaper and lines the bottom of the fireplace with it, and piece by piece we burn up that lousy ramp.

It doesn't take long. The stuff ignites like kindling. It's a loud, fierce blaze, and every crackle is like the cry of a dying ghost.

Soon the last of it is in the fireplace, burning away. There's just one more thing to do.

"Go ahead, Mickey."

I don't need to be told what to do next. I lift the Captain's photo off the mantel and set it flat on the blaze, back side down. The flames curl around the edges of the frame and then the glass cracks, and the image of that monster burns up like an autumn leaf. Then I do the same thing with the Burning Angel photograph.

At last the fire stops roaring, calms down into a red-glowing pile of embers that'll die out by dawn. I put the screen in front of the fireplace and turn to Lynn, who's actually fallen asleep on the couch. It's been one hell of an exhausting exorcism.

I lift her in my arms and head for the stairs. I think I'm going to like being a man.

She opens her eyes, surprised but not startled to see that she is being carried.

"I love you, Mickey."

The words I'd been dying to hear . . . for a moment they make me weak at the knees. I have to pause and gather my strength before continuing the trip upstairs.

"Well," I say, "it's about time."

"But, baby, I don't think I'm ready to express it just yet."

"Good. Neither am I. Let's just fall asleep. That's what old married couples do."

She giggles. "Is that what we are?"

"That's exactly what we are. We've been married since we first set eyes on each other. There's just been this twenty-year delay to the honeymoon."

"Can we take your boy to Italy some day?"

"Sure we can."

"I want to see his face when he sees the Sistine Chapel."

"I want to see *your* face when *you* see it."

We strip down and cuddle like children, back to back. She

falls asleep first, and then it's my turn. But sometime in the middle of the night she reaches for me, or maybe I reach for her, or maybe we reach for each other.

Anyway, it happens. It finally happens the way it's supposed to happen, as naturally as a tide coming in.

And just like that, I understand why I always got lousy grades in math, right from the first grade. The teacher always used to insist that one plus one is two, but I knew better. If you're one of the lucky ones, one plus one is One.

CHAPTER THIRTY-FOUR

The next day I called Belachek the private eye. He grabbed the phone on the first ring, and when he realized it was me he laughed out loud.

"Hey, good news, kid! You're off the hook."

My stomach began churning. "I don't understand."

"The envelope, please! The results are in, and . . . the child is *not* yours! You can breathe easy, my friend."

I could barely breathe at all. "Wait, wait . . . what are you saying?"

"I'm saying you are not the boy's daddy. And I apologize for any distress this matter may have caused you."

My tongue tasted salty. I had to swallow before I could speak. "Who's the father?"

Belachek chuckled. "God only knows. And I got a feeling that God's the only one who'll ever know."

It was the second-worst news of my life, next to Lynn Mahoney running away from home. It was unacceptable news. I could not accept it. I would not accept it.

"Could the test be wrong?"

"The test?"

"Yeah, I mean . . . Sharon said I was the father, right?"

"Well, she was wrong. Wishful thinking on her part, is my best guess. You know."

"What do you mean?"

"Figure it out. This Benny clown dumps her, she goes a little crazy. Sleeps around for a while, has a few flings . . . kinda thing that's out of character for a woman like her, you know? Compared to the other candidates, your genetic matter must've looked pretty good to her. So when she had to pick a father, she picked you."

In his smarmy way, Belachek was calling her a slut. I couldn't have that. This was the child's mother he was talking about, my child's mother.

"You're way off base, man. She wasn't like that."

"You're defending her?"

"She's not around to defend herself, you shithead!"

I was taking it out on the wrong guy. Belachek was just doing his stinking job, and I wasn't doing much to keep his friendship.

He was quiet for a moment, gathering himself.

"Hey. Mr. DeFalco. What's goin' on here? You should be dancin' in the street!"

"Who else knows about this?"

"I got the results five minutes ago. You're the first to know. By law, I gotta tell you first."

I shut my eyes, said a fast prayer to whoever might have been listening.

"Mr. Belachek," I all but whispered, "please don't tell anyone else. I want that child."

There was absolute silence on the phone for what seemed like hours. I thought maybe we'd been disconnected, but then Belachek's voice came through, soft and clear.

"This," he said, "is too fuckin' weird."

Suddenly he wasn't a private eye, he was a parish priest, and I was confessing everything to him. I told him about Lynn, how she was my real-life inspiration for "Sweet Days," the most amazing human being I'd ever known.

I told him how she'd broken my heart and run away and now I had her back at last, but we couldn't have kids of our own.

Belachek listened, sighed, and chuckled once again, a very different kind of chuckle from the first one.

"This is a new one," he said. "Tell you the truth, I don't know what the hell to do now."

But I knew what to do, absolutely and positively, for maybe the first time in my ridiculous life.

"Look. Your job was to find me, right?"

"Yeah."

"Which you did. The DNA test was for *my* sake, right?"

"Yeah."

"Does anybody else even know about the DNA test?"

"Just you and me."

"It never happened."

"I beg your pardon?"

"I never agreed to it. You never took my cheek cells. Tear up those test results. Burn down the lab, if you have to. Do what you gotta do."

I was rolling, now, like a manhole cover down a steep hill. Nobody and nothing could stop me. . . .

"You found me, and you told me I was Aaron's father, and I believed you. No reason not to believe you. I had unprotected sex with Sharon on the boat, and she got pregnant. End of story. Now I'm ready to assume full responsibility for my child."

I laughed out loud with a surge of gleeful hope. "It's in the *stars,* man! And Lynn . . . Jesus, man, Lynn will be the best mother any kid could have. I swear it on my soul, if I even have a soul anymore. . . ."

I ran out of words. My sales pitch was done. It would work, or it wouldn't. I could hear Belachek breathe, each breath a little less jagged than the previous one, until at last his breathing evened out. He'd come to a decision. I got down on my knees, shut my eyes, and squeezed the phone to my ear until my cheek throbbed.

"You're rewriting history, you realize," Belachek said.

"Yeah, well, these particular pages of history could use a little polish. I can live with it if you can."

Belachek was quiet, long enough for a drumroll that was actually the hammering of my heart.

"Mickey," he whispered, "we both gotta go to our graves with this, you hear what I'm sayin'?"

Victory. I started to cry, fought to control my voice. "I hear you, Mr. Belachek. Right to the grave."

"I mean, you can't even tell your wife."

"She's not my wife yet, but that won't be a problem. After I hang up this phone, I won't even tell myself what we both know."

I got to my feet, knees throbbing. It was all settled. Belachek chuckled for the last time.

"Man, this is a first in my business," he said. "A guy in the middle of a paternity rap who actually *wants* to raise a stranger's child. Who'da believed it?"

"Hey, Mr. Belachek. Don't you get it? *Everybody's* a stranger's child. Nobody really knows anybody in this fucked-up world. But God damn it to hell, there sure is nobility in the attempt, isn't there?"

It took him a moment to reply. I think he was stunned by what I'd said.

"Yeah," he agreed at last, "yeah, I guess you're right about that, kid."

"Stop calling me 'kid.' I'm a father now."

I had to go back on my word to Belachek. Lynn and I couldn't have secrets anymore. Lousy secrets had kept us apart for twenty years. I waited until we were packing up her stuff.

"Lynn, listen. It turns out I'm not the baby's father."

She set down an armload of clothes, sat down on the bed as if the bones in her legs had dissolved.

"Oh, God. Well. I guess this changes everything."

"No. Everything's the same. We still get the baby, because nobody knows who the biological father is."

I explained the logistics of what I'd gone through with Belachek, and the deal we'd cut. She looked at me in disbelief. She was either thinking I was crazy, or wonderful, or maybe both.

"Mickey. Are you sure this is all right with you?"

"It's better than all right."

"How do you figure?"

"It's a perfect balance now. The baby's not mine, and he's not yours. He's ours."

She looked at me as if she believed it, got to her feet, and fell into my arms as if she had no plans of ever letting go.

Listen to me when I tell you that I am a man who has certainly known sweet days.

Once the wife of a Beverly Hills record producer gave me a diamond-studded watch, just for singing my song at her teenage daughter's Sweet Sixteen party. A few days later I went on tour and carelessly left the watch in some hotel room.

What was it worth? Ten, maybe fifteen grand? Didn't matter. Whatever its value, I couldn't be bothered to backtrack and search for it under seat cushions. I didn't even phone the hotel to ask about it. Whoever found it could keep it, as far as I was concerned.

And why? I've thought about that. Close as I can figure, it was because backtracking would have been like returning to the past, and that's where Lynn lived, and that was too painful a place to visit.

So I lunged forward, ever forward, even as the sweet days grew

sour and I wound up a homeless man on a beach. I'd hit rock
bottom.

One good thing about hitting bottom—if you've still got any
heart left, you can push off and swim back to the top.

It's my last day in Little Neck, our last day in Little Neck. We're
off to a town in the Berkshire mountains, where Lynn lived just
before coming home to take care of her mother. There's a
stream in the woods where she wants to dump Ruth's ashes.
We'll find an apartment, and for the first few months I'm going
to look after the baby while Lynn gets her old job back at a local
bank.

Just two days earlier I'd gotten a letter, the one and only piece
of mail that came to me during my weeks in Little Neck. The return address was a law firm on West Forty-third Street. I opened
it reluctantly, because letters from lawyers rarely spelled good
news for me, but this one was different.

> Dear Mickey,
>
> You told me not to get involved in this matter,
> but an obedient lawyer is a useless lawyer, as far as
> I'm concerned. I've done a little digging and it
> seems to me that the contract you signed when
> you sold the rights to "Sweet Days" has a couple of
> holes in it. I'm going to see if I can make those
> holes bigger. No charge, my friend. Give me a call
> in a month or two. I should know something by
> then. Hope it worked out with that woman. You
> never did tell me her name, did you?
> Sincerely,
> Rosalind Pomer, Attorney at Law

It's Lynn, Rosalind. Lynn Ann Mahoney.

Lynn's mother had a rusty red Dodge Dart that nobody had

driven in years. Steady Eddie DeFalco has given it a real thorough once-over—points, plugs, the works—and a set of new tires, to boot. That's his going-away present. It should make it all the way to that town in Massachusetts where little Aaron is waiting to be picked up by his parents.

On moving day the car is loaded with two suitcases (her stuff), one green duffel bag (my stuff), and her mother's ashes, in a plain gray can.

"Let's get the hell out of here, Mickey."

"Got to stop and say good-bye to my parents."

"Of course."

I drive to Glenwood Street. The car rides well. Steady Eddie knows his stuff. It's Saturday, not yet eight in the morning, but I know I won't be waking anybody as I pull up at the house and beep the horn.

My parents come outside to say good-bye. They are going to deal with Eileen Kavanagh and the sale of the Mahoney house, which is going on the market as a "fixer-upper" and a "handyman special." They promise to come and visit their grandson. As far as they know, he is their biological grandson. As far as I'm concerned, it doesn't matter who his father is. Lynn and I are his parents. That's all there is to it, and it's as much of a truth as there is in this world.

My own parents look as if they have come to the end of a long, rocky ocean voyage. I'm leaving them, and they can't hide the relief they feel over this, and why should they? They can go back to the way they were, before I dropped in on them like a human grenade.

My father hugs Lynn, long and hard, then reaches out to shake my hand. I see a round bandage on his upper arm.

"Hurt yourself, Dad?"

He shakes his head. "Your mother's got me on the nicotine patch. Figures it'll help me stop smoking."

"It's probably a good idea."

He shrugs. "It won't last. I'll keep smokin' and get double the nicotine buzz. Maybe I should take a nicotine suppository, too, go for the trifecta. Which reminds me."

He puts an arm across my shoulder and slips a wad of cash into my shirt pocket.

"What's that?"

"Couple hundred. Had some luck at the track yesterday. Get yourself a baby carriage."

He takes me in a long embrace and is wet-eyed when he breaks it off.

My mother has just finished hugging Lynn and turns to me.

"Michael."

"Mom."

"Oh, *Michael.*"

"Thanks for taking care of me, Mom."

She hesitates before speaking, clears her throat to quell a tremor in her voice.

"I found something you might want to take," she says, and hands me an old marble-backed notebook. I open the cover, and right there on the inside are the faded ink lyrics I'd scribbled for a little song called "Sweet Days."

"Mom. Jesus!"

"You know I never throw anything out." She hugs me and kisses my cheek.

"Good-bye, Michael. Be happy."

"See you soon, Mom. Use the good silver once in a while."

"Maybe tonight."

I'm up for this long drive. I feel so strong, I can't imagine ever needing to sleep again. Nobody ever talks about the strength that comes with hope, maybe because most people never get their hope back once they lose it. It's a real gift, the second time around.

Lynn stretches and yawns. "Know what's wonderful, Mickey? I'm sleepy."

"Why's that wonderful?"

"Because I haven't really slept right for about twenty years."

"What's that mean?"

"It means . . . I trust you."

I feel a tingle that goes all the way down to my hands on the steering wheel.

"Funny, I'm the opposite. I have all this energy. Maybe because I'm finally awake, after twenty years of dreaming."

"Well, if we have any hopes of making it, we've got to even this thing out. If you're wide awake and I'm fast asleep, we're screwed."

"At least we wouldn't fight."

"Good point."

We're not even out of Little Neck when Lynn dozes off. As we head down Northern Boulevard I see Rosie Gambardello plodding along, bound for work at the International House of Pancakes. I wave to her. She freezes as she stares at me, expecting maybe that I'm going to jam on the brakes and yell at her for those stupid things she said on *Hollywood Howl,* but my son is waiting for me, and there's no time for old grudges.

Soon we're on the highway, heading north. Lynn is in a deep sleep. Her hands are together as if in prayer and she's placed them between her face and the upholstery, a pillow for her cheek. There's a pout to her lips, as if she's dreaming that she's a little girl, a little girl being denied a bowl of ice cream because she won't finish her vegetables.

My God, she looks beautiful. A man could write a song about a sight like that. Good thing is, I even have the notebook to write it in.